I HEART CHRISTMAS

Lindsey Kelk is an author, journalist and prol[i]
tweeter.

Lindsey loves living in New York, expensive sho[es?]
professional wrestling and wondering whether or
not it's time for bed. Lindsey dislikes too much
frosting on a cupcake, being so far away from
London, spiders and not being in bed. Lindsey is
indifferent to sushi and dogs that are smaller than
a cereal box.

Lindsey has written eight novels: *I Heart New York*,
I Heart Hollywood, *I Heart Paris*, *I Heart Vegas*, *I
Heart London*, *The Single Girl's To-Do List* and
About a Girl. You can find out lots more about her
here: http://lindseykelk.com

LINDSEY KELK

I Heart Christmas

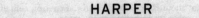

HARPER

Harper
An imprint of HarperCollins*Publishers*
77–85 Fulham Palace Road,
Hammersmith, London W6 8JB

www.harpercollins.co.uk

A Paperback Original 2013

2

Copyright © Lindsey Kelk 2013

Lindsey Kelk asserts the moral right to
be identified as the author of this work

A catalogue record for this book
is available from the British Library

ISBN: 978-0-00-750150-2

Set in Melior by Palimpsest Book Production Limited, Falkirk, Stirlingshire

Printed and bound in Great Britain by
Clays Ltd, St Ives plc

Partly for Bernard's dancing, partly for Matt's beard and entirely for Terri White.

ACKNOWLEDGMENTS

Dear everyone, please accept this virtual hug as the Christmas card I won't have time to send and know that I have asked Santa to put you all on the 'nice' list. He says you're golden. Rowan Lawton, thank you for being everything that you are and for stopping me from licking Brian Cox at dinner that time. Thank you to everyone else at Furniss Lawton and James Grant, especially Liane, Blaise and Georgie (what happens at karaoke, stays at karaoke) and Izzy, John and Will, thanks for suffering so quietly through the Kelktails madness.

The day Lynne Drew says 'sod it, she's gone mental' will be the day HarperCollins give up on me so thank you Lynne for not saying it yet. Couldn't do it without you. Same goes to Thalia Suzuma, you are ridiculously supportive, understanding, bloody good at your job *and* you're doing unsupported shoulder stands. I'm so jealous. There are a thousand people to thank at HC but massive tinsel-covered lovin' goes out to Lucy, Jaime and Martha who genuinely suffered me this year. Sorry. And sorry in advance for next time.

I can't use emojis here which really limits my emotional expression. But to everyone on Twitter and FB, you're my advisors, my sounding board, my gossip buddies and most importantly, the reason I do this. Thank you so much. Meeting so many of you this year has been incredible (especially my Kelktails gang!) and I am genuinely touched by every message I receive – if I don't get time to reply, it's only because I'm writing another bloody book, not because I didn't do a little cry while I was reading it. I literally couldn't do this without you, I mean, HarperCollins just wouldn't let me.

I'm always being asked where my inspiration comes from and whether or not it's hard being a writer. If it weren't for these people, there would be no books, just a lot of red hair, attention-seeking issues and a drinking problem. Thanks to all of you, I get to call that 'being a writer'. Emma Ingram, Ana Mercedes Cardenas, Sarah Donovan, Rachael Wright, Jackie Dunning, Julie Allen and Rebecca Alimena, as well as Tracy Solomon and Michelle Dortignac – thank you for picking me up and putting me back together again, as required.

And to Jack Murnighan, Terri White, Della Bolat, Beth Ziemacki, Ryan Child and Ilana Fox, without everyone else, this book wouldn't be here. Without you, I wouldn't be here. I don't have the words to express it.

Which is a bit shit when you think what my job is.

CHAPTER ONE

'Can you explain to me exactly why I'm dragging this thing through the streets of Brooklyn,' Jenny asked, huffing and puffing behind seven feet of majestic Christmas tree, 'when you have a perfectly acceptable husband to do these things? What's the point in being married if he's not going to carry heavy shit for you?'

'Because we're strong, independent women who don't need men to carry things for us,' I offered, shivering as I fumbled for my front door key. 'We are woman, hear us roar.'

'I am woman, hear me call a delivery service to do this so I don't have to,' she grumbled through a mouthful of the finest Douglas fir. 'Where is Alex anyway? Isn't this the kind of cutesy shit you two should be doing together?'

'He's out, somewhere.' I shuffled backwards, pulling Jenny and the tree towards the lift and pretending not to see the trail of pine needles. 'God knows.'

'You really make marriage sound like a dream,' she replied.

Getting the tree up to our floor would not be the

perfect crime. Our building super already disliked me with a fiery passion. I couldn't quite work out if it was because he had trouble with my accent and never quite understood what I was saying or because I still couldn't remember which bin was for recycling and which was for rubbish. Or there was a small chance that it was due to all those times I'd locked myself out at three a.m. when Alex was away on tour and I'd had to call him to let me in. Regardless, the fact of the matter was, he just wasn't that keen on me and this unquestionably seasonal, yet unrequested new carpet of Christmas tree needles in the lobby was not going to go down well.

'I don't know where he goes.' I tiptoed backwards into the lift, trying not to fall over my own feet. Again. 'That boy is a wanderer and it's too bloody cold for me to wander with him. Besides, I wanted to get the tree. I wanted to do it with you, oh bestest friend in the entire universe.'

Jenny poked her head around the tree to fix me with a narrow-eyed stare.

'He said you couldn't have a tree yet, didn't he?'

'Yes, ma'am,' I nodded.

'And why not?'

'Because I still haven't cleared away all the Thanksgiving dishes,' I admitted. It wasn't like I hadn't put them in the dishwasher, I just hadn't taken them back out again. For over a week. 'But I needed it. It's been a weird day.'

'You're disgusting.' She yelped as she pricked herself for the eighteenth time in two minutes. 'And it's been a weird day so you picked up a Christmas tree? You couldn't just buy shoes like normal people? You're what's weird in this scenario.'

'Something's going on at work,' I said, jabbing at the buttons and willing the doors to close faster. 'I'm sure of it. Delia and Mary are being all whispery behind closed doors.'

'Don't you and Mary share an office?' Jenny asked. 'What are you doing, following them to the ladies' room?'

'Um, yeah, we have separate offices now.'

Mary, the editor of *Gloss*, and I had started off sharing a big, beautiful office but since I apparently couldn't stop singing show tunes when I was trying to concentrate and occasionally enjoyed the odd YouTube video of kittens with narcolepsy, she'd had a wall put up in the middle of the room. I tried not to take it personally. If she couldn't appreciate my celebrated (by me) rendition of 'I Know Him So Well', that was her loss.

'Something's definitely going on, though. They've both had time blocked out in their diaries and—'

The silver doors slid together for just a moment, before springing back apart to let another passenger inside.

'Not the super, not the super, not the super,' I whispered into the branches of my glorious tree.

'Hi, I'm Jenny.'

Before I could deliver my admittedly paranoid work theories, Jenny interrupted me with her best 'hello, you're a hot man' purr. Nestled behind the bulk of the tree, I might not have been able to see either of them but I could hear her sparkliest smile twinkling through her introduction. Lowering myself into a squat, I squinted through the branches to get a better look at her target but all I managed was an eyeful of sap and the suggestion of some very shiny brown hair.

3

'Oh, uh, hi,' a deep voice that most definitely did not belong to my gnarled Italian super replied. 'I'm Doug.'

'Doug?' Jenny repeated his name like it was the most interesting thing she had ever heard. I wondered whether or not someone had actually pressed a button. I was desperate for a wee. 'You must be new to the building, right?'

'Pretty new,' he confirmed. I leaned back against the wall of the lift and pushed up onto my Converse tiptoes, trying to get a look at this 'Doug'. If that was his real name. 'You live on the top floor?'

'More or less,' she replied, with a tinkly laugh that made me want to punch her in the boob. 'I'm a Manhattan gal. This is my best friend's place, which I guess means I almost live here, right?'

'Nice to meet you,' I shouted in his general direction through a mouthful of tree. Which did not taste as good as it smelled. 'I'm Angela.'

'Oh shit,' Doug replied. 'I didn't know you were hiding in there. Hi.'

'She's behind the tree,' Jenny explained. Doug made an 'oh' sound. Doug was clearly not the sharpest knife in the drawer.

'This is my stop,' he announced as the bell sounded and the doors opened on the third floor. 'Have fun.'

'Oh, we will,' I heard Jenny promise. 'We always do.'

'You massive slag,' I said as the doors closed quickly, slicing through the sexual tension. 'Haven't you got a boyfriend?'

'No, I don't have a boyfriend and I was just flirting.' Somehow Jenny managed to find a way through the tree to punch my arm. 'Relax, Mom.'

4

I paused, thought better of my question, then asked it anyway. 'Was he hot?'

'Super hot,' she sighed. 'He looked like Clark Kent. Real gentleman. Can I set off your smoke alarms? See if he comes to help us?'

'That'll be a fun one to explain to Alex,' I muttered, pushing Jenny backwards out of the door as we arrived at my floor. 'Oh, sorry, darling, we burnt the apartment down to see whether or not the new neighbour downstairs was as chivalrous as Jenny assumed he was after a fourteen-second conversation.'

'Screw you,' she replied, giving me the finger for extra emphasis.

'A real lady, worthy of a real gentleman,' I smiled over the top of the tree.

One hour, two arguments and three beers later, the Christmas tree was safely(ish) in its stand and towering proudly over my apartment. It only leaned ever so slightly to the left and somehow we'd managed to string the fairy lights without throttling each other, but sheer exhaustion and desperate thirst meant we'd been forced to pause in the decorating for a beer break.

'So, you didn't finish your story.' Jenny picked a single stray pine needle from her sweater and tossed it on the floor with disgust. She was so thoughtful. 'What's going on in the office?'

'I didn't finish because you were too busy cracking on to "Doug" to let me finish,' I stated. 'Actually, I'd barely even started.'

'Then stop whining and start now,' she said, curling her legs up underneath her. 'What's the goss at *Gloss*?'

Gloss had launched ten months earlier and, against all odds, it was doing really, really well. While other

5

magazines were disappearing from the stands, our weekly freebie was everywhere. We had even launched an enhanced iPad edition that people were actually paying for – it was crazy. And while I was the first to put my hand up and say the editorial was fantastic (possibly because I was deputy editor), it really was all down to Delia. She was an incredible business-woman and no one on earth was able to say no to her. Every time I saw her, I wanted to do a little dance and sacrifice a goat. Or maybe just give her a Kit Kat. Admittedly, I saw her less and less as the magazine got bigger and bigger. I knew her grand-father, Bob, the president of Spencer Media and ultimately our big boss, was grooming her to move up in the company and while I was happy for her, I wasn't ready for her to disappear from the mag. Bob was basically the Donald Trump of publishing, which might have sounded like an exaggeration if I hadn't known for a fact that Delia and The Donald were on first-name terms. While the New York billionaires' club was bigger than you might think, it was still pretty cliquey.

'There's nothing specific,' I said. 'It's just a feeling. Mary and Delia have been in and out of each other's offices all week and they've both been very quiet around me or so—'

'They've been quiet or you've been extra loud?' Jenny asked. 'It is December. I figure you've been running around in some ugly Santa sweater singing holiday songs since the first, right?'

'Don't interrupt me.' She didn't need to know that was exactly what I'd been doing. 'They've been weird, all right? Something is up.'

'You didn't think to just ask them?'

I stared at her revelatory concept. Oh Jenny, you and your common sense.

'Um, no?'

'Right,' Jenny sighed, 'because why would you do something as obvious as that?'

'Oh, fuck off.' I hopped up and grabbed two fresh beers from the fridge, popping the tops and handing one to Jenny. 'I want everything to be OK, that's all.'

'You'd know if it wasn't,' she reassured me. 'You're a pain in the ass like that.'

I nodded slowly, considering her sage advice. Tomorrow, I would march into Mary's office and ask what was going on. Definitely tomorrow or the day after. Although maybe it would be better to wait until Monday. By Monday, I would totally know when I was going to ask.

'We ought to be drinking mulled wine.' I frowned at the bottle of Brooklyn lager, changing the subject. 'Or at least eggnog.'

'Mulled wine takes too long and eggnog tastes like shit,' Jenny pointed out. While my old Topshop jeans and Splendid T-shirt were speckled with a year's worth of dust from the tree ornament boxes, Jenny's black leather leggings and white cashmere sweater looked like she had just slipped them on. Probably because she'd been about as much help as a chocolate teapot as soon as she'd taken her coat off. 'Besides, you're the one who insists on living in hipsterville. I don't think you would find either of those things on Bedford Avenue.'

'I can sniff out Christmas like Rudolph the red-nosed bloodhound,' I said, sipping the cool, bubbly goodness. 'Christmas makes everything better, even hipsters.'

'Nothing makes hipsters better,' Jenny disagreed. 'Give me a man in a suit any day.'

'Aren't you dating a hipster?' I reminded her, putting my beer down and grabbing my handbag while I was still sober enough to climb the stepladder. 'And haven't you been doing so for some time?'

'Yeah, I think that might have come to a natural end, you know?' she said, watching me drag the stepladder away from the wonky Christmas tree and position it underneath the air-conditioning vent. 'What the hell are you doing?'

'I'm going to hide a copy of *The Great Gatsby* in the ceiling,' I explained, holding up a small padded envelope. 'It's Alex's Christmas present and I know he'll go looking for it if I don't hide it.'

'I think you're confusing Alex with yourself.' Jenny eyed my climb up the ladder with badly hidden nerves but didn't offer to get off her arse and help. 'Never had him pegged for a reader.'

'Unlike you, he reads all the time,' I replied, straining to open the vent cover. There was a reason I let boys do things like this, feminism be damned. 'I've tried to get him to watch telly like normal people but he won't have it.'

'I read,' she protested, flat on her back across the sofa. 'Like, every day.'

'I don't know if self-help books actually count as reading.' I finally got the vent open enough to slide the book inside without trapping my fingers. 'And have you read them all yet? When do you know if you're self-helped?'

'Self-improvement is a process, Angela,' Jenny announced. 'It's a journey without a destination.'

'It's a journey that's keeping Barnes & Noble in business,' I replied. 'What's going on with Craig?'

'Nothing. Ever. That's kind of the issue.' She pulled

a thick strand of shiny hair upwards until the curl straightened out, then let it spring back down onto her face. 'I think I'm ready to date a guy who wants to take me out for dinner instead of ordering pizza. There are only so many evenings a girl can spend watching *Breaking Bad* until three a.m. without going totally crazy.'

'Yeah,' I agreed, wondering whether or not that number was as high for Jenny as it was for me.

'Dude, can you believe Erin has two babies? Two of them. It's crazy.'

'It is weird.' I pretended not to notice that she'd changed the subject. I figured we'd get around to whatever was really bothering her sooner or later. 'One minute there were no babies, now there are two babies. It feels like she moved away or something.'

Our friend Erin had recently rebranded herself from a super-hot PR maven into a baby-making machine. As soon as she was married, she got pregnant with Arianna and as soon as Arianna was sitting up straight, she was pregnant with Thomas Junior. Obviously, she wasn't quite so available for manicure dates and spur-of-the-moment cocktails as she used to be.

'I know, I talked to her yesterday for the first time in a week. Says she's coming back to work super soon.' Jenny made a clucking noise. 'But, dude, one baby and your own business is one thing, but two? It's not going to be easy.'

'Erin has two babies.' I rested my head on the cool steel of the stepladder and shuddered. 'I can't even process the fact that she has one. It's madness. It's like you having a baby.'

'And why wouldn't I have a baby?' Jenny looked up sharply. I saw her tightly drawn mouth and arched eyebrow and closed my eyes. Oh bollocks. 'What? I'm fundamentally unbabyable?'

'That's not what I meant.' I was too tired to pick my words as carefully as they needed to be picked. It had been a long day, I'd just put up a Christmas tree and I was halfway inside an air-conditioning vent. Me and my bright ideas. 'I only meant that it's strange that when I moved here, we were all single and going out and dating different guys and stuff and now Erin's got two babies, you've been dating Craig forever, I'm *married* to a *boy* and it just seems weird when you think about it.'

There. That should do it. And now to shuffle backwards out of the air-conditioning vent and safely back down the ladder. Piece of piss.

'So you think it would be weird for me to have a baby? You think I wouldn't be a good mom?'

Oh, for fuck's sake.

'No, I'm sure you would be amazing,' I said, shuffling half an inch at a time, clenching my hands into tiny, tight fists and then stretching out my fingers as far as they would go. A yoga teacher had once told me it would calm me down in stressful situations. She was incorrect. 'What's this all about? Where's it coming from?'

'Well, I've been thinking,' Jenny said, sitting up and fluffing out her hair. 'I want to have a kid.'

I paused on the ladder, took a moment and considered my response.

'You mean you want to have a baby at some point in the distant future?'

Jenny shook her head. 'I mean I want to have a baby now.'

I breathed out slowly, puffing up more dust, and

spun my wedding ring round and round on my finger. Maybe if I rubbed it hard enough a genie would appear and I could wish some common sense into my best friend.

'I've been thinking about it,' Jenny said, launching into her clearly prepared speech before I had a chance to get a word in. 'There's never going to be a better time. I've got a great job with great maternity benefits and I'd absolutely be able to work around my pregnancy. So many of the girls in the office are pregnant right now, Erin's been talking about opening a day care centre in the building.'

'In the building?' I asked.

'Next to the gym,' Jenny nodded.

'Of course.' I raised my eyebrows and tried to restrain the tutting noise I was desperate to make. 'Where else?'

Sometimes I forgot Erin was obscenely wealthy. Most people would just get a childminder but why bother with that when you could open your own nursery?

Jenny had been working for Erin's PR company for a couple of years and she was good at it. She was also good at making rash decisions without thinking about the long-term effects on her life. Usually it meant spending a month's rent on shoes, dip-dying her hair badly or indulging in the odd love affair with a complete dickhead, but a baby? This was a worry.

'I've got a great apartment, great friends, I'm healthy, financially stable and I want a baby.' She sounded so pleased with herself, I didn't quite know what to do. 'Why wouldn't I do it? The longer I wait, the harder it's going to be.'

'I'm going to say something controversial now,' I

11

said, shuffling down the ladder with three drinks' worth of utter grace. 'But is Craig, who is still techni-cally your boyfriend as far as I know, the best candidate for Father of the Year?'

I tensed, gripping the metal handlebars, expecting her to pull the ladder out from under me. Instead, she laughed. It was tough to say whether or not a shot to the chops would have surprised me more.

'Oh Angie, Craig?' Something I'd said had clearly tickled her. 'No way! Craig can barely look after himself. And it's been fun but we both know it isn't serious.'

I was confused. Did we know that?

'We, you and me, or we, you and Craig?' I asked.

'We, me and everyone.' She spoke very slowly, rolling her eyes. Really? I thought. As though I was the mentally unstable one in the situation? 'Craig knows this is what it is. He's not ready to have a baby.'

'But you definitely, definitely, super certainly are?' I trod as carefully as humanly possible, metaphorically and literally. After all, a slap could still be in the offing. 'This is the biggest decision you'll ever make, Jenny.'

'Which is why I've been thinking about it so seriously, Angie.' She gave me a gentle, knowing smile. I assumed she'd been working on it as her 'maternal' look. 'It's all I've thought about for, like, days.'

'Days?'

And that was the precise moment when I lost my shit.

'Like, a week. Two weeks,' she muttered into her beer bottle. 'Since Erin had TJ.'

'You've been thinking about it for days?' I knew I was shrieking but I had absolutely no control over the volume or pitch of my own voice. 'You can't make a decision like this that quickly, Jenny. Just because someone you know recently heaved a tiny person out of their vagina doesn't mean you should do the same. If Erin jumped off a cliff, would you jump after her?'

I jumped off the bottom step and gave her the frowning of a lifetime.

'It's hardly the same,' she snapped back. 'I want a baby.'

'And I want a unicorn to fly me to work every day but that's not going to happen, is it?'

'Unicorns don't fly!' Jenny shouted.

'That's not the point!' I shouted back.

We stared at each other in silence for a few moments, Jenny sipping her beer, me imagining how useful a flying unicorn might actually be. Anything else was too traumatic to think about.

'I have an appointment with my ob-gyn tomorrow after work,' Jenny said quietly after a couple of minutes. 'I was going to ask you to come with me but if you don't feel comfortable, I'll ask Sadie.'

'Of course I'll come, you daft cow,' I replied, lifting up her legs and dropping onto the sofa. Clearly I was going to have to go along, if only to make sure she didn't accidentally fall on someone's penis en route. 'I just don't want you to rush into anything that's permanent. Life-changing.'

'Like running away from home and moving to New York without knowing a single soul and ending up married to one of the only decent men left in the Tri-State area and landing your dream job?' She pursed her lips and raised her eyes to the ceiling.

Ooh, the sneaky cow would use my own silver-lining fuck-ups against me.

13

'Yes, exactly like that,' I replied with a gentle slap on the back of her head. 'Because if I hadn't met you and listened when you tried to talk some sense into me, I would have been back at home by now, either living with my parents or, God forbid, married to a horrible man who was cheating on me.'

'Whatever,' she replied, setting her empty beer bottle on the floor and slapping me back. 'But you'll come with me tomorrow? To the doctor's?'

'I'll come to the doctor's with you.' I held her cold, damp hand in mine and gave it a squeeze. 'But I'm staying at the head end. I'm not getting involved with anything in stirrups.'

'You're such a prude,' she sniffed, pulling away and turning her nose up at my filthy sweater. 'I would totally take a look at your cervix if you asked me to.'

'And I never, ever will,' I promised.

'Well, would you look at that – we have a tree.'

I heard the door close behind Alex an hour or so after Jenny had left, while I was busy adding the decorations to my masterpiece. It was taking longer than I had anticipated and I'd already cried twice. Dressing the Christmas tree always made me emotional. As did drinking four beers in an hour and a half with my wannabe-babymama best friend.

'We do,' I said, turning my face up for a kiss as he tossed the mail on the coffee table behind me. 'I was on my way home and Jenny was coming over and I thought, well, we might as well pick it up and save you a job at the weekend.'

'You're so thoughtful,' he replied, looking over at the blatantly-still-full dishwasher. 'The dishes are still totally in there, aren't they?'

14

'I love you so much. Have I told you how much I love you?' I replied with another kiss. 'Isn't it pretty?'

'It's beautiful,' Alex replied, picking up a silver bauble and hanging it on a random branch. 'Like you.'

'Charmer.' I waited until his back was turned and his attention fully on finding a beer before moving the bauble to a more suitable spot. 'Where have you been?'

'Around,' he said, leaning against the kitchen counter and wiggling his eyebrows at me. 'I was gonna get a haircut but I didn't.'

'Around?' I carefully placed a blown-glass Santa Claus on a low branch of the tree. 'You are an enigma, Alex Reid.'

'I know, I'm trying to cultivate an air of mystery so you don't get bored of me.' He popped open his beer and took a deep drink. 'How was your day? How's Lopez?'

'Something weird is going down at work – my money is on an alien invasion – there was half a mouse in someone's sandwich at lunchtime and Jenny has decided she wants to have a baby.' I added a delicate silver star above the little Santa. 'What do you fancy for dinner? Don't say half a mouse.'

To his credit, Alex didn't even look fazed. Instead, he just sipped his beer and nodded slowly, keeping his eyes on the tree.

'Half a mouse?' he asked, swinging the beer bottle between his thumb and forefinger. 'Was it fried at least? Everything tastes good when it's fried.'

I smiled and felt my shoulders drop. Just being in the same room as him made my life a thousand times better. I let my attention waver from decorating the tree for a moment, just long enough to get a good look at the hottest man I had ever had the privilege of touching. His green eyes were dark and heavy against his pale skin and his cheeks glowed from the cold outside in a way that not even *Gloss*'s beauty editor could replicate. He gave me a questioning smile and brushed his too-long hair out of his face, tucking the fringe behind his left ear. I still wasn't quite sure how I'd managed to lock him down but, sparkle sparkle, the two rings on my left hand reminded me I had pulled off that miracle.

'Can I help with the tree or should I keep a safe distance?' He hovered by the tree for a moment, before settling on the arm of the sofa, poking around in the ornaments.

'I'd stick with a safe distance,' I admitted, stopping myself from slapping his hands away from the glittery box of joy. 'This is not me at my best.'

'I know, you're a tree Nazi,' he said with a half-yawn. 'My mom was the same, I get it. So, what do you want to deal with first? The aliens, the mouse, Jenny or my hair?'

Finishing off his yawn for him, I shook my head and picked out a pretty glass snowflake. 'Start where you like, they're equally unpleasant.'

'I didn't see anything on the news about an invasion of the body snatchers today, so I think you're OK there.' He rolled his head from side to side and stood up, wrapping his arms loosely around my waist as I tended to my tree. 'And I don't think there's much we can do for the mouse.'

'It was not a dignified end,' I replied, revelling in the feeling of his body pressed against mine. It never got old. 'But it definitely woke everyone up for a bit.'

'I can see how it would.' He pulled my hair away from my face and held it back in a makeshift ponytail, making me catch my breath. I was conflicted. As nice as it was, these were not the ideal conditions for tree trimming. 'And as for Jenny, you know how she is. She's seen a baby, she wants a baby. Last time I talked to her, she was obsessed with those dumb little dogs, right?'

'She was quite intent on Pomeranian ownership, yes,' I agreed, my heart beating a fraction faster as Alex slid his hand down my hair until it rested on my shoulder. He wasn't the only one who needed a haircut.

'Right, and she forgot soon enough.' His breath was warm on my skin and I was just tipsy enough to have developed a sudden case of the raging horn. 'And I can't see Craig pushing a stroller any time soon, so I wouldn't let that worry you too much.'

'I don't think she's really involving Craig in her plan.' I spoke in a whisper in case my voice broke and tried to turn around to face him, but instead Alex tightened his grip around my waist, pinning me in place. He carefully took the snowflake bauble from my hand and hung it somewhere on the tree. I stared at the floor and tried to steady my breath. Where he had stuck the ornament didn't seem terribly important anymore. I was so fickle. I tried to keep my breath even as he ran his fingertips down my back but it was all too much when I felt his teeth against my ear. I heard a tiny gasp escape from my lips and Alex had to pull me backwards just to keep me upright.

'Maybe you shouldn't worry about Jenny's plans so much.' His voice was low and warm in my ear. 'Maybe you should only worry about my plans.'

'Why?' I asked, clasping my hands over his to stop

them from moving lower and to stop me from toppling over into the Christmas tree. 'Are they dangerous?'

'Only if you don't do as you're told,' he replied, spinning me round for a kiss. Even though his eyes were dark and dilated, he was still smiling. My stomach fluttered and I felt myself blush before I kissed him back. 'You're going to have to finish the tree later.'

'Sounds fair,' I squeaked, following him happily into the bedroom, tree be damned.

Afterwards, when Alex was fast asleep and I was too restless to sleep, I padded back into the living room in my knickers, picking my jumper up off the floor where it had been abandoned and slipping it over my head. I turned out the big lights and perched on the edge of the sofa, just as Alex had an hour earlier, picking up his abandoned beer and taking a sip. It was flat and a bit warm. So obviously I kept drinking it.

'American beer is like pop,' I told the tree. 'Practically shandy.'

But that was the good thing about Christmas trees, they never judged. They just stood in the corner, looking all stately and wonderful, reminding you that it was the most wonderful time of the year and that all would be well. I had always loved Christmas, ever since I was tiny, and every year I worked my arse off to make sure the season was as jolly as the many, many adverts on telly promised that it would be. But this year . . . this year was going to be the best Christmas ever. Since I no longer had the Boots Christmas catalogue to tell me It Was Time, I now had to rely on the red Starbucks cups, the Coca-Cola advert and my own in Christmas-dar, honed from decades of seasonal celebrating. I'd spent months searching for the perfect present for Alex and finally found a first edition copy of *The Great Gatsby*, his favourite book, which I hoped would make up for the time we saw the movie, which I loved and he hated. It really was the closest we'd come to divorce – there had been a distinct threat of legal action in his eyes as we walked to the subway that night.

As well as excelling at gifting, I'd been squirrelling away my favourite things for months. Not quite whiskers on kittens but there were some brown paper packages, tied up with string. Louisa, my best friend from forever, had been sending care packages from England ever since the Boots Christmas catalogue came out. I had assorted advent calendars, boxes of crackers and endless supplies of Ferrero Rocher, After Eights, Quality Street and Cadbury's Roses hidden away in the top kitchen cupboard. I hoped she hadn't forgotten the savoury selection . . . On top of the British Christmas essentials, I'd already ordered my turkey and, following a Thanksgiving nightmare that involved a paring knife, a stubborn carrot and the tip of my left little finger, many pre-prepped vegetables. I would still be making the pigs in blankets myself, though, I wasn't a complete heathen.

Christmas was going to be perfect. I hadn't taken more than two days off since the wedding and I was completely exhausted. For the first time in forever, I'd booked an entire week's holiday and, quite frankly, I was going to Christmas the shit out of myself. I wanted to OD on the season of goodwill to such an extent that the sight of a candy cane would make me vomit by the end of it.

As long as it had been since I'd had time off, it felt

even longer since me and Alex had spent quality time together. Now I was working full-time, it seemed like every weekend was filled with chores and obligations. I hated for him to feel like he should do the food shopping or the laundry in the week just because he wasn't working a nine-to-five in an office, mainly because when I wasn't working a nine-to-five in an office, I sure as hell wasn't doing the washing. But fitting real life around work did mean some of the shine had gone off our relationship. There were no last-minute jaunts to watch him play international festivals or days spent lazing around in McCarren Park just because we could. The week was going to be all about us and I couldn't bloody wait.

Seven straight days of festive fun, culminating in twenty-four hours of just me, Alex, loads of food and an entire day sat in front of the TV, playing with my presents. And just in case he didn't quite come through on the gifting front, I'd picked up a couple of things for myself on one of my Christmas shopping binges and informed my mother she owed me the money. I was a very considerate daughter.

The lights on the tree twinkled on and off in an unfathomable pattern, echoed by the lights of the city outside the window. I closed the drapes on Manhattan and stared at the tree. I couldn't remember how I'd set them not to blink last year but then I couldn't remember how I'd made my wireless printer work two days earlier so that wasn't such a shock. I just wanted them to be the same as they had been. I just wanted one thing to be predictable for one moment. And that moment needed to start with Jenny. Alex was probably right, she would have her heart set on something else soon enough. And if she didn't, I'd just have to remind her how horribly Erin had suffered through both of her pregnancies – the morning sickness, the uncontrollable lactating, not being able to get into a single pair of her beautiful, beautiful designer shoes for over a year.

Emptying my beer, I picked up a stack of mail from the coffee table and leafed through the assorted flyers and bills. One was a reminder that I was due for a check-up at my own gynaecologist. It had been a year already? If there was one thing you could say about the US healthcare system it was that they were thorough. As long as you had insurance anyway. I pressed my hand against my belly and, just for a second, I stopped wishing it was flatter and pushed it out against my palm. I had spent so much time and energy over the years trying to get thinner, the idea of suddenly ballooning up, full of baby, was terrifying.

Halfway down the mail pile was a thick cream-coloured envelope with mine and Alex's name written in elegant script. Ooh, the first Christmas card of the season! I smiled beatifically at my Christmas tree. It felt good not to be the only seasonal crazy in the city.

But it wasn't a Christmas card. It was an invitation.

To the wedding of Mary Stein and Bob Spencer.

CHAPTER TWO

'You're getting married?'

'Good morning, Angela,' Mary replied without looking up from her computer when I raced into her office and slammed the door the following morning. The door-slamming was accidental but it did add to the dramatic effect.

'You're getting married to Bob?'

Mary took a deep breath, pushed her glasses up her nose and looked up at me with all the patience she could muster. Which with Mary was never that much.

'Delia told you?' she asked, carefully rolling up the sleeves of her crisp white shirt. Everything about Mary was crisp – her steel-grey bob, her Manhattan-born-and-bred accent, even her eyeliner. 'I told her I wanted to tell you myself.'

'Delia didn't tell me,' I said, taking an unoffered seat. I felt like such a shambles in front of Mary. She was almost the same age as my mother but always a thousand times more put together than me. I'd left the house in the same old Madewell pencil skirt I'd worn the day before and a neon pink and white striped

T-shirt. Somewhere in the bottom of my trusty old Marc Jacobs handbag there was a bright blue Paul & Joe jumper that absolutely failed to bring the entire outfit together. My spring–summer hand-me-downs from Jenny were on the brighter side this season. 'I got an invitation. To the wedding. Your wedding, to Bob. Bobbity Bob Bob Spencer Bob.'

'I don't think we'll be using his full name in the vows.' Mary pulled a face and immediately began clicking through screens on her Mac. 'They went out already? That's a week early. Honestly, you just can't hire the right people these days.'

'Oh no, what a nightmare.' I rapped on the desk for her attention and repeated myself. 'Mary, you're getting married to Bob Spencer?'

'Well, if I weren't, the invitations would be kind of an elaborate joke, wouldn't they?' Mary took off her glasses and I could swear I almost saw her smile. 'Yes, Angela, I'm getting married to Bob.'

She paused and waited for me to speak but I didn't have anything. No words. Not even swear words. Which was odd for me. After a quiet sigh, she picked up her phone and punched in an extension number.

'Delia, could you come down? Angela appears to have become mute.' I watched, still silent, and this time there was definitely a smile on her face. 'Yeah, I checked, she's still breathing.'

'I knew something was going on.' My voice found itself before I managed to exercise any control over its volume. 'I mean, not in the sense that I had any sort of actual idea but I knew you were up to something. So that's why you've been having all these secret meetings with Delia.'

'Kind of,' Mary replied.

'Kind of?' Brilliant. I loved it when Mary was vague. That was my favourite. 'What do you mean, kind of?'

'My getting married isn't the only change on the horizon, Angela,' she replied. 'Delia and I wanted to have everything ironed out before we presented you with the new plan. So there wouldn't be any reason for you to panic.'

'New plan?' I panicked. 'What's going on? Is *Gloss* closing? Have I been fired?'

It had to be all the pens I'd 'borrowed'. I couldn't help it, I was a stationery klepto. I feverishly tried to work out how many had found their way into the bottom of my handbag so I could replace them but there was no use, I'd literally had hundreds away.

'You haven't been fired,' Mary said with a sigh. 'You always jump to the worst possible conclusion. Why on earth would you be getting fired?'

Don't say the pens, don't say the pens, don't say the pens . . .

'I've nicked loads of pens.'

'I'm not even going to dignify that with a response.' She pressed her lips into a thin line and shook her head, just as the office door opened and Delia appeared. 'Thank Christ, you're just in time.'

'Have I missed anything?' Delia asked before leaning down to kiss me quickly on the cheek. She smelled like angels would smell if they happened to have spent a spare half hour in Bergdorf with a Black Amex.

'Angela just confessed that she is heading up an international stationery smuggling cartel,' Mary replied. 'But apart from that, no.'

'So nothing then,' Delia said, smoothing down her perfect pencil skirt and slipping into the big comfy chair. 'Right. Where do we start?'

'Mary's getting married to Bob.' I was shouting again. 'Your granddad, Bob.'

'Yeah.' Delia looked at Mary, then looked at me. 'I know about that one.'

'And you didn't tell me?'

How to go from shouting to squealing in two easy steps by Angela Clark.

'OK, I'm taking this over.' Mary clapped her hands together and leaned across her desk. 'Angela. We have a lot of good news to share. And a lot of it concerns you.'

'Now I know I'm not going to like what you have to say,' I replied, smoothing down my unironed pencil skirt and wishing I'd worn something more appropriate for running away. 'Spill it.'

'Delia has been promoted,' she said simply. 'As of January first, she will be VP of business development and acquisitions for all of Spencer Media.'

'Oh my God, that's amazing!' I turned to stare at my friend with wide eyes. 'I'm so proud of you. You're literally superwoman. This is incredible.'

'Thanks, Angela,' Delia said, blushing a pretty pale pink. 'It's kind of amazing.'

'It's totally amazing.' I could feel myself tearing up and tried to fight back the stinging in my eyes. Mary would not appreciate blubbing in her office. 'Mary's getting married, you're getting a promotion . . .'

'Watch it, Clark,' Mary warned.

'Watching it,' I replied with a sniff.

'But it does mean I won't be around quite so much at *Gloss*,' Delia said, placing her hand on my knee and looking at me with big, earnest blue eyes. 'We're the reason I'm getting this job. I told Grandpa there was no way I'd sign off on us completely, but there will be a new publisher. I'll be executive publisher.'

Now was not the time to freak out, I told myself, pasting on a smile and patting Delia's hand in a way that I hoped was reassuring and not threatening. I wasn't sure, though. Delia was an amazing businesswoman, this was only ever a matter of time. I knew this was coming, I just wasn't actually ready for it.

'And the new publisher will be brilliant,' I told her. And myself. 'Don't you worry about me and Mary. We'll muddle through.'

'OK.' Delia gave an awkward laugh and turned towards Mary. 'Your turn?'

'I'm not going to dick around here, Clark,' Mary said, as casually as humanly possible. I felt my heart rate soar and my face blanch. Thank God I was already so incredibly pale. 'When Bob and I get married, I'm taking a three-month sabbatical.'

'But you and Bob are getting married on New Year's Eve.' I felt my bottom lip start to quiver. 'That's in three weeks.'

'Plenty of time to get you where we need you,' she replied with a half-smile.

'Where do you need me?' I could hear my voice getting weaker and weaker. They couldn't actually send me to prison for nicking some pens, surely?

'We want you to hold down the fort while Mary's away,' Delia explained. 'We want you to be the interim editor of *Gloss*.'

Ridiculous wasn't a good enough word for it. We needed to make up a new one – this was supercalifragifuckedup. I took back everything I'd ever said about Delia being a good businesswoman. Clearly she'd gone completely insane. Power made some people mad.

'Angela?' she said, reaching out for my hand. 'You've gone quite pale.'

'OK, one thing at a time,' I said, clearing my throat and pointing at Delia. 'You're leaving?'

'Not leaving, I just won't be around for the day-to-day,' she clarified. 'But you'll have a new publisher who you can help hire to support you.'

'So you're leaving,' I corrected her. She sighed and nodded. I turned and pointed across the desk. 'And you're leaving?'

'I'm going on sabbatical,' Mary confirmed. 'For three months.'

'And when you've both left,' I said, taking a deep breath, 'you want me to be the editor of the magazine?'

'Yes,' Delia said, beaming.

'Interim editor,' Mary qualified, not beaming.

And that was the part I was having most trouble with.

Absolutely, I'd been a writer of sorts for years and I'd been working as a journalist since I'd moved to New York three and a half years ago, but this was sudden. This wasn't something that happened. I'd be a laughing stock. Other than Delia's savvy publishing, one of the reasons *Gloss* had done so well was because people loved Mary. She was an institution in the industry, she was respected. I was a random English girl who came to meetings with toothpaste down her jumper. And occasionally Ready brek.

'You'll have a new deputy. We can talk about whether we promote internally or look for an external hire.' Delia had clearly practised her argument before

27

coming to me. She really was very clever. 'And we're going to hire you an assistant to help out with your schedule and manage the office but you can do this, Angela. I've talked to Grandpa about it and so has Mary and he's willing to take a chance.'

Mew. I quickly translated that into the truth. Bob Spencer thought promoting me to editor, even temporarily, was as good an idea as I did. Unfortunately for Bob, I was just about contrary enough for that to convince me to give it a go.

'*Gloss* is your baby, don't turn this down.' Delia grabbed hold of my wrists and shook her blonde ponytail at me. She really was so much stronger than she needed to be. 'If you think about it and you really don't want to do it, we can find someone else. It won't be hard to fill the position. But with me and Mary out of the picture, if you and the new editor don't get along, who knows what would happen.'

Awesome. So if I took the job I didn't have a clue how to do, there was every chance I'd run my magazine into the ground, and if I didn't, there was every chance a new editor would kick me out. And this new, hypothetical editor didn't even know about the pens.

'Do I have any time to think about it?' I asked both of them. I really wanted Delia to let go of my wrists so I could bite my nails but she wasn't going to. Probably for the best. 'Just a day would be . . . I just need until tomorrow morning.'

'I told Grandpa I'd let him know at the end of the week,' Delia said, a small smile breaking on her face. 'But I knew you wouldn't need that long. Anna Wintour, eat your heart out.'

'I've heard she doesn't have one of her own, that's

why she has to eat other people's,' I said in a weak voice. 'Will I have to start wearing a suit?'

'Maybe not a suit but you will have to look into getting an iron,' Mary answered quickly. 'Really, they're not that expensive.'

'You realise, if I agree to this,' I said, flexing my wrists as Delia let go to give herself a little clap, 'I'm going to be an emotional wreck. And I'm probably going to have to start self-medicating and drinking at lunch and keeping pills in my desk and everything?'

'Oh, Angela.' Delia jumped up and pulled me to my feet for a hug. 'You're a real journalist now.'

'Yeah, a hardened artery away from a Pulitzer,' Mary added. 'Delia, you want to leave us to it? So we can discuss the finer details?'

I stared at Delia, begging her to say no and insist we all immediately leave the office and fly to Vegas to celebrate, but instead she broke our hug and nodded as sombrely as possible, which was not sombrely at all, and headed for the door.

'You're going to ace this,' she said with a wink. 'In three months you'll be begging Mary to take another trip. Trust me.'

'Of course,' I nodded, waving her away with a smile on my face and waiting for the door to close behind her. 'For fuck's sake, Mary, what are you thinking? Please don't leave the magazine.'

'I assume you mean, please don't leave *me*?' She gave me her most teacherly look and frowned.

'Yes,' I replied, pulling my chair closer to her desk. 'Of course that's what I mean.'

'It's time, Angela,' she shrugged. 'Bob is taking a step back from the business. I've been at this desk or one just like it for more than thirty-five years. I want to actually see the world rather than write about it. Preferably while I still have control of my bladder. I think we're leaving things in very capable hands.'

'Yeah, Delia's,' I said, torn between wanting to give her a big hug and wanting to cling to her leg and beg her not to go.

'And yours,' Mary said. 'As weird as it feels saying this, I'm not worried about *Gloss* or you. You're smart, you're driven and you care more about this magazine than anyone. Plus, you've been working for me for nearly four years. If you haven't picked up what you need in that time, you never will.'

I suddenly regretted dedicating so much time to beating my high score on Candy Crush Saga during all those editorial meetings.

'You'll be fine,' she went on. 'And I'm only ever as far away as the end of the phone. Or more likely an email – I might be overseas. Bob is talking about chartering a boat.'

A sudden vision of silver fox Bob and his blushing bride giving it the full *Titanic* on the front of some mega-yacht popped into my head. *I'm flying, Bob!* And try as I might, it would not go away.

'You can't fuck this up, Angela.' Mary snapped her fingers in front of my distressed-looking face. 'This magazine is idiot proof. I'm not going to sit here and puff up your ego by telling you how amazing you are, desperately trying to convince you that you can do a job you know perfectly well that you're capable of.'

'I am capable,' I repeated. Only I wasn't sure of what.

'Exactly,' Mary agreed. 'This magazine might have been your idea but I've been the editor since launch.

It's my baby. There's no way I'd sit back and watch someone run it into the ground for fun.'

It was the closest thing to a compliment she'd ever given me.

'Any other concerns?' she asked, turning her attention back to her computer.

'So, you and Bob, eh?' I said, standing and making a clucking noise. 'That old devil.'

'Go get a coffee and try not to speak to anyone until you're properly caffeinated.' She raised a hand to wave me away. 'And don't slam the door on the way out or I'll fire you before you can take over.'

I assumed she was joking but that didn't stop me closing the door extra quietly, just in case.

By the end of the day, I was ready to jack it all in, let Alex knock me up seventeen times, move to a farm in the middle of nowhere and be milked like a cow until the end of my days. Even though I hadn't technically accepted the job, it seemed the entire office already knew what was going on and I wasn't quite sure what to do with myself. There were cover lines to come up with, future features to approve, freelancers to look at and now apparently I needed to attend lots of exciting circulation meetings and schedule all sorts of thrilling executive appointments that almost all involved Excel spreadsheets. I hated Excel spreadsheets. Someone in finance had emailed me about something called a pivot table three times and I'd already come out in a rash. On the upside, I now had hot and cold running coffee, morning, noon and night, hand-delivered by writers who had barely acknowledged my existence before today, and someone from an entirely different magazine who was looking to

31

make a move to 'the most exciting publication in the company' brought me a bagel. Power, it turned out, was delicious but exhausting. I was fairly certain, if it weren't for the three and a half venti Starbucks I'd put away, I'd have passed out at my desk by five p.m.

My brain was buzzing with numbers and pictures and Taylor Swift's love life and I desperately needed to hear the voice of someone normal. Reaching for my phone, I dialled the only number I knew would help me make sense of such a ridiculous twenty-four hours.

'You've reached Louisa. I'm not around to take your call right now but leave a message and I'll get back to you as soon as I can.'

With an audible sob, I replaced the handset and cursed the Atlantic Ocean. I couldn't really complain when Lou wasn't able to take my calls – she had an actual baby to keep her busy and, to her credit, she had never been one of those mothers who made it sound easy. I'd known Louisa my whole life and no one had ever been better suited to motherhood – her mum used to joke that she would have changed her own nappies if she'd been able – but even she couldn't paint parenthood as a walk in the park. Lou was obsessed with baby Grace. Since the second she had popped out of her vajay-jay, she had been her everything. Lou had left her job when she got pregnant and now it even felt like her husband, Tim, barely got a look-in. The last time we had spoken, she didn't even know what had happened in the last season of *True Blood*. It was that serious. But she was pragmatic and honest and she always knew just what to say to make me feel better. When she answered her phone.

'Hey, only me,' I told the beep. 'Just feel like we

haven't talked in ages. Give me a call when you can. Love you.'

The second I hung up, the phone rang again.

'Louisa?' I was almost too excited.

'Angela?' a confused voice, not Louisa, replied. 'It's me. I'm waiting in the lobby?'

'Jenny?'

Of course. I suddenly remembered, the doctor's appointment.

'I'm sorry. I'll be right down.'

There was no rest for the wicked, or for friends of Jenny Lopez.

Although she was wearing her 'take me seriously' shoes and most resolute face, I could tell Jenny was nervous. She talked about her plans for Jenny Junior all the way up Madison but I couldn't quite tell whether she was trying to convince me or herself that it was a good idea. I listened quietly, making encouraging noises often enough to sound supportive but not regularly enough to sound thoroughly enthused. Because I wasn't. I heard my phone chiming inside my Marc Jacobs satchel just as we arrived but since Jenny had turned absolutely ashen, I decided to let it ring through to the answer phone.

'It's just a doctor's appointment, nothing to worry about,' I reminded her, taking her hand and giving it a squeeze.

'I know,' she said with absolutely zero conviction. 'I just want to ask some questions.'

She stopped outside the building and looked up at the skyscraper.

'Can we get drinks afterwards?' she asked.

'We can,' I agreed.

'Because I won't be able to drink once I'm pregnant, right?' her voice shook a little, even as she laughed. 'Better make the most of me while you can.'

'Let's go in.' I pulled her through the fancy gold and glass doors and smiled at the doorman. If she was this nervous going in to ask questions, maybe Alex was right, maybe this phase would be over before New Year's. 'We'll be late for the doctor.'

The doctor in question was in fact Erin's gynaecologist and former college roommate, Dr Laura, and her surgery looked more like a spa than any office I'd ever had the pleasure of visiting on the NHS. There were orchids where there should have been browning rubber plants, copies of *Vogue* and *W* instead of a 1996 *Take a Break* summer special and I couldn't see a single broken Etch A Sketch anywhere. I kept waiting for someone to offer me a manicure.

'Jenny?' Dr Laura Morgan opened a frosted-glass door into the plush waiting room almost as soon as we had sat down. 'And Angela! Wonderful. Come this way, ladies.'

Obviously, I'd heard that doctors in America were loaded and I'd met Laura a couple of times before, at Erin's wedding and then at assorted baby-related events, but I hadn't realised quite how, well, glossy she would be at work. Her hair was tied back in a perfect shiny black ponytail and underneath her slim-fitting white coat, she was wearing a gorgeous white silk shirt and camel-coloured skinny trousers. As a general rule, I hated women who looked good in trousers, primarily because I didn't, and she looked amazing. The nude patent Louboutins didn't hurt either. I had a minor sulk about my Topshop ankle boots and then reminded myself that I had owned

Louboutins once upon a time, and I would again. Just as soon as I considered myself enough of a grown-up not to fuck them up the first time I wore them. Besides, as I reminded myself every time Delia pranced into the office wearing them, there were other shoes in this world. Just none that were quite so pretty.

'So, Erin said you wanted to see me.' Laura waved us into her cushy office, all pale greys, fresh whites and soft pinks, and called out to her assistant for coffee. Her assistant was dressed head to toe in flowered scrubs, topped off with a your-last-minute-appointment-is-keeping-me-here-after-hours scowl. I noted that the designer shoes weren't uniform for everyone. Poor cow. 'Or at least she said Jenny wanted to see me. What can I do for you?'

'I want to have a baby,' Jenny declared, leaning forward in her overstuffed armchair, confidence back ten-fold. 'And I just want to make sure everything's in working order.'

'That's exciting news,' Laura replied, glancing at my worried expression and then back at Jenny's wild-eyed mania. 'I just want to check, I'm not going crazy, am I? You two aren't a couple?'

'Jesus Christ, us?' Jenny looked at me in horror. 'Shit, can you imagine?'

'I think what she's trying to say is no,' I translated. 'I'm here for moral support.'

'And her husband wants to put a baby in her too,' Jenny added. 'But she's all "la la la, I don't need a baby right now", right, Angie?'

'Shall we deal with one crisis at a time?' I asked, giving Jenny my best 'behave yourself' glare. She ignored it, as usual. 'We don't need to worry about me.'

'Well, I'm not worried about either of you.' Laura

tapped her pen against her desk and remained impressively calm. 'You both look pretty healthy, you're not an age risk, I can't really see any issues. But I'm super happy to do a physical, get some blood work done. There are a couple of tests I can run to make sure your hormone levels are where we'd want them and then after that it's really all down to you and the baby daddy. Or daddies in this case.'

'That sounds great,' Jenny breathed out, her shoulders slumping inside her black blazer. 'I mean, I don't technically have a baby daddy right now but I want to know that everything's working as it should be.'

'Uh, that's OK.' Laura looked slightly puzzled for half a second and then went back to tapping her pen. 'But this is something you're looking into imminently?'

'Yes.'

On cue, Laura's assistant opened the door with three cups, a coffee pot, a jug of boiling water and assorted teabags, cream and sugar options. I was so far away from home. The best I'd ever got at my doctor's at home was a paper cup of tap water when I needed to do a urine test and couldn't go. Somehow I was certain it was all Margaret Thatcher's fault.

'I see a lot of single women in their thirties who just want to check things out and, you know, there are a lot of options these days,' Laura said, taking a cup and pouring herself a stiff black coffee, into which she emptied three packets of Splenda. 'I can always refer you to a therapist if you want to talk through your feelings. Before you start any kind of process.'

Clever Dr Laura. I gave her a small, thankful smile as I made myself a cup of Earl Grey. Send Jenny to a psychiatrist who would take one look at her before forcibly applying a chastity belt and throwing the key into the East River.

'Maybe.' Jenny ignored the drinks and started drumming her fingers against her folded arms. 'Can we do the blood and hormone tests now?'

'Sure we can.' Laura took a calm sip from her cup before setting it down and pressing a button on her phone. 'I'll have Theresa set everything up in the next room. We can do both of you at once.'

'Both of us?' I immediately poured boiling water all over the floor. 'I'm fine. Really.'

'I want you to,' Jenny said, turning on me in a heartbeat. 'And it can't hurt to know everything's OK, surely?'

'What's to know?' I whispered with a smile. It was hard to be startled, pissed off and still polite to a doctor all at the same time. But you had to be polite to doctors, my mum said. 'I don't need this. I'm not doing it.'

I was prepared to do a lot of things for my friends, including and not limited to doctor's visits on a Friday night, holding back their hair while they vomited into my lap and even watching multiple *Saw* movies, but this was something else. She was literally asking me to bleed for her. And it wasn't even because she needed the blood.

'Obviously, this is all between us.' Laura stood up and rearranged her white coat. 'Just a friendly favour to you guys. It doesn't need to go on your records, it's just a fun thing to try.'

'How is getting a needle jabbed in my arm a fun thing?' I asked both of them. 'Ever? Unless you're a smackhead?'

'That . . . that's a joke, right?' Laura suddenly looked

very concerned. 'Because that kind of thing definitely affects these tests.'

'I'm not a smackhead,' I groaned. 'I just don't think I need these tests.'

'Do it for me,' Jenny pleaded, gripping my hand in hers and practically dragging me out of the lovely, calming office and following Laura into an altogether less artfully lit room full of medieval-looking medical equipment. And there it was. The chair. With the stirrups. I felt my vagina seize up in protest.

'I'm just going to take a little blood,' Laura said over the not at all reassuring sound of snapping rubber gloves. 'And then we'll do a urine test. You don't need my help with that. The results will be back in a couple of weeks and they'll show us generally how you're looking, what your hormone levels are like and how many eggs we're dealing with.'

While eager beaver Lopez shrugged off her blazer and rolled up her sleeve, I took a moment to think about my eggs. I couldn't say I'd given them the time of day before, unless I was cursing one of them for chaining me to the sofa with a hot-water bottle and an entire jar of Nutella while it took its own sweet time to mosey on out of my cramping uterus. But people talked about bad eggs all the time. What if I only had bad eggs? Sure, they had half a chance, they were going to be fertilised with Alex's super sperm, but there was still every possibility they'd get my dad's indigestion and my mum's asthma and my fallen arches. High heels hurt me. I didn't wish that on my future child. But what if that was all that was left? Asthmatic, gassy babies who couldn't walk in anything over a three-inch heel. That took modelling and prostitution off the table for future career choices. What if my next period was the last decent egg? My last chance at birthing a professional footballer or Nobel peace prize winner or *X-Factor* semi-finalist?

'Angela, your turn.'

Jenny was carefully prodding a tiny round plaster on the inside of her elbow as Laura advanced on me with a length of rubber tubing and a hypodermic needle.

'You ready?' she asked.

'No,' I replied.

And, dear God, was that the truth.

CHAPTER THREE

One of the most common phrases I heard in New York was 'go big or go home'. Usually, this made me very happy. Everything was more over the top here – the people worked harder, the bars opened later and there was bacon in everything – but today, even the weather was acting like a real New Yorker. Whoever had upset the wind and brought the brutal sleet shower that slapped me in the face when I stepped out of my apartment needed a kicking. It was days like this that I was reminded I was not a true New Yorker. A born-and-bred city gal would have pulled on her North Face jacket, muttered 'fudgedaboudit' and gone about her business. I stood on my doorstep in a duffel coat and a fancy scarf that became immediately sodden, and whimpered until a cab buzzed by. I couldn't think of a day I'd been happier to stick out my arm and jump inside. This was an open-minded city but murdering commuters because you had had too many drinks and not enough hot dogs the night before was generally considered a no-no and, I imagined, it was especially frowned upon at Christmas time.

As soon as we left the doctor's office, Jenny and I had headed straight to the St Regis for 'dinner'. Only dinner turned out to be a bowl of bar nuts and three martinis, a choice that was neither nutritious nor conducive to an easy morning commute. Thank God it was perfectly acceptable to wear sunglasses indoors in December in this city. My comfy, comfy leggings, cocoon-like Club Monaco sweater and battered old Uggs combo had been frowned upon by the girls in the office but I was fairly certain I'd got the greasy egg, bacon and cheese sandwich past them without anyone detecting it. My satchel was going to stink for weeks. Stink like heaven.

No sooner had I sat down to take my first bite than my phone began to ring. I picked up as quickly as I could, just to stop the noise, fumbled with the handset for a moment and finally managed to answer.

'Angela? It's Mandy from human resources. The first interviewee for the assistant position is here. Are you on your way up?'

The assistant position. Interviews. I had to sit in a room and talk to strangers about a job I didn't really want to give them. I looked longingly at the greasy paper bundle in my handbag and sniffed.

'I'll be up in five minutes,' I croaked into the phone. 'How many are there?'

'Eight,' Mandy replied. 'Five minutes.'

For a moment I wondered if HR at Condé Nast spoke to Anna Wintour like that. Taking one delicious bite out of my sandwich before trudging back out of my office, I figured they must. Even a Prada-wearing devil had to hand in her appraisals on time, surely?

Of course, the interviews were torture.

Even if I hadn't had a seventeen-piece orchestra

41

tuning all their instruments at the same time inside my head while my stomach behaved like it was on a roller coaster, on the deck of a cruise ship, travelling through very choppy waters, it would have been unbearable. In fact, trying not to vomit was pretty much the only interesting thing I had to focus on throughout. One after another, shiny-haired, impeccably dressed and wildly overqualified boys and girls filed in, sat down and showed me the result of their very expensive childhood orthodontist work and even more expensive education. Not one of them had a single, solitary hair out of place and not a single one of them had woken up with a little bit of their own sick on them. Was it weird to feel intimidated by your own potential assistant? Alistair, Chessa, Tessa, Betsy, Beatrice, Sarah, Sarah and Sara were all exactly the same human being. Well, Alistair obviously had some differences from the girls but he was wearing very expensive designer shoes and did also like kissing boys, so not that many. They were fashionably put together but not making any sort of statement. They had all attended expensive, liberal arts colleges and had degrees that had great potential to be entirely useless in the outside world. They all lived on the Upper East Side with their families or had just moved out to Brooklyn and they all had an uncountable number of internships under their belt. Basically, everything added up to 'they were all really rich'. It wasn't like I'd grown up without two pennies to rub together, or like I hadn't met some very rich people in my time in New York who weren't entirely dreadful, but something about that soft-focus sheen that money gave a person made me nervous. The idea of having to ask someone to go and get me a coffee when they had never had to light up the inside of their handbag with their pay-as-you-go mobile looking for a last pound coin to pay for their kebab on the way home from Wetherspoons made me feel a bit, well, weird.

As the interviews dragged on, I discovered that they were all perfectly nice and had excellent interview skills. They all wanted to work in journalism and they were all so excited about the opportunity to work on a magazine as fun and as fantastic as *Gloss*. Blah blah blah. Why hadn't anyone thought to bring me a snack as a bribe? After the first hour, I would have given them my job if they'd have just given me a bag of Doritos. As soon as Tessa had finished telling me about her award-winning humanist-slash-beauty-slash-kitten fancier blog and wafted out of the room on a cloud of Chanel, I leapt to my feet and told Mandy I had an important conference call that meant I absolutely had to get back to my desk. There was no way I could sit and discuss the subtle differences between Sarah's English major and feminist theory minor versus Sara's English major and quite blatant cocaine addiction minor. I felt like I'd just interviewed the entire cast of *Gossip Girl* and I needed a quiet sit-down.

And so that was exactly what I was not about to get. As I sloped back to my desk, I spotted a blonde head poking up from the chair in front of my desk. Delia. At least she might take sympathy on me, I thought, cheering slightly at the thought of some empathetic nodding. And most importantly, she wouldn't judge me when I ate the shit out of that cold egg sandwich.

'Fuck me,' I announced, pushing the glass door open and letting it close loudly behind me. 'Interviewing is too hard. All I want to do is bury myself in a vat of Ben & Jerry's and eat my way out.'

'Ew.' Delia wrinkled up her tiny, surgery-free nose and gave me the filthiest look she could muster. Which would have been a strange response for Delia, if it had in fact been Delia. But it wasn't. Of course it wasn't, because today was turning out to be a day of complete and utter shittiness and that could only mean one thing. Delia's twin sister Cici had come to pay me a visit.

Fucking. Brilliant.

I sank down in my chair and stared at her. It was like being in the same room as a spider – I wanted it to go away but I didn't dare take my eyes off it in case it came to get me when I wasn't looking.

'Cici,' I said eventually.

'Angela,' she replied, wiping off the look of disgust and replacing it with a bland, easy smile I recognised from the poor little rich girls I'd just interviewed.

'I am too tired today.' I prayed she would make it quick. 'Can you just punch me in the face and leave?'

Cici looked at me blankly for a moment and then threw her head back in a terrifying laugh that I'd previously only seen written down in Jenny's most manic text messages. 'Oh, hahahahahaha. That's funny.'

'Is it?'

Just for a moment, I really wished I'd had a panic button installed under my desk.

'Yes?'

I breathed in, breathed out and waited but apparently she really didn't know what I was talking about. Cici sounded the same but, while I couldn't quite put my finger on it, something was very slightly off. Her super-trendy outfits had been replaced by a pair of bootcut jeans and a regular-looking sweatshirt and her hair, gorgeous as it was, didn't look like it had seen a straightening iron in, well, at least five seconds. Maybe she was dying? I peered under the table. She was wearing trainers. No heels. Perfect for a speedy getaway.

'Oh.' Finally, she clicked. 'Because you think I hate you and, you know, all that stuff that happened.'

When Cici said 'all that stuff that happened' I assumed what she meant was the time she'd had my suitcase blown up at the airport in Paris and tried to sabotage my career by blackmailing my assistant into screwing me over. Or maybe when she got me fired, which meant I almost lost my visa and could have been deported. Or maybe it was the time she tried to destroy *Gloss*, the magazine her very own sister was working on, before it had even launched. Of course, I had responded to this evildoing with grace and maturity and had risen above the whole thing. Aside from the time Louisa almost beat the living shit out of her. But that was totally by the by.

'If you're not here to ruin my life, or at the very least Christmas, what do you want?' I asked. I was too weak to get into a scrap again, although throwing up on her would be new and, I imagined, quite effective.

'So, Deedee told me you need a new assistant.' She flicked her hands out to the side in a kind of jazz hands gesture. Her nails were all chipped and bitten down. Cici Spencer hadn't had a manicure . . . OK, she was definitely dying. 'So, like, I'm here to be your new assistant.'

More often than not, in situations where most people would have been rendered speechless it was my unfortunate habit to let out a string of expletives and unintelligible noises. However, in this instance, I was quite simply gobsmacked.

'I know we've had some issues in the past,' Cici went on, ignoring the horror on my face and the fear in my eyes. 'But I've totally changed. I've been in India at a yoga retreat.'

As if to convince me that this complete and utter spiritual shift was complete, she tugged on a tiny plait, interwoven with gold and red threads, hidden in her hair.

'I was there for six weeks.'

For a moment, I was very worried that I had actually drunk myself to death the night before and this was some sort of purgatorial test but a quick and painful pinch of the arm proved that whether I liked it or not, this was happening.

'So, you went to a spa in India, got your hair done and now you're a new person?' I just wanted to get all my facts straight before I called the police.

'I mean, they called it a spa,' Cici said with a raised eyebrow. 'But, you know, I didn't dare sit in the steam room on my own and I had to take my own towels. And for some reason there were, like, cows and elephants everywhere.'

'Because you were in India?' I suggested.

'Yeah, at a spa,' she repeated.

'Right.' I used my last reserve of strength to stand up and press my hands onto the desk, trying my hardest to look stern and as though I wouldn't fall over if a kitten pushed me with a whisker. 'This has been fascinating but you have to leave. I'm sure you've got whatever hilarious kick you were after out of my outfit anyway.'

'Listen, Angela.' Cici flushed bright red and stood

up until we were face to face. Except for now she was about five inches taller than me, even in trainers. Albeit nice ones. 'I really have changed and I really want to make a new start. I guess in some weird, abstract way, I sort of kind of feel like you and I owe each other an apology.'

'That is interesting,' I said as my psycho alarm began to blare inside my head.

'But clearly you want to hold a grudge.' She sniffed and feigned a sad face. 'I guess spending all that time soul-searching and working out how I can be a better person, how I can make my pops and my sister proud, I guess all that was for nothing.'

'It would seem so,' I said with as much sympathy as I could muster. 'I hope you at least got a good massage out of it.'

'You've changed.' Her eyes flashed, as though she was being hard done by, as though she might actually be able to squeeze out a tear. 'I know you don't believe it but I liked working with Mary when I was her assistant, you can ask her.'

'Well, yeah,' I admitted. 'But I'm fairly certain you never accidentally on purpose dropped a picture of a huge penis in any of her PowerPoint presentations either, did you?'

'You have changed, Angela,' she nodded, smiling. 'What, now you're a big shot editor with your dumb dip-dye colour job, you're too big and important to give a girl a second chance? And FYI, I wasn't even going to mention your cruddy outfit.'

'By my count, this would be your fifth chance,' I pointed out. 'And it's not dip-dye, I just haven't had time to get the roots done.'

'Whatever,' she snapped. 'Namaste.'

I watched Cici and her wounded karma flounce all the way down the office, confusing the newbies who thought she was Delia in a never-before-seen huff and scaring those who remembered her from her previous reign of terror at Spencer Media. I fixed my eyes on her tiny bottom until she was safely in the lift and safely out of the building. And then I sat down. And then I sighed. And then I threw up in my bin.

My name is Angela. I am disgusting.

Two hours later, I was still sat at my desk, surrounded by Christmas cheer I was struggling to feel and desperate to get outside into the fresh air. But sadly, if I wanted to take any time off the following week, there was a lot of work to be done. I'd already had an email from Mary saying they needed me in on Monday but I was still hoping to take the rest of the week off. Four days of fun was better than none.

I rubbed my eyes to stop them from blurring as I stared at a page of mascara reviews, only to pull away my fists covered in blackish brown smudges. I'd been looking at my computer for too long and I was a long way from being finished yet. There was every chance I shouldn't have spent half an hour streaming the *Come Dine With Me* Christmas special after Cici left but how else was I supposed to get back my seasonal spirit? That girl brought out my inner Grinch. Before I could focus my eyes back on the screen, my iPhone rattled across the glass top of my desk, flashing up a name that made me very, very happy.

'Hello!' I screeched, mentals and mascara smudges completely forgotten.

'Clark, get your arse outside. I'm freezing my bloody balls off.'

Even though it was not Santa, I would have been hard-pressed to be more excited. This was someone who gave much better gifts and visited far less regularly.

'On my way,' I replied, hanging up and clapping my hands. The magazine could manage without me for ten minutes. Probably.

'All right, you old slag.' As soon as I stepped out of the Spencer Media lobby James Jacobs, my absolute favourite formerly closeted gay actor from Sheffield, threw his huge arms around me and squeezed until I squeaked. I hadn't seen him since my wedding, despite repeated promises and four a.m. text messages swearing he'd swing by the next time he was in New York. Oh, to be so jet-set-slash-busy doing it with boys. We hugged it out while I wrapped my not nearly warm enough but very cute Theory duffel coat and jumped up and down, half because I was so excited and half to warm up my feet. It really was bloody freezing.

'Why didn't you tell me you were coming to visit?' I demanded, still mid-hug. Sometimes his hugs went on a bit and I couldn't quite breathe but they were very lovely. 'Or are you on the run?'

'How did you know?' he asked, letting me go and holding me at arm's length to get a good look. 'I'm here for work and to tell you to get your hair cut. Where do we go?'

'We could just go upstairs?' I suggested. 'I've got an office with walls and windows and everything.'

'As impressive as that sounds,' James said, patting me on the top of the head, 'I'd rather not.'

'Because of the celebrity mags?' I asked, all sympathetic and understanding.

'Because I shagged one of the blokes who works on

reception once and never called him,' he replied. 'So, where are we going?'

I thought for a moment. He didn't want to go to the office, I didn't want to go to the Bubba Gump Shrimp Company and neither of us wanted to stand in the street freezing our nuts off, which did not leave us with many options. Looking up at James, six foot something, glossy brown hair, huge eyes, cheekbones that would slice bread, I frowned. Did he have to be quite so bloody tall and gorgeous? If we couldn't go somewhere he wouldn't be recognised, we had to go somewhere no one would care. Somewhere people had other things to think about. Somewhere in Times Square . . .

'I know just the place.' I grabbed his hand and dragged him down the street. 'I'm a genius. Follow me.'

'You're a genius?' James shook his head and folded his arms. 'Sometimes, Angela Clark, I worry.'

'Embrace it,' I replied. 'It was close, it's quiet and no one in Toys R Us a week before Christmas gives a shit about you. They just want a Buzz Lightyear or Teletubby or whatever the kids are into these days. Plus, I've got a bag of Sour Patch Kids in my handbag so you'll even get a snack. What more could you want?'

When most people were stressed or unhappy, they went to look at the ocean or hang out in the park. Others opted for retail therapy – Holly Golightly went to Tiffany, Jenny Lopez went to Saks Fifth Avenue, I went to Toys R Us in Times Square. Admittedly, it was a bit odd when I didn't have any kids of my own but I had yet to find anywhere else within ten minutes' walking distance of my office as distracting as the giant animatronic dinosaur in the Jurassic Park section of the store. When Bergdorf put one of those in, I'd walk the extra ten blocks. Until then, I was staying here.

'Sour Patch Kids are not a snack,' he said, taking a handful anyway and raising his voice over the extra-loud music. 'Jesus, I haven't eaten this much sugar in about seven years. Incredible. Your logic troubles me.'

'But you do admit it's a kind of logic,' I said, 'so that's something.'

'If anyone tweets about this, I'll kill you,' he said, pausing to offer the kids in the My Little Pony car below us a dazzling smile and flip his curly brown hair away from his face. Yes, he clearly hated the attention. 'And if I get motion sickness, I'm going to throw up on your shoes.'

I crossed my legs, tucking my Uggs under the seat, and hoped he was joking. It was a miracle I'd never thrown up on them, I'd be damned if someone else was going to do it.

'OK, what's going on?' I asked, popping a handful of sour sweets in my mouth and leaning back to enjoy the ride. 'Aside from making my Friday complete, what are you doing here?'

'You can't tell anyone,' James leaned in to whisper in my ear with unnecessary but very welcome theatrical flair. 'I just auditioned for a musical.'

I stared at him with a completely blank expression. 'Fuck off.'

James. In a musical. Ha. Yes, he was an actor and yes, he was as gay as the day was long but he was far from camp and, above all else, he was a boy from Sheffield. It just wasn't possible. Boys from Sheffield weren't in musicals. They could be in bands but they could absolutely, positively not be in musicals.

'I did! I just auditioned for a musical!' he insisted, just loud enough for everyone in the shop to update everyone they knew on every form of social media known to man. So much for subtlety. 'I'm serious.'

And according to the slightly annoyed glint in his eyes, he was.

'Hollywood wasn't enough?' I sipped my water and tried to rein in my excitement. I loved a musical – it was my not-so-secret secret shame. The fact that tickets were so incredibly bloody expensive was the only thing that stopped me from singing along with *Pippin* every single night. Well, ticket prices and the fact that everyone I knew would disown me. 'Which one?'

'*Les Mis*,' he replied casually as he popped another sour sweet with relish. 'God, I've missed junk food. Maybe I'll get really fat next year and then do *Dancing with the Stars* to get it all off.'

My heart stopped. My eyes widened. Had he just said what I thought he had?

'*Les Mis* as in *Les Miserables*? As in the best musical ever made? As in I know all the words and sometimes when I'm in the shower I like to pretend I'm Eponine and you can never, ever, ever repeat that as long as you live?'

'Yes, Angela, you mental, that *Les Mis*,' he said. 'You know they're reviving it?'

'Of course I know they're reviving it,' I answered in a near shout. 'There is a blog, James. There are several blogs. I cannot believe you auditioned for it. Who are you playing?'

'Well, if I get it,' he said, very clear about the 'if', which I ignored, obviously. 'Jean Valjean. You know?'

I did know. And to communicate this, I pressed my hands to my heart and nodded because I was entirely without words. Twice in one day. It was a new record.

'And yeah, I had the audition this morning so I flew in last night, met the producers, sang my song . . .' He raked a hand through the too-long hair that now made all sorts of sense and shrugged. 'I'll know in a few days if they want to see me again, so I thought I'd stick around.'

'I'd invite you to stay but it'd be the sofa or the airbed and I am sure you are far too fancy for that,' I said, trying to pretend I didn't want to talk exclusively about the fact that he was potentially going to appear in my all-time favourite musical ever.

'Don't worry about it.' James pulled a face and stretched his arms out along the back of the car. He was clearly enjoying himself, even if he wasn't prepared to admit it. 'I'm staying at the Mondrian. And you know I don't do Brooklyn. It gives me a rash.'

'You've never been to Brooklyn,' I pointed out. 'But if you're going to be here over Christmas, I'm going to force you over at gunpoint. I'm going to do a Boxing Day thing. Jenny'll be around. And probably Graham and Craig. You remember Graham?'

'Graham?' James furrowed his brow into a vision of contemplation. He was so handsome. When I was thinking hard, I looked like I needed the bathroom, or was about to cry. Because sometimes when I had to think that hard I did cry. 'Is he the one I met at your wedding?'

'Yes,' I replied, practising my judgey face for when I got back to the office. 'In England and in New York. He's the bassist in Alex's band? Very tall, handsome, glasses? You had sex with him several times?'

James clicked his fingers and nodded. 'Oh yeah. Nice guy.'

'And so memorable.'

'It was ages ago,' he said, as though I was being entirely unreasonable. 'We hooked up, we weren't the ones getting married.'

'I suppose it is easier to remember the names of everyone you've ever had sex with when you can count them all on one hand,' I replied. 'Names, dates of birth, identifying marks, names of parents, allergies and medical issues.'

'I can't decide if you're my hero or the saddest woman I ever met.' James squeezed his arm around my shoulders, elbowing Woody and Buzz in the face. 'Poor lamb. Tell me all about it. Have you got the seven-year itch a bit early?'

'No,' I protested, horrified at the very thought. 'I wouldn't cheat on Alex. Not even with a Hemsworth.'

'What about both Hemsworths?' he asked.

I paused for a moment.

'Nope,' I declared. 'Not even both Hemsworths and a Gosling.'

'Shit, that's serious,' James clucked. 'You really should think before you say such things.'

'I mean it,' I said and I did. 'Let's be honest, I was never very good at dating. I'm perfectly happy to have retired early.'

'Sounds nice,' he said, contemplative for a second. 'But yeah, there comes a time when enough's enough. But what can a boy do when he's ready for a change?'

'Secretly pop over to New York without telling his friends,' I suggested, 'and audition for a part in a musical?'

'Oh Clark, you're not as green as you are cabbage-looking, are you?' He smiled and gave my shoulder another squeeze. 'You can be quite perceptive sometimes.'

I smiled. Upsettingly, it was the nicest thing anyone had said to me all day.

'So what's going on?' I asked, smiling broadly at the bored-looking shop assistant who was in charge of shoving people on and off the ride. I wondered if anyone ever fell off. I wondered if anyone ever jumped off. It would be a hell of a way to go.

'Nothing really.' He peered over the edge of our car and tapped out a beat on the side of the carriage. I noticed the stubble on his cheeks, the dark shadows under his eyes. I'd assumed they were evidence of too much travelling and fun times but maybe not. 'Just feeling a bit shit, a bit lonely. It's been a long time since I've had someone around.'

'And that's what you want?' I covered my mouth so as not to offend him with a mouthful of neon goo. 'A boyfriend?'

'I want something,' James said, looking behind us. Buzz and Woody seemed to understand. 'I want someone to text stupid things to, not just a picture of my knob and *my place at twelve?* I'm thinking about moving to New York permanently actually. LA feels a bit tired.'

'Obviously I would love that.' I decided to ignore the dick pic part of the debate. That was an issue for his agent, not me. 'You really think the dating prospects are better here than in California?'

'That's what I hear,' he replied with a shrug. 'And it's a better place to raise a family for me, I think.'

'Everyone has gone baby mad.' I dug my hands deep into the pockets of my coat and tried to remember if I'd taken my Pill that morning. 'Is there something in the water?'

'You too?' James broke into a real smile. 'That would be amazing. Imagine, our little babies growing up together, going to school together, beating each other up, having incredibly awkward sexual encounters and then crying about it all in therapy twenty years later. Amazing.'

'Well, as special as that sounds . . .' I couldn't quite return his big grin but I mustered up the ghost of a smile so as not to let him down. 'It's not me just yet. Alex, maybe. Jenny, yes. My friend, Erin, just had her second.'

'You're not ready?' he asked.

I fiddled with my engagement ring and shook my head.

'I just pulled a half-empty, family-sized bag of Sour Patch Kids out of my handbag and that was supposed to be my lunch,' I said. 'No, I'm not ready. How am I supposed to take care of a baby? I am a baby.'

'You know what they say, there's never a right time,' he said, taking another handful of sweets and throwing them into his mouth. 'But I have just crossed you off my surrogate list.'

'Thank you.' I scooped up the rest of the sweets into my hand and folded the bag as small as possible to avoid filling the bottom of my satchel with sour sugar. Again. 'It is appreciated.'

'You say Jenny's feeling broody?' James did not extend the same mouth-covering courtesy to me that I had shown to him. Gross. 'She seeing someone?'

'Yes, she is, and sort of, but maybe not by now. She's being ridiculous. It's totally out of nowhere.'

'Hmm.' My favourite gay leaned forward, elbows on knees, swinging the carriage forward. I just managed not to squee with delight. 'Biological clocks are pretty intense, Clark, and she's a couple of years older than you, isn't she?'

'I know,' I said, feeling a tiny bit guilty. 'I'm not giving her a hard time, or at least I hope I'm not. I just don't want her to rush into something this massive and then regret it. I don't know if she really wants a baby or she just doesn't want to be on her own. I don't think dating Craig has really been the relationship of her dreams.'

'Which one is Craig?' he frowned.

'The one in Alex's band that you didn't have sex with,' I said. 'I hope.'

'I definitely only did the one in the glasses,' he said, squinting with the effort of remembering. 'But I think I remember him. He's hot.'

'He is,' I acknowledged. 'But I don't think he's particularly thinking about the future right now. He's a straight, good-looking thirty-two-year-old musician in Brooklyn. That gives him the emotional maturity of a nineteen-year-old anywhere else in the world.'

'Alex manages monogamy,' James said, his foot tapping along to 'Frosty the Snowman' as he spoke. 'Maybe you're just being cynical.'

'And I fully expect to wake up from my coma and find out Alex was all a dream any day now,' I replied. 'He is not the norm here, you know that. Dating is hard. I think that's a bigger problem for Jenny than the baby thing. I just don't think she wants to admit it.'

'It'll all come out in the wash,' he said with a yawn. 'You'll get the truth out of her eventually. Probably when you're hammered.'

'You know me so well,' I said, wincing at the thought of ever having to drink again. I could not hold my ale like I used to and that was saying something. 'Why don't you come over for dinner? I'll call her, we'll get her liquored up together?'

'In Brooklyn?'

'Yes?'

'Oh, Clark,' James replied with a friendly smile. 'How many times? I Don't Go There.'

You had to admire a man who had his principles.

CHAPTER FOUR

'Are you planning on getting out of bed at all today?'

I opened one eye and squinted up at an unusually perky-looking Alex Reid. Instead of hiding from any sort of natural light, which was how I found him almost every single morning, he was up, dressed and sat on the edge of the bed, holding a steaming cup of coffee. Weird.

'No?' I closed my eye and pulled a pillow over my head.

It was Saturday. A quick shuffle of my feet confirmed my body was entirely covered by the duvet and I didn't need a wee. There was absolutely no good reason I could see as to why I should move at all.

'It's just that I kind of need you to get up so we can go check in on your Christmas present.'

I opened both eyes. I moved the pillow. I looked at my husband.

'Give me fifteen minutes,' I replied.

A little over an hour later, Alex and I emerged from the deepest, darkest depths of the G train, thirty minutes from home and in the middle of a neighbourhood I barely knew.

'We're in Park Slope?' I asked as he took hold of my hand and squeezed it through my bright knitted mittens. 'I should not be wearing shorts.'

'It's below freezing,' Alex replied. 'That's why you shouldn't be wearing shorts.'

'What are we doing?' I asked, looking left and right at quiet, orderly streets. 'My Christmas present is in Park Slope?'

'Your Christmas present is in Park Slope,' Alex repeated, nodding his head and pointing with the hand that held mine. 'This way.'

I was full of questions but Park Slope was a library of a neighbourhood, shushing me before I could speak. Alex and I didn't hang out this south of Williamsburg often. Or ever actually. Brooklyn was a big borough, full of diversity and adventure, but for the most part, there were three different kinds of neighbourhoods. There was the trendy, hipster part where people rode their bikes everywhere and had ironic moustache tattoos on their fingers, there were the incredibly dodgy bits where I was too scared to get off the subway, and then there were the yummy mummy, super-swanky parts with lots of trees, lots of iPads and lots of odd shops that sold things like artisanal mayonnaise or handcrafted hats. And only two things united all three areas – a fierce love of Beyoncé and men with beards. Park Slope was the epitome of the third type of neighbourhood.

Everywhere I looked, there were attractive couples in their gym clothes pushing elaborate prams and drinking from reusable water bottles, well-groomed women walking expensive-looking dogs and coffee shop after coffee shop after coffee shop. I knew that somewhere nearby there was a huge, beautiful park where Alex's band, Stills, had played at a festival the summer before and I'd been saying I was going to come back and visit for months on end but, like so many things I was 'going to do' in New York, I still hadn't got around to it. But I did remember that Park Slope in the summer had been beautiful, all sunny skies and green trees, and if it was possible, today it was even more picturesque. The streets we strolled down were orderly and clean, punctuated with stately trees and lined by big brownstones, the kind of houses that made me want to put on my best shoes, sit on my stoop and flag down a yellow cab. Inside, I saw warmly lit trees and menorahs, and almost every other door had a beautiful red-ribboned wreath hanging outside. Even though we were half an hour away from Manhattan, this looked like the New York you saw in the movies and it made my heart sing.

'You really have no idea where we're going?' Alex asked, sheepdogging me down another street, away from the coffee shops and past a church and a synagogue and another church. With its own coffee shop. 'I can't believe I've actually been able to keep a secret from you.'

'I've been busy,' I explained, looking up at the street signs and trying to work out what he was talking about. 'Is it food?'

'No, it's not food,' he sighed. 'It's better than food.'

'Seriously, I got dressed before midday on a Saturday and you're not even going to feed me?' What was better than food? 'Was that Anne Hathaway? She lives here.'

'You got half dressed,' he reminded me. His eyes were shining so brightly I couldn't help but smile.

'These are the things I worry about when I'm away on tour. And no, I don't think it was Anne Hathaway.'

'It might have been.' I was trying not to be too grumpy but Alex (and anyone who had ever spent more than half a day with me) was well aware that I was difficult when I was hungry. 'You don't know.'

'Yeah, I do know because it was a fourteen-year-old boy.' He squeezed my hand and stopped short in the middle of the street. 'We're here.'

But we weren't anywhere. We were stood in the middle of 9th Street, right between 8th and 9th Avenues, looking at nothing with no one in sight.

'Alex?' The front door to the brownstone in front of us opened and a tall, glossy woman with too much too blonde hair appeared, smiling at my husband.

'Hey, Karen,' Alex replied cheerfully, heading up the steps and pulling me along behind him. He pushed me in front of him to shake the woman's outstretched hand. 'This is Angela.'

'Mrs Reid, so nice to meet you at last.' Karen was older than me – I guessed at least somewhere in her mid-forties, although it was so hard to tell with well-heeled New York women. Either there was some Botox at play or it was a very impressive fake smile she was shining right at me. 'Alex has told me so much about you.'

'Um, it's Angela, please.' Flummoxed as I was, I'd be buggered if I was going to be called impolite. By a complete stranger. Who appeared to have some sort of close relationship with my husband that I knew nothing about. 'And it's Clark. Not Mrs Reid. I didn't change my name. When we got married. Because of work and . . . you know.'

Karen's eyes flitted over to Alex with mild concern. Apparently she did not know.

'Right,' she smiled again, although this time more like I was a puppy with three legs, and beckoned us inside. Alex gave me a gentle shove through the front door and a slap on the arse. It did not make up for how incredibly confused I was. 'Shall we go inside?'

A thousand scenarios were running through my head but none of them seemed quite right. She was an artist and Alex was going to have our portrait painted. She was a chef and Alex had bought me (sorely needed and often referenced) cooking lessons. She was a very unfortunate prostitute and Alex thought it was time to spice things up in the bedroom. Oh God, that was it. She was some sort of sex teacher. We had drunkenly made a 'no three-way' sex vow before the wedding but what if my recent sexy bedtime ensemble of a promotional Smirnoff Ice T-shirt and topknot weren't doing it for him? Things had been a bit quiet in the bedroom of late but I was so tired from long hours at the office and Alex was up all night working on new songs. How had I let things get so bad? I should have been *Fifty Shades of Grey*ing the shit out of him every night, I should have—

'You have to tell me what's going on in your head right now,' Alex whispered, 'because your face is a fucking picture.'

'Alex, tell me what's going on right now,' I replied, having adequately scared myself shitless.

'So, you'll be apartment one. The basement and backyard are all yours. Two and three are up the staircase and they have the rooftop.' Karen gestured absently up a dark, wooden staircase to my right and then unlocked the door on my left. 'Shall I give the two of you the grand tour or do you want to do the honours yourself?'

'I'm going to take it from here, if that's OK,' Alex said, giving Karen a half-nod and holding his hand out to take the keys from her. 'We'll see you outside?'

'Of course,' she said, beaming back at the pair of us. 'Congratulations. It's a beautiful home. Perfect for a new family.'

'Thanks.' Alex waited for Karen to leave and then locked the door behind her. Leaning against it, he smiled awkwardly out from underneath his floppy fringe, hands shoved deep into the pockets of his leather jacket. 'So, yeah. Merry Christmas.'

Karen was not a sex teacher. She was not going to teach me the art of sensual massage. This was not a well-concealed brothel. This was . . . well, I still wasn't sure. I looked up at the tall white tin ceiling. I looked over my shoulder at the huge empty room with its enormous bay windows, elegant fireplace and shiny hardwood floor. I looked back at Alex. He looked completely out of place and so incredibly happy.

'This?' I pointed at him, then at myself, then at the floor. 'You rented this apartment?'

'I bought this apartment,' he said, not budging from the doorway. 'It's ours.'

I suddenly felt very, very sick.

'You bought this apartment? It's ours?' I couldn't really make words of my own so I repeated his, trying very hard to keep my voice even and my legs straight. 'This is our apartment? That you didn't tell me about? That you bought? Without telling me?'

'I'm feeling like maybe you're not as excited as I had hoped you would be.' He advanced on me slowly, hands held out, either to hug me or hold me off, I wasn't sure. 'It was supposed to be romantic. It's an amazing apartment, babe, let me show you around.'

64

It was too much. Before he could take another step, I sank to the floor, crossed my legs and rested my head in my palms, hiding behind my hair. Alex had bought an apartment. In Park Slope. Without asking me, without telling me, without even hinting that he was thinking about moving. Usually, I couldn't get him to order from a new pizza place without having to bribe him with sexual favours. I couldn't even begin to understand what had possessed him to do this.

'Don't freak out, OK?'

I heard my husband outside the safety of my hair but I couldn't quite look up, not just yet.

'I was talking to this guy down at the recording studio and he told me he was selling and I came by to take a look and all I could think was how perfect the place is, how much you would love it,' he explained. 'Listen, Angela, there's an office for you, there's even a soundproofed room downstairs in the basement that I could turn into a studio. The guy used it for practice but it would be perfect for recording. And there are two bedrooms so we could have a place for guests or, you know, maybe a nursery.'

Oh, no.

After a series of deep, calming breaths I remembered from the single yoga class I'd taken three years ago, I parted my hair and peered out at the man I had married. Alex was squatting in front of me, an earnest look on his face that was somewhere between 'what's wrong with you?' and 'I know I've fucked up.'

'Alex, you bought an apartment without telling me,' I croaked. 'What happened to us telling each other everything?'

'It was supposed to be a surprise.' he offered with a double thumbs up.

'A surprise is a Kinder Egg,' I replied, reminding myself to focus on the matter at hand and not on whether I wanted a Kinder Egg. Which of course I did, I wasn't made of stone. 'This is a house.'

Alex bit his lip and reached out to take my hand. 'Can I show you around?'

Dizzy, I pushed myself up off the floor, ignoring his outstretched hand, and dusted off the back of my shorts. With a sigh, I rolled my eyes at his sad puppy face and allowed him to lead me around the seemingly endless apartment. He was right – it was beautiful, it was perfect, it had everything. Where our current apartment, our home, was brand new and sparkling, this place had character. It was all original features and sympathetic remodelling. The rooms were plain and empty but they were also big and airy and full of light. The bathroom had a roll-top bath – my interior design kryptonite. I was powerless against it. And then there was the garden. Actual grass in an actual outdoor space that was bigger than the average paddling pool. Slowly, I started to see how our lives could fill the space. My desk in the office alongside a big, squishy armchair for reading-slash-online shopping, our bed in the bedroom by the enormous sash window, Alex's instruments lining the room of his new studio . . .

Once I'd got over myself, I could see exactly what he could see – this place was made for us. Maybe not the people we were when we met but the people we were now. I couldn't imagine scared, fresh-off-the-plane Angela rolling up to a leafy Park Slope address with her Marks and Sparks weekend bag, a spare pair of pants and a crumpled bridesmaid dress, but this Angela? Even in my denim shorts and specially-shipped-from-Marks-and-Sparks black tights, I could see it. If I squinted. I was absolutely the sort of woman who lived in a place like this and went out to buy her husband freshly baked bagels on a Saturday morning. Or at least the kind of woman who thought about it, fell asleep again and ended up eating Corn Flakes and illegally streaming *Ant & Dec's Saturday Night Takeaway*.

'Well?' Alex hadn't spoken in an age. He looked genuinely worried. 'What do you think?'

'Can we afford it?' I asked. I was my mother's daughter after all.

'You can't,' he replied, gazing at the fireplace as lovingly as I had ever seen him look at me. 'Seriously, you make no money for the hours you work, it's crazy. But, you know, I've been saving for this for years and with the advance for the new album . . .' He stopped getting it on with the apartment fixtures momentarily and looked back at me. 'We'll be flat-ass broke for a while until we let the other place but yeah, we can afford it.'

And that was when I realised. He must have been planning this for ages. While I'd been all late nights at the office and dragging myself through Monday to Friday so I could sleep through the weekend, Alex had been quietly working away and plotting our future. The sneaky, wonderful git.

'What do you think?' he asked in a soft voice I loved.

'I think it's amazing,' I said, mentally punching myself in the ovaries for not being appropriately grateful for what a wonderful man I had. 'I can't quite believe it but it's amazing. You're amazing. Thank you.'

Alex smiled down at me then cupped his hands around my face and kissed me for what felt like a very long time.

'Just don't ever, ever do this again,' I said, actually punching him in the belly. 'Because I will fucking kill you.'

'Duly noted,' he laughed, rubbing his stomach and pushing me away. 'Not that I can imagine we'll need to move for a very long time. This is going to be a great place to raise a family.'

I pulled him back to me, pressed my head into his chest, ignoring both his family comment and the fleeting concern as to whether or not I was still getting an actual Christmas present.

'Eurgh,' I mumbled into his sweatshirt. 'I hate moving.'

'Oh, yeah . . .' Alex's voice wavered slightly. 'I figured the sooner the better so I kind of started arranging that already.'

Here we go. I held my breath and counted to ten.

'That's awesome,' I said, as positive as possible. 'So after Christmas, yeah?'

'Next week.' I felt him tense up but there was no fun in punching him when he was expecting it. 'A week from today.'

'You want us to move house, across Brooklyn, in seven days?' I shrieked, composure forgotten. So this was what hysteria felt like. 'Four days before Christmas?'

'I'll do everything,' he replied as quickly as was humanly possible. 'I'll hire the movers, I'll get the new stuff we need, I'll make sure it's perfect. I just thought it would be nice to do Christmas in our new home, you know? And you're taking the week off so you'll be around to make sure I don't fuck up.'

'And we have plans for that week,' I said. 'It was supposed to be relaxing.'

'Really?' He raised an eyebrow and looked away. 'Fighting my way around an ice rink in Central Park isn't really my idea of relaxing.'

'Well, it was supposed to be fun,' I clarified. I turned to take a wistful look at the roll-top bath. Roll-top baths made everything better. 'And I just wanted us to spend some time together.'

'It'll all be fine,' he said with false certainty. 'You can still go off and do all your holiday stuff while I organise the move.'

I stared up at him, trying not to look disappointed. Disappointment had a terrible tendency to be misread as ungratefulness and that wasn't what I was feeling. The whole point of taking this week off, the whole reason I was more excited about this Christmas, even more so than any other, was because I was finally going to be able to spend some time with him. And while it was true, moving house did mean spending time together, I had a funny feeling it wouldn't be quite so romantic as holding hands beneath the Rockefeller Center Christmas tree.

'We'll figure it out, I suppose,' I said with sagging shoulders. 'I don't know what else to say.'

'Whatever it is, can you say it outside?' Alex rubbed the back of his neck and pulled the keys out of his pocket. 'I just remembered we left Karen out there and she's probably frozen to death by now.'

On the doorstep, Karen was talking on her phone, shivering against the winter wind that had sprung up while we were inside. Well, at least the frozen face thing made sense now – Karen was an estate agent, she could afford Botox and she faked smiles for a living. I stared back over my shoulder as Alex locked the door. A new house was definitely better than cooking lessons. Or a three-way.

After saying our goodbyes, Alex wrapped a leather-clad arm around my shoulder and began chattering away about home improvements as we hunted for a place to get brunch in our new neighbourhood. As we walked, I tried to ignore the overwhelming feeling of panic that was growing in my stomach. My poor, tiny brain was too confused to process what was going on and so the rest of my body was having to pick up the emotional slack. I knew everything that was happening was incredible. Alex had bought us an actual, honest to Santa, real family home, I had been handed an amazing opportunity at work and I was about ten minutes away from eating several thousand pancakes, but I couldn't fight the feeling of being completely swallowed up. Somewhere along the line I'd gone from having nothing better to do than take a week off to watch chestnuts roasting on an open fire to taking over the magazine and moving house in a week. Had everyone forgotten who they were dealing with or had I?

CHAPTER FIVE

I didn't know anyone who jumped up and down and cheered for Monday mornings but since I'd started at *Gloss* I'd taken Monday dread to a whole new level. Before, it meant replying to all the emails I'd ignored on Friday, a bit of a telly hangover from *Mad Men*, *Game of Thrones* or *True Blood*, depending on the time of year. Now Monday meant press day, which meant checking, rechecking and re-rechecking every word on every page of the magazine. *Gloss* might only have been a teeny, tiny weekly but there were still a good deal of stern looks, raised voices and little cries in the toilets. Mostly Mary took care of the stern looks and raised voices while I, admittedly, was the one having a little cry but now, since she was off on the Love Boat, I had the pleasure of being in charge of the whole shebang. There had been a time when I thought working on a proper magazine at a proper publishing company would be all glamorous like *The Devil Wears Prada* but in reality it was turning out to be very stressful and a lot of hard work. Like in *The Devil Wears Prada*. And so far Stanley Tucci had yet to appear to cover me in free Chanel, although I was still hopeful. Hopeful or stupid. I needed a fairy godfather to keep me in designer goods and empowering speeches.

For the want of an avuncular gay mentor, I let Delia drag me out for lunch. Even though I really wasn't supposed to be out of the office on press day, I really needed to update her on Cici's nervous breakdown. It was only fair.

'I can't believe how long it's been since we went out for lunch.' Delia speared a piece of lettuce and munched away happily, as though it was real food. 'Hasn't it been ages?'

I nodded in agreement, and shovelled a mouthful on quinoa down my throat, wishing I hadn't ordered quinoa. One day I would learn not to order something just because I'd seen Jamie Oliver going on about it. It was horrible. We'd settled on The Breslin for our powwow which was always a bit more trendy than I wanted it to be. It was the kind of place that said 'totally come in jeans!' but then when you came in jeans it raised an eyebrow as if to say 'oh, you came in jeans.' But it was far enough away that there wouldn't be anyone else from the magazine there, yet close enough that I could escape without being missed. Plus, the food was delicious. As long as you didn't have the quinoa.

'I'm so glad you were able to sneak away,' Delia said as the waiter refilled our water glasses with impressive stealth. 'It's like we never have time for each other anymore. Hanging out with you was the best thing about *Gloss*, it really was, not that I'm not really excited about the new role. I'm really excited. But I'll miss you.'

'Yeah, I didn't think I'd see you before the Christmas party,' I said, eyeing the bar for celebs. There was a man who looked a bit like Michael Fassbender three tables over but when he stood up he was so short that if it was Michael Fassbender, I didn't want to know. Why kill the dream?

'Holiday party,' Delia corrected me. 'Non-religious.'

I pouted but said nothing, persevering with my grains.

'But I'll be there. I'm glad you're coming. I never know anyone I actually want to hang out with and I have to go because Grandpa would go crazy if he heard I didn't go, even though he never goes, but still he expects me to go which is complete double standards, you know?'

If my food hadn't been so bloody awful, I might not have noticed that Delia was rambling. I stopped chewing for a moment and tried not to freak out. Delia was nervous. Delia was never nervous. What was going on?

'The exec floor is really dull,' she carried on, sipping water quickly and then punching her fork into yet more lettuce. 'I don't think they're even doing secret Santa. Isn't that awful? Grandpa says I'll get used to it but I don't know . . . Maybe it is too soon, maybe I don't have the experience. I suppose we'll see. How's your appetiser?'

'It's horrible,' I said, with fear in my heart. Whatever was going on, I really wanted to know before my main course arrived because if I was getting fired, I was changing my order to the burger and getting a cocktail while I still had a company credit card. 'Delia, what's wrong?'

'Why would anything be wrong?' she asked in a

73

voice so high pitched it hurt my ears. 'I'm just a little stressed. That's all it is.'

Now I knew she was lying. Delia Spencer had never been stressed in her entire life. She was so in control, I had wondered more than once if she wasn't actually some sort of media magnate cyborg, created by her grandfather to take over the family business. The only evidence to the contrary was her sister. Oh. Fuckity fuck. Of course, her sister.

'Delia,' I put down my fork. If she was going to say what I thought she was going to say, I was in for enough punishment, I didn't need to suffer through another mouthful of superfood. 'Is this about Cici coming in yesterday?'

She pursed her lips, looked down into her lap and nodded.

'You mean your new assistant, Cici?' she asked with unwarranted optimism.

'You can't mean it?' I asked. She couldn't. I hadn't had a memo about everyone in the world going completely insane so this must just be a very, very late April Fool's joke.

For a moment, there was an awkward silence at the table that had never existed between me and Delia before. I waited for her to laugh and tell me she was taking the piss and of course she didn't genuinely expect me to have her clinically insane identical twin working on our magazine, on our baby, that we had fought so hard for, but she didn't. She just sat there, pushing some sad little leaves around her plate and waiting for me to say something else. But I didn't. I couldn't.

'I know everything you're thinking,' she said after realising that I wasn't going to speak. 'And you're completely within your rights. I know it seems crazy to even think about having Cici around after, well, after everything.'

'Can I get you ladies anything?' An overly chirpy waitress in a shirt and tie appeared behind Delia.

'Do you have anything that's like a cosmo?' I asked, unable to take my eyes off Delia. 'Doesn't have to be a cosmo but is definitely as strong as a cosmo?'

'Uh, sure,' she replied, with almost as much fear in her eyes as there was in mine. 'Anything for you?'

'Whatever you get for her,' Delia muttered, throwing back her water in preparation for something harder hitting her stomach.

'Two cosmos then,' the waitress replied, backing away as fast as she could. Sharp instincts. She'd go far.

I took a deep breath, trying to calm down, but my heart was racing and I had a really bitter taste in my mouth. It could have been the quinoa but I was fairly certain it was just straight-up bile.

'It's going to sound dumb,' Delia said, resting her elbows on the table and wiping her hands over her face, 'but she really has changed.'

'Because she spent a month at a spa in India and got a dodgy hair wrap?'

'Maybe,' she said, pulling on her ponytail. 'And maybe because Grandpa threatened to cut her off if she doesn't get another job.'

'So make her your assistant if you want her around so badly.' I was trying, but failing, not to squeak when I spoke. 'She'll be putting anthrax in my cappuccino within a week.'

'Don't you breathe in anthrax?' she asked, reaching for her phone to Google it.

'That's not the point,' I yelled, slapping the phone out of her hand. 'There's no other job in the entire company, the entire Spencer Media empire, that you can shove her in? I don't believe it for a second.'

'Of course there is,' Delia replied. 'But she wants to work at *Gloss*. We sat down and talked and I genuinely, genuinely think she's changed. And for what it's worth, I think she feels guilty about all the stuff she did to you, and to us. I'll keep an eye on her, I'll make sure she's not up to anything, you have my word.'

'You can't babysit your psycho sister while you're running a publishing company,' I sighed as it dawned on me that I wasn't getting a say in this. The deal was as good as done. 'I just can't believe you're doing this to the magazine.'

'There are two ways to look at it.' Delia's cheeks were red from embarrassment. I hated that she felt so uncomfortable, hated putting her in a position where she was torn between work, friendship and family. Unfortunately, I hated her sister more so she was just going to have to get used to it. 'There is a chance that I'm right, that she isn't lying and has finally woken up to what a total bitch she used to be. In which case, she's really smart and she's going to be an asset to the company. She's a good assistant, she's super smart, she kicks ass and she looks after her own.'

'Because she's always been so wonderful to you,' I said, arms folded, bottom lip out, the full grumpy chops.

'I was never her own,' she admitted. 'But she's loyal to her friends and you have first-hand experience of how far she'll go when she's committed to achieving something. Maybe we'll be able to use her power for good?'

'Maybe,' I nodded. 'Can I just use your phone to check if Hell has frozen over?'

'The other way to look at it is this,' Delia said, ignoring me. Probably rightly so. 'My grandpa is eventually going to cave and give her a job. Would you rather it's the job she says she wants, in a place where you can keep an eye on her and have the whole staff keep her in check? Or would you rather she was somewhere else in the business, pissed off that you – in her eyes – have screwed her over again and dedicating every moment that she could be answering your phone to destroying your career?'

Well, when she put it like that . . .

'You're going to make me hire Cici as my assistant,' I said, hardly believing the words as they came out of my mouth.

'I'm not going to make you do anything,' Delia replied. 'Because I'm not an asshole. But it's genuinely the best idea I have come up with. I've been over it a thousand different ways and I can't think of a better solution. I know you don't trust her and I don't expect you to. It's hard enough for me to give her another chance but really, I do believe she's different.'

'I know, she's been to India and has forgotten to get her nails done.' So this was how it felt to be backed into a corner. 'She's an entirely different person.'

'She's been volunteering,' Delia lowered her voice as though she were telling me a terrible secret. 'At the park. With old people. She hates old people. Honestly, it's freaking me out. That's one of the reasons I want her somewhere I can keep an eye on her. At first I thought she might have hit her head or something but it seems to be sticking.'

'So it's not just that she's got an inexplicable vindictive streak just for me,' I asked, making sure I had my mad ducks in a row. 'You now think she's actually psycho?'

Delia looked pained. But not pained enough to throw herself on the floor and beg my forgiveness. Why hadn't I just hired Tessa or Blair or Serena van der Woodsen when I had the chance?

'If I do this,' I said, thankful for the massive pink cocktail that was set down in front of me as I raised my hand and started counting off conditions on my fingers, 'and I do mean if, there's a trial period, she actually has to come into the office every day and do work, she's not allowed to spit in, on or around me, or anything I might consume.'

'I mean, it sounds reasonable,' Delia nodded. 'She really does have the potential to be so good. She worked for Mary for an age and you know how tough she can be.'

I did know how tough Mary could be. I also knew she had never arranged to have an entire suitcase of borrowed and slavishly saved up for designer clothes – not to mention one very special pair of Louboutins – *blown up* by French airport security for shits and giggles.

'And you know, she didn't suggest this, I did, so it's not part of a plan.' She took a tiny sip of her cocktail, politely ignoring the fact I had already almost finished mine. 'I promise.'

'Which is just what she would say if it was part of a plan,' I replied.

'But you'll give her a shot?' Delia asked, her eyes

sparkling ever so slightly. From hope or booze, I wasn't sure.

'I suppose I'd better get used to the taste of laxatives in my tea,' I nodded, resigned, reluctant and terrified. 'Might help me lose a couple of Christmas pounds.'

'Hey Angela.'

I wouldn't normally be so surprised to hear a man's voice shouting my name but since I was hiding in the ladies', trying to find the strength to put on a brave face after lunch with Delia, it was a bit of a shock.

'Yes?'

'Angela, you in there?'

'I'll be out in a second,' I shouted back, stashing the second finger of a Twix back in its wrapper and down into the deepest, darkest depths of my handbag. Eating chocolate in the toilets really was a new low but then so was hiring Cici to be my assistant. 'Give me a minute.'

'Great, I'll put the beauty pages on your desk.'

Another fun fact I had just found out about press day – I couldn't even go to the toilets without Jesse, our managing editor, hunting me down like a dog. God help me if he found out I'd actually left the premises for lunch, let alone had a drink.

Most of the time I liked Jesse. He was the same age as me, lived in Williamsburg and knew all the words to Taylor Swift's latest album, even though he played guitar in an indie band and looked like a super hipster. And because he worked on a women's fashion magazine, he knew an awful lot more about nail varnish than your average bloke. If he'd been gay, he'd have been my gay best friend. Since he was sadly straight, he'd had to settle for the role of my work husband, meaning that it was his responsibility to bring me snacks whenever he left the office and make sure I was never without the latest *Game of Thrones*-inspired meme. Aside from his general, personal qualifications, it was hard to find a good managing editor and I was delighted when Mary had managed to lure him away from the low-paying but high-credibility music paper he'd been working on to come to *Gloss*. You really had to have a mental imbalance to love being a managing ed, all that time spent checking and correcting and making sure no one had snuck any dirty acrostic poems into the feature articles or teeny tiny penises into celebrity fashion spreads. Not that anyone in our team would do that. Except for maybe me. And Jesse genuinely loved it.

Back at my desk, surrounded by every Christmas card the office had received, some delightful fluffy reindeers I'd picked up at Target and several Alexander Skarsgård posters, I stared down at the beauty pages, willing myself to read every single word, to see each syllable and to start caring about what eyeliner Selena Gomez was wearing this week. It wasn't Selena's fault. Usually I'd be thrilled to know that she mostly used MAC but that I could achieve the same effect with Maybelline (even though I knew you couldn't really) but I had a lot on my mind. Jenny and her baby banter seemed like something that had happened a million years ago and the new house in all its leafy Park Slope glory would be something I worried about when we actually had to move. In four days. Right now, I had enough on my plate. I had to work out how to work with Cici without either killing her or inciting her to kill me. Maybe if I sent back all my Christmas presents and just asked for one little miracle instead . . .

My office phone, appropriately wrapped in silver tinsel, rang quietly, as if afraid to interrupt my review of Jennifer Aniston's best and worst hair days.

'Hello?'

I hated not being able to see who was calling, I thought as I answered. There was something so threatening about answering the phone not knowing who it was. Of course, I could have just peeled the *Twilight* stickers off my phone so I could see the screen but that would have been too easy.

'Angela, it's your mother.'

Aah. Because so far, today had been far too easy.

'Hello, Mum.' I closed my eyes and pinched the bridge of my nose, hoping it would calm me. It didn't. I had no idea why people did that. 'Are you all right?'

'Everything's fine,' she replied in a voice that implied that was, in fact, not the case. 'I was just wondering if you'd heard from Louisa this week?'

'No,' I said, sitting up straight. 'I've been trying to call her but she's busy. Why? What's wrong? Is she OK?'

'Oh, I'm sure she's fine,' Mum said. 'Not that I'd know, she never comes round with that baby.'

'Well, she's probably busy taking it to see her mother and not mine,' I replied. 'Or doing, you know, stuff.'

'No need to be snippy,' she sniffed. 'So, you haven't heard? It hasn't been on the Facebook?'

'Has what been on the Facebook?'

It was sometimes quite difficult not to lose my patience with her.

'Well, her next door told me and she said she'd heard it from Janet who works in the hairdresser's but you know what she can be like.' My mum took a sharp breath and the phone line crackled with silence for a second. And then she started again. 'So I don't know whether it's true or not. But that's what they're saying.'

'You don't know what is true or not?' I asked. At least she was right about one thing – her next door was a right old cow.

'That Mark and that Katie are having a baby.'

Oh. Mark, my ex-boyfriend, my ex-fiancé, and 'that Katie', better known as the blonde tart he cheated on me with. They were having a baby.

'Well, that sounds very nice for them, Mum,' I said, pulling at the ends of my hair and trying my best not to care. 'Did they say when?'

'You don't sound very bothered.' My mother had clearly expected more of her only child. Maybe some oohs and aahs or even a few tears. And she might have got them if I hadn't already had such an incredibly shite day. 'I haven't forgotten him showing up here on your wedding day.'

'What do you want me to say?' I really didn't have enough emotional mileage to deal with this non-bombshell. A man I'd broken up with nearly four years ago was having a baby with a woman he'd been involved with for, well, more than four years. Unfortunate maths aside, I really didn't feel that affected.

'He shows up at your wedding, causes a scene and then just goes and has a baby with someone else willy-nilly?' Mum said in disbelief. 'And you don't care?'

'Not really,' I said. And I didn't. Part of me wanted to but that part was busy working out what it would do the first time Cici left a rat in my desk drawer. The rest of me was fully aware that I had a really rather spectacular husband of my own at home, so meh.

'Well, it's just you've been married more than a year

now and he's having a baby . . .' Aah, so that was it. 'They're not even married yet, you know.'

'It's not a race,' I pointed out. 'Mark isn't winning because he's having a baby first.'

Mum made an unconvinced humphing sound.

'And anyway, I'm married and he isn't.' I was fairly certain that meant I'd won. If it was a race, which it wasn't. But if it was . . .

'I know you're busy with your career,' she said, taking special care to pronounce the word career with all the disdain she felt that it deserved. 'And you know we're very proud of you—'

'Tell her I'm proud of her as well,' I heard my dad shout down the line.

'I said "we". Be quiet, David,' she scolded. I smiled. 'As I said, we're very proud of you, me and your dad, but you're not getting any younger, Angela.'

A fact I was completely aware of and did not wish to be reminded of again.

'We don't need to have this conversation,' I said, putting a verbal black line through the topic. 'We're not ready, that's all there is to it.'

'No one's ever ready for a baby,' she replied. 'If me and your dad had waited until we were ready for you, we wouldn't be having this conversation. But never mind me, the last thing I want to do is be accused of interfering.'

'The last thing,' I sighed. 'Listen, Mum, I've got to go. I've got loads to do and—'

'Well, there's something else I wanted to talk to you about as well,' she said before I could hang up. 'Just very quickly . . . Me and your dad are coming over to you for Christmas.'

'What?'

My grip tightened around the handset and I sat straight up in my chair, begging her to start laughing.

'We were talking about it last night, how we haven't seen you in ages and how you're so busy with your career.' Pause for a distasteful swallow. 'And how if you do decide to start trying for a baby, you shouldn't really be travelling anyway and so we just did it! We booked the flights. Your dad did them on the internet.'

'What?'

'Surprise!' Dad bellowed from across the room. 'Merry Christmas!'

'What?'

'Dad'll send you an email message with the details so you can meet us at the airport,' she said, sounding considerably more cheerful than she had at the beginning of the phone call. 'Love to Alex.'

And with that, she hung up.

Love to Alex? Love to bloody Alex? It wasn't too long ago that my mother would only refer to the love of my life as 'that musician' and now he was getting sent love? It was just all too much. I had my Christmas plan. I could work the move in, I could deal with Jenny and I could manage Cici, but my parents? In my house for all of Christmas with no warning? I couldn't cope with any more surprises.

Without even replacing the receiver I reset the line and dialled Alex as fast as I could.

'Alex,' I wailed when he answered. 'Mum just called to say they were coming for Christmas and I'm freaking out and I don't know what to do and they can't come, they can't, please tell me they don't have to come.'

'Um, OK?' he replied. 'I'm in the furniture store. If I send you a picture of a sofa, can you let me know whether or not you like it?'

'ALEX!'

'Right, your mom, sure,' he sighed. 'I'll fix it. And don't freak out if I'm not home when you get in tonight. I have an appointment with a builder at the new place.'

'The new place,' I said, trying to find a way out from underneath this horrible cloud of shittiness that I had just created for myself. I was a horrible daughter. 'OK.'

'And it's forecast to snow,' Alex's voice crackled. For some reason, American phone lines were always a bit rubbish. 'So don't stay late if you don't have to.'

'I never stay late if I don't have to,' I muttered. 'I'll see you later.'

He really hadn't grasped the enormity of the situation. Probably because his parents lived upstate and he saw them about once every five years or at family weddings and/or funerals, whichever came first. My family were not his family. They were selfish and wonderful and passive aggressive and there was a reason I was perfectly happy to have them on the other side of the ocean.

'Love you,' he replied before hanging up.

With my face flat on my glass desk, I stared down at my black Jimmy Choo biker boots and sniffed. You knew things were bad when they couldn't put a smile on my face. I'd had plans to drag Jenny out to dinner and then to see *The Nutcracker* but there was no way I'd be out of the office in time to make it. So that was day one of my Christmasgasm effectively ruined and if I couldn't find a way to convince my parents that Christmas in New York was a terrible idea, the whole thing would be buggered. With a sob, I turned back to the beauty pages, throwing myself into the many different looks of Beyoncé. Whether I liked it or not, my big week off was starting to look about as realistic as the virgin birth.

'I'm totally leaving,' I announced to my favourite ASkars poster, stretching my arms high above my head. He gazed down at me with brooding approval. It was just as well I'd married my Alex and not Alexander. I would have got really annoyed having to find the weird Swedish characters on my phone every time I wanted to text him.

Enough was enough. It had been a great big bastard of a day and I needed to go home. Jesse had put the final pages to bed half an hour earlier and everyone else was long gone. Attempting to get ever so slightly ahead of myself, I'd stayed to answer all the emails I'd ignored over the course of what would go down in history as the worst Monday ever, but I realised when I signed off an email to the head of finance with three kisses and a smiley face that was I done for the day. While my lovely week of vacation was now nothing but a dream, I had at least snagged Tuesday off and Alex had promised me his undivided attention for twenty-four hours. I had really struggled to decide what to do with him. Ice skating? Christmas shopping? A train trip upstate to walk around some lovely woods? To be fair, given the day I'd had, I would settle for a duvet day and the odd reassuring pat on the head. But it felt good to know I was going home to something warm and comforting following a day of stress and clinically certifiable insanity.

On my way out, I ran my fingers over all the empty desks and boxy computer screens, feeling a rumbling of professional pride. OK, so I struggled with my personal relationships from time to time and I had just broken my mother's heart but workwise, things were objectively on the up. The *Gloss* office might be the least sexy office in the entire Spencer Media building but we were still in the building and that was an epic achievement. Yes, it smelled of fish on Tuesdays but that was because the canteen served fish on Tuesdays and we were right by the canteen. Some of the team considered that a negative, although I wasn't quite sure why. Better to be the crappy office next to the Spencer Media canteen than to have no office at all. Plus, I was greedy.

The first time I'd visited Spencer Media three and a half years ago, to talk to Mary about writing a blog for *The Look*, I had thought my heart would beat right out of my chest. The thought of being right in the heart of Times Square – the theatres, the shops, bright lights, big city, the naked cowboy and suspect adults dressed as Elmo . . . But tonight I just wanted to get home without tripping over Spider-Man or being invited to a comedy show. Alex had been right, it was snowing by the time I left, but the fresh chill of the air felt good on my face. I fell into step with the rest of New York as we rippled down the subway stairs, everyone moving in the same direction without saying a word. The station was crowded and when I finally made it onto a train, it was even worse. I slung the strap of my satchel over my head, pulling it in closer to my body. No matter how long I lived here, I would still treat the subway with suspicion. The subway and every single human being alive.

This close to Christmas, travelling in the city was always a chore. Commuters crossed with Christmas shoppers and every train car was full of musicians or dancers trying to make some money from the out-of-towners.

Usually I didn't mind it. More often than not, I forgot my headphones in the morning and who didn't like watching four kids performing the *Thriller* dance on your way home from work? And while Jenny was against mariachi in all its forms, I loved a jaunty tune on the L train. But tonight, it was too much. Between everyone's giant winter coats, the bags and bags and bags of shopping, there really wasn't room for two Spanish guitars and an accordion. With my face pressed against the metal bars separating the privileged few who had forced their way into a seat and the rest of us sardines, I closed my eyes and tried to block out enthusiastic strains of 'Feliz Navidad' but there was no point. Thank God I had my tree at home. Oh my God, we were going to have to move the tree.

'Oh!'

We were just pulling into 1st Avenue station when I felt someone grab my arse. And not in a particularly friendly way. If there was such a thing.

'A crowded subway is not an excuse for an inappropriate touch,' I shouted at the squish of people pouring off the train before giving the rest of my fellow passengers an accusatory stare for good measure. I couldn't even be slightly flattered – in this crush, whichever perv had copped a feel had hardly been driven to it by the sight of my fabulous rear. He probably just went round all the carriages with his hands out, hoping not to run into one of those blokes who left their fly open 'by accident'. Unless . . . oh cockingtons. Unless he wasn't as much a perv as someone who went around feeling people's arse pockets for things he could steal. Things like the iPhone I vaguely remembered shoving in my back pocket when I was being rushed onto the train without enough time or room to open my bag. Brilliant. What a fabulously shitty end to a fabulously shitty day.

Brooklyn was always colder than Manhattan and the winter wind blew in sharp off the water, pinching my face with sleet as I climbed the subway steps and ambled down the street to the apartment. This I would not miss. I rummaged around in my bag, mitten-covered fingers searching for sharp, shiny keys, muttering to myself about my lost phone and wondering who was enjoying my vast collection of pictures of other people's pets. Bath, beer, bed. Bath, beer, bed. It wasn't much to ask for, just five quiet minutes out of an entire twenty-four hours.

'Angela?' Right there, on my doorstep with a suitcase in one hand and a toddler in the other, was Louisa. 'Merry Christmas!'

CHAPTER SIX

Ten minutes of taking it in turns to use the toilet later, I was bribing the baby to be quiet with the last of my stash of Cadbury's Buttons, while Louisa installed us on the sofa under several blankets, clutching steaming mugs of tea. Unfortunately, coming inside and warming up had given Grace a newfound burst of energy but somehow it had rendered her mother mute. Louisa hadn't said a single word since she'd come out of the bathroom.

'So . . .' I was completely dazed. 'Surprise visit?'

Lou nodded with an enormous smile then shuffled further under the pink fluffy blanket that Alex had tried to get me to throw away several thousand times. She stared vacantly around the apartment, her light blue eyes red and tired looking.

'Nice tree,' she commented, taking a tiny sip of tea. 'Lovely flat, Ange, really nice.'

'We're moving in a week,' I replied. 'Louisa, seriously, you've never so much as surprised me with a phone call. Is everything OK?'

'Everything is fine,' she said, stretching out the word

fine for about half an hour. 'I was just sat at home the other day and me and Gracie-pants were watching *Miracle on 34th Street* and I thought, I need some Angela time. So we booked a flight, we packed a bag and we came. What's not OK about that?'

'Nothing,' I said, reaching over to press my hand to her forehead. She was still cold from standing on my doorstep but she didn't seem to be sickening for anything. 'Why didn't you call me from the airport at least?'

'I've been calling you for the last hour,' she replied. 'But you weren't answering.'

'Oh yeah.' I remembered the friendly neighbourhood iPhone thief. 'I had my phone nicked. So that's it? You were watching TV and you just thought, hmm, flying to New York seems like a good idea?'

'And what exactly went through your mind when you nicked off without a second thought as to the rest of us?' she asked, blowing gently on her steaming hot tea.

Aah, touché.

'I didn't have a husband at home and it wasn't a week before Christmas,' I said in my defence. 'Tim doesn't mind?'

'Nope.' She glanced over at my goddaughter, Grace, who had made herself right at home in front of the TV. She noticed her audience, rolled onto her back and showed us her knickers. Hardly a novelty for me – I'd seen her mother do that lots of times.

'Is he going to come out too?'

'He's very busy.'

This was all just so un-Louisa. Granted, she wore the trousers in her household but she hadn't gone anywhere without Tim since he was eighteen and kissed a fifty-year-old for a dare at a Grab a Granny Night on a boys' holiday in Magaluf. He'd called Louisa sobbing and we'd sat up all night watching *Pretty Woman* and weeping because that's what TV told us we should do. They made up three days later when he came back, all sloped shoulders and sunburnt nose, bearing an apology, a coral necklace and a massive bottle of Archers. All was forgiven. And it wasn't just her Tim-less state. Something was definitely off about her. The short sentences, the brief answers. Of course she was tired but even an exhausted Louisa was a nosy Louisa.

'Well, I'm very happy to see you,' I said, making the conscious decision to tread lightly. 'And I know Alex will be giddy as a kipper for some time with Grace. I think he's a bit broody at the moment.'

Louisa paled ever so slightly and then recovered with a laugh. 'I'm sure Alex will be a fantastic father,' she commented, with an edge to her voice that I wasn't used to. OK, yeah, definitely something going on. 'Can't picture you at mummy and baby yoga, though.'

'Tell me about it,' I replied, sipping my tea. 'So how long are you staying? Not that I'm trying to get rid of you.'

'What day is it today?' She pushed a wisp of wavy blonde hair off her face and rubbed her eyes. 'Tuesday?'

'Monday.'

I couldn't really call her for not knowing what day it was. I'd gone into the office on a Saturday by accident twice in the last six months, although as far as Alex knew, it had only happened once.

'Um, maybe a week? Is that OK?' she asked.

'Of course it is.' I put my scalding tea down and gave her as big a hug as I could muster. 'I just wish you were staying for Christmas.'

'Well, we could, you know.' Louisa's eyes lit up. 'Wouldn't that be lovely?'

'I'm pretty sure Tim would have something to say about it,' I joked, head on her shoulder. 'But I'd be very happy. Things have been batshit here lately and you are a bloody sight for sore eyes.'

Across the room, Grace started clapping at the TV. Oh, she was a *True Blood* fan too.

'Oh shit, Grace, don't look at that,' I shouted, scrambling for the remote while Louisa darted across the room and scooped her child up into her arms.

'Hi,' Grace said, clambering away from her mother and settling herself against my white cotton shirt, pawing me with sticky fingers. Because what this shirt was really missing was chocolatey handprints. 'I'm Grace.'

'Gracie, this is your Auntie Angela.' Louisa lovingly patted Grace's blonde hair down, oblivious to the dry cleaning disaster happening in front of her. I hadn't realised what a mini-me she had become from all the photos Lou had posted on Facebook. It was frightening how alike they were. 'You remember Auntie Angela, don't you?'

'Yes.' The baby beamed her approval by sticking her hand directly in my face. 'Anala.'

'I've been called worse today,' I said, kissing her forehead. She smelled all milky and weird. 'Thanks, Grace.'

'She's in a real chatterbox phase,' Louisa said,

looking far too proud for someone who had just let their child watch two vampires going at it for ten or so minutes. 'And she wants to touch everything.'

'So I see.' I looked at my blouse and said nothing. 'I can't believe she's already a year old.'

'Nineteen months next week,' Lou sighed. 'It's mental. Doesn't seem like two minutes since I was bringing her home from the hospital.'

'I feel like I would fixate more on the part where you heaved her out of your vagina,' I commented, relaxing into my toddler hug. It was odd but it wasn't so bad.

'Well, yes, you would,' she replied. 'But it really is best to just put that behind you as soon as you can.'

'Do you think you'll have any more?' I asked, thinking of how quickly Erin had taken to churning them out. 'Is Tim desperate to turn out his only manly man mini-me?'

'You know, I am so tired,' she said, snatching a giggly Grace out of my arms and standing up. 'Shouldn't we get the airbed out or something?'

'Don't be stupid.' I stood up as well, mostly to make the moment less awkward. 'You can sleep in my room. Me and Alex will go on the airbed.'

'You don't actually know where the airbed is, do you?'

'I know where it isn't,' I replied. 'Go on, get ready for bed and I'll see you in the morning. I've got the day off so we'll do something fun.'

'Brilliant,' she leaned in to kiss me on the cheek. 'It's so bloody good to see you, Clark.'

'Bloody good to be seen,' I said, slapping her bum and giving Gracie a kiss all of her own. If anyone asked about the stains on the shirt, I'd just tell them it was a new Mary Katrantzou print and really, who would be any the wiser?

It was another hour before Alex arrived home, all chapped cheeks and watery eyes. I silently accepted a quick kiss while he took off his three outermost layers and started excitedly relaying all of our moving news. Leaning over the back of the sofa, I watched as he went straight into the kitchen, debating the value of full-service movers versus hiring someone to do the heavy stuff and us doing the rest with the band's van, carefully stepping over Grace's toys and moving around Louisa's suitcase. I didn't even laugh until he opened the fridge, ignored the dozens of juice cartons and premixed formula, and reached right in for a Coke.

'Craig and Graham will totally help,' he said, collapsing on the sofa and staring at the Christmas tree. 'And it's not like we have that much . . .'

I placed my hands on his shoulders, leaning over to kiss him on the cheek.

'Angela?'

'Alex.'

'Why is there a box of diapers under the tree?'

'We have a visitor,' I said, kissing the other cheek and clambering over the back of the sofa to join him. 'Louisa and Grace are here.'

Alex closed his eyes, shook his head and opened them again.

'What?'

'I know,' I said, snuggling up to him as close as I could. 'Unexpected. They're in our bed.'

'Is she OK? I mean, that's not super like her, is it?' He raked a hand through his hair, a look of concern on his face.

He was the best. Whatever past life Angela had had to get me this man in this life, I couldn't thank her enough. At this point, I was starting to believe there was a good chance that I had been Jesus. Or at least one of those people who hand out free cheese in the supermarket.

'I think,' I replied. 'She's being a bit vague and she doesn't want to talk about Tim, like, at all, but I'll find out tomorrow when she's not so knackered.'

'Cool.' He kissed the end of my nose and sighed. 'I gotta tell you, I kind of thought, just for a second there, those diapers were your wacky way of telling me you were pregnant.'

I laughed. And laughed. And then laughed some more.

'What?' Alex looked at me. 'It's such a crazy idea?'

'On top of moving and starting the new job and everything else?' I asked. 'Yes. It's such a crazy idea.'

'I don't think it would be so bad,' he said, draining his drink and turning his attention to me. 'I think it would be kind of awesome actually.'

'Grace has been here for two hours,' I said, pointing at the chocolate-covered rug and the chocolate-covered me, 'and she has decimated the apartment.'

'I just figured you'd been in the Nutella again,' he said, his fingers dancing around the buttons on my shirt.

'That was one time,' I replied, slapping his hands away. 'And there's a baby in the next room. Control yourself, man.'

'Fine,' he pouted, fastening me right up to the throat and kissing my nose. 'I'll go get the air mattress out the basement.'

Aah, the basement. Of course.

'You can stay there and think up baby names.' Alex stood up and stretched with a great big grin on his face. His stupid, handsome face.

'But I've already got you a present,' I shouted after him as he vanished through the front door. 'And it doesn't need changing five times a day.'

One of my biggest concerns about motherhood had always been how early I would have to get up in the morning. At six fourteen the following morning, that concern was proved to be valid.

'Anala!' Grace leapt onto the airbed, displaying no interest in how ironic she was making her name. 'Aah.'

Without another peep, she crawled under the covers and draped herself across me, thumb in mouth, eyes wide open.

'Hey, Grace,' Alex said, rubbing the sleep out of his eyes and yawning loudly. 'Do you remember me?'

'No,' she replied without even looking at him. Graceless and tactless. Admittedly only nineteen months old but still, when did a girl gather her manners?

'Morning,' Louisa sang out as she sailed out of the bedroom, looking as though the last twenty-four hours hadn't even happened. 'Shall I put the coffee on? Hello, Alex, sorry to wake you up so early. Madam doesn't understand the concept of jet lag.'

'No problem,' Alex replied, rolling off the airbed and subtly adjusting his boxers while he thought no one was looking. 'Let me make the coffee, you take a seat. It's not really that early.'

He was such a filthy liar. Alex Reid never saw the wrong side of ten a.m. if he could help it. I'd had to develop a full-on stealthy getting ready system so that I could sneak out of the apartment in the morning without waking him up that mostly involved getting dressed in the bathroom and trying not to fall over. It had a fifty–fifty success rate.

'So what are the grand plans for today?' Louisa breezed, appearing above me with a sippy cup and outstretched arms. 'Christmas in New York. Dazzle me.'

I handed over the baby, now fully aware of why Louisa had such awesome, toned arms. 'I don't know.' I looked longingly at Alex. So much for our day together. 'What do you want to do?'

'I don't know,' Lou said. 'We did all the touristy things when we came out for your wedding. You're the Christmas addict. Surely there's something fabulous me, you and Gracie could do together?'

'We could go ice skating?' I suggested. 'Would she like that?'

'Bit too young, I think,' she replied. 'What would you be doing if I wasn't here?'

I eyed my husband's backside as he bent over the coffee maker, trying to work out why it wasn't making coffee, and coughed. 'I don't think you'd want to do what I'd be doing if you weren't here,' I said, wondering when would be a good time to tell him he needed to plug it in first. 'Christmas shopping?'

'Ooh.' Louisa's face lit up. 'I could always do with grabbing a few bits. Might not be the best thing to do with madam here, though. She hasn't quite grasped the concept of "not everything is mine" yet.'

Alex, having finally woken up enough to locate the 'on' switch, sat down beside Lou on the sofa and ruffled Grace's hair.

'I can look after Grace if you guys want to go off into the city?' he suggested. 'I don't mind.'

'That's really sweet,' Lou said as Grace turned to eye her wannabe babysitter with suspicion. 'But she can be a real pain in the arse if you're not used to kids. I'm saying that and I love her. I couldn't put you through it for an entire day.'

'What if it was just half a day?' he said. 'I'll take the morning shift so you guys can shop and talk shit about me and Tim and then I'll find something fun for us to do all together this afternoon?'

'You, sir, are a genius,' Lou said with a smile. 'How does that sound to you, Angela?'

It sounded to me like she was right – Alex was a genius. He knew I needed some alone time with Louisa to find out what was going on and he knew that if I entered Bloomingdales with Grace, I was likely to exit without her. To think he was willing to throw himself onto that adorable blonde grenade for me . . .

'It'll be good practice for me anyway, right, Ange?' Alex hoisted Grace onto his lap, earning himself a punch to the nose, followed by a hug. 'Log some babysitting hours before we get one of our own.'

Louisa turned her head towards me very slowly, an incredibly smug look on her face and eyebrows quirked so high they were practically in space.

'Good practice,' I replied weakly. 'I'm going to go and have a shower then.'

Mew.

New York had decided to give us a break with the weather, and as we trotted up the subway steps at 59th and Lex, the sun shone happily and the air was fresh. The snow that had fallen the night before had all but vanished, and, if it weren't for the Christmas carols blaring out of the speakers outside Bloomingdales, you might have mistaken it for a fresh spring day. Something I would have been hard-pressed to mistake for anything else was the sexy silhouette of one Jenny Lopez as she strode up the street to meet us. While hiding in the shower, I realised I was going to need help with Lou – in the shopping *and* interrogation stakes – and Jenny was an expert at both. A quick email exchange later and she had called in to the office with a personal day and was on her way to Bloomies. She and Louisa had experienced what was fair to say a bumpy start to their friendship but they had been so far up each other's arses at mine and Alex's wedding the summer before, I was almost surprised that Lou had shown up on my doorstep and not Jenny's.

'Lou Lou!' Jenny bounded across the street with little to no concern for the 'Don't Walk' sign and barrelled straight into Louisa, spinning her around and almost knocking us both to the ground. 'Ohmigod, you look amazing! How do you look amazing? You just got in yesterday? You should look like shit. You should look like Angie. Angie, how come you look like shit?'

Louisa looked like a woman reborn, all shiny hair, rosy cheeks and clothes that didn't need ironing. I looked as though I'd been woken up at six a.m. and had spent the night sleeping on an air mattress next to a man who had forgotten all duvet-sharing etiquette, for no apparent reason.

'Hi, Jenny. Thanks. You look nice.'

'Well, duh.' She threw her long, curly ponytail over her shoulder and gave me a cursory peck on the cheek. 'So what's the plan?'

'Christmas shopping?' I said, pointing up at the best

department store in the entire world. 'Shameless indulgence? And then maybe a cheeky midday beverage?'

'First stop for you is the make-up counter because you need all of the make-up.' Jenny waved her hand in my face. My sad, unmade-up face. 'Jesus, Angie, it's always like I'm starting over with you.'

'This is what you get for trying to do nice things for people,' I sulked, letting the two of them bully me through the doors as they cackled to each other.

I'd given Jenny a very brief overview of the situation in my email and warned her that my unexpected visitor wasn't really feeling terribly chatty about whatever was going on so we'd probably need to use a softly-softly approach. But, of course, softly-softly to me wasn't the same as softly-softly to La Lopez. We had only been wandering around the second floor for five minutes when she started.

'So, Lou Lou,' Jenny said, picking up a Kooples blazer, scrutinising it for a second and then putting it back with a tiny shake of the head. 'What the fuck is going on?'

'Hmm?' Louisa let out a confused noise while fingering the price tag of an extortionately expensive plain white T-shirt. 'What's that?'

I bit my lip, hovering at Lou's side and wondering whether or not to intervene. Maybe this hadn't been such a good idea.

'You, here, what gives?' Jenny thrust a cropped black cashmere jumper at me and carried on her questioning. 'Kind of a weird thing to do, don't you think?'

Folding her arms over her boobs, Louisa looked at the floor and shook her head. Nope, this definitely wasn't a good idea.

'I don't know what you're talking about,' she replied,

her voice becoming very crisp and proper. 'I'm just here to see Angela. Just a last-minute trip, that's all.'

She waited for Jenny to respond but when our personal shopper-slash-interrogator shrugged and moved on, we both let out a sigh of relief.

'You know the last time someone turned up on New York's doorstep with zero notice, it was this chick.' Jenny pointed at me before adding a silver studded T-shirt to the growing pile in my arms. I had a feeling she was trying to keep my hands busy so I wouldn't be able to get involved in any potential violence. 'And we all know what that was about.'

'Hmm.' Louisa appeared terribly interested in a charcoal crop top, decorated with a diamanté studded skull. Not something I would have chosen for her myself, but . . .

'So tell me,' Jenny continued, suddenly stepping right into Louisa's face. 'What's going on?'

For one impossibly tense moment, I had no idea what was going to happen. Louisa's pale skin turned flame red and she started to vibrate. Either she was about to turn into the Incredible Hulk or . . .

'Tim is cheating on me,' she wailed at the top of her lungs. And with that, she began to weep hysterically, falling to her knees, clutching Jenny's ankles. 'He's having an affair.'

A startled-looking shop assistant froze beside me, eyes wide open, while the rest of Bloomingdales whispered amongst themselves.

'Excuse me.' I held out the clothes in my arms. 'I was wondering if you could start a room for us.'

Two minutes later, we were safely installed in a private dressing room with a very strong pitcher of mimosa, far from the main shopping floor. Apparently, having a nervous breakdown in the middle of Bloomingdales had its perks. Jenny, having switched from bitch mode to fierce protector, had all but carried Louisa into the changing rooms, giving anyone who looked at her the evil eye, while I apologised profusely to everyone we passed. Not that I thought we really had anything to apologise for but because I was English.

'Lou, are you OK?' I knelt down in front of the crumpled blonde mess that used to be my best friend, and poked her arm gently. I didn't know where to start. 'Do you want to go home?'

She didn't move or speak or even sniff. I knew first-hand how exhausting a good two solid minutes of hysterics could be, so I sat back on my heels and looked to Jenny for advice.

'Here, drink this.' Jenny handed Lou a very full glass of booze before turning to the nervous-looking assistant who hovered at the door. 'We would like to try on all of your clothes,' Jenny instructed. 'Like, everything. Theory, Marc, Vince, Maje, Sandro, Equipment, Current/Elliott . . . you get the idea? I want sequins, I want sparkle, I want leather pants, denim, dresses and everything in the store made of cashmere.'

'What sizes?' The girl was visibly shaking.

'Like, a six? A six.' Jenny looked at me for confirmation. 'Sixes, eights if they run small. We're gonna buy a shit-ton of stuff so if you could make sure we get the good stuff and not the shit over at the front end of the floor, that would be awesome.'

'I'll be right back,' the shop assistant replied, backing away uncomfortably. Poor cow.

Jenny joined me on the floor with her own glass of

fizz and gave me a 'here goes' glance. 'You're gonna feel better when you tell us what's been going on,' she promised. 'And you're gonna feel even better than that when you drink that mimosa.'

Louisa nodded softly and pushed her hair behind her ears before sinking the drink on command. She took a deep breath, wiped a finger underneath each eye to smear away some of the runny mascara and held her glass out for a top-up.

'It's my fault,' she said with a hiccup. 'I should have seen it coming. It was just like you and Mark. Everything was fine and then one day, I woke up and he wasn't there.'

'He left?' I pushed myself up to my feet, ready to run all the way to England to punch Tim Smith in the face. 'He walked out on you and Grace?'

'No, that's not what I meant.' Lou wrinkled her nose, looking all crumpled and small. 'He just wasn't *there* anymore, you know? Physically he was but mentally, he was somewhere else. So I thought about it and it all made sense. Late nights at the office, Saturday at the football, Sunday at tennis. Tennis, Angela. We both know what tennis means.'

'Well, for me, tennis meant my ex was boffing his mistress,' I agreed. 'But it doesn't mean Tim is cheating on you. Tim loves you. Tim is a good person and not a snivelling, coward of a shit of a man. And Grace, he would never do this to Grace.'

'She's right,' Jenny cooed, rubbing a soothing hand up and down Louisa's back. 'Maybe he's not cheating? Maybe he's just an inconsiderate shit who needs his ass kicking?'

'I read his texts,' Lou whispered. 'Yesterday morning, before he went to work. And there were all these messages from a woman called Vanessa. I don't know anyone called Vanessa.'

'That doesn't mean he's having an affair,' I said, clutching at every straw I could find. This couldn't be happening. I refused to believe that perfect Louisa and lovely Tim could possibly be in this situation. 'That just means he's getting texts from someone called Vanessa. I bet it's someone at work.'

'And I bet she's fat,' Jenny added. I rolled my eyes and ignored her best attempt at comfort.

'Whoever she is, she's texting my husband in the middle of the night, putting kisses at the end of her messages and talking to him about stupid bloody man stuff that I don't know anything about.' She took a tiny sip of her second mimosa. 'What kind of woman texts a man about golf and her car's engine and sends him pictures of a round of shots?'

'To be fair, it doesn't exactly sound like she's trying to seduce him,' I said with careful diplomacy. 'I mean, a text about golf isn't the same as a picture of her tits, is it?'

'No, it's worse,' Jenny said. 'That's some sneaky girl shit, Angie.'

'Yes!' Louisa exclaimed, pointing at Jenny. 'She's all "ooh, I'm just like one of the boys except I've got boobs and exciting parts where you can put your thing, and did I mention I'm so much more fun than your wife?"'

'Oh yeah.' I often forgot about those girls. Or at least I tried to. Toxic.

'I bet she plays computer games and always eats bacon sandwiches and loves football and even though she has beautiful, long hair and Bambi eyes, she never, ever wears make-up.' If nothing else, Lou had already perked up a bit. 'Because make-up is for girls and she's just one of the lads.'

'Even if he's texting this *woman*,' Jenny said, spitting out the word as though this Vanessa's gender were questionable, 'he might not be doing anything. Maybe he's just going through a shitty patch and didn't know how to talk to you. Have you tried to talk to him?'

'Talk?' Louisa smiled weakly at herself in the massive mirror behind us. 'We don't talk. What time will you be home? What do you want for dinner? Say goodbye to Grace for me. That's it. He's never home and I'm *always* home. Last Friday, he didn't come home at all.'

'But he had a reason, surely?' This was not looking good for Tim.

'He was on a stag do with some boys from the office and he text to say he was so wasted he was going to stay in their hotel room,' she said. 'But how likely is that? Bunk down with the boys in a Travelodge or just get in a taxi and come home? The next day he was a wreck.'

'Because he really was hungover?' I suggested.

'Because he was guilty,' she corrected. 'He's a guilty, lying shit. I can feel it in my bones, babe, I know it.'

And then it was time for hysterical tears, round two. Jenny and I sat back on our heels and looked at each other without anything more helpful to say. This really couldn't be happening. Louisa and Tim had been together since we were kids. They were that really annoying couple who always finished each other's sentences, held hands wherever they went and, most annoyingly of all, seemed to genuinely like each other all the time. I knew things had been harder since they'd had Grace, because when was adding a baby to the mix easy? But this just seemed so unlikely. Tim wasn't a cheater. Tim didn't have the balls to be a cheater.

'So what did he say when you said you were coming here?' I asked, hoping to stem the sobbing. 'Did he freak out?'

'Well . . .' I spotted a fleeting look of sheepishness run across her face before she quickly replaced it with righteous indignation. 'I haven't told him, have I?'

'LOU!'

Jenny beamed with pride and nodded with approval.

'Damn right, girlfriend,' she said, clapping.

'Oh, you stop it.' I slapped her hands away. 'You really cannot get away with saying "girlfriend". And she needs to tell Tim where she is.'

'I text him to say we were going to my mother's for the night,' Lou said. 'He doesn't know we're here. It was all those texts. I've known for ages something's been going on and I've been so miserable and then I read them and they went back weeks, Ange. All I could think was that I needed to get away and obviously I couldn't go to my mother's.'

'Well, obviously,' I admitted. She might as well have gone to my mother's.

'And I just wanted to see you. I knew you'd make me feel better.'

I softened, just for a second, and the sobbing began again. It was quieter this time, sadder. 'I really don't know what to do,' I said, stroking her hair as the dressing room door opened and the petrified-looking shop assistant pushed in a rack of clothes, waved a disembodied hand at us and closed the door again, without even entering.

'We'll fix it,' Jenny promised without any actual

way of knowing whether or not that was possible. 'You did the right thing, Lou Lou. Let him see how he likes being home without you and Gracie for a couple of days. He'll rethink his situation.'

'I guess.' Lou tried to look hopeful but failed.

'But she needs to tell him that she's gone,' I pointed out, 'or he won't know that he's supposed to miss her.'

'I gave someone else some advice once,' Jenny said, pushing herself up to her high-heeled feet and browsing the rack of clothes pulled by our invisible friend. 'It's OK not to be OK. You're going through some stuff, it's not all going to feel better when you wake up tomorrow. And that's not your fault.'

I bit my lip and watched, my heart breaking for my best friend, while Jenny picked out a pair of leather leggings, just like hers.

'And the person who took that advice turned out OK, huh, Angie?'

'What?' There suddenly seemed to be an awful lot of PVC in this changing room. 'You gave someone advice?'

'You. I gave you advice.' Jenny looked less than impressed. 'Maybe you didn't turn out so good after all. Did someone drop you on your head this morning? Lou Lou, try these on.'

Louisa took the leather leggings and blanched. I couldn't help but smile – after everything she'd just told us, the thing that threw her was a pair of bloody trousers.

'We'll give you a minute,' I said, taking Jenny's hand and yanking her out of the changing room. Lou nodded, looking a little relieved, and took another sip of her mimosa. If Jenny had been right about anything, it was that the booze seemed to make things better.

'I can't believe that asshole,' Jenny hissed once we were safely back on the shop floor. 'I ought to cut his balls off.'

'If it turns out he is cheating on her, I'll hold him down while you take the first snip,' I replied. 'With a pair of rusty barbecue tongs. But for now, we just need to calm her down. We can't go back to Grace with her in this state.'

'Shopping is totally calming.' Jenny held out her hands, as if I hadn't noticed we were still in a store. 'We'll work this out.'

'Fine, but I think we should just give her ten minutes on her own before we go charging back in there telling her what's what.'

And by we, I of course meant Jenny.

'Whatever. I'm going to pee.' She fluffed out her ponytail. 'And then I'm going to buy shoes. Any shoes. Coming?'

I looked around at all the racks of Christmas party dresses and felt my fingertips begin to prickle.

'I'm going to see if they've got this jumper I wanted for Alex downstairs,' I said, exercising previously unforeseen self-control. I wasn't sure I liked it. 'See you back here in ten minutes?'

'Ten minutes,' she agreed, flouncing off to the ladies'. Jenny-less, I pressed the down button on the lift and stopped, stock-still.

What if Tim really was cheating on Louisa?

The thought hadn't actually occurred to me before that moment. Obviously he was in her bad books for a good reason but in all honesty, I just assumed he was being a bit shit and a bit stupid. What if he was having an affair with this Vanessa woman and Louisa nicking off had just given her all the more time and freedom to get her feet under Louisa's beautiful modern country table. It wasn't as though Tim would be the first husband to cheat on his wife after their baby was born. I could imagine how left out he must feel, how hard it must be for him not to be her entire world after getting all of her attention for the last fifteen years. And he had some great role models to turn to – my ex had been one of his best friends and his affair had turned out just great. He was engaged to the woman he cheated on me with, everything had come up trumps for him. Perhaps there was more to this than I wanted to believe.

The men's department wasn't quite as busy as the women's floors but there were plenty of harassed-looking gents trailing their partners and patiently lifting their chins while jumpers and shirts were held up against them for consideration. Shopping anywhere in New York in December was a trying experience but I loved coming to Bloomingdales any time of year. In spring it was full of bright colours and the hope of summer, in summer it was a delicious swirl of air conditioning, and in winter it was all sparkly party dresses, giant Christmas trees and happy shoppers. The season of goodwill concentrated into a single store. Even when the queues were long and I had to wait ten minutes to go to the toilet, there was something about Bloomies that always put a smile on my face and it wasn't just the 10 per cent tourist discount I always got, even though I'd been living in the city for years. Trusty British driver's licence.

'Hey, Angela?'

I was happily stroking a preppy blue on blue striped jumper, wondering what kind of sexual favours I'd have to trade Alex to convince him to wear it, when I heard a voice I recognised.

'Jesse.' I reluctantly turned away from the kitten-soft jumper and gave him a quick hug and an air kiss. I was turning into such a twat. 'I'm busted.'

'Yeah, right,' he said with a laugh, grabbing the blue sweater from behind me and holding it up against himself for approval. I nodded and gave him a thumbs up. 'I saw you were out today. Getting your Christmas on?'

'What on earth makes you think I'm excited about Christmas?' I asked, altogether too aware of how awful I looked. Jesse was one of those men who always looked perfectly put together, even when he was super casual. I assumed it was something to do with being six feet something and having a perfect beard.

'I don't know. The light-up reindeer in your office are kind of a hint,' he said, tossing the blue jumper over his arm. 'Looking for something for the party on Friday night?'

'The Christmas party?' I was so beyond excited about my first ever proper honest-to-the-son-of-God-whose-birthday-we-were-celebrating office Christmas party.

'Holiday party,' he said. 'We're not allowed to call it a Christmas party because there are lots of different religions represented at Spencer Media, Angela.'

'Oh, yeah.' I would never be politically correct enough for America. 'Are you Jewish?'

'Catholic,' he replied. 'Mostly. I'm yanking your chain.'

'Right.' I raised my eyebrows and forced myself not to sigh. Sometimes, America . . . 'Am I still allowed to be Christmas shopping?'

'As long as you don't say the "C" word in front of HR,' he confirmed. 'Who's the sweater for?'

'My husband,' I said, holding up the jumper again and frowning. 'Alex. Alex Reid. I didn't change my name. But I'm married. To Alex.'

There was a good chance I was over-explaining but for one, I felt bad that I'd been caught Christmas shopping when the rest of the office was slaving away and two, not to put too fine a point on it, Jesse was hot. And hot men made me nervous.

'Aah, the mysterious Mr Angela.' Jesse stroked his chin through the stubble and smiled. His eyes were very blue. His hair was very black, a little bit like Alex's, only shorter. Of course he wasn't as handsome as Alex, I reminded myself quickly, and as sexy as that beard might look, it would almost certainly give a girl a rash. 'He's a sweater guy?'

'Against his will, on special occasions,' I said, trying not to sound as awkward as I felt. 'He's a perennial jeans and T-shirt kind of a man.'

Why was it always so weird to see someone you worked with outside work? I spent between eight and twelve hours a day with Jesse, five days a week, and had never so much as coloured up when he tipped me the wink in the office but three minutes of casual conversation in the Bloomingdales basement and I felt like a complete slag.

'I feel him,' Jesse said, clearly not awkward at all. 'I only dress up for you.'

'Huh?'

'In the office?' he gave me a huge grin. 'I figured jeans and tees every day would be pushing my luck. With Mary mostly.'

'Oh, of course,' I agreed quickly, nodding so hard I

thought my head might fall off. 'Yeah, she can be a bit strict. Although I'm a bit more casual off duty, as you can see.'

Better to bring up my bag lady ensemble than have him say nothing then run back to the office and tell them all what a tramp I was. Not that there was a single person in that office that hadn't walked in on me trying to get some sort of stain out of some sort of clothing in the last year.

'I like it.' Jesse flicked some presumably very real dust from my shoulder. 'Totally punk.'

'Totally what I was going for,' I said, relaxing a little. 'You're Christmas shopping too?'

'Yeah.' He waved the blue sweater in the air and rolled his blue eyes. 'I'm doing so well. We both know I'm gonna end up wearing this before I give it to my brother. I can't cope with going out to do laundry in this weather.'

I nodded in agreement, bathing silently in the glow of the brand new washer and dryer in our new apartment. Soon, my precious, soon.

'You're in Williamsburg, right?' he asked, digging around in his Manhattan Portage messenger bag. 'You should come to my band's show Thursday night. You haven't seen us play before, right?'

'I have not,' I said, taking the flyer and scanning it quickly. Music Hall, Thursday at eleven. So past my bedtime, but super close to my apartment.

'Yeah, we're R5-D4.' He pointed to the band at the top of the list. 'It's a dumb name.'

'No, it isn't,' I said reflexively. I had no idea if it was dumb or not. 'Ooh, you're headlining.'

'Yeah, it's our friend's night,' he shrugged. Bless him for being so blasé about it. I'd once heard someone say there were a hundred blogs on the internet for every one that had a reader. If that was true, there had to be a thousand bands in Williamsburg for every one that only ever played in their friend's basement. Thursday night at Music Hall was nothing to be sniffed at. 'It should be fun, though. You should come. I'll put you on the list.'

'I'll try.' It was as committal as I could be. 'As long as you don't quit and leave me in the lurch looking for a new managing editor while I'm looking after things for Mary.'

'We're a long way from quitting our day jobs,' he promised. 'As you'll see if you come to the show.'

'Maybe Alex'll come,' I said, more wondering to myself than to Jesse. 'My husband. He's a musician, he's in a band.'

'Yeah, I know,' he said with another shy smile. Bloody Americans and their perfect teeth. If I weren't dead against it, I'd have been pitching Jenny's empty womb for rent at that exact second. Smart, handsome and brilliant gnashers. She could do worse. 'I love Stills. They were like my favourite band when I was in college.'

College? How old was he? How old was I?

'I should go,' Jesse said, looking at his watch. 'I ran out as soon as Mary wasn't looking but I had better get back before the staff meeting.'

'You're making me feel so guilty.' I pushed my dirty hair out of my face and held my head. 'Tomorrow is going to be hard work, isn't it?'

'Maybe I won't mention I saw you.' Jesse tapped his nose and tossed the sweater over his shoulder. 'Secret Shoppers Anonymous.'

'I wouldn't hate you if you didn't.' I dug my hands

deep in my jeans pockets, feeling a bit odd again. 'I'd better get back upstairs. See you tomorrow?'

'At work or in Macy's?' he asked as I walked away.

'Make it Barneys and you've got yourself a date,' I laughed before immediately blushing from head to toe. 'A shopping date. Obviously.'

'Too late,' he deadpanned, turning to the cash desk. 'I'm going straight to HR when I get back to the office.'

And even though I was smiling as I walked away, I still felt a little unsettled. The Americans were a litigious people.

When I got back up to the second floor, I had a sneaking suspicion that Jenny wouldn't have been able to keep clear of the changing room and give Louisa the space she so clearly needed. After a quick scout around the shoe section proved fruitless, I ran back to the changing room.

'Jenny, I'm just not sure,' I heard Louisa protest inside. 'I don't think it's really me.'

'Don't be dumb,' Jenny replied. 'It's all wipe clean, baby sick proof. It's totally practical.'

When I threw open the door, I was treated to the sight of Louisa clad in a backless leather bustier and leather trousers so tight I could more or less see exactly where Grace had come into the world.

'Help?' she said, afraid to move in her towering high heels.

'Doesn't she look awesome?' Jenny stood beside her masterpiece and gave me a double thumbs up. 'Hell of a makeover.'

'Hell seems about right,' I said, fighting a smile that would not be welcomed by either of my friends. 'I reckon we probably ought to get back home soon, relieve Alex of his Grace-sitting duties?'

'Oh, yes please,' Louisa nodded, immediately bending down to take off the ridiculous stripper heels Jenny had chosen for her. 'I'm sure she'll be missing her mummy.'

'You two suck,' Jenny announced, hands on hips. 'I hope you know that.'

'We do,' I said, throwing an arm around Louisa's shoulders and squeezing them in a half-hug. 'And we're fine with it.'

CHAPTER SEVEN

'They're totally unconscious,' I announced, quietly closing the bedroom door on Grace and Louisa, both completely sparked out on my bed at three in the afternoon. Alex nodded from his cross-legged position in front of his record racks. Someone had had a very busy morning pretending to start packing up the apartment. He was surrounded by record sleeves, some I recognised, some I didn't, all showing the careful wear and tear of being played often but with love.

'Jet lag's a bitch,' Alex said, sliding a Nirvana album into the slots of a special packing crate. 'They must be exhausted.'

We'd been out of the house for nearly five hours and Alex had filled one box. But he had been on babysitting duty and I couldn't imagine he'd allowed Grace anywhere near his precious vinyl collection. I was only allowed to touch the records if I washed my hands and even then I was forbidden to drop the needle on the record player, following an unfortunate scratching incident with my dad's Police record when I was five. I still couldn't believe my dad remembered that. Or that he had told Alex within fifteen minutes of meeting him.

'Can you believe all this Tim stuff, though?' I had filled him in on the basics with a series of exclamation mark-filled texts on our way back in the cab. 'I just can't get my head around it.'

'Yeah, it's too bad.' Alex cleared a spot beside him for me to sit down. I stretched out along the floor, pulling the Ramones T-shirt I'd borrowed in my rush to get dressed that morning over my bare belly. 'I liked that guy. I hope they can figure it out.'

'What did you and Grace get up to?' I said, resting my head in his lap. 'She went out like a light.'

'I took her to the park,' he said, pushing away the rest of his records and stroking my hair away from my face. 'She's a maniac. I thought my legs were going to fall off chasing her around the dog run. Word of advice, never let a kid see a puppy if she can't actually have it. I had to bribe her to stop crying with all the candy on earth.'

I decided to keep that information from Louisa, just in case.

'So you're over the baby crazies?' I asked, bridging my neck to look into his green eyes. 'One morning with a toddler was enough?'

'Are you kidding me?' He leaned down to plant a kiss on my nose before carefully placing my head on the floor and pushing himself up to his feet. 'I loved it. I was, like, the best dad ever. And seriously, I wish I'd had a kid to drag around when I was single – I've never been hit on so many times in my life.'

'Well, that's nice to hear,' I said, giving him the dead eye from my spot on the floor. 'You massive shit.'

'I only took one phone number,' he said with a smirk, kicking me in the hip with love. 'So are you

118

going to stay down there or help me pack up some of your shit?'

'I'm going to stay down here,' I replied. 'The floor is good. There's no magazine, or move, or mental friends, or evil assistants, or uninvited parents. There is just the floor.'

'And what's going to happen when you have to get off the floor?' he asked, crouching behind the tree to turn on the still blinking lights. He knew me so well. 'And all those things are still problems?'

'Move to Lapland?'

Alex grinned and pushed his hair out of his eyes. He still hadn't had it cut and I was still happy about it. My mum wouldn't be impressed, though.

'Shall we take this one at a time?' he suggested.

I shrugged and stretched out my arms and legs, making a snow angel in the middle of all the records.

'So, I really haven't had a chance to tell you but I am stupid impressed at the fact they made you editor of your magazine.'

'Interim editor,' I said with faux modesty. I knew I liked him for a reason.

'Whatever, I think it's pretty hot.' Alex began taking books off the bookcase and carefully stacking them in one of the empty boxes by my feet. 'My wife, the editor. And you're going to be awesome at it so let's stop pretending that's a problem.'

'Well, when you put it like that,' I replied, gazing lovingly at my tree. And then my husband. And then my tree.

'You don't have to worry about the move at all. I've got that all covered,' he swore. 'And Delia has promised that the evil assistant isn't going to give you any shit, correct?'

'She has,' I admitted. 'But really—'

'Then you worry about that when you need to.' Alex cut me off with his wacky common sense. 'I get why you're freaking out but if you told Delia you'll give her a chance, then I say give her a chance. Maybe she's on some new meds or something. People do change, you know. Occasionally.'

Hmm. This time I just concentrated on the tree.

'As for the other two, they're not even problems. Louisa needs a few days to straighten herself out. I bet when she wakes up from her nap, she'll be ready to get back on the plane.'

I wasn't so sure about that one but I was too tired to argue. Glancing over at my advent calendar hanging on the kitchen cupboard door, I wondered whether I could sneak tomorrow's chocolate without Alex noticing.

'And yeah, your parents coming over could be kind of stressful but it's Christmas,' he said. 'It might be fun to have the folks around. Isn't that what the holidays are all about?'

'You've never spent Christmas with my folks,' I reminded him. 'Imagine my mum the day before the wedding, times a million. Annette gets stressed which means I get stressed which means you, my love, will get stressed.'

Alex blanched slightly and paused in his packing.

'I just figured they might bring a bunch of those awesome orange cookie cake things,' he admitted. 'Can't they just get drunk and pass out like normal people?'

'I've already got Jaffa Cakes, I was just hiding them so you didn't eat them all before Christmas,' I whined. 'And no, they can't. Well, my dad can and will but

120

my mum will be a massive pain in the arse. I really wanted it to be just us. I wanted our Christmas.'

Alex put the books in his arms into the box and walked back over to me, stepping over my waist and kneeling down. Pulling me up against his chest, he pressed his lips against mine in a long, tender, quiet kiss before wrapping his arms around me.

'We'll work it out,' he said. 'But whatever, we've got this afternoon, right?'

'Right,' I said, hugging him tightly and smiling over his shoulder. 'Want to stop packing and eat the secret box of Jaffa Cakes?'

'Yes, I do,' Alex replied, a smile in his voice. 'It's all going to be OK. By New Year's, you'll wonder why you were getting so worked up.'

'I hope so,' I said as he dragged me to my feet and carried me into the kitchen.

'Now, where are you hiding those goddamn Jaffa Cakes?' he asked, dropping me in front of the fridge.

I laughed, climbing onto the kitchen counter and rifling through a cupboard, retrieving the secret snacks. OK, so this wasn't quite the same as the entire week I'd planned to spend snuggled up on the sofa with him but it was better than nothing. Jaffa Cakes made everything better.

Wednesday morning saw me back at work, entirely against my will. Alex, Louisa and Grace had bundled themselves up and trotted off to Prospect Park to meet some actual reindeer. It had literally taken every ounce of restraint not to call Mary, quit my job and trot off with them. Gutted wasn't the word. And so, instead of singing 'Rudolph' at a bunch of very confused deer who probably weren't really enjoying lots of random people singing 'Rudolph' at them for eight hours a day, I was getting ready for the arrival of my new assistant.

Louisa and Grace had slept right up until tea time and we'd spent the evening as a happy bunch, eating pizza and watching *The Muppet Christmas Carol*, never once mentioning Tim's alleged infidelity. It had been a happy evening and the whole time I was stuffing my face with pizza I was at peace, but as soon as the girls turned in and me and Alex took to the airbed, I became restless. It was all well and good for Alex to tell me my problems weren't really problems but the more I thought about them, the more I was relatively certain that they were.

Taking an A4 pad out of my desk drawer, I drew up a quick list. Number one, moving house. Number two, Cici. Number three, my parents. Number four, Louisa and Tim. Number five, Jenny's baby fever. I quickly drew a line through number five. Jenny hadn't mentioned anything the whole time we were together on Tuesday so I figured she'd already forgotten about her baby crazies. The chime of a credit card machine was louder than her biological clock after all. The rest of the list needed some consideration. Number one was starting to give me a rash. Alex had booked movers for Saturday morning and not only had we only packed up one box of records and one box of books, we had number four to take into consideration. What if Louisa was still here on Saturday? She certainly wasn't showing any signs of packing up and going home, despite Alex's assurances that she'd be ready to jump back on the plane. But what could I do, other than be a good friend? I couldn't call Tim and grass her up. I couldn't force her to leave when she wasn't ready.

This one was tricky. Almost as tricky as number three. My parents. Try as I might, I couldn't get excited about their unexpected visit. I'd tossed and turned all night long, trying to think of a nice and inoffensive way I could suggest they not bother but I had nothing. It wasn't as if I never wanted to see them again, I just hadn't prepared. The house wouldn't be ready – the house or my nerves. If they had wanted to come for Christmas, I needed a good six-month warning to make sure I had an adequate number of guest towels. My mother would be mortified if she knew I hadn't changed the sheets for Louisa and Grace but, quite frankly, the laundry needed doing and I just didn't have that many sheets.

And that left number two. On cue, my borrowed-from-Alex ancient iPhone 3 buzzed into life, revealing a text message made up of nothing but fifteen different happy emojis and an exclamation mark. I wasn't quite sure what the ghost with a sticky out tongue meant but mostly I took this to mean that Cici was on her way.

'Hey,' Jesse stuck his head around my door. 'You OK, boss?'

'Oh God, don't call me that,' I groaned, shoving the notepad underneath my keyboard. 'I'm fine. Just waiting for the devil to show its horns.'

Jesse was well aware of my history with Cici. He'd heard all of my war stories over the last few months and I would be hard-pushed to say whether he was more scared or excited about her impending arrival. I had a suspicion that he was nursing a crush on Delia and the prospect of her slutty, bitchy twin had to be a little bit exciting to the straight male staffers, i.e. Jesse. Of course, if I'd told him she was a saint who nursed sick children back to health on her weekends, he wouldn't have been even slightly interested. Men were strange creatures.

'Want a coffee or anything?' he asked. 'I'm going down to Starbies.'

'I would love a coffee,' I said. What would I do without him? 'Thank you.'

'Any time,' he said with a salute, ducking back out the door.

Really he was a saint. Which made the next person to appear in my office the devil incarnate.

'Good morning, boss.'

Looking up from my computer screen, I felt the blood drain from my face as I saw Cici stood in my doorway wearing a great big scarlet smile. The red of her lipstick matched the soles of her shoes, which immediately got my back up. Loubies on her first day. She couldn't have stuck with her gap-year chic for her first day? Of course not. I forced myself to give her the benefit of the doubt – she probably hadn't worn them purposely to piss me off, it just wouldn't have occurred to her not to wear them. I wondered what kind of person I would have grown up to be if I'd popped straight out of the womb and into a Gucci babygro. If Gucci made babygros. I should ask Erin, she'd know.

The promise of gainful employment had clearly lured Cici out of the kibbutz collection couture and into the hairdresser's. Gone was the braided strip, back was the manicure. Her hair looked so glossy, I assumed she'd had every strand coated with diamonds. The gems that hadn't been ground down and sprinkled liberally about her person hung from her ears, her throat, her wrists and her fingers. Everything about her sparkled.

'Our first day together!' Cici squeezed her shoulders

up around her ears in an effort to look cute and waited for me to exhale (it had been a minute, I must have been turning blue) before she stepped over my threshold. 'So, I got your coffee. Caramel macchiato, right? I checked with Deedee.'

She held out a huge Starbucks cup, her nail polish matching her lipstick. Presumably it was so the blood didn't show.

'I already had HR reroute all of your calls to my phone and obviously I'll have your inbox and your calendar from now on so anything you want me to handle, just tag it and I'll reply for you.'

'You have my inbox?' I gingerly accepted the coffee and put it down on my desk, waiting for it to jump up and attack. No way she'd go for anything as subtle as poisoning. 'There's no need for that, really. I think I can answer my own emails.'

'Relax,' she said, sipping her own coffee, presumably black, presumably calorie-free. 'I'm not going to be printing out Alex's love letters and hanging them in the bathroom.'

She actually had the nerve to giggle.

'The more you trust your intuition, the more empowered you become, the stronger you become, and the happier you become,' Cici declared as though she was quoting some great philosopher as she brushed invisible lint from her snug black sweater. 'I know trust takes time.'

'Wise words,' I replied. I wasn't interested in playing games. I was even less interested in getting shanked in an alleyway outside the office but these were the chances we took in life. 'Not yours?'

'Gisele Bundchen.'

'Aah, one of the great philosophers of our time,' I commented.

'No, she's a supermodel,' she corrected me. 'She's, like, Brazilian?'

'Yeah.' I tried to see if anyone was watching this but the office looked half empty. Why was there never a good material witness around when you needed one. I eyed the security camera, completely unconvinced.

'I think we're going to get along super well.' Cici clicked her red nails together, not asking my imagination to work too hard turning them into claws. 'I'm not here to cause trouble, Angela, I'm here to get ahead. I want to be part of the business, like my sister, and if I really put my mind to it, I don't think it's going to be too long before I'm exactly where I want to be.'

She clicked her fingers, gave me the guns and winked.

'You're going to have me shot?'

'We are going to have some fun, huh?' she laughed. 'You and me. Give me a week and you'll be calling me your BFF. Trust me, I'm way more fun than Deedee. We should get cocktails. Oh, let's get cocktails tonight!'

'I would love to but I'm planning on poking myself in the eye with a red-hot poker,' I replied. 'Maybe you should go and find your desk?'

'You crack me up.' She trotted out her over-the-top laugh again, pressing a hand into her side for good measure. Clearly, it was splitting. 'We really are going to make a great team.'

'A great team,' I muttered, picking up the coffee and regarding it with caution. Maybe she had just spat in it, I thought, taking a sip. It tasted normal. But then, weren't most laxatives taste-free these days?

The rest of the day passed fairly uneventfully. I'd spent a couple of hours with Mary and Jesse, going over the online approvals system we had just installed to speed up the approvals process on press day, and a couple more going over features proposals that Mary refused to look at on the basis that I was going to have to learn how to make my own decisions sooner or later. I didn't think she needed to know I made most of my decisions with the Magic 8 Ball app on my phone. Alex and Louisa had both sent hatefully adorable photos of the three of them visiting the reindeer and, at last count, I had eaten seven gingerbread Christmas trees. I'd tried to enforce a strict 'all staffers must eat' rule with the team but they were far more interested in fitting into designer sample sizes than baked goods. Fools.

'Hey, boss!'

That really was going to start to grate very soon.

'Cici,' I replied without taking my eyes off my screen. I hoped that if I didn't look directly into her eyes, she wouldn't be able to steal my soul. 'Are you leaving?'

'Yeah, we're going to get cocktails, right?' She zipped up a tiny leather jacket and wiggled her hips in a little dance. 'Cocktail time for the girls.'

'Did you just sing at me?' I asked, slightly stunned. 'You didn't really think we were going to go for drinks?'

I couldn't work out if I was more shocked at the look of disappointment that flitted across Cici's face or the fact that I almost felt a little bit guilty for causing it.

'Yeah, no, right.' She tossed her honey-blonde hair over her shoulder and fixed a blank expression. 'You probably have plans.'

'And so do you?'

'Well, obvies,' she laughed. 'I'll see you tomorrow.'

Happily, before I could open my mouth and insert my foot directly inside, my phone rang.

'I'd better get this,' I said, snatching up the handset before she could. 'See you tomorrow.'

'Tomorrow,' she mouthed, closing my office door behind her. It sounded so much like a threat.

'Hello?' I rubbed the heel of my hand across my forehead, hoping to erase the last three minutes of my day.

'Hi, Angela? It's Laura,' a woman's voice announced. 'Dr Morgan?'

'Of course, hi,' I replied, a beat too late. 'Sorry, bit of a mad moment.'

'Oh, is now not a good time to talk?' Laura asked.

I looked down at my desk, over at my messy meeting table covered in notes from the day's meetings and then at all the emails lit up in big bold type in my inbox. When was there a good time to talk?

'Now's fine,' I answered. 'What's up?'

'I got your test results back today and I really just wanted to go over them with you,' Laura's voice trod a fine line between casual girlfriends and professional courtesy. I was immediately on edge. 'Any chance you could come down to the office, maybe after you finish up at work?'

'Not really.' Without warning, a wave of nausea rushed right over me. I gripped the handset a little tighter and breathed out slowly through my mouth. 'Can't you just tell me now?'

'I don't really like to discuss test results over the phone,' she replied, leaning further towards a more professional tone with every syllable. 'It's much better to explain everything in person.'

'Without wanting to be a drama queen,' I began. I absolutely wanted to be a drama queen. What was wrong? Was I pregnant? Was it triplets? Did I have some horrible symptomless disease? Oh God, this was from that time I dropped my Danish on the kitchen floor and ate it anyway. The ten-second rule didn't exist after all! 'I'd really rather know now. I just can't make it over there today.'

'OK,' she said with a reluctant deep breath. 'I don't want you to panic about anything because, really, it's nothing major.'

'I'm not panicking at all,' I said with a light laugh. Which was very strange because inside my head, all I could see were flashing red lights accompanied by sirens and the word 'PANIC' flashing over and over in ten-foot-high fluorescent letters.

'Now, I want you to know, nothing is conclusive and none of the tests we did revealed any incredibly serious conditions, they just give us a guideline with regards to fertility,' she said. I was trying to listen and ignore the big scary panic disco that was going on in my head. 'Your overall health is great and you are ovulating which is fantastic.'

'Fantastic,' I repeated. Not a word I had applied to ovulation before.

'But one of the tests did show your hormone levels were a little lower than I would like, given that you're not immediately considering starting a family,' Laura said carefully. 'And that you have fewer eggs than might be considered typical at your age.'

'I see. And what exactly does that mean?' I asked, as though I was asking her how one might go about baking a Victoria sponge without the requisite ingredients.

'It means you might have some fertility challenges,' she replied. 'And the longer you leave it, the harder it might be to conceive naturally.'

She let the news sink in for a moment but I wasn't

sure whether or not she was waiting for a response. If she was, I didn't have one, so she was buggered.

'I'd love for you to come in so we can talk about some options,' she went on. 'There's really no need to panic, this doesn't mean you're infertile. There's absolutely no reason why you wouldn't be able to conceive naturally and have a perfectly healthy pregnancy, we'll just need to stay on top of the situation.'

'But sooner would be better than later,' I said, way more calmly than I was feeling. 'If I wanted to have a baby naturally.'

The word 'naturally' stuck in my throat. How else did you have a baby?

'Sooner would be better than later,' she said with emphasis on the 'would'. 'But there are a lot of options, Angela. I really would like you to come in and talk. Seriously, I had a woman come in last week who froze her eggs when she was three years younger than you and she's just had twins. And we're a long way from even contemplating egg freezing.'

'Egg freezing.'

'It's an option,' Laura said. 'A long-term option. For women looking to put off pregnancy indefinitely.'

'Egg freezing.'

'Angela?'

'Egg freezing.'

'Angela, are you OK?' Laura's professionalism was slipping over into concern. 'Is anyone there with you?'

'I'm fine,' I whispered to stop my voice from cracking. I was not going to cry on the phone to a doctor, my mother would kill me. 'I'm OK. Thanks for letting me know.'

'You need to come in and see me so we can talk about this some more,' Laura insisted. 'I can make some time tomorrow. Whenever works for you. Just let me know.'

'Did you call Jenny yet?' I cradled the phone between my ear and my shoulder, freeing my hand to wipe away a tear that hadn't quite made it out. And I wasn't going to bloody let it.

'I haven't,' she said. 'I wanted to talk to you first.'

'She's fine?' It was a statement more than a question.

'She's fine,' Laura confirmed, softly.

'Can you not mention anything about this when you call her?' I asked, embarrassed.

'Of course not. I absolutely wouldn't discuss your test results with anyone else. So you'll email me with a time for tomorrow?'

'I will,' I said, sniffing with resolve. 'I will.'

'And maybe if he's around, bring Alex?' she suggested.

'If he's around.' Alex. The resolve seeped away, along with any measure of strength that was stopping the tears that welled up behind my eyes. 'Thanks for calling, Laura.'

Without waiting for her to reply, I hung up. It was rude and my mother would be endlessly disappointed at my treatment of a health professional but I figured it was better to be thought of as abrupt than the woman that sobbed uncontrollably down the phone to a doctor she barely knew. I turned my chair to face the window, the bright lights of Times Square blurring into colourful smudges. I didn't even know why I was crying. It was like Laura said, there wasn't anything majorly wrong, my hormones were just a little bit low, that was all. And there was no reason why I couldn't have a baby naturally. People went through worse than this every single day and right now there wasn't even anything to go through. Apart from telling Alex that we might have a hard time having kids. How did I even start that conversation? *Merry Christmas, honey. I know you really want to have kids but surprise! No such luck.* All at once, I wanted him there with me and I never wanted to see him again. I wanted him there to hold me and tell me everything was OK but I just couldn't imagine how I was going to look him in the eye. Even though I wasn't quite sure how, somehow I felt as though I'd let him down.

Picking up my phone, I looked at the photo of Alex, Louisa and Grace huddled around a small, distressed-looking reindeer and smiled. They looked like the perfect family – handsome dark-haired husband, beautiful blonde wife and the perfect mini-me daughter. Only the blonde's husband was three thousand miles away and possibly porking some bird called Vanessa while the dark-haired husband's wife was going to struggle with a mini-me of her own. Dropping the phone on the desk, I pulled my notepad out from underneath the keyboard. Problems one to five suddenly seemed a little bit silly.

Bollocks.

CHAPTER EIGHT

By the time I arrived back at the apartment, I had come to what I considered to be an ingenious solution to my problems. I would just ignore them. I'd been looking forward to Erin's tree-trimming party for weeks and I wasn't going to let a little issue like potentially never being able to have children even though my husband had nothing but babies on the brain ruin my evening. After a twenty-minute cry in the shower and half a bottle of eye drops, even I couldn't tell anything was wrong with me.

'Who's ready to trim a tree?' I asked, stepping out of the bathroom and into the living room to a round of applause from the ladies of the house. Grace's eyes lit up as she slapped her chubby hands together. Alex nodded his approval from the kitchen, where he was shoving a Jaffa Cake in his mouth, hoping I wouldn't notice.

'You do scrub up very well.' Louisa gave my gold sequinned BCBG shift dress an admiring nod. I did a spin, making sure I could get around in the obscenely high Brian Attwood heels I'd nicked from the fashion desk on my way out. I hadn't worn the shoes in an age and they were a risk but they made me look skinny so I couldn't really see what choice I had. 'You still need a haircut, though.'

'Well, I'm not quite at the point where Vidal Sassoon can come in and give me a trim while I'm at my desk,' I said, checking my handbag for lip balm and chewing gum. 'Nice jumper.'

'Thanks, it's yours,' she replied, stroking the silver sparkles on her shoulder. 'And I'm pretty sure Vidal Sassoon is dead.'

'All the more reason why I'd struggle to book him for a trim them.' I clacked my hastily applied stick-on nails on the kitchen top. 'Shall we get off?'

'Hey, chill.' Alex wandered out of the bedroom, fussing with a skinny black tie against a white shirt. 'I called a car. It'll be here in a second.'

Talk about scrubbing up well. Whenever Alex ventured into the wild world of formalwear, I wanted to drag him around the streets of New York, shoving him in random women's faces and screaming 'this is mine!' Totally rational.

'Don't Auntie Angela and Uncle Alex look glamorous?' Lou said, hoisting Grace onto her lap and stretching her little arm out towards us. 'Don't they look like neither of them spent twenty minutes trying to get chocolate out of your hair this afternoon?'

'Yeah, sorry about that,' Alex muttered, turning to me so I could fix his tie. Adjusting a tie was something a sexy, grown-up woman did in movies. It made me feel like Julia Roberts in *Pretty Woman*, except without the casually overlooked prostitution part. I just hoped he never actually needed me to tie it for him because I had no idea how. 'I left her alone with a cookie.'

'You never leave me alone with a cookie,' I sulked, stepping back to admire my handiwork. Outside, a car horn sounded as Alex helped me shrug on my coat while Louisa did the same with Grace. The irony was not lost on me. 'Come on, gang, let's get our Christmas on.'

One of the biggest problems with moving to New York was accepting that coffee house waitresses and wannabe actors did not live in big, beautiful lofts in the West Village. In truth, the only people who lived in the West Village were extraordinarily rich people. People like my friend Erin. But, as we stepped inside the beautiful townhouse on Perry Street, I remembered that it had cost her not only over a million dollars but forty years of slogging away for eighty hours a week and three failed marriages. When you really thought about it, that was probably a lot to pay for a house, even a really nice one.

'Angela!'

I was awkwardly handing my coat to a middle-aged woman wearing a black maid's dress and a face like a slapped arse when Erin appeared in her own hallway. 'Alex, it's been an age. And Louisa, so excited that you're here! There's a crèche in the next room, feel free to offload this little cherub.'

She tweaked Grace's cheek and planted kisses on the rest of us before literally snatching Grace out of Louisa's arms and handing her over to a waiting nanny. Grace took the whole thing with a surprisingly good attitude, waving happily at us as she was whisked away through a dark wooden door. Before Louisa could react, Erin placed a glass of champagne in her hand.

'Merry Christmas,' she said, giving Lou a 'drink up' gesture. 'Enjoy the night off while you can.'

Stunned, Louisa did as she was told and Erin turned her attention to me, wrapping me in a bear hug that belied her tiny frame.

'I'm so glad you're here,' she whispered in my ear, mid-hug. 'I feel like a zombie. It's so long since I've done anything like this. You look amazing. I feel like shit.'

In reality, Erin's son, Thomas Junior, was only two weeks old and we'd been to brunch literally twenty-four hours before she gave birth. And while she might have felt like shit, she looked amazing. I might not have been able to get the hairdresser into the office but Erin had certainly had him round to her house. Along with a personal shopper and a make-up artist from the look of it. Her floor-length black dress made her blonde hair shine and the simple T-shirt cut of the gown stopped the heavy satin material from looking too much. It was a simple elegance I could never get away with, although I did think I'd look all right in the enormous diamond chandelier earrings that peeped out from her half-up, half-down do. Truly, Erin was the best example I knew of how the other half lived. West Village townhouse, Wall Street banker husband, her own PR company, private jet, summer house in the Hamptons and ski lodge in Vermont. It was insane. Sure, Delia was from family money but she hadn't been spoiled and since the woman never left the office, it was easy to forget about the black Amex in her wallet. But Erin had worked hard for what she had and she was committed to making the most of it, and for that I couldn't knock her. I could be insanely jealous, but I couldn't knock her.

'Come through,' she said, grabbing my hand and leading the way with a half-full glass of champagne. 'There are so many people you need to say hello to before we get shitcanned with Lopez.'

Music and laughter from another room suggested we weren't the first to arrive. Stricken with sudden social anxiety, I was relieved to feel Alex's hand on my waist. He was a total champ to come to the party. Wall Street bankers and Manhattan socialites were not his cup of tea and the poor boy had already put in a full day entertaining my emotionally compromised best friend and her toddler, all while planning our move in three days' time. He deserved a medal. But instead, he was getting a hearty handshake and a slap on the back from Erin's husband, Thomas, and being presented to all of his banker buddies.

'This is Alex,' I heard Thomas announce. 'Hell of a guy. He's actually in a band. He lives in Brooklyn.'

The Brookes Brothers gang stared at him as though they'd just been told Alex lived on the moon and sold crack for a living. I made a mental note to make it up to him in sexual favours as soon as we got home. It wouldn't exactly be a hardship.

I tottered along behind Erin, letting her drag me through clumps of well-dressed but decidedly unsparkly party guests, while she nattered on to Louisa about the difficulties of childrearing under the influence.

It wasn't hard to tune out. Erin's house had been transformed from a chic West Village townhouse into a winter wonderland. Every available surface in my office and apartment was covered in reindeer, snowmen, bells, tinsel, twinkling lights, candy canes and cotton wool snow. And if there was already something on the surface, that something was now wearing a miniature

Santa hat. I liked to think of my Christmas decorating style as enthusiastic and fun. Erin's Christmas decorating style was, like the rest of her house, bloody beautiful. Classic Christmas crooners were piped through an invisible sound system and there were beautiful glowing candles on high shelves, safely out the way of clumsy guests, i.e. me. And in the corner of the main reception room was a towering Christmas tree of glory. Truly, it was a thing of beauty but much to my utter dismay, it was already completely decorated. Wasn't this supposed to be a tree-trimming party? From top to bottom, the eight-foot giant glowed with hidden fairy lights and tasteful gold- and silver-toned decorations. Classy. I always envied these kinds of trees but at heart I was a mishmash of decorations girl. I had baubles on my tree that I had made in Brownies when me and Lou were tiny, I had decorations from all of my travels, pieces friends had bought, things that reminded me of special times. Erin's tree only really reminded me that I still hadn't worked out how to stop my lights from blinking on and off like a mad man.

'What's wrong?' Erin asked, handing me a glass of champagne. 'You look like someone just told you the holidays were cancelled. Here's a clue – they aren't.'

'Your tree is already done,' I said. Heart. Broken. 'I thought we were going to put all the stuff on it?'

'Oh no.' She gave a tiny tinkling laugh and placed her hand on my arm. 'I had someone come over and do it. Dressing the tree is such a chore. Now we get to concentrate on the fun part!'

I smiled happily, nodding while I died on the inside. So much for my mega-fun Christmas evening that was going to take my mind off all the messy, stressy bollocks that was threatening to send me mad.

While Erin and Louisa carried on chatting, I tiptoed closer to the tree. A proper lungful of piney goodness would make all this better. Except, I couldn't smell anything. Because the tree didn't smell of anything. Because the tree was fake. Peering in between the densely packed branches, where I was expecting to see a thick, woody trunk, was just a chunky green plastic pole. Christmas fraud! I turned to look back at Erin, trying to think of an appropriate way to express my dismay. With no better option, I decided it was best expressed in consuming as much alcohol as humanly possible. I'd been robbed of decorating the tree – hell, I'd even been robbed of an actual tree – but I'd be damned if I was giving up all Christmas traditions. There was nothing else to do but get really drunk.

'Angie!'

The inimitable call of Jenny Lopez sounded across the room, shaking me out of my sulk. She strode in, her flatmate Sadie hot on her heels. I abandoned the tree of lies and made my way over to my friends, determined to turn things around, determined to have a good time.

'Hey, Lou Lou.' Jenny threw herself on Louisa, leaving bright red lipstick smudges on her cheeks. She was wearing a purple silk jumpsuit with towering gold strappy sandals and a matching belt around her tiny waist. Her hair was everywhere. Sadie was almost wearing a silver Hervé Léger bandage dress.

'Hi,' she breathed, leaning ever so slightly forward to suggest air kisses on both of my cheeks. 'I just flew in from London. I'm really fucking tired.'

'It's good to see you too,' I replied. Sadie was a model. This meant she occasionally forgot how actual humans were supposed to act in social situations. 'Merry Christmas.'

She blinked twice, moved her mouth into a smile that didn't meet her eyes and then whispered something to Jenny before vanishing.

'She OK?' Louisa asked.

'Sure.' Jenny waved away our concerns and waved over a waiter. 'She's just gonna go do some coke and then she'll be fine.'

'Oh.' Louisa looked startled for a moment before resetting her face. 'Is that . . . is that normal?'

'Not for normal people,' I replied on Jenny's behalf before she said something that might upset Louisa's delicate, suburban temperament. 'If I'm a bit tired, I have a Diet Coke and a sit down. But Sadie isn't normal people.'

'Fair enough,' Lou muttered, looking around the party with new eyes, trying to work out who was just a regular Manhattanite and who was a raging gak head. Following her gaze, it actually wasn't that hard to tell.

'So what's going on, Lou Lou?' Jenny asked, taking a glass of champs from the waiter. I wondered how many bottles Erin had ordered and whether or not France was worried about running out. 'Have you spoken to that dirtbag husband of yours?'

Lou coloured up slightly, far too English to consider such a conversation at the party of someone she barely knew. But unfortunately for her, Jenny wasn't concerned about such things. Or, actually, any things.

'Not yet,' she admitted. 'Honestly, I'd rather not talk about it tonight. Can we just have a lovely night out and talk about it tomorrow?'

'Sure,' Jenny replied in an unprecedented display of tact and understanding. 'Do you guys have plans tomorrow night? Shall we get dinner? Make it a real girls' night?'

'Oh, I'd like that,' Louisa nodded. 'Are you free, Angela?'

I nodded. 'I have to be at work again but I can be out at a decent time,' I replied. 'And you know Jesse in my office? His band is playing. He said he'd put us on the list if we wanted to go and see them play?'

'Jesse?' Jenny's eyes sparkled. 'I don't remember a Jesse. Is he hot?'

'I suppose so,' I said, trying not to blush. 'But I have to work with him so can you try not to accidentally fall on his penis right away?'

'Honey, it's never an accident,' she said, finishing her drink with a loud smacking sound. Classy gal. 'And I make no promises.'

'I need a wee,' Louisa whispered as Jenny waved the waiter back before he'd even got halfway around the room. 'That girl's not going to make me do drugs in there, is she?'

'No,' I promised. 'As I understand it, she's not that generous with her coke anyway. You can pee. Just remember, just say no.'

'I'm gonna find some food. You want anything?' Jenny asked, reaching out to sweep away an unseen smudge on my cheek. 'You look beautiful, by the way.'

'I'm OK, thanks,' I said with a smile. 'I'll be here.'

'Things all good?' she asked, leaning her head to one side. I knew her Dr Jenny, amateur psychologist pose very well. 'You seem a little off.'

'Just work stress,' I shrugged. I didn't keep things from Jenny. She always knew exactly how to help me work through my problems but how could she help me with this? Here she was, desperate for a baby but

141

without a dependable man in her life, and here I was, married with a happy husband ready to knock me up as soon as I said shoot and the only thing standing in the way of us getting pregnant tomorrow was me.

'I knew it,' Jenny said with a grimace. 'It's Cici, right? She's already being a total fucking troll? That's it, I'm having her killed. Happy Christmas, that's your gift – I'm putting a hit out on that bitch.'

'I've thought about it but there's too much of a chance they'd get Delia by accident,' I laughed. 'Really, don't worry about me. I'll be fine, just need another couple of drinks.'

'Then I will make sure you have them,' she promised. 'Can't have my Angie pouting at Christmas, it's too weird.'

I watched her go, feeling weirdly better and worse at the same time, before turning on my increasingly painful heel and stumbling off into the next room. Another tastefully decorated tree, slightly smaller than the last, sat in the corner of the room and groups of people, some I recognised, most I didn't, stood talking and laughing and clinking glasses. I had just found a quiet corner complete with comfy sofa when I spotted Alex stroll into the room, searching, presumably, for me. I waved silently, trying to get his attention without attracting anyone else's, and then ducked down, sprawling out on the sofa. As much as it was possible to sprawl in skintight sequins and two pairs of Spanx.

'Hey there, you,' he said, a tired expression on his handsome face. 'Hiding already? We've only been here for ten minutes.'

'Says you,' I said, clinking my glass against his. 'You're bored of the boys already?'

'I'm not banging groupies, we're not going skiing and I have not improved my golf handicap since Erin and Thomas's wedding,' he replied, 'and so we ran out of shit to talk about pretty quickly.'

'You don't play golf,' I said, frowning. 'And you don't bang groupies.'

'Both things that disappointed the fellas.' Alex sipped his champagne and closed his eyes. 'What brought you in here? You OK?'

I took a quick, deep breath and readied myself. This was it. This was the time to tell him about Dr Laura's call, to ask him to come to the doctor's office with me and hold his hand and have him make everything better.

'Everything's fine,' I said, ignoring the angel on my shoulder who was repeatedly slapping me around the face. 'Did you have a fun day? I'm sorry you got stuck on Louisa-sitting duty.'

'I don't mind.' He rested his hand on my bare thigh. 'It's like hanging out with you, if only you still thought you had to make an effort to be nice to me. And Grace is awesome.'

'Yay,' I replied weakly.

'I asked Louisa what was going on with Tim.' Alex reached up to loosen his tie a little, simultaneously and unconsciously tightening my ovaries.

'And what did she say?'

Clever Alex. Of course he could get away with just asking the question the rest of us were pussyfooting around, he had a penis. Penises had no tact.

'She said everything is fine and that she talked to him earlier but she was kinda vague and dismissive.' He sounded doubtful. 'I asked if she needed any help getting shit organised to fly back to the UK but she just went quiet and changed the subject.'

'Lou is a big believer in not addressing anything that she doesn't have to,' I acknowledged. 'Very big into stiff upper lips.'

Alex nodded and idly ran his hand up and down my leg. 'I don't think she's talked to Tim, though. Kinda smelled like bullshit.'

'I wouldn't be surprised,' I said. 'Whatever's going on, I don't believe he'd be all super cool about her and Grace nicking off to America without telling him. I'm sure I would have had a passive-aggressive phone call by now.'

'Maybe you could talk to him and find out?' Alex asked. 'Like, maybe email him or something?'

'I could but she'd kill me.' I shook my head. 'At best, I'd be interfering which is enough to get me a slap and if she really hasn't called him, she might just go for broke and kill me.'

'Sometimes friends interfering isn't so bad,' he said, meeting my eyes with a smile. We'd definitely had more than one helping hand along the way, whether we liked it or not, but Louisa was not me. I was a bit useless and not terribly good at saying what needed to be said. Lou was so proud and, generally speaking, a far more capable human being than me. While I occasionally needed some sense slapping into me, Louisa was far more likely to slap you right back.

'I'll talk to her tomorrow.' I peeped inside my handbag at the blank screen of my new-old iPhone. 'Even if she hasn't called him, realistically, how long can this go on? It's Christmas in a week, I think he's going to notice if she's not there.'

'Depends whether or not Louisa is right about him cheating,' Alex theorised. 'If you took off with my kid in the middle of the night, I wouldn't sleep until I knew where you were. Tim doesn't seem to be trying that hard to get them back, even if he thinks they're with her mom. Don't you think that's weird?'

'Yes,' I admitted. 'But Tim wouldn't call Louisa's mother unless his life depended on it. She's a right old cow.'

'I guess I got lucky with your folks,' Alex said.

I waited a moment for the punch line.

'What?' he asked.

'Never mind,' I replied. Bloody men.

'And I'm not complaining about having Gracie around,' he smiled, nudging my foot with his, unaware of the agony I was currently suffering. 'It's good to get some practice in, right?'

'I told you I'm not getting you a baby for Christmas,' I said, ignoring the sharp pain in my gut and the tears burning behind my eyes. 'It's in a week and they take ages to order.'

'Maybe we should get home soon and practise then.' The hand on my thigh slid upwards, underneath the hem of my skirt. 'Make sure we're doing it right.'

My stomach flipped as I pushed his hand away gently and stood up, ready to make a hasty, tear-free dash for the bathroom. I needed extra time in my heels.

'Hands to yourself, Reid,' I said, as lightly as possible. 'I'm off to the bathroom. If you really want to go, I don't mind. You didn't have to come, I know you hate it.'

'I don't hate it.' He rolled his eyes. 'It's just not what I would do with my Wednesday if I had a choice. Because if I had a choice . . .'

'I'll see you in a bit.' I leaned against the door frame,

half to look cute and half so that I didn't fall over. 'I love you.'

'I love you too,' he said. 'Now go pee. This is a really nice house and I don't want to have to explain any accidents to the stockbroker boys. They're already disappointed in me as it is.'

On my way out of the bathroom and into the kitchen, I caught sight of Louisa. She was stood with her back against the wall, almost pinned into position by one of Thomas's douchier co-workers. I remembered him from Erin's wedding and as far as I could tell, his only redeeming feature was that he was friends with Erin. The man was so utterly charmless and bland that I now couldn't remember his name. Jenny hadn't even bothered to learn it on the day and had christened him Douchenozzle for the want of something more memorable. I started over to rescue Lou but as I tottered on, I realised she was smiling. And not only smiling but laughing. Every time the Douchenozzle opened his mouth, she threw back her head and gave a crazy throaty laugh that I'd never heard from her before. In fact, the only person I had heard it from was Jenny Lopez, the Man Whisperer. I stopped beside a small coffee table and scooped up a handful of nuts, ignored the fact that they weren't dry roasted as they should be, and watched, curious.

Whatever they were talking about was apparently the most fascinating and hilarious thing Louisa had ever heard. Her eyes were sparkling and her cheeks glowed pink against her pale skin, set off by my sparkly Marc by Marc Jacobs jumper and her skinny black trousers. I watched as she crossed and uncrossed her ankles, obviously a lot more comfortable in the Jimmy Choos she had borrowed from Jenny than I was in my own shoes. I leaned against the arm of a duck-egg blue Eames chair and smiled a little. It was nice to see her looking happy. What harm could a little flirtation do? Maybe it would do her good to chat to another man for five minutes, help her remember what she was missing at home. Which was a perfectly good theory until I watched her reach up to brush some invisible lint off Douchey McDouche's shoulder with her left hand. A hand that was noticeably less sparkly than it had been fifteen minutes earlier. She had taken off her wedding ring.

'Louisa,' I barked, pushing up off the chair and marching over, ignoring the burning in the bottom of my feet. 'There you are.' I forcibly inserted myself between my best friend and Douchnozzle with a dark look on my face. 'Sorry,' I said, without sounding the least bit apologetic. 'I need a minute with my bestie here. You don't mind?'

He paused and looked over my shoulder at Louisa, clearly upset at being shunted out of what he had thought was a sure thing.

'It's my period,' I shouted. 'I need to talk to her about my period. Which I'm having.'

He backed away, slowly at first and then very, very quickly, not uttering a single word. Louisa on the other hand had several words ready and none of them were very nice.

'What the bloody hell was that?' she screeched as I took the glass of champagne out of her hand and knocked it back in two big gulps. 'I was bloody talking to him. And you haven't got your period. What the bloody hell, Angela?'

147

'Louisa,' I said, giving her back the empty glass, 'where is your wedding ring?'

My best friend glanced down at her bare hand and reddened, her cheeks flushing from pale pink to a beet-red stain.

'You think everything is so easy.' She stared at me for a moment, as though she was about to say something else, but instead she pushed straight past me and marched across the room to the French doors.

It was below freezing and beginning to snow on the streets of Manhattan but behind the high garden walls of the wealthy, unseen outside heaters meant it was spring-like all year round, even as the snowflakes fluttered to the ground. Louisa barged past a group of smokers, not bothering to apologise. I followed, delayed by my footwear, and found her literally fuming. Louisa was smoking. An actual cigarette.

'Lou!' I hadn't seen her smoke since Freshers' Week, back when it was both big and clever. 'You don't smoke!'

'I don't do a lot of things, Angela,' she pointed out. 'And I'm sick of it.'

'So you're going to start smoking?' I asked. 'Couldn't you start with something ever so slightly less carcinogenic?'

Louisa stared back at me, a challenge in her eyes that I knew well. When you'd been bickering with someone for the best part of thirty years, you got to know their 'you're not the boss of me' expression. But I wasn't backing down. Instead, I countered with my hands stuck to my hips, lips pursed and eyebrows raised. Rather than say anything, Lou raised the cigarette to her lips and took a drag. She then erupted into an epic coughing fit and threw the cigarette onto the floor while she doubled over. I stamped out the amber tip and placed a hand on her back, rubbing gently and shaking my head. The other smokers looked over for a moment before deciding they were far more interesting than us and turning back to their conversation.

'Nicely done,' I commented once Lou had her breath back. 'Very sexy. You should definitely take up smoking as your new hobby.'

'Oh, piss off,' she replied, catching her breath. 'That tastes like shit. Why do people do it?'

'Why don't I go and get us a drink and you can sit there and think about the answer to that question?' I suggested. 'You silly cow.'

A couple of minutes later, I was back with two glasses and a bottle of champagne. I really couldn't cope going up and down in these shoes and there was no way I was taking them off outside – patio heaters or no patio heaters, it was still bloody December.

'Before you start,' Louisa said, holding out her glass as I filled it up to the brim. 'I wasn't doing anything, I was just talking to him. And I took my rings off because I didn't want to spend the night explaining to people why my husband isn't here.'

'Couldn't you just lie?' I asked, topping off my own glass.

'Ooh, that sounds like fun,' she replied with a stern look.

'Fair enough. I'll give you that this isn't an ideal situation.'

She sipped her champagne, shaking her head.

'But you are going to have to deal with it sooner or later.'

Louisa sighed, looked up at the sky, an inky black smudged with hazy greys and yellows from the nearby skyscrapers of downtown.

'Can it be later?' she asked. 'Or at least tomorrow?'

I looked at my friend and saw the sadness in her eyes. She looked frustrated and tired.

'I just don't know what to do,' she whispered.

'I don't think any of us do,' I replied. 'Ever.'

'In that case,' she raised her glass and took a deep breath, pasting a smile on her face, 'there's only one thing to do. Cheers.'

'Cheers,' I replied with a smile. 'And merry Christmas.'

'Merry Christmas,' she said with a grin. 'Let's show these people how we do a party.'

It was difficult to say exactly how or when the party stopped being a civilised get-together and became a sixth form piss-up of epic proportions but I do know things escalated very quickly. One minute the main reception room was full of grown-ups talking about their holiday plans, their 401ks and assorted other topics I couldn't even start to follow. The next, Jenny had stormed the liquor cabinet and was playing shot girl, encouraging the head of mergers and acquisitions at Merryll Lynch to do a body show from the coffee table and Louisa had found the stereo, replacing the delightful Bing Crosby CD with *Now That's What I Call Christmas*. Most importantly, after two shots of tequila, my feet didn't hurt anymore and that was in itself a Christmas miracle. Douchenozzle took a shot and started the dancing, tossing his tie across the room and even Sadie stood on the side of the makeshift dance floor and swung her hips moodily, entirely out of time with the music. I figured it wasn't her fault. She hadn't grown up listening to Noddy Holder screaming 'It's Christmas!', she didn't understand.

'Ange, babe, I'm so happy.' Louisa bopped over to me, her blonde hair tied up in a quick ponytail on top of her head. She flung her arms round my neck and began to spin me around in a circle. 'This is awesome. Totally what I needed.'

'Me too,' I shouted over the music. Alex was in the corner, his tie hanging loosely around his neck, playing DJ with my iPod. 'I'm having the best time.'

'This is what Christmas should be,' she called back. 'Just friends and fun and not stressing out about stuff.'

'Who's stressing?' Jenny jumped into the middle of our dance hug, sending us all into shrieks and squeals. 'Hey ladies!'

'Angela's stressed about everything,' Louisa slurred, still shimmying from side to side. 'And I'm stressed about Tim. Except I'm not because I'm dancing.'

'So, you don't be stressed about Tim and you don't be stressed about everything,' Jenny declared, a bottle of Patron in her hand. 'S'totally cool. This is what we'll do Christmas Day. It'll be awesome.'

'But my mum,' I whined, feeling and sounding just like a teenager. 'I totally can't cope with her coming out.'

'Gimme your phone.' Jenny took a swig from the bottle and then placed it behind her on a table that didn't exist. Ignoring the thud as the empty bottle hit the carpet, she made beckoning motions with her hands, demanding my phone. Pawing through my evening bag, I pulled out the phone and handed it over. 'Ew, Angie,' she wrinkled her adorable nose at my ancient technology. 'OK, so you just call and you say . . .'

She scatter-tapped the screen of my phone before holding it to her ear, twirling a curl around her index finger.

'Hey, Mom and Dad, this is Angela. I'm really, really freaking out about everything ever right now because, like, I have shit going on, you know? I have a job and I'm moving house and I have to get Jenny an awesome Christmas gift for being so awesome, so you can't come over for the holidays. So don't come. OK, I love you. Bye!' she tossed the phone back in my handbag and snapped it shut with a flourish. 'And that's how we deal with parents.'

'Oh my God.' Louisa was doubled over again but this time with laughter. 'I so want to be there when you make that call to your parents.'

'So this is where the party's at?'

'James!' Throwing my bag onto the sofa behind me, I ran across the room and leapt into James Jacobs' arms. 'You came!'

'You texted me and told me to,' he replied. 'You know I always do as I'm told.'

'Did you get the job?' I asked as he swung me around in a tight circle. 'Did you?'

'I got the job!' he sang at the top of his lungs. 'Are you excited?'

I had no words and so instead I hugged him so tightly he began to choke. So I let go.

'Where's the hostess?' James coughed. 'I should say hello.'

'Of course. Erin, where are you?' I slithered out of James's arms until I was on the floor, clutching his hand tightly in mine and pulling him across the room. But it seemed that the party had been all too much for the host. Erin was curled up on the sofa, seemingly fast asleep, my beaded evening bag resting against her legs where it had landed. 'It's OK, isn't it Erin? I invited James.'

'The more the merrier,' she whispered. She looked genuinely peaceful and entirely at rest. Motherhood truly was a miracle. 'Hi, James.'

'Hi.' He raised a hand but she was asleep again, or at least pretending to be. It was understandable that he might be confused about what was going on. Before he made it into our private party, James had come through at least two rooms full of bankers, stockbrokers and women who hadn't danced since their first facelift. The rest of the original guest list was nearly as into the revised agenda for Erin's tree trimming as the rest of us. But perplexed as he might be, when we hugged again, I detected a distinct whiff of whiskey and cigarettes on his breath and so it didn't take him long to get into the party spirit.

'We should take Gracie home soon,' Louisa hiccupped as we all pogoed to Cliff Richard. 'I am so drunk, it's disgusting.'

'Alex is sober, he'll look after us,' I replied, pointing over to his DIY DJ booth, or rather where Jenny had fenced him in behind three dining chairs. 'And he's totally obsessed with your baby. Not in a Jimmy Savile way, though.'

'I know, he loves her,' Louisa shouted back. 'He wants you to have a baby.'

'I know,' I panted. I could not stop bouncing or, I was quite sure, my feet would fall off. 'Eurgh.'

'Slow dance,' Jenny screeched, leaning over one of the dining chairs and pawing at the iPod, shoving Alex out of the way. Too sober for his own good, Alex held his hands up and stepped away. 'We need a slow dance.'

'Fine,' he said, clearly miffed. 'But it totally doesn't fit with the rest of the set.'

It was heartwarming to know he was even a super muso nerd when it came to DJing for a bunch of drunk girls in a living room dance party, no matter how fancy that living room might be. But there was no time to feel that sorry for him as the music started up.

'Now, I've . . . had . . .' Jenny took to the middle of the floor and pressed her hands to her heart, making sure we all knew just how much she was feeling the music. '. . . the time of my liiiiiife.'

'Oh.' Erin suddenly opened her eyes and perked up. '*Dirty Dancing*?'

It was only when she was upright that I realised she was wearing a Santa hat. I wondered whether or not I'd put that on her. In true end-of-sixth-form-disco style, the girls and their gay gathered in a group hug, ambling around the room, singing every word straight into each other's faces. It was reassuring to know that some things translated. No matter where I might find myself, no one ever put baby in a corner.

'Do the lift!' Jenny shouted as James began to strut up and down the room, plucking the Santa hat from Erin's head and giving it his best Johnny Castle. 'Do the lift!'

'Yeah!' I was hopeless when it came to mob mentality. 'Do the lift!'

'No, Angie, you do the lift,' Jenny explained with a sigh. 'Jesus, woman.'

'Oh no.' I shook my head, padding my feet up and down, fighting off the burn that had returned now I'd stopped running around like a mad woman. 'I can't do the lift.'

'Do the lift.' Jenny, Erin, Louisa, Sadie, Douchnozzle and some random woman I'd never seen before in my life all stood behind James, chanting and clapping 'Do the lift.'

'Even Baby didn't do the lift,' I yelled as they made room. James bent down and prepared himself. 'I'm not that bloody heavy,' I muttered as he flexed his knees.

I looked around, waiting for Alex to rush in and stop me, to save me somehow. But instead, he was leaning against one of the dining chairs, clapping along with the others. This was definitely something I was saving for any future divorce papers.

'But I don't want to,' I wailed, even as I tottered across the room to make enough space for my run. 'Seriously.'

'Do the goddamn lift!' Jenny screamed.

Before I could second-guess myself, I focused my eyes on James and started to run across the plush carpeting of the West Village townhouse. Seconds later, I felt myself soaring up into the air, high over the handsome head of my six-foot-something buddy, arms aloft.

'I'm flying, Jack!' I shouted, ecstatically happy.

'Wrong movie,' Louisa replied. 'You amazing, daft mare.'

'Ready to come down?' James asked as the room exploded into applause. 'My arms are killing me.'

'Yes, please,' I nodded, slightly out of breath and gazing at the top of the Christmas tree. Eye to eye with the angel, I gave her a wink and silently apologised for judging her tree earlier in the evening. It was a beautiful tree, magnificent even. It didn't matter that it wasn't real, it was still awesome.

'Ladies and gentlemen, a round of applause for Angela Clark.' James placed me carefully on the floor as the song came to an end and held my arm aloft, victorious. 'I can't believe I didn't drop you.'

'I can't believe I didn't fall over,' I said, rubbing his back. 'Amazing.'

I wasn't quite sure how but it seemed that someone had replaced my shoes with stilts while I was up in the air. As soon as James let go of my arm, I felt my ankles give way. Reaching forwards, I stumbled backwards, falling arse first into the Christmas tree. For a second, I thought it was all over, that my epic spill was karmic punishment enough for the lift going so well, but no, the universe wasn't quite done with me yet. The branches of the tree gathered around me, obscuring the frozen faces of my friends as the tree wavered, swaying from side to side for a moment before settling upright again. And then promptly collapsing on top of me. For the first time that evening, I was actually happy that Erin had opted for a piece of plastic crap that might leave a bruise rather than send me to the hospital. There was nothing Christmassy about a coma.

'Um, is anyone out there?' I called, waving one useless leg at the assembled masses. 'Alex? Help?'

'Well, I guess you will need to come over and help decorate it now,' Erin said as my tinsel blinkers were lifted and Jenny and Louisa dragged me out from underneath the tree. 'Are you OK?'

'I'm fine,' I assured her, struggling to my knees and then my feet. Before promptly falling right back onto my arse.

'Oh, for fuck's sake,' James sighed. I spun my entire body round to see him and Alex holding the tree in the air. 'I say we just leave her under it until New Year's.'

Lying back, I closed my eyes and waited for someone to hoist me upright. It wasn't the worst idea I'd ever heard.

CHAPTER NINE

It was safe to say, the following morning was not my finest. It had been months since I'd had a genuine hangover in the office and now I was on my second inside a week. Unfortunately, this was not an area where experience made things easier. This hangover made the last one feel like I'd been for a spa treatment. We had left the party (to be entirely accurate, I had been carried out of the party over James's shoulder, while Jenny propped Louisa up and Alex took care of the actual baby amongst us) and I had spent most of the evening throwing up tequila while Alex held back my hair and fed me Advil and dry toast. When my alarm went off at seven a.m., I seriously considered actually chopping off my own legs rather than getting up to go to work but instead I threw up once more, downed a strong, black coffee and called a cab.

'Hey, boss!'

Standing outside my office door, Starbucks in hand and a smile on her face, still, was Cici.

'I can't,' I croaked, my throat sore from all the attractive puking. 'Not today. I just can't.'

'Oh, are you not feeling well?' she asked, following me into the office like a very well-dressed lapdog. Today's seasonally inappropriate outfit was made up of over-the-knee socks, a pair of leather shorts and a red silk pussy bow blouse. As someone who actually had got dressed in the dark, it was difficult to see her in that ensemble, in December, and not ask serious questions about her sanity. 'Can I get you anything? Advil? Ginger ale? Coke?'

'Actually, a Diet Coke would be really good,' I said, collapsing in a sweaty mess in my chair.

'Oh, sure, a Diet Coke to drink, that's what I meant,' she said, glancing around the ceiling and frowning at the security camera. 'I'll be right back.'

'Don't rush,' I whispered, switching on my computer.

It was Thursday. My original plan for Thursday was to visit the Christmas market in Union Square, buy some more shit that I didn't need and then go to a boozy screening of *Elf* with Alex at the Nitehawk cinema but now I was sitting in my office, staring at a nodding dog toy and willing myself to keep my morning coffee down. I could not face the indignity of throwing up in my rubbish bin. Although, if I did, would Cici have to clean it out? Before my stomach could make a decision, my phone rang, snapping me out of my nauseous reverie and reminding me I was at work. Which was a win when you thought about it.

'Angela, it's Mary,' my boss barked down the line. 'I need to go over some of these cover lines for next week. Are you free now?'

'Free,' I replied, forcing every ounce of strength into my voice. My arm and my ankle throbbed from where the tree had collapsed on top of me, suggesting my painkillers were wearing off and I just wasn't ready for that. 'Cici's just run out to get me a drink and then I'll come in?'

'Nice to see the two of you getting along,' she replied without a trace of emotion in her voice. I had to assume she was taking the piss. 'See you in five if the hangover abates.'

I replaced the handset and looked up at the camera Cici had eyeballed moments ago.

'Paranoid,' I whispered, rubbing my temples. But I still turned my chair around to face the window before popping more ibuprofen and dropping a Berocca into a bottle of VitaminWater.

'And all of that makes sense?' Mary asked for the third time in an hour.

'It does,' I lied, scribbling nonsensical notes in my notebook that I had to believe would suddenly become incredibly enlightening as soon as I got back to my desk. 'All of that makes sense.'

'Right, so that's everything,' she said. 'You know everything I know. Well, obviously you don't but you get my point.'

Hmm.

'Any other things you want to discuss while you've still got me?' Mary wiggled the cordless mouse next to her Mac, clearly hoping that I would in fact not have anything to discuss. Unfortunately for Mary, she was shit out of luck. I had hit a wall and I had to talk to someone.

'Alex wants to have a baby,' I replied.

Mary froze.

'I did mean issues regarding the magazine but that seems like a valid issue.' She spoke calmly and quietly. 'I know this isn't going to be a very forward-thinking, feminist thing to say, Angela, but getting pregnant now wouldn't be the best thing for your career. Maybe you're only interim editor for now but who knows what's next? Have you two talked about it?'

'He really wants to have a baby,' I nodded. 'And I might have trouble if we wait that much longer.'

Saying it out loud felt insane, like I was talking about someone else or something I'd seen on TV.

'I would never tell a woman to choose between her career and her family,' Mary replied, her face softening for just a moment. 'But even in this day and age, in this industry, I've got to tell you, having it all is a myth.'

'But you managed it,' I said. 'Lots of editors have kids.'

'Lots of editors have very unhappy second and third marriages,' she replied. 'And I managed it so well, it's taken me three decades to finally find a way to be with the man I love. I couldn't be happier right now but it breaks my heart to think about all the things Bob and I will never have.'

I nodded to show I was listening but I was totally lost for words. Was Mary really telling me I couldn't have my job and a baby? Not that I wanted a baby. Probably. At the moment. For a while.

'I can't say I would have made different decisions if I'd had a crystal ball when I was younger, but as you get older you do start to realise people are more important than you might like to think. Or at least more important than I wanted to believe.'

'You chose your career over Bob?' I asked. 'Back, whenever it was?'

'It wasn't the Dark Ages, Angela,' she said, straightening a stray strand of hair. 'It's not really that simple but, for the sake of a shorter story, I suppose I did.

Bob was already a very rich and successful man when we met. I wanted to be successful in my own right. He wanted a wife.'

'So what happened?' I was curious to hear the ballad of Mary and Bob. As long as she left out the dirty bits.

'He met his first wife, I met my ex-husband,' she shrugged. 'It's not a long or dramatic story. My marriage didn't work out because I put my job first.'

'Because you were really in love with Bob?'

'Because I loved my job more than I loved my husband,' Mary admitted. 'What was important to me mattered more than what was important to us. I love my kids but the family always played second fiddle to my work. That's not something I'm proud of.'

It was weird to be having such a frank conversation with Mary. We'd spent hours, days, discussing stories, slaving over publishing plans and magazine roughs but we'd never really talked about her life, her family. And now I was starting to wish we hadn't bothered. She was scaring the shit out of me.

'Are you saying you wish you hadn't had your kids?' I gave my thumbnail a quick nibble and hoped Mary hadn't noticed. She hated nail-biters.

'I'm saying it isn't easy,' she replied with diplomacy. 'If your heart is in one place, it's hard to give something else everything it deserves. Everything it needs.'

'But relationships are about compromise, aren't they?' I had definitely read that somewhere. Possibly in *Gloss*. Possibly in one of my articles. 'Surely you can manage work and a family these days? We've got iPhones now, we can do anything.'

'I don't think Apple are really thinking that far ahead,' she replied. 'Actually, they probably are. But I digress . . . I'm lucky I've been given a second chance to get what I really want. Too many people choose pride and ambition over love. Not just men. It's probably a lot more women these days when you think about it. Damn, we should write a feature about this . . .'

'Then you don't think you can have a family and a successful career?' I asked.

My kingdom for a peppermint latte.

'I think you can have whatever you put your heart and soul into.' Mary rested her elbows on her glass desk and leaned towards me. 'You're taking on a job that is going to demand everything you have, at least for a while, until you find your rhythm. A baby needs all that and more. From you *and* Alex. And you'll need each other.'

'Alex and I are fine.' I knew that was at least a fact. 'Really, there's no problem there.'

'Babies don't always mean to cause problems but sometimes they do,' she said with a shrug. 'What if you have a baby and end up losing the job while he goes on to have his enormously creatively fulfilling musical career? You won't resent him at all?'

'I can't imagine resenting Alex for anything,' I said softly. 'But I can see how that might not be much fun.'

'And what if you don't have the baby then he goes on tour and he's so mad at you, he gets drunk one night, the unimaginable happens and he accidentally gets someone else pregnant?'

'Alex would never,' I replied, quick and certain. 'He wouldn't.'

'I'm not saying he would.' Mary leaned back in her chair. 'I'm just saying he could.'

'Sometimes, life is a complete bastard, isn't it?' I said, nibbling on the end of my biro. 'I mean, a complete shitter.'

'You know, if this is bothering you that much, it must be bothering women,' Mary said, wearing her ideas face. 'You could always write a piece about it.'

'Not a bad idea,' I mused, scribbling down her suggestion. 'Might help me make some sense out of it.'

'Might make matters worse,' she said with a warning. 'But it would make a great article.'

'You know, it always looks so easy on the telly,' I sighed. 'You just pop it out, stick it in a papoose and the next thing you know it's in college.'

'The fact that you're referring to your future child as an "it" does not fill me with hope,' Mary said with a doubtful expression. 'They're usually one or the other.'

'Usually,' I repeated. 'But not always?'

She shook her head, more in disgust than confirmation, and turned back to her computer screen.

'Brilliant,' I muttered, standing up to leave. 'Now I've got something else to worry about.'

'Hey, Angela.' Jesse called me over as I was crossing the office, trying to decide between a trip to the bathroom or the canteen. I either needed something deep-fried or I needed to throw up again – it was wide open. 'You still coming tonight?'

'Tonight?' I looked blankly at my work husband. Had I made plans and forgotten?

'The gig?' He waved a flyer high in the air. 'At Music Hall?'

'Oh, God, right,' I nodded, the urgent need to line or empty my stomach abating. 'Yeah, I'm meeting my friends for dinner but we'll definitely try to make it.'

'What's this?'

Like all the best villains, Cici appeared from out of

nowhere, plucking the flyer from Jesse's outstretched hand and pursing her red lips. 'Music Hall? Where's that?'

'Williamsburg,' Jesse said, his face full of fear and the horn. I glanced over at Megan, the beauty editor who sat opposite Jesse, and she rolled her eyes in response. It must be hard being a man, knowing that something was so awful but desperately wanting to put your penis in it anyway. I imagined it was a little like my love-hate relationship with Ben & Jerry's, only with added peen.

'Oh.' Cici looked desperately sympathetic and handed back the flyer as though she might catch something from it. 'I'm sorry.'

'No, it's really OK. You should come,' Jesse said quickly, looking to Megan for support. Megan's eyebrows were so high up her forehead I was amazed we hadn't had a call from air traffic control asking her to bring them back down. He had no help coming there.

Cici laughed, slapping Jesse on the back and then waving her hand at him.

'Oh, you're funny,' she said, holding a finger horizontally underneath each eye to avoid mascara smudges. As if fembots could cry, even if it was from laughing at people. 'I should come. Hilarious.'

Jesse sat in his chair, confused and embarrassed and not sure why, as Cici sashayed away and Megan began to laugh.

'Dude.' She shook her head slowly, never looking away from her computer screen. 'Dude.'

'What just happened?' Jesse asked me, utterly perplexed.

'Nothing good,' I replied, tossing him a gingerbread Christmas tree for his troubles. 'Nothing good at all.'

Deciding against a snack-slash-puke pitstop, I turned

back to my office and swished my mouse to bring my computer back to life. Ignoring the IM full of smiley faces from my seemingly lobotomised assistant, the email from Dr Laura's office asking me to schedule an appointment and the picture message from Jenny that showed a can of sugar-free Red Bull and a slice of pizza, I opened a new Word document and began to write.

My husband wants to have a baby and I don't.

There it was, all written down in black and white.

My husband wants to have a baby and I don't. Not as in, I don't ever want to have a baby, but more I really like my life right now and I'm somewhere in the middle of the scale of mildly scared through to thoroughly petrified at the thought of heaving a living person out of me and then being expected to keep it alive for the next eighteen or so years before I send it off to college, full of hopes and dreams and resentment, and finally get my life back.

I looked at the first paragraph and frowned. Did it sound selfish? Maybe a little. But then maybe I was being a little bit selfish.

I realise that doesn't sound terribly motherly but then that could be why I don't think I'm ready to become a mother. Every time my husband raises the issue, I want to throw a box of cereal on the floor and shout But I'm the baby! – *hardly the best qualification for parenthood. But regardless of whether or not I'm emotionally stable (or mature) enough to have a baby, a recent trip to the doctor's office suggests I might not have a lot of time to make my decision. It might be a baby now or a baby never, and I have no idea what to do.*

As well as a husband, I have wonderful friends, I'm about to move into a beautiful new home and I have a job that I love, a career that I have worked hard for and am thrilled to see develop. But I can't ignore that nagging voice deep inside that says none of it matters until I have a kid. I should clarify – I don't mean I'm hearing a soothing, earth mother coo that's compelling me to fill my womb with offspring. Rather, it's a scratchy cackling that sounds a bit like my mother crossed with anyone who ever played a witch crossed with dial-up internet. It's not a nice voice, it's a voice that tells me women shouldn't feel fulfilled or inspired by their careers. It's the same voice that tells single women they're not good enough until they've got a boyfriend or that they really ought to lose ten more pounds. It's the judgemental chorus that we all hear and we all know we should ignore but can't. It's too loud.

As women, we're constantly trying to keep all our balls in the air – friends, family, careers, relationships. And it's not that guys don't have the same concerns, it's just that maybe they're able to prioritise a little easier. When they decide they're ready to start a family, they choose a mate, they settle down and maybe they hit the bar a little less often (gasp). Perhaps they even move out of Manhattan. But as women, we have to be ready to give up so much more. Imagine telling the Wall Street banker he had to take a year out of his job and hope it was there when he wanted to go back to it. Consider sitting down with the marketing director and saying 'well, you're going to gain about forty pounds which will be a bitch to get off, and you'll be exhausted all the time and maybe you'll throw up for three months but it'll be OK after that. Until you actually have the baby and you're completely incapable of maintaining a simple train of thought for more than fifteen seconds.'

But what happens if you're not ready to give up anything?

What if you bought into the idea that you could have it all?

Pausing to take a sip of Berocca-spiked VitaminWater and read over what I had written so far, I couldn't help but frown. I couldn't even have a week off work, let alone have it all.

Of course, this is a much bigger issue than whether or not I have a baby. When men get what they want, they feel powerful. When women get what they want, they feel selfish. For centuries, female artists have complained of feeling marginalised, pushed out of history and significance because their primary focus in life was supposed to be childrearing and taking care of their family. It was all right for men to sequester themselves, hole up in isolation for months on end working on a masterpiece, but I imagine that could have been a bit difficult if you were breastfeeding your youngest and needed to get tea on the table for half past four. If a woman put her career in front of her family, whatever career that might be, she was seen as a monster. What I want to know is, do we still look at women that way? Is it still taboo to say, I'd love to pop out a couple of babies, darling, but could we possibly wait until the end of the third quarter so I can see what the profit line looks like going into budget season?

I live in New York City, a town dominated by successful, wonderful women, but I can't tell you whether or not they're all happy women. We're judged by men, we're judged by ourselves and, worst of all, we're judged by each other. If I decide I'm not ready to have a baby right now, the thing I'm most scared of is what people will think. Maybe they'll think I don't really love my husband and that I care more about my job than I do about him. Maybe they'll think I'm a horrible, unloving human who is utterly selfish. Or maybe they'll think, well, she really struggled with the decision because it took her a while to find her passion and she wasn't ready to give it up. And the reason I worry that people will think these things is because I think them.

They said we could have it all. They never said it would be easy.

I pressed apple-S to save the draft and emailed it to Mary before I could think better of it. And then I remembered Mary wasn't the editor anymore, I was. Eek. Staring at the screen, I couldn't help but wonder. Was I afraid or was I being selfish? Was I scared of having a baby or was I scared of what it would mean to not have a baby? I sat back in my chair and exhaled, rubbing my forehead with the palm of my hand. I was definitely right about one thing – it definitely wasn't going to be easy.

CHAPTER TEN

By the time I got home that evening, I was weirdly buzzed and excited about the night out. It was strange what a day of deadlines could do for a girl. And so instead of crawling into my pyjamas and my bed, I pulled on my skinniest jeans, added Alex's most washed-out, wrecked band T-shirt and filled my hair with so much dry shampoo I looked like a troll doll. Once I had applied my blunted Bad Gal eyeliner pencil, sharpened it up and applied it again, I considered myself ready to go out in Williamsburg.

'That's some big hair you've got going on.' Alex walked through the front door, dropping a brand new stack of packing boxes on the sofa and his door keys on the coffee table. 'What's up with that?'

'Go big or go dirty,' I explained. 'Are you sure I can't lure you out tonight? It'll be fun? Probably?'

'As much as you're selling it . . .' He stood up, his black T-shirt and blue jeans covered in dust. I was a bad housewife. 'Last night was enough excitement for me.'

'Me too,' I admitted, clambering over the boxes to

get a hug. He smelled sweaty and disgusting and amazing. 'But I promised Jenny and Louisa we'd go for dinner.'

'Can't argue with ladies' night,' he said. 'And besides, I get to play babysitter.'

'You're getting very good at it,' I replied, rubbing on lip balm and checking the time. 'Louisa is just putting Grace down. We won't be late, I swear.'

'No worries,' he said, slipping his hand inside my back pocket and giving my bum a squeeze. Aah, romance. 'I have so much to do. I might have been a little overoptimistic on our packing schedule.'

I looked around at all the full and half-full boxes in the living room. It was weird watching him pack up our little apartment. Even though I hadn't lived there that long, I had managed to amass enough stuff to qualify for an intervention on *Hoarders*. My collection of vintage glasses, bought in bulk on eBay once a year when *Mad Men* came back on, were already wrapped in newspaper and carefully stacked in the kitchen. The assorted prints I'd bought at every craft fair I went to were in a pile next to our books, unframed and unhung, despite what I had said when I bought them and, most terrifyingly, there was my wardrobe. I'd told Alex to leave it to me since 'it wouldn't take long' and swore that I would be able to 'whack everything in a couple of suitcases on Saturday morning'. When I'd said it, I'd believed it but having just spent an hour poking around in there for an outfit, I wasn't quite so sure anymore. He was going to have a fit when he saw the number of ballet flats I owned. I was almost certain they were multiplying in there . . . If only I could stop losing the left shoe, I wouldn't need to keep buying new ones. Packing for a boy was so much easier – Alex had nothing but guitars and records and clever boy books. No make-up to organise, no bras to fold or shoes to box, and that was before I even got to the handbags. How did you move handbags? I couldn't let him chuck them all in a bin bag in the back of Craig's van, that would be sacrilege. Maybe I could take them with me in a taxi, one at a time. It would only take a month or so.

In the corner of the room, the tree stood tall, twinkling on and off like a mad man, daring Alex to try to pack it. I loved that bloody tree. If only because it hadn't tried to launch itself on me. Yet.

'Shall I stay and help?' I asked, clutching the leather strap of my satchel and turning back to my hard-at-work hubby.

The thought of a night in alone with Alex was suddenly very tempting. It might have only been three nights but it felt as though Louisa and Grace had been with us forever.

'No, you go. I'm a pain in the ass when I'm trying to organise stuff,' he said as the buzzer went. 'Lopez?'

'Lopez,' I nodded, pressing the button to let her in the front door. 'Play nice.'

'I always play nice,' he said, tucking his hair behind his ear and getting back to work. Sticking the Sharpie in his jeans pocket, Alex dropped back onto the floor in front of the sofa and began building up a huge pile of flattened boxes I hadn't seen. He was so good. 'I guess we're lucky that we both have flexible jobs so our kids won't need a nanny. I hate the idea of sticking them with some stranger for hours on end.'

'So what else needs doing, move-wise?' I asked, changing the subject completely. 'There's really nothing I can do?'

'There's really nothing you can do,' he confirmed. 'The furniture guys are coming Saturday morning, Graham and Craig are helping me move some boxes and the more delicate stuff tomorrow and the new furniture is being delivered Monday. By the time your folks get here Tuesday, it'll be like a goddamn show home, I swear. And I'll even have time for a haircut.'

'And by the time they leave on Saturday, it'll be like the seventh circle of Hell,' I replied, momentarily having forgotten they were coming at all. 'I just hope the tree survives the move.'

'If I have to go into Prospect Park and chop a tree down, I promise you will have your perfect Christmas tree,' he said, eyes trained on forcing the flaps of the half-built box in his hands. 'That or we'll cover Craig in tiny little lights and have him sing "O Tannenbaum" until New Year's.'

Floppy hair or no floppy hair, Alex Reid really was the best.

'Ange.' Louisa tilted her head to one side, a tumble of blonde waves dropping into my eyeline as she spoke. 'Angela? You with us?'

'Hey.' Jenny gave me a poke. 'Earth to Angela?'

Even though they were right – my mind was somewhere else entirely – I gave them a grin and raised my Diet Coke in a toast. I was excited to be with my girls but I was also ready for my bed. We'd eaten a mound of seasonal tacos at La Superior, all the while trying to sing along to Mexican versions of classic Christmas songs, and then skidded through the fresh snow, all the way back up to north 6th Street ready to see Jesse storm the stage.

'Don't make me pinch you,' Jenny threatened. 'You

know I need the same amount of attention as a five-year-old child at all times. What's up, doll? All that hairspray freeze up your brain?'

Somehow she had coiled her massive amount of hair into a normal-sized topknot and pared her make-up back to a slash of bright red lipstick, to match her bright red skinny jeans. Even though it was minus five outside, she was wearing a cropped black T-shirt that revealed just a hint of toned torso and slipped off one shoulder. She was a fashion magazine's interpretation of 'hipster' and she looked fantastic.

'Nothing is up,' I lied perfectly. I was surprised how smooth I was – it had been a while. 'I'm just tired. Busy day at work. I'm excited to be out now, though, honest.'

'I'm knackered,' Lou admitted. She had turned her silky blonde hair into a head full of sexy waves, perfectly set off by precise cat's eye make-up and pretty pink lips. I felt bad dragging her into a dirty, sticky club. She looked as though she should be sipping tea and eating very tiny, expensive cakes somewhere not here. Well, until you looked down at her outfit. I couldn't imagine anyone other than Grace had seen that much of her boobs in a very long time. 'We could always just go back and hang out at yours? Or call it a night? I'm not fussed.'

I knew I liked that girl.

'No way.' Jenny stamped a tiny snowbooted foot. 'I dragged my ass out to Brooklyn, we're staying out. Plus, it's ten thirty already, your friend is on at eleven, we can't go until we've seen him, right?'

'You're right,' I agreed, shouting as the DJ started a super-loud song I didn't recognise. 'I do want to see them. I've heard they're good.'

I chose not to mention that I had heard that from Jesse.

'Is this the place we came to see Alex's band that time?' Jenny asked, glancing around at all the glasses-wearing gig-goers. 'You know, when you first moved here?'

'Um, yes.' I pretended to have to think for a moment but obviously I had every moment of our entire relationship stored safely away. 'It is.'

'It's almost reassuring to know that these places are the same all over the world,' Lou said, shifting from foot to sticky foot. 'The floors are covered in God knows what and everyone's high as kites. Everyone even looks the same. I'm positive I saw her over there on the 98 bus last week.'

I wanted to be positive that she hadn't but who knew? Hipsters got around these days. Just because they looked like they'd found their outfit on the floor of a chazza shop and then slopped it around the toilets of a second-rate shopping centre didn't mean that they weren't actually the artistic director of some international ad agency. Or Cara Delevingne. I could never tell.

'So what's up, Angie?' Jenny was never one to let sleeping dogs lie. Or napping dogs. Or dogs that were just trying to change the subject until they were allowed to go home and pass out. 'You might as well tell me before I force it out of you.'

I didn't fancy force.

'Really, it is just that I've had a shitty day.' It was a straight-out lie – once the hangover had faded, I'd actually had quite a nice day. 'I had to write this article and, you know, I was really looking forward to having some time off this week, spending it with Alex. Feels

175

like I got all excited about Christmas and now the whole thing is going to pass me by.'

'We'll make up for it tomorrow,' Louisa said, looking a little sheepish. 'I'm sorry we're in the way.'

'You're not in the way at all,' I promised. 'Not even a little bit.'

Another lie. As much as I loved waking up to see Louisa every day, hearing her laugh whenever Alex pronounced 'oregano' or 'aluminium' and telling me how pretty I looked, having Grace in the apartment was exhausting and I was constantly on edge as to whether or not Lou had spoken to Tim. So far, she'd admitted to texting him to say she'd be away for another day or so because she was ill. So she'd admitted to lying. Which was a great development.

'Well, something's up with you and it's not just being a bit grumpy about missing out on Christmas shopping,' Lou frowned. 'Out with it, Ange.'

'Fine.' I did some quick thinking and let out a huge sigh. 'I'm really not loving having Cici in the office. But I promised Delia I would try it and I feel like I've got to give it a go.'

In searching for a lie, I'd actually managed to find the truth. I did not love having Cici around and not because she was being a bitch but because she was being so nice. Being on my guard all the time was even more tiring than trying not to drop an F bomb in front of my goddaughter.

'You know I don't condone violence,' Louisa said, reaching out to stroke my hair and pulling her hand away quickly. However good it looked, it did not feel nice. 'But yeah, I think in this instance, you're going to want to get ready for some fisticuffs.'

'I'll kick her freaking ass.' Jenny waved away our

concerns with the flick of a wrist. 'Dude, seriously. She's crossed you for the last time. Crossed all of us. Do you think she wants me to beat the shit out of her again? No, she does not.'

'I can't imagine it's top of her agenda,' I admitted. 'But she's got to be up to something, hasn't she? She can't genuinely want to come and work with me. For me, even. Delia must be suffering from some sort of sibling blindness.'

'I wouldn't trust her as far as I could throw her,' Lou agreed. 'But she probably doesn't weigh very much and I am quite strong from lugging Grace around these days so even that might be too far.'

'And that's it?' Jenny still didn't look convinced. 'You're just worried about when that psycho is going to reveal her true demonic form?'

'What else would it be?' I enquired with innocence and a raised eyebrow. I really was good at lying. I ought to try to get more use out of it.

'Nothing. I just talked to Dr Laura this afternoon, is all.' She flicked her eyes over at Lou, as if to check it was OK to ask in front of her. Unfortunately I didn't have a code to tell her that it was not. 'I thought maybe she called you with, I don't know, news?'

'Why have you been to the doctor's?' Louisa flew into a panic immediately. Which was why I hadn't said anything in the first place. 'What's wrong with you?'

'Nothing is wrong with us,' Jenny replied, placing a calming hand on Louisa's shoulder and bringing her back down to earth. 'I went in to get checked out because I'm going to have a baby—'

'You're having a baby?' Louisa's voice was very, very, very high pitched. I was fairly certain there were some dolphins off the coast of Scotland complaining that she was a being a bit squeaky. Without another word, she snatched the beer bottle out of Jenny's hand and slapped me on the arm.

'What did I do?' I yelped, rubbing my injury.

'You let her drink pregnant,' she screeched. 'I can't believe either of you would be so reckless—'

'Lou, chill,' Jenny interrupted and took her beer back, taking a sip before explaining. Because she was Jenny. 'I'm not pregnant. I meant I'm going to be trying for a baby soon and I dragged Angie along with me. She took the same tests. I was just kinda thinking maybe you got news.'

'Does that make more sense?' I asked Louisa with a sweet smile.

She shook her head. 'Not really. What do you mean you're trying for a baby?'

I settled back on my barstool. Here we go, I thought. Louisa wouldn't put up with Jenny's nonsense. She'd be back onto a Pomeranian in fifteen minutes or less.

'I know it might not make total sense to everyone,' Jenny explained, giving me the evil eye. 'But I just can't think about anything else.'

'Oh, I understand completely,' Lou agreed quickly, wiping the invisible smile right off my face. 'When it hits, you're buggered. Have you spoken to Craig about it?'

'Actually, yeah,' Jenny replied, clearly relieved. 'And I think he gets it. We agreed that we should take a break while we work stuff out but, you know, even if I decide to do this with a guy who isn't going to be actively involved, I don't think he's my baby daddy.'

'Well, I'm glad you're taking it seriously,' Louisa rested a hand on Jenny's arm in sisterly support. I felt like a complete shit, albeit a complete shit who was living in a parallel universe. Of all people, I would have expected Louisa to be on my side of the Jenny–baby fence. Lou was the first one to call me when a girl we went to school with, who now worked down the post office, got pregnant without a man on the scene. She was a whole two days ahead of my mum on that one, which was a record. Unmarried mothers were hardly front-page news in New York but Louisa was a big believer in the family unit. Or she had been. I hadn't considered the fact that we were dealing with a new Louisa now. This wasn't the happily ever after Lou I'd always known and loved. This was the freshly scorned 'even if he swears his undying love, he'll only cheat on you with some slag who texts him the golf scores while you're at his cousin's christening' Louisa.

'So you didn't hear from her?' Jenny asked, turning the attention back to me. 'No news?'

'Why would I get weird news?' I laughed, hoping it would cover the bumps in my voice. I wasn't doing this here, I just wasn't. 'I think she called earlier and left a message. I haven't had time to check my messages, what with all the meetings and the babysitting and slutting up to hang out with you two.'

'That does take some time,' Jenny said with a half-serious smile. 'Well, OK then. You call her back tomorrow, though, right?'

'Of course,' I breezed. Again, that one wasn't entirely a lie – I would call her tomorrow. At some point. 'But you spoke to her? You're all good?'

'I'm all good to go,' she nodded, before taking a chug of beer. So maternal. 'I have, like, wonder womb. Millions of eggs, superb thick lining. It's like a fetal memory foam mattress in there. She says I shouldn't have any problems as soon as I want to try.'

'And I'm asking as an absolutely delighted and supportive friend,' I said, holding my beer bottle away from my face in case of sudden attacks. 'But you're still sure you're going to try soon?'

'Let's not talk about it tonight?' Jenny compromised and I nodded in acceptance. That was becoming our group catchphrase. Regardless, I was pleased Jenny was healthy. Maybe knowing she was ready to get pregnant at any time would take the pressure off her to do it right away, but at the same time, it made my heart ache a little bit more. Here was Lou, already a mother to a wonderful little girl, and Jenny, who was apparently going to be able to pop out a baby at the drop of a hat. Or more like the drop of her knickers. And then there was me.

'I might be ready for a hair of the dog,' I said, finishing my Diet Coke and smiling at the girls. 'Who wants what?'

'I'm all right actually,' Louisa said, her English rose complexion blushing a delicate shade of green. New York was starting to catch up with her. 'I hope your friend is on soon, I'm going to be asleep before I know it.'

'Get me the same?' Jenny raised her beer bottle and pulled Louisa in for a supportive half-hug but instead of cheering her, it just seemed to make her retch a little bit. Fantastic, I was almost certainly going to be holding her hair back to puke in a bin on the way home and she hadn't even had a drink. Sneaky, delayed jet lag hangovers.

The bar was dark and crowded but I managed to shuffle my elbows in between a girl with a half-shaved head and a man wearing a reindeer jumper and a kilt. Oh, Williamsburg. Actually there was a lot of seasonally themed knitwear. Part of me was delighted to see the season of goodwill being embraced so readily and part of me wanted to punch out every hipster that thought it was funny to take the piss out of the most wonderful time of the year. Damn them and their irony. Leaning into the bar, I wiggled my elbows outwards until I was safely squeezed in and waited to make eye contact with the bartender. And waited. And waited. It was difficult to be patient at a bar when you were still sober. At least the pounding music meant I didn't actually have to bother thinking my own thoughts. It was a huge relief.

'Well, hello there.'

A gentle poke in the shoulder was followed by a weird half-hug from behind. And no one wanted anything weird from behind. Ever. I craned my neck to try to identify my snuggly assailant only to a) discover it was Jesse and b) turn Jesse's appropriate air kiss into an entirely inappropriate lip-on-lip mega smooch.

'Well, that's a nicer hello than I expected,' he said with a laugh, smoothly brushing off my burning shame. 'You made it.'

'I made it,' I confirmed, rubbing his accidental kiss from my lips, dying a little inside. 'I'm not having a lot of luck with the bar, though. I think they can tell I have a full-time job and don't play keyboards for anyone. They won't sell me a PBR.'

'Here, let me.' He placed his hands on my waist and pulled me away from the bar, switching our places. If I hadn't already snogged the man, I'd have felt a bit awkward. Instead I just watched as he waved a couple of reddish-coloured tickets at the bartender and pointed to a backlit fridge. Seconds later, he turned around with two cans of PBR and a pair of full-to-spilling shot glasses, one resting on the top of each can. 'Whiskey, OK?'

'More than,' I said, taking the can and the shot graciously. 'Only I was supposed to get one for my friend, Jenny.' That and the fact that I hated whiskey, but turning down a free drink would be rude. And stupid.

'So, how about we shoot the whiskey and then I give you both the beers? I shouldn't drink before a show anyway,' he suggested. 'We got a deal?'

I didn't drink whiskey. Whiskey made me very sick. But here in the land of the cool kids, without Alex acting as my hipster beard, I felt something like peer pressure for the first time in a very long time.

'Deal,' I replied, picking up the whiskey, touching plastic cup to plastic cup and knocking it back in a oner. That was the easy part. Keeping it down was another matter entirely. Jesus Christ, it was disgusting. Maybe this was the whiskey that had necessitated the invention of a pickleback. The only thing that could possibly wash away the foul taste in my mouth was a shot glass full of brine.

'Oh man.' Jesse tossed his shot glass into a nearby bin and laughed, rubbing his mouth with the back of his hand, smearing the inky black stamp that marked him out as over twenty-one. 'That was pretty gross. Sorry.'

'Oh, don't be.' I squeezed my eyes together one last time and waited to see if the shot was going to stay down. It seemed like I was going to be lucky. 'It wasn't that bad. I love whiskey. I've had worse.'

Three lies in one sentence. What was wrong with me? Jesse had changed since we left the office and while there wasn't an epic difference in his outfit, his smart trousers had turned into jeans and he'd switched the striped shirt for a worn-out plaid alternative. Basically, he'd turned the preppy dial down just enough to play up his hipster hotness. His dark-rimmed glasses looked more edgy than office and his hair seemed ever so slightly more mussed up than usual. I imagined he paid a lot of money to make such a simple haircut so very versatile. Alex had maintained that he cut his own hair for months after we met, until I finally got him to admit he went to some ridiculously fancy Soho stylist but had, on occasion, been known to trim his own fringe when on tour. One day I would get him to admit that he'd had a manicure for our wedding but that felt more like a deathbed confession.

'Did Alex make it?' Jesse asked, leaning into my ear so he didn't have to shout quite so loud. 'I'd love to say hi.'

It was weird hearing him say Alex's name. I guess we never really chatted about boyfriends and girl-friends at work. Or husbands and wives. I didn't even know what his girlfriend was called. Or whether or not he had one. Or several. Several was most likely.

'He couldn't make it,' I said, pulling a regretful face. I hated that I felt the need to exaggerate every gesture when I was in a loud bar, it was such a sign of my age. 'We're moving on Saturday.'

'Yeah, you've mentioned it,' he laughed. 'Park Slope, I hear.'

'About a thousand times?'

'A thousand and one?'

Jesse's tight smile brought out a pair of dimples

under his stubble that I'd never noticed before. He really was very good-looking. I wondered for a moment if he might be gay. Wondered-slash-wished. This would feel less weird if he was a big old gay. And then I could set him up with James! But sadly, my gaydar picked up more activity when Alex wore his red skinnies and sang Taylor Swift songs in the shower. Jesse was definitely hetro.

'I think I'm just trying to convince myself it's really happening,' I confessed, the disgusting aftertaste of the whiskey fading away into a pleasant burn that made the ugly jumper party around us faintly more tolerable. 'I can't believe we're moving to Park Slope. I can't believe we're leaving Williamsburg. I can't believe it's going to take me an extra fifteen minutes to get to work in the mornings.'

'I hear the F train is way more reliable than the L train,' Jesse offered. 'But yeah, that's got to be weird. It's, like, where grown-ups live.'

'I know,' I said, wide-eyed with agreement. 'And I'm not one! They're going to kick me out as soon as they realise we haven't got a blender or a bread machine.'

'I'll get you a stroller as a housewarming present,' he said. 'Then you can park it outside and they'll leave you alone.'

I opened my mouth, fully intending to laugh, but instead some sort of dying seal impression escaped. Jesse's eyebrows shot up underneath his shaggy hair.

'Stroller!' I shouted in a voice so high it made Louisa's scandalised reaction to Jenny's baby news sound like she was being voiced by Brian Blessed. 'Ha! Stroller!'

'OK, so, anyway, I gotta get backstage.' Jesse handed

me the second can of PBR and began to back away. So, we had found our limit. 'Uh, I'll see you after? Or at work tomorrow?'

With a resigned nod and overenthusiastic smile, I held up the two beers and thanked him again before scuttling back through the ironic Santa hats and Ramones Christmas covers to find Jenny propping Louisa up against a rusty-looking iron railing, eyes all glittery, hands held out for her drink.

'Who was that guy?' Jenny asked, peering over my head into the crowd, trying to get a look at my runaway editor. 'He was super cute. Did he buy you drinks? Did you tell him you were married? Did you tell him I'm not married?'

'That's Jesse,' I explained, slightly more concerned with Louisa's clammy-looking face than Jenny's instacrush. 'He is super cute, he is the one playing tonight so he had drinks tickets, and he knows I'm married, but I didn't get a chance to alert him to your relationship status, I'm sorry.'

'Ange, I'm really sorry but I think I'm going to have to go home quite soon,' Lou bleated, slipping backwards down the railings until she was crouched in a tiny ball, elbows resting on her knees, sweaty hair resting on her face. 'I think I might be a bit sick.'

'What did she eat at dinner that we didn't?' I asked Jenny, crouching down beside my bestie, rubbing her back and pretending I couldn't hear her gipping. 'Oh man, she's not good.'

'I ate everything.' Jenny held out her hand to take my still unopened beer. Lou was clearly going to be a two-handed situation. 'I always eat everything.'

'True. She's probably still hungover from last night.

185

She's not used to drinking like you.' I didn't mean to sound like her mother but sometimes . . .

Cue the dead-eyed stare.

'She's not used to drinking like us,' I corrected myself and then shook my head. 'No, really, you. She's not used to drinking like you. Even I can't keep up with you anymore.'

'It's delayed jet lag,' Louisa mumbled, coming directly to her new friend's defence. 'I'm just tired, that's all.'

I nodded, agreeing to make her feel better, but being tired didn't usually make me throw up on my shoes, my friend's shoes and the shoes of one or two strangers who were stood nearby but didn't seem to notice. Thankfully.

'Oh, bloody hell.' I delved into my Marc Jacobs satchel, desperately trying to keep it out of the puke, and handed Lou a tissue to wipe her mouth. The bag was battered but it had yet to be christened with vom and when that time came, I at least hoped it would be my own. 'OK, let's get you out of here. It's not far, it'll be OK.'

'I feel better now,' she protested, wobbling all the way up to her feet. 'And you want to watch your friend's band. I'm better, honest.'

'I know.' I kept my arm wrapped tightly around her waist and shook my head silently at Jenny as soon as she opened her mouth. She closed it quickly into a tight cat's arse of a pout. 'But I'm really tired and we've got the day off tomorrow. I thought we might get up early and take Grace to Central Park so I reckon it's bedtime. Is that OK?'

'Oh yeah, that sounds nice,' she agreed, blinking a couple of times before managing to stand almost entirely on her own. 'I am actually quite tired.'

Hurrah. The sneaky 'I know you're OK but I'm not OK' reverse psychology. It always worked. As long as you didn't try it on Jenny.

'Well, if you guys are pussying out, I'm going to stay here and watch the band,' Jenny said, stroking Louisa's hair back from her face. 'Get some rest, OK?'

I'd expected Jenny to be more annoyed – she hated cutting a night short and she had little tolerance for a lightweight. It was amazing that we'd been friends as long as we had.

'Text me when you get home?' I asked, knowing full well that she wouldn't. 'And get a cab, don't take the train.'

'Of course I'm gonna take a cab.' She gave me a hug and brushed Lou's hair back from her face, looking for a puke-free spot to plant a kiss. Eventually she decided on the forehead before handing her back over to me. 'I'll call you tomorrow.'

'Do you want to come to the park?' I asked, feeling Louisa begin to waver at the side of me. I really had to get her home. 'Or we could meet you for lunch?'

'I have to be in the office tomorrow,' she pulled a face. God forbid. 'And I have a lunch thing already. But I wanna help with the move and I said I'd hang with Lou Lou and Gracie while you're at your work party tomorrow night.'

Oh yeah, the office Christmas party. Sorry, holiday party. Hopefully Jesse wouldn't have had time to tell every single person we worked with that I had snogged him and then had a complete psychotic breakdown when he mentioned a stroller before we had time to mix the punch.

'OK.' I inclined my giant hair towards Louisa, the helmet-like quality providing a last defence in case she decided to puke on me again. 'I'll talk to you tomorrow. Love you.'

'Love you,' Jenny replied with a jammy kiss to the cheek.

'Ew, did someone throw up in here?' A girl with Zooey Deschanel hair and Deirdre Barlow glasses baulked to the left of us.

'And that's our cue to leave,' I muttered, dragging Lou through the crowds and out into the frigid, puke-free night.

CHAPTER ELEVEN

'Angela, I think I'm dying.'

'You're not dying.'

'I am, I think I'm dying.'

I glared at my best friend. She didn't look well but she was definitely still in the land of the living. Just.

For the briefest of moments, just before I'd slid underneath the crappy guest duvet the night before, I'd imagined that I might get a lie-in on Friday morning. Louisa had passed out the second I got her into bed and poured two Advil and a pint of water down her throat (she hadn't even woken when I scrubbed her face clean with three face wipes. I was a sort of good friend), I finally had a whole day off and we were going to Christmas the shit out of the city. But no.

For the last twenty minutes, we'd been perched on a bench in Central Park watching Grace chase some very hardy squirrels while the sky tried to snow and Louisa tried not to throw up. I couldn't believe there was anything left inside her. I had given up trying to sleep and had moved into the bathroom to be on hair-holding duties at about six a.m. when she'd decided to bring up everything she'd eaten or drunk since she'd arrived. Despite my best efforts to persuade him otherwise, Alex had excused himself from spending the day with me to get on with the packing. While I was sad, I knew I couldn't really kick his ass – we did have to move after all. I just wished that I could have had my one perfect New York Christmas day.

Instead, I'd ridden in a cab on the way into Manhattan, while Louisa held her head out of the window like a bandana-wearing dog, clutching a sick bag made out of three Duane Reade bags 'just in case'. It was all very traumatic, mostly for me. Grace seemed to find 'silly mummy' hilarious. Silly mummy was struggling to raise a chuckle.

'Do you want some water?' I asked, delving deep into my bag, rummaging through the assorted bits and pieces I'd collected on our way up to the park. 'Or orange juice? Or Pepsi? Or a biscuit?'

Traditionally, poorly Louisa required options. And I often required biscuits.

'Can I take more headache tablets yet?' she asked, loosening the scarf around her neck as I tightened mine. I recognised the post-pukey sweats and while I sympathised, I didn't want to have to explain to Gracie that mummy popped her clogs a week before Christmas because Auntie Jenny had the constitution of an ox and the liver of post-mortem Oliver Reed whereas mummy, it seemed, did not.

'No, it's only been two hours,' I replied, shaking the bag to locate the Advil. God help me if we'd lost the Advil. 'Have some water.'

Reluctantly, she did as she was told, happy to have an excuse to remove her leather gloves (technically my leather gloves), and sipped teeny tiny drops of water. While Louisa gathered herself, I looked around the park. New York really excelled itself when it came to Christmas. Everywhere you looked people were smiling, holding hands and wandering off on another winter adventure. Horse-drawn carriages rolled along the winding paths, the horses' bells ringing as they trotted by, and the icing sugar sprinkling of snow covered the sparse winter grass with storybook perfection. I kept waiting for one of the snowmen in Sheep Meadow to spring to life and dance for us, possibly before revealing himself to be a maniacal serial killer.

'She's so excited about the ice skating.' Lou pointed at her toddler who apparently had not noticed that she was still very much on solid ground and was already twirling and leaping like a loon, a one-legged pigeon playing the reluctant Dean to her enthusiastic Torvill. 'I just need a minute. I don't think I'm safe to be on skates yet.'

'I don't think you're safe to be more than five feet away from the toilet yet but, you know,' I said, 'needs must when the devil shits in your teapot.'

'I feel like he's shit in my something,' she replied, still a very fetching shade of green. My mother would have called it puce because she liked to sound fancy and superior whenever someone had a hangover who wasn't her. I kept my opinions to myself. Just.

'So . . .' I shuffled deeper inside my big, padded coat and nosed my scarf up over my mouth. No time like the present for an uncomfortable conversation. 'While you're feeling so well, I'll just ask. Have you spoken to Tim yet?'

'No.'

It wasn't really a reply that left itself open for debate but since she'd been in New York for almost five days and had apparently made zero plans to go home, it seemed to me as though she might need a bit of a push.

'Not at all?'

'He text me yesterday,' she replied, the weakness in her voice transforming into steely resentment. 'To see how Grace was.'

'I know I'm not going to make myself popular,' I said, turning towards her, pulling my scarf down to reveal my face. Fuck me, it was cold. 'But you've got to talk to him. You can't actually just be in a different country to your husband and hope he won't notice. And maybe I've watched too many episodes of *Law & Order* but I'm pretty sure it's illegal to take his baby out of the country without telling him.'

'Ange, he hasn't even noticed,' she said, looking up at the heavy sky. 'He genuinely believes I'm at my mother's. I've been in America since Monday. It's days until Christmas and he thinks I'm still at my mother's. I bloody hate my mother. But he wants to believe me because then he doesn't have to feel guilty, does he?'

'I don't know,' I admitted. 'I don't know what's going on. And until you talk to him, neither do you. Really, Lou, I'd have you stay forever if it was up to me . . .'

Her face lit up with a spark of colour.

'But it isn't.'

Poof. The spark was gone.

'I want you to be happy and I want what's best for you and Grace but that isn't hiding here and pretending nothing's wrong.'

'You know, it's really hard hearing that from you, don't you?' she said, slowly screwing the cap back on her water bottle. 'Miss Successful Runaway of the Century?'

'I wasn't married and I didn't have a baby,' I said gently. Just like she was wavering on the line between reluctant acknowledgement and snarky chastisement, I was treading the fine line between supportive and patronising. 'And you know I love Grace but I would make a horrible co-parent.'

'Alex would be good, though,' she mused with a sniff. 'And you'd learn how to manage. And Jenny would help.'

'Jenny would be drunk,' I said with a smile and a gentle nudge. 'I think she's enjoyed having a new playmate a little bit too much.'

'I've enjoyed it too,' Lou admitted. 'I know it's a terrible thing to say but sometimes I wonder if I didn't rush into having kids. Not that I'd change it for anything.'

I didn't know what to say. So I didn't say anything.

'I know Alex is desperate for a baby but honestly, Ange, if you're not one hundred per cent desperate, don't do it. It's so hard and it's such a test. I wanted Grace so much, I used to wake up in the night, dreaming about being pregnant. It was all I could think about. But I knew Tim wasn't totally into it at the time. I just assumed he'd come round once she got here.'

I opened my mouth to tell her about Dr Laura's phone call. I knew this was the time to have her hold my hand while I returned one of the three messages she had left me so far that morning. And I also knew I wasn't going to do it.

'But he didn't?' I asked instead.

'He did,' she said, with reservation in her voice. 'But it was overwhelming. Everything happened too quickly and it was so . . . so much more than I had anticipated.'

I looked over to Grace. She was now armed with a stick. Squirrels of Central Park beware. She was definitely a handful.

'She took up all of my time and I let her. Everything else sort of slips if you let it.'

It wasn't hard to imagine. Me the size of a house, covered in baby vom, the size of a house, wearing something delightful from the Kim Kardashian plus-plus-plus-size pregnancy line while Alex swanned around our beautiful brownstone looking like his regular god-like self. I couldn't imagine it would take too long before his eyes started to wander, even if his hands and his penis took longer to follow. At which point I would obviously have no choice but to chop them off and keep them in a jar on top of the telly to teach my future daughter that all men are evil.

Hmm. There was a chance I'd got a little bit ahead of myself.

'Ange?'

'Sorry, I was just thinking how right you are,' I said, reaching my mitten for her leather glove. 'I'm sorry I didn't realise. I should have. You're my best friend, I should have known you weren't happy.'

'I wouldn't have admitted it even if you'd asked me straight out,' she said, looking a little more human and a little less sad. 'But you're right.'

'About?'

It was something I heard so rarely, I needed it explaining.

'Sorting this out. Calling Tim. Sorting myself out.'

'What's the worst that can happen?' I asked.

'It turns out I'm right, that he is cheating on me, that the only man I've ever loved, the father of my child, the only relationship I've ever had is over because he's replaced me with some slag from the office who likes *darts*.' She really spat the word out. 'And I'm alone with a mad baby who resents me for driving away her daddy and I never, ever find love again.'

'That doesn't sound brilliant,' I said. 'Best case scenario?'

'That he's a thoughtless tosspot who needs a kick up the arse?' Louisa suggested. 'Changing the subject entirely, what about Jenny?'

'What about Jenny?' I asked, readjusting my bobble hat. 'He's not knocking her off as well, is he?'

'Ha ha. I think she's serious about this baby thing, you know,' Lou said, some strength returning to her voice. It was always easier for her to talk about anyone other than herself. 'I know you think it's a phase but I'm not sure. I've been through it.'

'I don't know what to think,' I replied. 'She was serious about moving to LA to be a stylist. She was serious about going back to school to study as a psychologist. She's serious about working in PR for now. She was serious about marrying Jeff, about dating Sigge . . . It's not like I don't think she'd be a good mum, I just don't think this is the right time.'

'She's lonely,' Louisa said. 'It's hard. I understand.'

I leaned forward on the bench, wrapping my mittens around my hot chocolate and breathing in deeply. It was something I hadn't really thought about and now that I did, I felt horrible. Of all the shitty, stressful things I went through – was going through – I was never lonely. I had Alex. I had my work. I had Jenny

195

and Louisa and they had me, they knew that. Or at least I thought they did.

'I'm not having a go at you,' Louisa said.

It made my life so much easier when she read my mind.

'Anyone can be lonely, no matter how good their friends are. You must have felt that way before.'

'With Mark,' I said, nodding. 'But I feel bad that I didn't realise it was that bad for you. Or for Jenny.'

'Seems to me Jenny's been playing her cards pretty close to her chest on this one,' Lou said, placing a hand in the middle of my back. 'And you know me, I like to fix my own problems.'

'A baby isn't going to fix Jenny's problems.' I closed my eyes and stamped my feet on the concrete to get the blood moving again. 'But she doesn't want to hear it.'

While I attempted to process all of the crappiness, Grace inexplicably threw herself to the floor with a shriek. I jumped a mile, my heart pounding, but Louisa didn't even flinch. A split second later, Grace leapt to her feet and began to spin in circles, laughing her mad little head off.

'Don't worry,' Lou said, patting my hand and forcing herself to her feet. 'She does that sometimes. My little girl is mental. Ice skating will tire her out. I hope.'

'I see.' I pulled my scarf back up over my frozen nose and followed her across the grass. 'Tell me, would you say you drank a lot while you were breastfeeding or just a regular amount?'

In my mind, a work's Christmas do meant three bottles of red, three bottles of white and a couple of boxes of own-brand mince pies. If you were lucky. But my work's Christmas do wasn't a hastily arranged shindig with people karaoke-ing to 'Last Christmas' around the photocopier. This was Spencer Media's Annual Holiday Bash and I should have known better. With a skip in my step and reindeer antlers in my bag, I left Alex, Grace and Louisa packing, hiding in boxes and passing out on the settee respectively, thinking I'd pop into the party, get my air guitar on to 'Merry Christmas, Everybody' and be back home in time to pretend to understand all the jokes on *The Daily Show*. And then I arrived at the party.

Before I'd even got past the velvet rope, I managed to slyly lose my antlers in a bin in case the massive bouncers searched my bag and refused to let me in due to the fact I looked like I was planning to have fun. I was suddenly very aware that this was not going to be a Fun Party. This was going to be a Cool Party.

Mew.

Spencer Media held almost all of its big shindigs at a restaurant in the Meatpacking District I never, ever went to. I'd heard amazing things about their parties – that they were filled with celebs, that they had the coolest DJs and the most delicious drinks. Obviously I never heard much about food but it was a New York media party – people didn't eat in front of each other. And while I'd heard lots of exciting things *about* the Spencer parties, I'd never actually *been* to one. I'd either been too busy working or watching *Top Model* on Jenny's living room floor or chasing Alex around the apartment with a cold teabag. We had been married for more than a year, we had to make our own fun.

'Angela!'

The party was a mass of barely moving, barely

smiling skinny girls in tight dresses and shorter-than-average men in expensive suits. Happily, one of those tight-dress-wearing skinny girls was my tight-dress-wearing girl. Delia pushed past a long, narrow table covered in half-empty vodka sodas and pulled me into a very welcome hug. She smelled how she looked – elegant and rich. Her hair was pulled up in a messy bun, her make-up barely there but flawless and her short black dress fitted and sexy without being revealing. I was so happy I'd decided not to wear my Mrs Santa outfit and if I had the chance to go home and change, I'd probably go with a slinky black number instead of an Urban Outfitters sweatshirt covered in seasonal penguins and red sequin shorts. Perhaps if I had been in the office earlier, I would have got the 'absolutely no sense of humour allowed' memo.

'I'm so glad you're here.' Delia made no reference to my quirky ensemble but then she was used to me by now. 'This party's killing me. It's even more boring than Grandpa's board meetings.'

'Oh, I can imagine,' I replied. It was a lie. I couldn't. 'Where are all the *Gloss* people?'

'I haven't really seen anyone,' she said, grabbing two colourful-looking cocktails from a tray. I really hoped at least one of them was for me. 'I thought I saw Jesse earlier but no one else. Regular staffers never really come to these things, you know.'

I took a decent slurp through the straw without a blind clue what I was drinking. Thankfully it was good, so I was currently one for three on things I'd heard about the Spencer Media parties because the music was terrible and I hadn't recognised a single celebrity yet. I had seen a lot of size-zero girls who gave me the evil eye every time I came in shovelling a croissant down my gullet and tried not to make eye contact with me when I used the treadmill in the company gym once a month but no actual celebs.

'It is a Friday night.' Delia waved her hand around the room full of strangers. 'And we did actively hire people who wouldn't be impressed by a party like this.'

'But they didn't know it was going to be a party like this,' I protested. 'I told everyone it was going to be a super-fun proper Christmas party with plastic reindeer antlers and crackers and ugly men putting mistletoe through their belt buckles and they still haven't come.'

'I can't think why?' She creased her forehead. 'What the hell is a cracker?'

Honestly, I had to wonder what was wrong with people sometimes.

'What kind of office party doesn't even have a photo-copier for someone to scan their arse on?' I asked. 'I can't even see a Christmas tree.'

'Because it's not a Christmas party,' she reminded me. Again. 'It's a holiday party.'

'I could go off you,' I said. If she wasn't careful, I wasn't even going to give her the spare bit of tinsel I had in my handbag for her hair.

'So, how's your big week been?' Delia asked, clearly dancing around the elephant in the room. The iden-tical, psychotic elephant that should not be named. 'Any new drama?'

I shrugged. 'Louisa seems to have moved in indefinitely and may or may not be breaking several international kidnapping laws, Jenny is convinced she's going to have a baby with or without an active father and I have to

199

move house tomorrow even though I haven't actually started packing at all.'

'Oh.'

'I'm closing the magazine all on my own for the first time on Monday because your grandfather is taking my Mary upstate early, my parents fly in on Tuesday, I still haven't bought a turkey and I haven't been able to find a bottle of Advocaat anywhere in this city.'

'I see.'

'Oh, and your mental sister is still mental. But on the upside, sitting at my desk in absolute terror does make the rest of it feel like a piece of piss.'

'Angela . . .' Delia smiled but sighed at the same time. On anyone else it would have looked patronising, but on Delia it looked, well, patronising but she got away with it. She was after all a patron of several charities. Including me. 'If you're that against it, then we'll can it, I'll find her something else. I don't want you to feel uncomfortable in your own office.'

'Ignore me,' I said, my martyr complex growing stronger with every sip of my cocktail. 'I feel uncomfortable every time I eat saturated fat in front of the fashion editor. I told you I'd give her a chance so I'll give her a chance.'

'And I told you if she messes up, I'll fix it,' she promised.

'Just make sure there's a body for my mother to bury,' I replied. 'That's all I ask.'

'So you're not going to freak out when I tell you she just walked in?' Delia winced and nodded to the door behind me. I didn't want to turn around. I wanted to close my eyes and wake up in a double glazing sales office in Croydon with a paper crown on my head, singing 'Mary's Boy Child' with Tony from marketing. *Anywhere but here*, I whispered in my head, *anywhere but here*.

'Deedee! Angela!'

Steeling myself, I pasted a smile on my face and for the first time since I'd walked into the party was glad I hadn't worn anything nice or expensive or dry clean only.

'Look at you!' She glowed from head to toe. It made me sick.

'Look at me,' I said, my voice completely and utterly dead. Her diamonds made my sequin shorts look like a reject from the *Saturday Night Fever* costume department, although the red on her skin-tight satin mini-dress did bring out the red in my bloodshot eyes.

'You look awesome,' she said with complete sincerity. 'One thing I always loved about you, Angela, is you're an individual. You have your own look. I wish I was secure enough to make your brave style choices.'

'Do you need a drink?' Delia interrupted and pointed across the room before the ground could completely swallow me up. 'Because the bar is over there.'

'Oh, that would be fantastic, thank you,' Cici nodded at her sister. 'Anything really. Champagne would be great. Or a vodka soda. Anything but those awful mixed drinks they're trying to force on people, they're all sugar. It's disgusting.'

I prayed for Delia to punch her sister right in the face while finishing up my sugary, mixed drink in silence. Delia stood between the two of us in silence for a moment, looking at me, then at Cici, before necking the rest of her own drink and stalking off to the bar.

'So, boss,' Cici said, nudging me in the ribs and winking. 'Don't you think this week went so well? I think we're going to make quite the team.'

'You do?' I asked. My mind was playing a highlights reel of some of mine and Cici's greatest hits. If you put the Benny Hill theme over it, the whole thing was quite funny. If you didn't, it looked like a horror movie.

'Of course, I mean, we've been through so much, I feel as though I really get you,' she replied. 'And I have so many great ideas for the magazine. Spending this week getting to know the team really gave me so much insight. I believe this is going to be a fantastic collaboration for both of us.'

'A collaboration,' I repeated. This was entirely my own fault. If I hadn't been hungover when I was interviewing assistants, I could have just hired Rag, Tag, Cottontail, or whatever that lovely gay boy was called, and had nothing more to worry about than whether or not he was judging me for wanting three sugars in my coffee. 'You have ideas?'

'Oh, so many,' she confirmed, her eyes flashing with what I hoped was enthusiasm. It was that or she was off her meds. 'I've been a huge fan of *Gloss* since you started. I genuinely respect how you speak to every woman because, you know, I'm a woman.'

'Glad to have that cleared up,' I said, looking for Delia. I needed her. And more importantly, I needed a drink and I didn't care what that said about me. 'I did wonder.'

'You're so funny.' Cici gave me another blast of her practised, real-life LOL again and pressed her perfectly painted paws to her chest. Her nails were spike sharp and blood red, her fingers covered in platinum and gemstones. She might be a woman but she wasn't really everywoman. 'I'm genuinely happy that I'm going to have a voice in the media. At last.'

'Well, you know there isn't that much editorial work in your role?' I didn't want to upset her if I could help it but if it had to be done, I'd rather do it in a room full of witnesses. 'I think it's going to be very admin-oriented. As in totally. Forever.'

'Is that right?' her voice cooled by about fifty degrees and the enthusiasm in her eyes paled down to a general sense of amusement.

'Pretty much,' I said. 'So if that's not something you're really interested in, I would totally understand if you wanted to wait for a more active editorial role. At another magazine. Somewhere else. Far away.'

'Oh no.' Cici reached out one of her claws to brush my hair back from my shoulder and grasp me in her Vulcan death grip. It hurt. Dr Spock must have taught special classes at her Upper East Side prep school. 'I'm staying at *Gloss*. It's the right place for me.'

'It is?' I wondered if her nails were painted red so they wouldn't show the blood.

'It is,' she confirmed. 'And I don't think it's going to be so long before I have an active editorial role.'

I didn't say anything. There wasn't anything to say. Instead I smiled brightly and thanked my lucky stars that she wasn't planning to douse me in pig's blood at the party.

'So I'll see you Monday,' she said, releasing my shoulder with an expensive smile and a wink. 'I have plans. I'm excited.'

'Fan-fucking-tastic.' I smiled back as she melted into the party, people seemingly instinctively stepping aside for a Spencer. That or their internal psycho alarm was going off and they didn't quite know why. Luckily for me, I was fully aware.

'Where did she go?' Delia reappeared, two tall glasses in her hands, one clear, the others brightly coloured and full of elaborate umbrellas and neon-coloured straws. 'I had to stand at the bar and *wait* for her goddamn vodka soda.'

'She's just gone,' I said, taking one of the cocktails and the vodka soda. I'd earned them. 'Don't worry about it.'

'Well, I'm glad you two are playing nice.' She gave me a weak smile and the nice-twin version of Cici's nudge. 'Who knows, you might end up being friends, God forbid.'

I downed the clear drink with a shudder, ignoring Delia's wide eyes and setting the ice-filled glass on the tray of a passing waiter.

'I think God would forbid it actually,' I said, resting my elbows behind me and leaning on the table. 'But it is Christmas and we are due a miracle.'

'Don't count it out,' Delia said, leaning beside me. 'Stranger things have happened.'

After a smash and grab at the only tray of canapés that had come our way and fifteen minutes of intense debate over which of the Spencer Media girls looked sad because they hadn't eaten in the last month and which were just sad in general, I was forced to leave Delia to a gaggle of not-nearly-good-enough-for-her suits and hunt down the toilets. Obviously, because I was wearing the highest heels I owned, a pair of ankle-shattering Guiseppe Zanottis (purchased because they were on super sale and because Jenny said they made me look skinny – double standards, thy name is Angela), the toilets were up a set of extremely steep stairs. And because everyone was drinking, no one was eating and lots of people needed somewhere to do their drugs, there was a queue a mile long. I crossed my legs for as long as I could before resolving to find another loo – this was a big restaurant, it was part of a hotel, there had to be more than one ladies' room. Two seconds away from committing to book a room for the night just to have a wee, I finally found the wheelchair- and high-heel-accessible lav on the ground floor. And it was unlocked. Praise be to baby Jesus in the manger.

'Hey.'

I never would learn my lesson about knocking on individual toilet cubicles.

Thankfully, on this occasion, I had not walked in on a secret gay tryst, just my managing editor washing his hands. I silently thanked sweet baby Jesus in the manger that I hadn't been two minutes earlier. It was one thing to accidentally kiss him mid-hug, it was another to accidentally wander in while he was having a slash.

'Is this my secret Santa?' Jesse asked, half laughing and half trying to get out of the toilet. Since I was all desperate to pee, I backed up against the wall and let him past. 'Because you set a ten-dollar limit on gifts and I gotta tell you, you're selling yourself short.'

'Oh, I don't know,' I replied, trying very hard not to wee on my shoes. My bladder had seen the toilet. My bladder was not going to wait much longer. 'Ten dollars gets you a slap on the arse and if you're not out of here very quickly, quite the show.'

'I might be into the ass thing but I figure you can keep the show.' He closed the door as he left, leaving me just enough time to bolt it shut. Seriously, what was wrong with American men? Why couldn't they lock a toilet door behind them?

Unless he was waiting for someone. Unless Jesse had a secret party hook-up arranged that I had just completely ruined. Which I would feel bad about just as soon as I'd had the world's longest wee.

'Killer party, huh?'

Jesse was stood outside the loo, ducked underneath the metal staircase, when I eventually emerged in considerably less pain and miserable in the knowledge that now the seal had been broken, I would have to go again at least twice in the next hour. Stupid girl parts.

'You are taking the piss, aren't you?' I asked, accepting one of the two drinks he held out. Aha! Two drinks! So he was waiting for someone . . . I glanced around, looking for a likely suspect. I hoped to God it wasn't Cici because I couldn't accurately report that level of potential crash and burn to Megan in the office without having some sort of aneurysm. 'This is a disaster.'

'I know, right?' he agreed, resplendent in a dark green shirt and black jumper that looked very soft. His hair was halfway between its messy Brooklyn best and the tidy sweep he kept up for work. 'Just such a bunch of phoneys. I know they all work in our building but altogether? Just the amount of cologne in the air is affecting my allergies.'

'Oh yeah,' I hastily agreed when, really, I didn't give a toss about the 'phoneys'. If they were dancing round with their ties around their foreheads, singing along to 'All I Want for Christmas', I would have forgiven them anything. He was right, though, someone had gone a bit heavy on the old Lynx. It made me nostalgic for Year Ten. 'Yeah, loads of phoneys.'

'I bet they flipped their shit when you came in wearing that.' He pointed towards my sweater, sitting back on the radiator. 'No one here has a sense of humour.'

I knew he didn't mean to be offensive and I couldn't work out the best way to explain that there wasn't anything even slightly ironic about my outfit. What was more Christmassy than red sequins and a sweatshirt covered in ice skating penguins? But I didn't see a lot of point in alienating one of the two allies I had in the entire room so I just nodded, sat down next to him, drank my drink and waited for a better song.

'You know what?' Jesse, it seemed, was not prepared to wait for a good tune. I had a feeling our DJ didn't have anything with him that Jesse would consider a good tune. 'There's only one way to get through a party like this?'

'We leave?' I asked.

'No.' He took my glass from me and placed it on the floor beside his own before holding out his hand. 'We dance.'

'Do we have to?' It was fair to say I was a little bit hesitant. 'Because I did some dancing the other night and it did not end well for me.'

With a sigh and a shake of the head, Jesse bent down to pick up our glasses and waited for me to chug my cocktail before repeating his less-dramatic-the-second-time-around gesture.

'No one else is dancing,' I said under my breath as he led me right into the middle of the bar and in front of the DJ booth. 'You do know that?'

'No one else is going home to Brooklyn either,' he

said. 'No one else came on the subway, no one else is gonna get dropped off at the twenty-four-hour bagel place on Bedford. These are not our people, Angela, this is not our party. All we can do is claim a small piece of it. Dance with me.'

It was a bold and pretty accurate declaration and there and then, in the land of the free and the home of the brave, what else was a girl supposed to do? And he was right – I was absolutely going to Bagelsmith on the way home, even if I'd actually taken a taxi to the party, but there was no need for him to know that.

Whether it was happy coincidence or the DJ felt our commitment to making this party happen, but the music shifted from unfamiliar chart 'hits' that I barely recognised to classic eighties goodness. Nothing you'd want to listen to walking down the street but a catalogue of office party classics, and when someone was playing 'Billie Jean', it didn't matter whether you were in a super-fancy Meatpacking District holiday party or at your cousin Sharon's wedding reception, you just danced. The weak, brightly coloured cocktails might have gone straight through me but they'd had the decency to leave a bit of a buzz on their way out. As soon as I started moving my feet, I felt that wonderful sense of coordination that only comes with one too many beverages. Jesse was a genuinely good dancer, I was not, but I didn't care anymore. Everyone already had me pegged as a twat so I figured I might as well enjoy myself. After five minutes on the floor, I was convinced I could have won *Strictly*. Jesse spun and dipped me, completely ignoring whatever was playing as well as every other single person at the party and, for the first time since I'd walked through the door, I was happy. I was having fun. And it felt like Christmas.

Rick Astley was halfway through promising he was never going to let me down, run around or desert me when Jesse grabbed both of my hands and dragged me off the dance floor. Something magical had happened while I'd been concentrating on my moves and the entire bar had started dancing. The miserable girls were smiling, the short men were waving fists in the air and barely a single tie remained knotted. Jesse put his arm around my shoulders and nodded silently, smiling at the crowd.

'Our work here is done,' he said, waving his hand at the mass of uncoordinated bodies jumping up and down to Stock, Aitken and Waterman's finest. 'Man, I'm so proud.'

'As you should be,' I said, patting his back. 'This is going in your appraisal.'

'It's going on my résumé,' he replied before looking at his watch. 'You're taking the L too, right? Wanna jet?'

'These shoes are killing me.' Hardly a new sensation. 'Do you want to split a cab? I mean, it is Christmas.'

'I guess.' He gave me the same disappointed look Alex always wore whenever I demanded a taxi instead of the train and I made a mental note to pitch a feature based on men having to wear heels for a week and then seeing how many blocks they fancied walking to get on a bloody subway at one in the morning in December.

The night was freezing, but after our sweaty dancefest it felt refreshing. I hugged my arms tightly around myself, wishing I hadn't been such a stubborn Brit and had brought a coat with me, even if it meant standing in a queue at the coat check, while Jesse ran out into the middle of the road to flag down a taxi. Why had everyone decided the neighbourhoods with the worst paving would have the coolest bars? I considered it one of New York's great mysteries. The Meatpacking District was all cobblestones aka stiletto kryptonite and Soho and Tribeca were just as bad. How did Beyoncé manage? I could only assume Jay-Z picked her up and carried her to their car, as opposed to standing holding the door open, rolling his eyes as she picked her way carefully across the street, one stone at a time.

'It's not my fault, it's the street,' I said, crawling across the back seat and immediately turning off the in-taxi television.

'Nothing to do with your choice of shoes at all?' Jesse asked, slamming the door behind himself and giving the driver his directions. 'Dude.'

'I will not be told what shoes I can and cannot wear just because New York can't be bothered to pave its streets safely,' I maintained, immediately kicking the instruments of tootsie torture off my feet. Really, though, they were so pretty. 'I should sue. Someone's going to break their neck.'

'I hope it's someone from that party,' he replied without hesitating.

'Oh, ouch,' I laughed, pretending to be scandalised when I was actually delighted. I had not spent an evening in a room full of my favourite people by any stretch of the imagination. 'You're not a massive fan of the Spencer Media crowd, then?'

'It's not that I don't love my job, I do,' said the man who was insulting his company to his sort of boss in the back of a taxi on the way home from a corporately funded free bar. 'I've always been a word nerd. Once an English major, always an English major. But I just can't stand those kinds of people.'

Closing my eyes and cuddling up into the corner of the cab, I slipped my hands up inside my sweatshirt sleeves. 'And what kind of people are those?'

'Eh, I'm allergic to Manhattan, is all,' he yawned. 'I don't meet my people there very often.'

The lights of the city rushed past, dark then bright, dark then bright. Even half asleep, without looking I knew we were cutting through Soho, headed for the Williamsburg Bridge. New York got under your skin, the sounds and the stoplights acting as an internal GPS.

'Your people?'

'People with a sense of humour.' Jesse's voice seemed so far away. I was so tired. 'People with passion. Creativity. Honesty. A genuine drive to do something good that they enjoy and not just something cool.'

I had to laugh.

'Yeah, you do know you live in Williamsburg and play bass in a band, don't you?'

'What's that got to do with it?' He seemed genuinely confused.

'You're a total hipster. Seriously, you're like the king of them. Do you actually need those glasses at all or did you just buy them from Urban Outfitters like everyone else?' I opened one eye and nicked his specs, pushing them up my nose, just like Mary. He was clearly as blind as a bat. 'Oh. OK, fair enough.'

'I'm not a hipster,' he replied, from somewhere in the taxi, I assumed. I really couldn't see anything. 'I'm an artist.'

'Spoken like a true hipster.'

No reply. Typical bloke – he could dish it out but he couldn't take it.

I rolled my head against the sticky black leather seats and squinted at him through the very strong prescription lenses. 'You still there? I can't see a bloody thing.'

'I'm still here,' he replied, removing his glasses carefully, his face awfully close to mine. 'I'm always here.'

'In the cab?'

Jesse didn't make any attempt to back up and all of a sudden I did not feel brilliant about being in the back of a taxi with my friend.

'Hey, look,' he said, pulling a bit of wiry-looking twig out of his pocket and holding it up. 'Mistletoe.'

There wasn't time for a snarky comment, vocal protestation or even a timely slap. Before I could react in any way, shape or form, Jesse's lips were on mine, the mistletoe still in his lap. My first thought was to get his face off my face. My second that he wasn't even doing this right. Amateur.

'Jesse.' I regained control of my faculties and gave him a good old-fashioned shove as we turned onto Delancey and caught sight of the Williamsburg Bridge ahead, lit up like a string of fairy lights stretched over the river. A beautiful backdrop for some unexpected sexual harassment and impending violence. 'What the fuck are you doing?'

'I've got mistletoe?' He held up the offending bit of weed and wore the face of a saint. 'It's Christmas.'

I snatched the mistletoe out of his hand and lobbed it out of the cab window, the taxi whizzing away as it spiralled into the river. It wasn't even really mistletoe, it was just a bit of branch with a white flower on it. I was appalled. At the act and the fraud. How dare he take Christmas's name in vain?

'It's never OK to kiss your married friend on the lips, mistletoe or otherwise.' I was well aware I was raising my voice but this was surely a lesson that would benefit everyone, including the cab driver. 'You know I'm married. You can't possibly be that drunk?'

'But we hang out all the time,' he spluttered. 'And you always reply to my texts and you laugh at my jokes in meetings and we like the same stuff and you get me. No one else gets me.'

'I'm not getting you right now.' I slapped his approaching hand right back to the other side of the taxi. 'And I reply to your texts and I laugh at your jokes because you're funny and I'm polite and . . . Jesus Christ, is that really all it takes?'

'You get me,' he said again. 'I think it's because you're British. I've always felt really connected to British people.'

'Oh my God,' I groaned, palm to face. 'You did not just say that.'

'And your husband didn't come to the show and you kissed me at the bar, remember?' He wasn't going to give up, even though the cabbie had already turned the radio up to full blast. Even he wasn't interested anymore. 'You kissed me first.'

'I did not kiss you at the bar,' I shouted. There was a worry some people in New Jersey hadn't heard my indignation. 'I turned and you turned and . . . oh God, don't be stupid. Of course I didn't kiss you at the bar. I cannot believe you just did that.'

I shook my head at the insanity and held my hands out in front of me to ward off any further madness.

For five more minutes, we drove on without saying anything, turning onto Bedford Avenue, our silence soundtracked by an ironic cover version of 'Away in a Manger'. Oh brilliant, the universe wanted to play me Christmas songs altogether too late to save the evening. Eventually we pulled up at the corner of Bedford and N7th and even though it was past one and tiny snowflakes were starting to fall from the thick purple sky, the streets were littered with those too cool to care about the temperature. I'd seen heavier coats on girls out in Newcastle. Jesse coughed a small, embarrassing cough when the taxi driver turned to see what was going on. The bagel shop was right outside but I wasn't in the mood anymore. I was so angry, I wasn't hungry. Shit had got real.

'Get out the taxi,' I said, exhausted and embarrassed and in need of my bed.

'Are we still getting bagels?' he asked in a small voice.

'No, we are not still getting bagels,' I replied as evenly as I could. 'I mean, you can get a bagel, I can't stop you. I'm going home.'

'I'm sorry,' he said, opening the door and letting a rush of bitter air into the car. As if the atmosphere wasn't frosty enough already. 'I misread the situation.'

'Yes, you did.'

'And I've been drinking.'

'Yes, you have.'

'I'm really sorry.'

'I'm sure you are.'

Jesse tousled his hair away and readjusted his glasses for full hangdog effect. If I hadn't been sat on my hands just to stop myself from punching him, I

214

might have been moved to feel sorry for him. But I was, so I didn't.

'Are you gonna fire me?' he asked.

I opened my mouth to tell him not to be an idiot and that of course I wasn't going to fire him, mostly because I didn't think I actually had that much executive power, but instead I took a deep breath, looked at the tragic figure who was causing me to freeze half to death and gave him my best death stare. 'I'll see you on Monday, Jesse.'

Mary wasn't even officially gone for another two days and already the power had gone to my head.

'Can you drop me at Kent and N8th, please?' I said to the driver. All I wanted was to go home, take a shower, eat several biscuits and pretend the entire evening had never happened. No Cici, no Jesse, no distinct lack of mince pies and definitely no kiss.

'Angela, really, I'm sorry.' Jesse quickly grabbed the door as I reached over to slam it shut. If I hadn't been furious with him, I'd have been quite impressed. It was all very climactic movie scene, but I totally could have broken his hand. And I did have a precedent in that. 'I was drunk, I was stupid. It was nothing but a Christmas party fuck-up.'

'Oh, now it's a Christmas party,' I replied, letting him close the door since he wasn't even offering to pay for the taxi. Twat.

Seething, I sat back in the seat as the driver gunned the engine, waiting for the lights to change. This was how a grown-up would deal with something like this, I told myself. They would be an adult and be restrained and not give in to the urge for physical violence. I tapped my fingers on my knee, shaking with overwhelming waves of pissed-offedness mixed with unavoidable English guilt and unmistakable Angela awkwardness.

Oh, fuck it.

Before Jesse could vanish from sight, I leaned out the window, watching my breath fog up in front of my nose.

'Oi, Jesse,' I shouted into the semi-crowded street. 'You're a complete tosser. Merry bloody Christmas.'

And then I felt a bit better.

CHAPTER TWELVE

'Hey, you awake?'

I groaned, rolling onto my side and .shaking my head as much as I dared for the fear of puking.

'No,' I replied, curling my legs up underneath me. 'I'm asleep.'

'We're going back to the apartment to get the last of the boxes.' I opened my eyes to see Alex's knees in front of my face, followed by his hair, followed by his face. He really was due a trim. 'You want to start unpacking the kitchen?'

'No.'

'You want to lie on the floor and sulk about being hungover?'

'I'm not hungover.'

'Whatever.'

He was putting a polite face on things but I knew Alex was mad at me. Really, really mad. But he was also wrong – I really wasn't hungover. I hadn't been even slightly drunk when I got home from the party but I had been angry. Too angry to sleep. And so, instead of waking him up and telling him all about it, I had paced around the living room for a couple of hours, packed a few boxes and eventually passed out on the sofa after necking several disgusting shots of whiskey somewhere around four a.m. It had seemed like such a good idea at the time – I would drink myself into a visit from the sandman, I wouldn't wake up my husband with my psychosis and I would empty a bottle that then wouldn't need packing. But things hadn't quite worked out that way.

It turned out, what I considered to be excellent wife-ing, Alex considered shitty moving-day behaviour. But given that Graham and Craig had been on our doorstep at the crack of dawn and we'd been shifting boxes and furniture and huge fir trees for the last six and a half hours, there hadn't been a good time to sit him down and say, *Hey, baby, so that bloke in the office who I'm really good mates with? He snogged me in a cab last night! Oh! And before I forget, there's a sniff of a chance I might not be able to have kids. Ta-da!* I imagined this would be best framed with a cheesy grin and a double thumbs up.

And it definitely didn't feel like a conversation to have while Grace screamed bloody murder at being strapped in her pushchair and shipped off to Aunt Jenny's with her mum when all she really wanted to do was climb on top of all the moving boxes and throw herself onto the sofa, repeatedly. And I couldn't say I felt inspired to begin the debate when I was squeezed in between Craig and Graham while Alex drove us to our fantastic new apartment. The BQE was an upsetting bit of road at the best of times, all potholes and super-narrow lanes occupied by angry taxi drivers, and Alex was not a patient driver. Switching lanes every four seconds for twenty minutes was not good for someone with a stomach full of whiskey sitting in a car full of smelly boys. Well, to be fair it was only Craig that smelled, having not taken a shower, his reasoning being that moving would only make him smell more. And so we had started our first day in our new home with a fun undercurrent of passive-aggressive behaviour and a smelly man hauling boxes. It was beginning to look a lot like Christmas.

Given all of that, I could sort of understand why Alex was not ecstatic at finding me flat on my back, hidden amongst a cardboard city of moving boxes, pale, sweaty and generally pathetic. All he saw was a woman who had gone to her office Christmas party, had a few too many and failed to take into consideration that she had to move house the next day. Craig on the other hand had seemed quite impressed but that wasn't exactly an honour I wore with pride. I waited for the door to slam shut – our new neighbours must have been chuffed to monkeys at our arrival – and pulled out my phone, stretching out onto my back again and taking comfort from the fact that this was the only day of my life that I would be happy the heating wasn't on yet. The freezing cold floorboards were the only thing keeping the contents of my stomach where they were. I should have just got hammered, at least then I'd understand why I felt so awful. Guilt, exhaustion and misplaced rage left me feeling just as disgusting but without the added benefit of a 'poor me' attitude.

In an attempt to be a Good Daughter, I held my phone aloft and snapped a picture of the new and unpacked kitchen, adding the caption *ta-da* before sending it to my mother. We had a tap exclusively for filtered water. I had finally made it. She would be so impressed. So impressed in fact that she felt the need to call me not thirty seconds later. I stared at the word 'home' lighting up my borrowed iPhone's screen and considered my options. Red button, green button. Red button, green button.

She'll only bloody ring back, I told myself, squinting with one eye and prodding the green button with great reluctance. I got it on the second try and was inordinately pleased with myself.

'Well.'

She obviously wasn't in the mood for pleasantries.

'Hello?' I wondered how easy it would be to find the kettle, already fully aware that it would not be at all easy to find the kettle. 'How are you?'

'Oh.' Annette was not in a good mood. 'That's all you've got to say? How are you?'

'Was there something else?' I asked. 'Have they changed it since I was last home?'

'Don't come calling me with nothing but cheek after what you've done, young lady. I've been wondering how long it would take you to pick up the phone.'

'But you called me?' Now I was completely confused. 'What are you talking about?'

'I don't know if you were honestly hoping I was going to ignore the little message you left on the phone the other night or you were actually so very drunk that you don't remember it.' Her voice was stiff but loud. 'And if that is the case, then I am as worried as I am disappointed.'

Disappointed? She was disappointed in me? I hadn't heard her this genuinely angry with me since I lied about having a house party when they were on holiday and then she found dozens of empty beer

220

cans on the roof of the garage. Stupid sixth-form boys.

'Mum, I really don't know what you're talking about.' I wondered how many times I'd need to bash the back of my skull against these lovely oak floorboards before I rendered myself unconscious. 'Unless I've got an evil twin, I haven't spoken to you since you called to say you were coming for Christmas.'

'I don't suppose you consider leaving a drunk message the same thing as talking to me, do you?' she went on. 'Didn't even have the decency to call us when we'd be awake. If your father hadn't checked the 141 thing . . . But don't you worry, we'll be cancelling the flights. Don't want to let a little thing like Christmas with your family get in the way of getting Jenny an "awesome" present or all that terribly important "shit" you have "going on".'

Somewhere in the back of my mind something began to rattle and it wasn't something good. While my mum's voice positively dripped with sarcasm, it did sound a bit like something I might say but not quite.

'Are you still there?' she asked. 'Or are you busy doing that "shit" right now? I'm sure you're far too busy to talk.'

'Right, I can tell you're upset,' I said, wishing I'd had more than three hours' sleep. Or that I had drunk more whiskey. 'But I really don't know what you're talking about.'

'The message you left on the phone on Wednesday night,' Mum answered. 'Not that I could hardly tell it was you for the terrible American accent. Is that how you talk when you're with these friends of yours now?'

'But Wednesday I was at Erin's party and—' What little blood had managed to circulate all the way up to my face drained right away. 'Oh.'

Jenny. I thought she was just pretending to call my parents. Oh, fuck a festive duck.

'Oh?' She was not amused by my reaction. 'That's the best you've got?'

'Mum, I can explain,' I started, without any sort of explanation to back up the statement. 'It wasn't me.'

If it was good enough for Shaggy, it was good enough for me.

'It wasn't you?'

'It wasn't me.'

'Then who was it?'

Aah. Now this presented another problem. My mum loved Jenny. 'Loved' actually wasn't a strong enough word for the warm and fuzzy feelings my parents expressed when presented with their beloved La Lopez, and even if I threw her under the bus on this one, they were unlikely to believe me.

'Someone with an American accent?'

'Oh, come off it, Angela. I've never heard such a fake accent in my entire life.'

I did not foresee a successful career for my mother in forensics.

'Look, it really wasn't me and I'm very sorry. I feel awful,' I said with one hundred per cent authenticity. 'But I was a bit surprised when you said you were coming, that's all.'

'Oh, so now we'll get to the bottom of it,' she snapped. 'It wasn't you but you really don't want us to come.' She lowered her voice into a stage whisper. 'Your father is devastated. Devastated.'

'What's that, love?' I heard a very undevastated-sounding Dad call from the other room.

'And don't you worry, we've cancelled the flights. We're far too busy doing "shit" to come all the way out to New York just to see you.'

Oh GOD. I didn't know what to say to make things better. I didn't know what to say to stop my mum from swearing again. It was freaking me out.

'So you get back to your house and your friends and your job and we'll pretend we hadn't gone to all that trouble and expense. And remind your dad that we didn't need to come all the way to America anyway because no matter how much we miss you, our only child, especially at Christmas, you're far too busy to miss us.'

'Mum.'

'Don't Mum me. I'm going, James Bond is on.'

Nothing came between my mother and a lecherous old Scotsman.

It was never a good sign when my mum hung up on me and it was never a good sign when I felt like I was going to throw up immediately after a phone call. Given that I was dealing with both of those things at that exact second, I had to assume things were now, in fact, completely buggered. I let my hands drop onto my belly, still clutching my hot, clammy phone. What I'd give for a lovely, room-temperature, flat Diet Pepsi and a greasy slice of pizza.

Maybe, I wondered quietly to myself, *Alex would be less mad at me if they got back with the rest of the boxes and pizza was waiting for them. Maybe he would think it was a thoughtful act and not an entirely self-serving puke-avoidance tactic.* I picked up the phone again and swiped at the screen until I found the Grub

Hub app – until I had my new iPhone, I was working on very limited app selection and while I didn't have Facebook on here yet, I did already have three different food delivery services. Hmm. If only I actually knew our address.

Since pizza wasn't going to magically arrive and solve all my problems, I skipped back to the call screen and redialled Mum's number. It rang through to voicemail. I tried again. Nothing. On the third attempt, just as I was about to give up and get on a plane back to England to try and explain, my dad answered.

'Dad, it's me, don't hang up. I'm sorry. It's all a big misunderstanding and I'm sorry and please tell Mum not to be mad at me.'

'Oh, Angela,' he said with a big, fatherly sigh that made me feel worse than anything my mum had said. 'She's in a real temper this time. You shouldn't have left it so long to call.'

'But I didn't know about the message,' I protested. 'Which I know doesn't make a lot of sense but it really wasn't me. It was someone else. I thought they were having a laugh.'

'Having a laugh about not wanting us to come for Christmas?'

Hmm. I should have thought that through better.

'She's not going to change her mind, Angela. She says she doesn't want to come now.'

There was nothing like guilt piled on top of guilt to make you feel like complete and utter shite.

'It's just been so mad, Dad.' I knew I was whining but sometimes, with dads, whining worked. 'Work has been horrible and moving house is so hard.'

'What's the house like?' he asked.

'We've got a special tap just for drinking water,' I

said, turning my head towards the kitchen. 'It's mental.'

'What does she say?' I heard my mum screech over the James Bond theme tune.

'They've got a tap just for drinking water,' he called back. 'In the new house.'

'Well, la-di-da,' she replied.

'Dad!' I shouted. 'Don't tell her that! Tell her I feel awful and that I'm sorry and between work and the house and Louisa and Grace turning up on the doorstep . . .'

'What do you mean, Louisa turning up on your doorstep?' he interrupted. 'Louisa, our Louisa?'

Oh fucklesticks.

'Another one?' I offered, throwing some shit at the wall, hoping it might stick.

'Another Louisa and Grace?'

'Yes?'

'Angela Clark.'

Eeep, both names. Fuck, fuck, fuck, fuck, fuck.

'So let me get this straight, Louisa and Grace are in New York with you?' Dad sounded as confused as I felt. 'Without Tim?'

'No.'

'No what?'

'I don't know.'

It was worth a try.

'Angela . . .' Dad put on his best stern voice. It wasn't very good. 'I'm not on the wacky baccy now, tell me the truth. What's going on?'

'What's going on?' I heard Mum's voice coming closer and prayed that my dad would have the sense to keep this to himself.

'Apparently Louisa and Grace are over there,' he

said, not doing a very good job of holding his hand over the phone. 'Did you know?'

'Give me that phone,' Mum demanded. I winced and gave bludgeoning myself to death further consideration. 'Angela Clark, what's going on over there? Why is Louisa there? Why don't I know about this? Was she the one who called me?'

'No, Mum, calm down—'

'Angela, I don't like being lied to. Shall I hang up the phone and call Louisa's mother?' she threatened.

I couldn't believe something that had worked when I was fifteen still held water. Next she'd be threatening to take my TV out of my room and stop my pocket money. Oh God, TV. I hadn't asked whether or not Alex had had the cable transferred yet. I bit my lip and pulled my knees up, knocking them together. One crisis at a time, Angela, one crisis at a time.

'Right, I'll just give her a call then. I have been meaning to pop over with a present for Grace.'

'Fine. She's here.' I really hoped I never found myself in an interrogation situation. They'd only have to wave an orange jumpsuit at me and I'd roll over on anyone. Hopefully they would be after my mum. 'She's here. And you can't say anything to anyone.'

'Why would I say anything to anyone?'

'Because you're going to be mincing around the supermarket and you'll see her mum or you'll see Tim and you'll be all "ooh, is Louisa having a nice time in New York?" and they won't know what you're talking about and then I'll be in loads of shit and then you won't have anywhere to stay when you get here because Louisa will have actually killed me. Actually killed me.'

There was quiet on the line for a moment. Well, quiet and the opening song to *Live and Let Die*. Some things never changed.

'Why would I be in the supermarket?' Mum asked.

'Getting my pickled onions and Jaffa Cakes?' I was a bit surprised that was the part of my rambling nonsense she wanted to focus on but still, I was not one to look a gift horse in the mouth, however unlikely it was to come galloping into my life.

'Well, that won't matter now we're not coming anymore, will it?'

'It's a long story, Mum, and we're really busy with the move.' Another kick at the boxes beside me. I hoped they didn't have anything breakable in them. They did have fragile stickers on them but I'd been a bit free and easy with those. I liked stickers. 'I'll call you tomorrow. She'll probably be home by then anyway, but if you see anyone, don't say anything. You don't know anything.'

'I can't be responsible for the things I do and don't say, Angela,' she replied, all feigned innocence and breeziness. 'It's hardly going to be my fault if I see Louisa's mother when I've gone out specially to buy you pickled onions and her daughter's whereabouts happens to come up, is it?'

'So you are bringing me pickled onions?'

'No,' she replied, 'we're not. Call back when you're ready to apologise properly.'

I couldn't believe it. I had been transatlantically sent to my room.

Louisa was not going to be happy. At all. I pulled up a new text message and tried to work out what to say.

'I may have dropped the tiniest of bollocks. Call me?'

I tapped, debating whether or not to include kisses. I went with two.

Three seemed like overdoing it, considering.

Lou hadn't replied to my text by the time Alex got back from the old place so I decided she must be in the middle of a very intense deep and meaningful with her husband, and probably booking her flights back home at that very second. That or she and Jenny had fucked off out shopping and she hadn't taken her phone. Not taking her phone would be very un-Louisa-like behaviour, but then again just about everything everyone was doing seemed like very un-them behaviour at the moment. Except for me, obviously. Cock-ups as standard.

When the last boxes were safely installed in the spare bedroom and our moving buddies had been sent on their way, I had hoped that Alex would take pity on me and let me have a little lie down. It was Saturday after all. Traditionally, that involved a lot of lying down, and the metaphorical boat had been rocked enough already. But no. Alex wasn't through. Moving almost the entire contents of our apartment inside five hours on a Saturday morning wasn't enough. I had not suffered enough. Alex wanted to go to Ikea.

Now, I was a girl who had braved the Next summer sale not once, not twice, but thrice in my pre-USA days so I was no stranger to a questionable shopping decision, but this? This was mental. I thought it was adorable that he would risk getting puked on when he picked me up and fireman's lifted me out to the van and I sold myself on a lovely little story about a sorry-looking English girl scarfing seventy-five-cent hot dogs and bottomless paper cups full of pop while her wonderful husband pushed two trolleys around, single-handedly for so big and strong was he. But once we pulled into the car park and rode the *Gladiators*-style travelator up to the showroom, I was ready to kill myself. Literally launch myself over the balcony and spear myself on a reasonably priced coat rack. Ikea at two thirty on a Saturday afternoon, four days before Christmas. It truly was the seventh circle of Hell.

Moving to the States had taught me a lot about the world but few lessons had been more unsettling than the fact that Ikea is exactly the same all over the world. A Klippan is a Klippan is a Klippan. At first I'd been quite charmed by the fact. Knowing that you can go and sit on an identical version of your first ever settee when you're three thousand miles and seven years away from it can be quite comforting, but after a while it just gets creepy. But my horror didn't stop at the slightly shonky furniture and bargainous snacks. It wasn't just the Stepford horse-meatballs and the bags of one hundred tea lights that were identical in this flat-packed social experiment. Oh no, it was the people. And the people were fucking horrible.

After giving him a brief update on my parental situation, Alex turned to look at me with wide, sympathetic eyes.

'Can you grab a couple of those extension cables?' He pointed to a huge wire bin beside me while studying his shopping list, tiny pencil in hand. 'You can never have too many, right?'

That was it. His entire response.

'I think I'm going to cry,' I replied quietly, grabbing

three plastic-wrapped plugs and dropping them into the huge yellow bag hanging from my shoulder.

'Huh?' Alex looked up, a smudge of moving-day dust above his left eyebrow, almost hidden by his hair. I pasted on as big and bright a shiny smile as I could muster.

'I think I'm going to cry,' I repeated with as positive an attitude as possible.

Alex looked back at his list, nodding. 'Yeah.' He held up the dangling tag from a small, shitty coffee table. 'We'll get a drink on the way out.'

All the way here, Alex had been merrily explaining his theory that Ikea would be empty, that everyone would have already left the city or they would be on Christmas pre-visits but he couldn't have been more wrong. I hadn't seen this many people crammed into one shop since the Bloomingdales Black Friday sale.

From an anthropological point of view, it was fascinating. This one store featured a complete cross section of New York life. Only, I wasn't an anthropologist, I was a tired, grumpy cow who wanted to eat pizza and go to bed. No matter where we went, we kept bumping into a young Hasidic couple and I walked into a wall trying to work out if the woman was wearing a wig. Then I tripped over the sari of a gorgeous Indian woman. There were dozens of little Hispanic children running around, all seemingly committed to knocking me down, and my heart softened for a moment when I spotted a truly beautiful multi-ethnic gay couple wandering around holding hands. At least it did until the white guy slipped his hands down the front of the black guy's jeans and they disappeared into a fire escape. Slightly less romantic. And despite our differences, we all had one thing in common. Not a single one of us wanted to be there. Truly, the multi-lingual shouting and screaming was a beautiful thing. Sort of.

'What are we actually looking for?' I asked, dragging my feet along the floor and having flashbacks to trailing my mum around BHS in the summer holidays. 'Don't we have everything?'

'I need a couple of things for the studio.' He waved a hand around in a non-committal way. 'I figured we should get everything fixed up before we never get round to it.'

It was a fair point. We were pretty bad at putting off today what could be taken care of never, but I really didn't think we needed to take a tour of a fake family's 350-square-foot studio apartment at that exact second. Who wanted to fight with angry college couples over a twenty-dollar coffee table that was always going to be wonky no matter how much care you put into building it when you could be snuggled up on the sofa, watching telly and having a little nap?

'Hey, what do you think about this?' Alex called from inside one of the pretend bedrooms. 'Maybe we should get this for Grace?'

Snapping out of my fluorescent lighting-induced trance, I shuffled around two teenage boys, shoving each other into a test mattress, and followed Alex's voice until I found him stood in the middle of a romantically decorated powder pink bedroom, complete with country modern furnishings and lots and lots of florals. It was the anti-Alex room. And it turned out the 'this' he was referring to was a cot.

'Don't you think she's a bit big for it?' I said,

scratching my head. I really should have found the energy to wash my hair. Or at least put it in a ponytail. I really was disgusting. 'I mean, she's nearly two. Do two-year-olds sleep in cots?'

'This is one of those convertible things,' Alex explained. 'Look, you just pull the sides off and it turns into a bed.'

I felt as though I had walked into a parallel universe. My muso boyfriend in his dark and dusty denim finery, standing in the middle of a bedroom so pink and pretty it was making me want to play some Joy Division and cut myself.

'Yeah, I'm just not sure she really needs it.' The yellow bag rustled as I moved, the sound of a thousand crisp packets accompanying my general discomfort. 'They're going to be going home soon and then what will we do with it?'

'Then we'll have it,' he replied, struggling to ram the removable bars back into their slot. Great piece of craftsmanship, totally solid. 'For when we need it.'

Totally devoid of a better response, I let my face fall into a completely emotionless expression and used my last ounce of energy to throw myself on the bed behind my husband. It was not a comfortable bed but horizontal was my default setting and, you know, any port in a storm.

'We're not buying a fucking cot, Alex.' I thought it was best to be direct. And maybe shout a little bit. 'We don't need a cot because we're not having a baby.'

'We're not having a baby today, sure, but what harm could it do to get this now and then put it in the basement until we need it?'

He did not sound terribly charmed by my reaction. 'From the looks of it, it could do a lot of harm,' I said, not moving. I wasn't even sure if I could move. 'It's a piece of shit. But if you want to buy a non-existent baby a crappy deathtrap of a cot, don't let me stop you. In fact, why don't I just go and wait in the van?'

'Because I would fucking love it if you could try to show a hint of excitement about the life I'm attempting to build for us.' Alex didn't raise his voice, he didn't shout but he was not a happy man. 'You don't give a shit, do you? You haven't even tried today. Or ever actually since I told you about the new apartment.'

'Yes, I have,' I whispered. 'I do give a shit.'

Alex never swore at me, ever. I sat up on the bed and wished I hadn't. He looked so angry. It was an expression I didn't recognise on him. He wasn't even this mad when we found out Dan Humphrey was Gossip Girl.

'When?' he asked, throwing his arms out and letting them slap against his sides. 'Because all I've heard about is your magazine and your friend and your mom and dad coming over and your Christmas plans. I haven't heard shit about me. I haven't heard anything about us. I've been working my ass off trying to create this life for us, for our family, and all you care about is yourself.'

We were not going to have our first big, proper row in a pretend bedroom in Ikea. There wasn't even a real door to slam. There was, however, a growing crowd outside our set.

'You don't think you're overreacting a little bit?' I asked with wide, warning eyes. 'Where's this coming from?'

'I'm not really surprised that you're surprised. I haven't really been top of your agenda lately, have I?'

233

He kicked the leg of the bed and the whole thing wobbled. Really, Ikea did need to reinforce their furniture better. We couldn't possibly have been the first couple to go at it on a Saturday afternoon inside these four walls.

'You're always top of my agenda, the whole Christmas thing was about putting you at the top of my agenda,' I said, immediately feeling horribly guilty. 'OK, so yes, there's a chance I haven't been able to give the move as much attention as I would have liked but it has been a busy couple of bloody weeks. And you did sort of surprise me with it.'

'It's not just the move.' He looked like he was ready to explode. 'It's everything, Angela. I'm never your priority.'

'Can we not talk about this now?' Aside from my inherent fear of 'making a scene', I really wanted a time-out. I needed two minutes to work out what to say — my brain still wasn't firing on all cylinders, if it was firing at all. 'Can we do this at home?'

'No, we can't,' Alex replied. He did not share my fear of public embarrassment. He was a musician after all. 'I'm sick of waiting to talk about everything on your schedule. I'm sick of waiting for you to get home from work. I'm sick of waiting for you to finish up with Jenny. I'm sick of waiting for you to decide when you want to start being a grown-up.'

I felt my feet getting stompy. Fine. If we were going to do it, we were going to do it.

'What are you talking about?' I shouted at him. 'You're the one who sods off on tour. You're the one who vanishes into his studio for days on end. You're the one who doesn't know what bloody day it is.'

'That happened one time,' he thundered. 'And I had been working non-stop for three days.'

'But you're sick of waiting for me to come home from work?' I was more upset than angry but I didn't know how to tell him. So, obviously, I attacked. 'And you're the one accusing me of not being a grown-up? Tell me, what grown-up thing is it that I'm not doing?'

'Maybe not getting wasted the night before we move?' Alex was out and out yelling and every time he shouted, I could feel my temper rising higher and higher. Who knew I could be this angry and this hungover at the same time? 'Maybe enabling your friend's dumbass runaway behaviour? Maybe a bunch of other things?'

'Whatever it is, just say it,' I snapped, jumping up off the bed until we were face to face, on either side of the world's shittest cot. 'For fuck's sake, Alex, just say it.'

He stared down at me, his breathing hard and heavy, two red spots glowing in his pale cheeks. I had never, ever been scared of him before but I literally had no idea what he was going to do. And so, of course, he did the last thing I imagined he would.

'I want to have a baby,' he said, covering my hands with his own.

It was a good job the bed was right behind me because that cot was not strong enough to hold me up. I pulled my hands away and sank backwards, waiting to catch my breath. Alex stayed exactly where he was, his eyes still wild. I could almost hear his heart pounding over the tinny music playing over the loudspeakers. How had we got into this?

'And you thought the best way to go about that was to start screaming at me in Ikea?' I asked. 'Really?'

'No, I thought the best way would be to marry you,' he said, still not moving. 'And love you and be happy and wait and that it would just happen. But it didn't and you won't even talk to me about it. So then I figured maybe I'd buy us an apartment that would feel like a home but you didn't even seem to notice that had happened. So tell me, Angela, what am I supposed to do now?'

I closed my eyes to stop the tears from falling and shook my head very, very gently, breathing out.

'What if I don't want to have a baby?' I formed the words very carefully, smoothing out the telltale bumps in my voice.

'Now?' he asked. 'Or ever?'

I still hadn't been to see Dr Laura, I didn't know what she was going to tell me, but there, in that moment, it didn't matter what she was going to say. All that mattered was what Alex would say. If there was no baby, if there was never a baby, would I be enough?

I couldn't say anything so I just shrugged, forcing myself to open my eyes and look up at him through heavy wet lashes. All the fight was gone from him. He looked so sad. Without warning, he shoved the cot away from him, sending it crashing into the bed, and stormed off out of the bedroom, striding across the showroom floor. As I watched him go, I noticed everyone around us was frozen like waxworks, eyes trained on the show, until the second he passed by them and they suddenly snapped back to life. No one made eye contact with me – it seemed they had all taken a keen interest in the contents of their own giant yellow shopping bags. Abandoning my haul, I shuffled off the edge of the bed, climbed over the broken cot and headed straight for the outside world. Ikea really did terrible things to people.

'I just wanted to have a nice Christmas,' I shouted as he left. 'Is that too much to ask?'

My phone vibrated in the bottom of my handbag as I reached the entrance. Waiting for someone to activate the automatic door from the outside, I ran out into the cold, happy to feel air that didn't come through an air-conditioning system. It was freezing but it was sunny and I turned my face up to the sky, trying to soak in some vitamin D and convince myself that the world was still turning. With a deep breath and a brave face, I pulled my phone out, expecting to see Alex's name in big white letters. Instead it was Louisa. Blindly, I pressed the green answer button and praised her psychic abilities.

'What do you mean you've dropped the tiniest of bollocks?' she demanded. 'What have you done now?'

'How did you know?' I asked, clearing my throat and ignoring a man holding three hot dogs. Three. At once. Bastard.

'Because you sent me a text saying that you had dropped the tiniest of bollocks?' she said, the line crackly with a wind that wasn't present in Red Hook, Brooklyn. 'What's going on?'

'Ohhhh.' I really was outdoing myself today. 'Yeah. That. Um, it's probably nothing but I might have accidentally told my mum that you're here. But she promised she wouldn't say anything. Sort of.'

'You did what?'

Louisa didn't sound that pleased.

'It just came out,' I offered, my row with Alex still whirling around my head. All I could think was that I needed to stand under a shower for a really long time. 'Listen, can I come over? I'll fix it, I promise.'

'Shouldn't you be doing house-moving things?' she asked with a resigned sigh. 'Because I think you've probably done enough already.'

'She wants to come over? Tell her to come over!' I heard Jenny shout to Louisa. 'He's gonna be here soon. Tell her to bring Alex.'

'Who's going to be there soon?' I asked, twisting my wedding and engagement rings with my thumb at the sound of his name. 'What's going on?'

'Nothing that's going to make your day any better,' Louisa replied.

'I don't think anything could make it any worse,' I said. 'Believe me.'

Hanging up, I stared at my phone for just a second and then turned towards the car park, squinting to see our van. It was still there, Alex must still be inside. Leaving it any longer would just make things more difficult, I decided, and so I took it upon myself to be the bigger person and dialled his number. My heart thudded against my ribs when the call connected but with each unanswered ring it fell a little, until I was sure I felt it hit the bottom of my stomach when my call finally went through to his never-checked voicemail. If I learned one thing about Alex in the time that we'd been together, it was that when he was seriously upset, he needed to be left alone. Of course, for the most part I'd learned this through the process of other people upsetting him. Knowing I was the reason for the look on his face when he had walked off was almost too much to bear. Maybe if I gave him a while to cool off, took myself to Jenny's while he calmed down, we could talk properly in a while. When I'd had a lot of caffeine and a shower and time to think about how to explain everything I hadn't had a chance to explain in the past seven days.

'You win this round, Ikea,' I said, staring up at the giant yellow and blue sign. 'You can stick your hot dogs up your arse.'

The man beside me looked up sharply, half a hot dog sticking out of his mouth. I frowned and hung up the phone.

'Oh, not you.' I stood up and waved at a waiting taxi. 'Please enjoy your lunch.'

But it didn't look like he was much in the mood for hot dogs anymore.

CHAPTER THIRTEEN

Even though I knew the right thing to do was to leave
Alex alone, every second of the cab ride to Jenny's
was torture. I stared at my phone screen, refreshed
my email every minute and started writing about
fifteen different texts but it was all for nothing. Soon
an hour had passed without a word and I had a
horribly familiar feeling. We'd only ever had one row
this bad, two years ago, almost to the day, and
somehow that time we'd ended up getting engaged.
Of course, it wasn't because we were both so mature
and openly communicative that we were able to sort
ourselves out. Oh no. Our friends had more or less
knocked our heads together until we saw sense and
it was with an incredibly forced sense of optimism
that I arrived at my old Manhattan apartment, hoping
against hope that they would be able to do the same
thing again.

'Sorry it took so long. The bridge was a nightmare.'
I let myself in without knocking and shrugged off my
coat. 'I need coffee so badly. I really, really need to
talk to you.'

'Hello, sunshine. You look like shite.'

I stopped in the living room doorway, blinked twice and felt my forehead fold into a frown.

'James,' I said, both as a 'hello' and a 'what the hell are you doing here?'

'Angela,' he grinned.

James and Jenny weren't close. In fact, they barely knew each other. We'd hung out a few times and they'd chatted a little at my wedding but as far as I was aware, they weren't exactly brunch buddies. So what was he doing perched on her windowsill drinking a cup of tea?

'There's coffee in the pot.' Jenny, all bright eyes and bushy ponytail, sat on the armchair closest to James, positively vibrating with excitement. She had never been very good at keeping her mouth shut and she clearly had something she wanted to say. 'Come sit down.'

'Where's Lou?' I asked, backing slowly towards the kitchen counter, pulling my favourite mug out of the cupboard and filling it to the brim, only leaving room for enough sugar to put me in a diabetic coma.

'I'm in here,' she shouted from what used to be my bedroom. 'I'm just putting Grace down for her nap. Can you please tell me exactly what you said to your mother?'

'As soon as someone tells me exactly what's going on here.' I leaned down to the too-full mug to slurp my coffee before I even tried to pick it up. 'James?'

'Uh, didn't you say you really needed to talk?' Jenny replied before he could. 'And yeah, how come you look like you slept in the park last night?'

'Long story short,' I began. I could still feel my brows knitting together. Hopefully Sadie had bought me Botox vouchers for Christmas. Again. 'Work Christmas party last night, Jesse hit on me in the cab home, I got hammered, we had to move this morning and me and Alex just had a screaming row about having a baby in Ikea.'

'Alex wanted to have a baby in Ikea?' James placed his own coffee mug on the windowsill beside his huge thigh, only to have said thigh slapped by Jenny. 'Utter filth.'

'Bad boy,' she scolded. 'You know what she means.'

'And how does that play into you telling your mother that I'm in New York?' Louisa emerged from the bedroom, hands on hips, long blonde hair curling around her shoulders. I noticed the dark circles that had been so prominent when she arrived on my door-step were all but gone and her cheeks were glowing and pink. In fact, she just looked great in general. They all did. I felt like I'd arrived on the set of a makeover show, two hours too late. They were the 'after' shot, I was the 'before'. Or more like the 'never would be'.

'She called me and I wasn't thinking straight and she caught me off guard and she isn't going to say anything.' I shook my head, careful not to shake my coffee. 'I'm sorry. It was a massive cock-up.'

'Yes, it was.' Lou didn't move. 'I can't believe you've put me in this position.'

'It's not like I was planning on it,' I replied, really quite keen to find out what was going on with the odd couple over by the window. 'And being brutally honest, I wasn't the one who put you on the plane. You really do have to call him.'

'She doesn't have to do anything,' Jenny interrupted, her hand still on James's knee and now safely covered by one of his own. 'We've told her she can stay as long as she likes.'

'We?' I turned back to stare at the lovebirds. If I didn't know better . . . 'What is going on? Have you hit your head or something? You do know you're gay, yeah? And that she's a girl?'

'Oh, Angie.' Jenny stood up and clasped James's fingers through her own. 'Of course he knows I'm a girl. How else would I have his baby?'

Right. Of course. Made perfect sense.

'Have I actually gone mad?' I asked everyone in the room. 'I mean, seriously, have I lost it? Because if not, it would seem that everyone else alive has and that just seems quite unlikely.'

'I told you I wanted to start a family.' James looked far too relaxed for someone who had just dropped a baby bomb. 'And when you said Jenny wanted to have a baby, it all made sense. So I called her after the party, we went for lunch yesterday and I made a proposal.'

'You're getting married?' I squeaked. 'Because that worked out so well for Tom Cruise?'

'Not that kind of proposal,' he tutted. 'A co-parenting proposal. And Jenny said yes.'

'Is Tom Cruise gay?' Louisa asked from across the room. 'I didn't know that.'

'Of course he isn't,' James said with a theatrical wink. 'What planet have you been living on?'

'Isn't it perfect, Angie?' Jenny gushed, her excitement spilling over into a little hop. 'James is going to move into the city so he can be involved right through the pregnancy.'

'And I already have a real estate agent looking for townhouses,' James added. 'Even a couple in Brooklyn.'

'But don't get your hopes up,' Jenny warned me. 'I kind of have my hopes set on the Village, maybe near Erin.'

'Wherever the best schools are,' James replied in a see-how-serious-I'm-taking-this voice. 'Only the very best for our baby.'

It was all too much. Completely and utterly overloaded, I edged my way to the arm of the sofa and sat down, drinking my coffee in silence. It would have been wonderful news, Jenny had the man she'd always dreamed of – handsome, intelligent, rich and desperate to give her a family. Except he loved cock every bit as much as she did.

'I know you weren't one hundred per cent behind this,' Jenny said, letting go of her baby daddy's hand and coming over to the sofa. 'But that was before James. This really is what I want, Angie. And uh, we were talking about it before you got here, there's something else.'

'Can I?' James jumped up, all six feet something of him blocking the bright, bitter sunshine out of my eyes. 'Can I ask her?'

Jenny nodded and took hold of my non-coffee-holding hand.

'We want you to be the godmother.' James pushed his way onto the sofa behind me and threw his arms around my neck. 'And Alex to be the godfather.'

And that was when I burst into tears.

'Oh lord, Ange, can you not?' Lou ran to pull the bedroom door to as gently as possible. 'If Grace hears you, she'll start and then I'll never get her to sleep.'

'I'm. Sorry,' I choked, letting James take my coffee away and Jenny rub my back. Every part of my body was giving up on me. There was nothing to do but sob. I could feel my common sense giving up and packing its bags too. I mean really, what was the point? 'This isn't OK.'

'Don't be sorry,' Jenny soothed, holding me close while James patted the top of my head. 'It's fine. You're emotional, that's fine. Maybe we should have waited to tell you. I'm sorry, I'm just so excited. And you know you and Alex will work this all out. You always do.'

'I'm not sorry for crying.' I wriggled out of her arms and shook my head away from James like an awkward pony. 'I mean this, this isn't OK.'

Apparently pointing manically at the two of them wasn't clear enough.

'You can't have a baby with James,' I wailed. 'You don't know him, you don't love him. You cannot have a baby.'

'Do we really have to go through this again?' I recognised Jenny's expression. It was the same one she pulled whenever she had already made up her mind but knew that she was making a mistake. I'd seen it a couple of times this week but not on Jenny, on Grace. It was the same expression she made when she reached for a biscuit when she'd already been told no. 'If you can't be happy for me, Angie . . .'

'It's just like that time you wanted that Hermès Birkin.' I was clutching at straws but I had to try to explain what I meant in a language she would understand. 'Remember? You were saving and saving and you got halfway and then you couldn't be arsed to save anymore so you bought a knock-off and pissed all the money away. But you weren't happy with the knock-off, not really. You still really wanted that Birkin.'

'Do you have a point you're trying to get to?' she asked, clearly making an effort to control her temper.

'This baby idea, it's a knock-off.' I stood up and pulled my hair into a ponytail, securing it with an elastic band I pulled off a pile of paperback books on the coffee table. 'It isn't what you really want but it'll do. For now.'

'So you tell me, Professor Angela,' Jenny began, her voice saturated with sarcasm. She didn't like it when other people psych 101-d her. 'What exactly is it that I really want?'

'Oh, I don't know,' I said, grabbing the stack of self-help books. '*The Five Love Languages*, *Eight Weeks to Everlasting*, *Getting the Love You Deserve*. What do you think?'

'Oh, I forgot, it's so easy to find a relationship,' she snapped back, standing up, inches away from my face. 'All a girl needs to do is hop over the pond, grab ahold of the first guy she meets and then cry and mope when he tells her he wants to have a baby.'

'That's not how it was at all,' I replied, refusing to budge. 'And you know it wasn't.'

'Oh sure,' she said with a sour smile. 'Alex was the second guy, right?'

'Maybe you wouldn't have such a hard time finding a boyfriend if you hadn't wasted so long knocking off a married man,' I suggested. 'Heard anything from Jeff lately?'

'Please can you stop arguing,' Louisa begged us. 'You're both saying things you don't mean and you're going to wake Grace.'

'We wouldn't be able to wake her if she was in England, where she lives,' I pointed out. 'Would we?'

'Don't you start on me.' She stepped away from the

246

door, her voice hushed but just as serious as mine or Jenny's. 'You're totally out of order and you know it. You need to calm down.'

'And you need to call your bloody husband,' I shouted at Lou before turning to Jenny. 'And you need to fucking grow up. A baby isn't a toy, it's not this season's accessory. What are you going to do when he gets bored of playing daddy and you're all on your own with a baby and no boyfriend?'

'Hey.' James started to speak but was silenced by three knife-like stares. 'All right, never mind me.'

'Jenny's not asking you for anything,' Louisa said, practically running to Jenny's side. 'I haven't asked you for anything. We just wanted you to be a friend.'

'And instead we got a selfish asshole,' Jenny added. 'What a fucking surprise. It's all about you.'

'So I'm not allowed to have problems because I'm married?' I asked the two girls. James was still sat on the arm of the sofa but was staying absolutely silent. 'Because that makes my problems less valid than yours?'

'Your problems aren't problems,' Jenny spat. 'In fact, the only problem that you have is yourself. Maybe that's my problem too. And Lou Lou's. And Alex's.'

'Fine.' I threw the stack of books in my arms onto the hardwood floor with a clatter. On cue, Grace started wailing in the bedroom. 'I'll just get out of your way and then you won't have a problem in the world.'

'Good!' Jenny shouted.

'Good!' I shouted back, stomping out of the apartment and slamming the front door.

Well, that went well.

It was bitter on the street but I was so angry I could barely feel anything. People were drifting up and down

Lexington, most of them carrying shopping bags, all of them staring at their feet or their phones in a hurry to get somewhere. Everyone had somewhere to go except for me. I leaned against the building, my first real home in New York City, and stared blindly, trying to calm myself down. I could sit in Scotty's Diner for a while but I couldn't face the thought of food, coffee or the company that it would offer. I hadn't lived in this neighbourhood for two years and I still couldn't walk through the doors without getting twenty questions. There was the W hotel bar nearby but I wasn't dressed for it. I wasn't really dressed for anything but lying face down on the sofa and waiting for my mum to make it all better. Which just went to show you how dire things had become.

As my temper faded away, all I felt was sad and tired. I wanted to shower and then I wanted to sleep but going to the new apartment didn't feel right and I definitely couldn't pop back upstairs and ask Jenny if I could hop in the bathroom for half an hour. Which only really left me with one option. Well, two if you counted the gym at the office but really, who did?

New York got dark much earlier than London and the sun was already beginning to set when I reluctantly stepped out of the bathroom and into the empty living room at four in the afternoon. Wrapped in the pathetic excuse for a towel I had bought from Duane Reade on my way over (along with shampoo, conditioner, shower gel and all of the peanut butter M&Ms I could carry), I turned on the kitchen spotlights, hoping no one on Kent Avenue was especially interested in staring up through our curtain-less windows. The place looked huge without our furniture, and other than the tragedy of our air mattress, that now took pride of place in the middle of the living room, the place was completely bare. The wooden floors were much dustier than I remembered and I could see four round impressions where the feet of the sofa had been. Evidence of so many happy hours in front of the TV and under Alex. I rifled around in the Duane Reade bag looking for the very sexy pair of white cotton Hanes knickers I had purchased. I knew no one could see into the apartment, not really, but I still didn't feel great walking around with my arse hanging out. I wasn't Donald Duck.

Hopping up onto the kitchen top, I pulled out a bottle of full-fat Pepsi (desperate times, etc.) and opened the first bag of M&Ms, mindlessly popping them into my mouth one after another and staring out into space. It was Saturday evening in New York City and there were a thousand stories being told outside that window. Downstairs, in the fancy organic wine shop, someone would be stocking up for a dinner party. Across the water, girls all over Manhattan would be choosing outfits and trying to decide whether or not they could walk in their high heels for more than a block while boys would be sat watching sports with their hands down their shorts, vaguely wondering whether or not they were going to get lucky later that evening. Oh, the romance. And somewhere, a couple of blocks down from the Chrysler building and a few longer blocks east of the Empire State, Jenny and James and Louisa were going about their evening without me. Probably together. Probably happy. I sipped the Pepsi, letting the bubbles burn before shoving in an entire handful of M&Ms. Who was I trying to kid with this one at a time nonsense?

I didn't expect to hear from Jenny or Louisa, not yet, but I was starting to get upset that I hadn't heard from Alex. Only I could start a day moving into a gorgeous new home and end it wearing a pair of supermarket knickers in an empty old flat that looked like a crack den. I hopped down off the counter, taking my snacks with me, and collapsed onto the airbed.

'Merry bloody Christmas,' I said to the ceiling.

The ceiling. Christmas. Alex's Christmas present.

In all the rush of the move, I'd completely forgotten about the book I'd stashed in the air vent. Pouting, I stared up at the slightly skewed vent cover and contemplated my options. We'd taken the stepladder to the new apartment already so unless I wanted to go knocking on neighbours' doors, that was out of the equation. The airbed wasn't going to be much cop in getting up to the ceiling, which really only left one option. Rolling off the airbed, I stood under the vent cover and stretched my arm out to the kitchen worktop. It wasn't far at all, I could reach it easily.

'Piece of piss,' I convinced myself, clambering up onto the marble counter with all the grace of a drunk cat.

My bare feet seemed to cling to the cold surface, which was slightly reassuring, and before I could think better of it I tiptoed over to the edge, pushed the cover off the vent and reached my arm up into the air duct.

'Please don't let anything have crawled in here and died,' I prayed to the empty apartment. 'Or have crawled in here and lived.'

I couldn't feel anything furry, squelchy or bitey but I couldn't feel anything padded envelope either, at least not within my reach. Left without an option, other than waiting for my sanity to return, I gritted my teeth, reached both arms into the air vent and dragged my sorry self up. There was no wonder you only ever saw people in prison movies doing pull-ups – you'd have to have an awful lot of time and very little to do to make that seem like fun. I pulled my T-shirt down over my bare belly and shuffled along the metal vent, blinking until my eyes adjusted to the silvery darkness. There was a vague chance that this was not my brightest idea ever. Eventually I spotted the envelope, just a couple of feet beyond my grasp, and propelled myself forwards until I could grab it. If I weren't on my own, half-naked with no genuinely safe way of getting back out of the vent, it might have been fun. But I was so it wasn't. With the envelope secured, I began to back up, trying to work out how to get back to the very edge without the T-shirt riding right up to my nose or falling twelve feet to the floor. I let my feet find their way back out the hole and kept pushing backwards, waiting to feel the counter underneath my toes. And waiting. And waiting.

Hmm.

'Right,' I mumbled, my concern echoing into the vent, my non-existent stomach muscles tensing. 'I can't feel the kitchen top but I can't go any further without having to drop down.'

I really hadn't thought this out well at all. If I dropped in the right spot, I'd only fall a couple of feet onto the counter. If I missed, it was about ten feet down to the floor. Was that bad? Would I break something if I fell ten feet? And of course there was always the glorious proposition of falling half onto the counter, half onto the floor and breaking my neck in the process. I didn't love the thought of that. And so I did nothing.

I pushed myself back into the vent, just far enough that my stomach was flat against the cool metal, and waited for something to happen. Other than me panicking. That was already happening.

'Maybe I should try to get into someone else's apartment,' I wondered aloud, swinging my legs back and forth. 'I'm sure the man next door hasn't got a gun.'

But he had already left for the holidays, the annoying voice in my head reminded me. Gone off to Vermont to see his family. Someone in the building was baking and the delicious smell of cake only served to remind me that I'd eaten nothing but two handfuls of peanut butter M&Ms all day. I had, however, drunk quite a lot of Pepsi and pretty soon, whether I liked it or not, I was going to need a wee. I couldn't even read Alex's book – it was too dark to make out the words on the page. Well, wasn't this a fantastic way to spend a Saturday night? Half-naked, starving and desperate for a wee in an air vent. I had two choices – I could cry or I could do something.

The tears came before I'd even thought what that something could be.

I had no idea how long I'd been dangling out of the ceiling when I heard the key in the lock but it was long enough for me to have considered crawling far enough in to have a wee and then crawling back. I'd decided against it on the grounds of not knowing whether or not the vents sloped up or down. I immediately tried to shuffle my entire self into the ceiling but the passage was narrow, what with it not actually being made for a person, and panic made me even clumsier than usual.

'Hello?'

The air vent made the voice below tinny and un-familiar but I was fairly certain it was a man. Without a better plan, I steeled myself to put up a fight. Whoever this man was, this man with keys to my apartment and no concern about finding someone inside. Sheesh, it was as though he owned the place . . .

'Angela, are you in there?'

'ALEX!' I shouted, banging on the air vent. 'Alex, I'm in here!'

The echo really did not make me sound ladylike.

'Holy shit.' Obviously I couldn't see him but I could hear his voice was closer and, unless I was very mistaken, he was trying not to laugh. 'What are you doing?'

'Can you please just get me down?' I sniffed, over-whelmed with the emotional charge of the fact that he had come to find me, that I wasn't going to starve to death and be eaten by rats and that I was going to be able to have a wee on a toilet within the next five minutes. 'I left something up here.'

'Gimme a sec,' he replied, definitely laughing this time. 'I think there's a ladder in the hall.'

I wiped away a tear and rocked myself from side to side until I was as close to the edge of the vent as I could get without falling out.

'OK, there's no ladder,' he shouted. 'Can you wait while I go find one?'

'No,' I called back, panic levels rising again. 'Please can you just get me down? Please?'

'Can you fall and I'll catch you?' he suggested.

I shook my head, the tears coming again. Maybe if I kept this up, I wouldn't need to pee after all. There couldn't possibly be that much fluid left in my body after all the sweating and puking that morning.

'Are you shaking your head instead of talking to me?' Alex asked.

'Yes,' I admitted. 'I can't fall. I'll squash you and then you'll die and then everyone will hate me.'

'You won't squash me and I won't die.' I felt a warm hand on my foot. 'And no one hates you.'

'Everyone hates me,' I corrected him. 'How did you find me?'

'I looked everywhere for you in the store,' he said, squeezing my toes. 'But you weren't there so I called your phone and you didn't answer. Eventually I went back to the apartment and you weren't there so I figured you'd be at Jenny's.'

'I didn't get any calls.' I tried to squeeze his fingers back with my toes. It was a little gross. 'I had my phone on all day.'

'Yeah, well, I'm dumb. I was calling your old phone.'

'Oh.' I couldn't really call him on that, I'd done stupider things. Like climb into the ceiling of an empty apartment on my own on a Saturday night. 'So you called Jenny?'

'Yeah.' The hand around my foot tightened. 'I don't know what went down there but she is steaming.'

'I know,' I said. Having had some time to reflect, I felt pretty horrible. 'I messed up. Really messed up. She didn't say anything?'

'She said a bunch of things,' he said gently. 'None of which need repeating right now.'

'Alex, I'm so sorry.' I pressed my face into my hands and groaned. 'I've been such a twat lately. Such a complete twat. I'm sorry I haven't been around. I'm sorry I haven't been listening. I'm sorry I haven't been good enough.'

'Hey, don't,' he replied, tapping my calf. 'I guess I

got ahead of myself in the baby conversation. In that there wasn't even really a conversation.'

'I need to talk to you about that too.' I watched a couple of fat tears plop onto the metal vent and roll towards me. Thank God I hadn't had that wee. 'I went to see a doctor with Jenny the other week and had some tests.'

I felt him stiffen beneath me and really wished I could see his face.

'So, I don't really know anything but she said there might be some problems.' I breathed in, waited a second, and breathed out again. 'With me. Having a baby.'

'What exactly did she say?' he asked, his comforting hand turning into more of a clamp. 'Exactly?'

'Just that things weren't exactly where she'd like them to be?' I tried to remember her exact phrasing but I'd told myself this story over and over so many times I couldn't quite remember the original words. 'She wants me to go in for some tests. She didn't say it won't happen, just that it might not be as easy as it is for some people.'

A couple more tears plopped onto the air vent as my breath fogged up the metal in front of my face. Alex didn't say anything, didn't do anything – at least not anything I was aware of – so I decided to carry on talking. Because that always went so well for me.

'I didn't want to worry you about it yet,' I said. It was more or less true, I just hadn't actually scheduled a time when I did want to worry him about it. 'And I didn't think it was something we were thinking about right away so I just sort of, you know . . .'

'I know,' he said, his grip on my leg loosening a

little. 'But you also know I want to be worried about things. Not just this, all the things.'

'Um . . . then Jesse from work tried to kiss me last night, I think Cici is going to try and get me sacked, Jenny and Louisa aren't talking to me because I said some really horrible things to them and I'm worried that I'm going to pee on you if I don't get out of here in the next five minutes.'

'Jesus,' Alex breathed. 'Shall we just deal with this baby stuff first?'

'You've got five minutes.'

'OK, here's how I see it,' he started. 'I've been thinking about this for a while and I guess, yeah, I didn't mention it because I figured you would get there on your own and I wasn't in any kind of rush. But then Erin got pregnant again and then she had the baby and then Grace came to stay and you just didn't seem interested at all.'

'I was interested,' I protested weakly. 'Sort of.'

'You weren't,' Alex corrected me. 'And that's totally fine. You had so much going on with the magazine and, you know, I get that. I have my music, I know how it feels to want to create something, to want to see it succeed. That's kind of like a baby too, you know?'

'Mm-hmm,' I agreed. He was right, that was exactly how it felt.

'And you can't rush shit like that. But it didn't stop me being a little jealous that the magazine was taking you away from me.'

'Nothing could take me away from you,' I interrupted, slapping the side of the air vent for effect.

'OK, stop hitting things before the whole damn thing falls out of the ceiling.' He slapped my leg just as hard. 'And let me finish before you pee your pants. Like I said, I know it's irrational but I felt a little abandoned. And so I started looking for a new place, thinking maybe it would get you thinking.'

'Crazy idea but it would have been a lot easier to just ask me.'

'Since when was just asking you anything ever the easy option?'

He took my silence as tacit agreement. Which it was.

'And actually, I tried to start the conversation a bunch of times but you always shot me down,' he reminded me. 'So I stopped asking and I thought I'd stop thinking about it.'

'But you didn't?'

'But I didn't,' he agreed. 'And I guess earlier, I was just so tired and so frustrated that I lost my shit. And that's not OK. I'm so sorry. As soon as I walked away, I wanted to come back and make it right but I couldn't find you.'

'We were both tired and stressed. I was a dickhead as well,' I said, gently patting his shoulder with my right foot. At least I hoped it was his shoulder. 'Please don't apologise. I feel horrible about it.'

'Then it never happened,' he replied. 'And we never, ever have to go back to Ikea again. Unless it's just for the hot dogs.'

'Deal,' I replied, feeling the first smile of the day spreading across my face. I wasn't sure whether it was for the hot dogs or my husband but I was happyish and that was enough.

'But about this baby stuff . . .' Oh, Alex wasn't done. Damn him for wanting to have the full deep and meaningful while I couldn't get away. 'We'll make an appointment for the doctor first thing in the morning, right?'

I nodded.

'Are you nodding?'

'Yes.'

'Good.' One more squeeze of the foot for luck. 'And it's not because I'm trying to get you barefoot and pregnant, it's because we need to know. Whatever we decide, whatever you want to do, it's not healthy to have uncertainty hanging over you, babe.'

'I know,' I told the air vent.

'And it doesn't matter what the doctor tells us,' he said. 'You're still you, we're still us. We'll work this out however. And if you decide you never want a baby, regardless of what happens, I don't know, I'll get a puppy or something. There's no rush.'

'It's not that I don't want a baby ever,' I tried to explain the best way I could. 'I think a tiny little version of you would be amazing. I just want to be ready.'

'Then we wait until we're both ready,' Alex promised. 'All I want is you. A baby would be, like, the icing. Really expensive, poop-covered, cries-all-the-time-and-never-lets-us-sleep icing.'

'Way to sell it, Reid,' I choked on a happy sob. 'I really was going to tell you, it's just been one thing after another this week.'

'Yeah, getting back to that,' he said, raising his voice a little. 'What do you mean Jesse from work tried to kiss you?'

'Can you not punch him out?' I asked. 'I don't want you in prison over Christmas. Also, I really don't want to have to hire a new managing editor.'

'DUDES!' I heard the door being flung open and

riotous laughter filling the apartment below me. 'What is going on? This is some kinky shit.'

'Shut up and put up the ladder,' Alex sighed, letting go of my feet. 'Come on, she's stuck.'

'Craig?' I called. 'Is that you?'

'Yeah, I'm doing double duty as a moving guy and superhero today,' he replied, still laughing. 'Nice underwear, Angie.'

'Thank you.' I pressed my burning cheeks against the chilled metal of the vent and tried to be happy that any minute now I would be out of the ceiling and back on solid ground. The fact that I'd never live this down with Craig was something I'd have to deal with later.

CHAPTER FOURTEEN

I should have slept like a log on Saturday night but
instead I spent hours staring up at my new ceiling
while Alex snored quietly beside me. Every time I felt
sleep washing over me, I'd get a sudden jolt, a tension
in my shoulders. My arms and legs felt tight, like I
wanted to shake them, like I wanted to run, so I knew
something was wrong. I never wanted to run. I still
had nightmares about a personal trainer I'd hired for
a week when I started at *Gloss*. On a normal day,
moving house might have been enough to put me under
for a month and the stress of getting stuck in an apartment ceiling would, I imagined, be pretty exhausting.
But when I piled everything up on top of each other,
threw in the row with Alex, the apocalyptic battle with
Jenny and Louisa, my mum's transatlantic rage and the
assorted work dramaramas, it really was all too much.

I rolled over and reached for my phone, hiding
under the covers to avoid waking Alex. There was
still no word from Jenny or Louisa but I knew if I
could just get something out of one of them, I'd feel
better. Even if it was 'fuck off' it would be better than

this complete shut-out. It was still early in Jenny Land, barely even eleven, but Alex had passed out at ten thirty with half a slice of pizza in his lap and I was sure Jenny and Lou would still be awake, probably out somewhere, probably with James. I couldn't pretend it didn't sting that my three friends were getting along so well without me but I also couldn't pretend I was blameless. Maybe I had got too wrapped up in my own problems. I had kind of assumed Jenny and Lou would sort themselves out – after all, they were so much better at that sort of thing than me. Arguing with Alex, on the rare occasions it happened, made me want to call Jenny, buy ice cream and watch four hours of *America's Next Top Model* on her living room floor. Arguing with Jenny made me want to cut off a leg. Arguing with Jenny *and* Louisa made me want to cut off a leg and beat myself to death with the soggy end. It just wasn't right.

Louisa would be mad but I knew she would forgive me eventually. We were practically blood and, aside from that, I knew she was physically incapable of holding a grudge. Jenny on the other hand thrived on grudges. It had been ages since we'd had a blow-up and I had no idea how long it might go on for, especially if she really was serious about this whole baby thing. I opened my text messages and scrolled back, tapping the 'load more' button again and again. I was very happy no one ever saw our conversations. 'Why am I sat in my underwear eating cheese slices on a Sunday morning?' 'I just sent a sext to our dry cleaner by accident. He's into it – what do I do?' 'How many Harry Potter movies is too many Harry Potter movies for an American woman over thirty in one afternoon?'

Yes, she was insane but I loved her. I was a bit mad

we couldn't go to that dry cleaner anymore but still. I really didn't know what I would do without her.

'I'm sorry. Can you call me?'

It was a very simple text but for some reason, despite my alleged profession, it took me nearly twenty minutes to get it right. As soon as I pressed send, I felt better. At least well enough to get out of bed, eat half a slice of cold pizza and have a wee. And that was enough.

'Bagel delivery.' Alex appeared from behind a pile of boxes bigger than him and threw a small paper parcel into my lap. 'Have you actually unpacked a single box?'

I nodded, stuffing the bagel into my mouth and promising myself that I would go to yoga on Monday. I pointed towards the bedroom and chewed.

'Shoes,' I said from behind my hand. 'Shoes and handbags.'

'I'm glad the important stuff got figured out,' he replied. 'And now books?'

'I can't settle until all the stuff is on the shelves,' I explained. 'I'll feel better.'

'OK.' He held up his hands and began to walk away. 'Whatever works for you. I'll be in the bedroom putting away my one bag of clothes.'

'That's not something to be proud of,' I shouted after him, wrapping up the rest of the bagel and looking over at my phone for what had to be the hundredth time that morning. Jenny still hadn't replied and I hadn't heard a thing from Louisa. It was horrible.

'Hey.' Alex reappeared above my boxes, a sympathetic smile on his face. 'Until you get this Jenny thing figured out, you're totally useless to me. Go see her.'

'But we have so much stuff to do.' I pointed weakly at the bookshelves.

'I'm translating that into, "I'm a total pussy and I'm scared that she's still mad at me." Am I right?' he asked.

'Maybe,' I sulked. 'I text her. She hasn't replied.'

'Because she's probably still really mad at you,' he said. He was such a perceptive man. 'But she's not going to get less pissed off while you guys aren't speaking to each other. You know Jenny, she's just gonna stew. It's a Band-Aid situation, Angela, you gotta rip this one right off.'

'I know,' I admitted. Maybe cutting off my own leg would be easier than apologising. It wasn't like I used it that often. 'But we really do have so much left to do. I've got to work tomorrow and then Mum and Dad get here on Tuesday—'

'And it will be a ton easier for me to do it alone than having you moping in a corner, pretending to stack books.' He stepped over one of the smaller boxes and pulled me up to my feet. 'You have a big day at work tomorrow, right? So don't let this get in the way. Go see her.'

'Have you got any protective padding?' I asked, resting my head against his chest and giving Alex a huge hug. 'You know the stuff they put on when they're training police dogs?'

'You'll be fine,' he promised. 'And when you get back, the cable will be working.'

'Really?' I looked up with sparkling eyes. Yes, Angela, there was a Santa Claus.

'Really really,' he said, kissing me once and then breaking the hug. 'Now go before I get other ideas.'

'I'd say save those ideas for later.' I reached up on

my tiptoes to kiss him once more before slapping him on the arse and handing him my bagel. 'But if the telly's going to be on, you might struggle.'

It took a lot longer on the subway to get to Jenny's place from our new apartment but I was glad of the unplanned procrastination. I had run over a dozen different apologies, a few potential bribes and considered leaving the country. By the time I got to Lexington Avenue, I had settled on a straight-up 'I'm sorry', combined with the leftover peanut butter M&Ms in my handbag, and then accepting whatever torrent of abuse followed. It wasn't possible that either of them could make me feel worse than I already did anyway.

There didn't seem a lot of point in ringing the buzzer – she wasn't answering my texts, she was hardly likely to buzz me up – so I used my key, climbed the stairs and steeled myself. But even having spent an entirely sleepless night and a forty-five-minute train ride readying myself for this, I could not possibly have been prepared for what I walked in on. The apartment was a disaster. When I'd arrived on Saturday, I'd been a little bit sad at the lack of Christmas decorations. There was the little white fake tree with its pink baubles that Jenny put up every year but aside from that, she really hadn't gone big on the festivities. Apparently that had all changed at some point in the last twenty-four hours. As had the apartment's residents. Everywhere I looked there were people I either vaguely recognised or had never seen before in my life draped over the sofa, crashed out on the floor or, in one instance, puking in the kitchen sink. Nice. Every available surface was covered in red plastic cups and glitter. There was tinsel hanging from the light fixtures and someone had gone really heavy on a neon pink reindeer motif. Not my taste in seasonal décor but at least she was trying.

'Jenny?' I called out, picking my way through the stirring bodies on the floor. 'Lou?'

Someone on the sofa groaned but it wasn't anyone I knew. A couple of girls wrapped around each other on the armchair by the window looked like a couple of girls from Jenny's office but since they were wearing elf costumes instead of office-appropriate ensembles, it was really hard to tell. I sighed. No good ever came from waking up in an elf costume. Clearly there had been something of a shindig here and I wasn't quite sure how that married up with Grace taking a nap when I left. Abandoning my search of the living room after tripping over an empty bottle of Jägermeister, I stopped trying to be quite so careful and marched through the bodies and into my old bedroom. Instead of finding my childhood best friend and her lovely toddler, I found an unconscious James Jacobs and a blow-up Father Christmas, both, thankfully, fully dressed.

'I should have known you'd be behind this,' I said, tapping his face gently. James groaned, snored and rolled over. Apparently a gentle tap wasn't going to be enough.

'Ow! Fucking hell.'

But a decent slap was.

'Where is Louisa?' I demanded, all sense of contrition forgotten. 'And Grace?'

'Not here.' He held out a hand to shield his eyes from the non-existent sun in the darkened room and smacked his lips together a couple of times. 'God, I taste like a rat's arse.'

'I don't want to know how you know that.' I took

265

a cue from his blatant hangover and pulled up the blinds. Dear God, that room was disgusting. 'Where did they go?'

'I don't know, I'm not their keeper.' James tried to push his hair back off his face but his fingers got stuck in something sticky. Gross. 'Jenny was pissed off after you left. We decided to have some drinks, then she called some people and Louisa took off with the baby. She wasn't in the mood for it.'

'Lou or the nineteen-month-old baby?' I asked. 'I can't imagine why Grace wasn't up for shots. You seriously don't know where she went?'

I pulled out my phone and immediately dialled Lou. And to think that I thought I felt awful before I arrived.

'Well, wherever she is, she isn't picking up,' I told the shell of a man on the bed before me. 'She'd better be OK.'

'Funny how she didn't come and stay with you, isn't it?' he muttered into his pillow, earning a second slap for his troubles. 'Ange, I've got a massive hangover and, honestly, unless you're going to make me a cup of tea and get me a sausage sarnie, you need to piss off before I kill you.'

'Excellent parenting skills you're showing here,' I said, trying Louisa's mobile again. 'You two are going to be brilliant.'

I heard James making some sort of sobbing sound when I slammed his door, the boom echoing through the apartment and seemingly reviving some of the hangers-on in the living room. But they weren't the only ones I managed to wake.

'Who is making all that noise?' Jenny opened her bedroom door and clung to the door frame, looking as though she might collapse at any second. Her hair was everywhere and a tight little red jersey dress was riding up her arse to reveal a pair of black knickers. At least she was wearing some – that was progress in a way. 'Angie?'

'Jenny, where's Louisa?' I asked, kicking a man old enough to know better, sprawled out on the floor in front of me as he grabbed at my ankle. 'What went on last night?'

'We had a party. Chill.' She scrunched up her face and turned away as though she'd seen something upsetting. I couldn't wait until I got her in front of a mirror. 'Uh, she said she needed to do something . . . I guess she didn't come back.'

'Can't think why,' I replied.

'This didn't happen until way later,' she said, as though it was a perfectly rational excuse. 'Why are you here? Didn't you say everything you needed to say yesterday?'

'I actually came to apologise.' I was trying very hard not to sound completely sanctimonious but it was difficult to stand there and say, *I'm sorry Jenny, I'm sure you'll make a wonderful mother,* when there were six strangers in her living room, dry-heaving. 'But now I'm a bit worried about Louisa.'

'Who's worried about me?' The front door opened and I heard the telltale squeaky wheels of a pushchair behind me. 'Oh my God, what happened?'

'I had a party,' Jenny replied weakly.

'Jenny had a party,' I confirmed, crossing my arms and then immediately dropping them back by my sides. I was still on thin ice until I'd got all my apologies out. 'Where were you? I've been trying to call you.'

'My battery died.' She held up a dead iPhone while

Grace clambered out of her pushchair, delighted at the chaos in front of her. 'I went to stay at a hotel, give Jenny and James a bit of peace.'

I watched as Grace began poking the blond man in the back of the head repeatedly, probably waiting a moment too long before scooping her up in my arms.

'Anala,' she said happily, immediately resuming poking.

Like all martyrs, I endured. 'Why didn't you call me?' I asked, bouncing Gracie awkwardly on my hip and ignoring the stirring drunks on the floor. 'You could have stayed with us.'

'Didn't much feel like popping over after our chat in the afternoon,' she replied, instinctively tearing off a length of kitchen roll and mopping up an upset bottle of Bud.

'I came to apologise,' I said. 'I was bang out of order yesterday. You'll do whatever you need to do in your own time and I will never, ever say shit about it, ever again.'

I paused, looked around the room and then back at the half-human version of Jenny in the corner.

'And Jenny should totally have a baby, right away.'

'Oh, fuck you,' she groaned, turning towards the bathroom. 'I'm gonna puke.'

'I felt so bad disappearing off to a hotel last night but she was in such a bad mood,' Lou whispered while I continued to dodge Grace's barrage of tiny, sharp attacks. 'And Grace was fussing, I couldn't get her to rest, so I just thought, you know, a night of quiet might help.'

'Did it?'

'Didn't bloody get it, did I?' she said with a yawn. I noticed the dark circles had returned. 'Madam would not sleep for love nor money. Honestly, I thought I was doing this on my own back at home but I don't think I realised how much it helps just to have another human being in the house.'

'Right.' I resisted the urge to jump up and down shouting *CALL TIM!* and instead gave her a very understanding nod.

'Don't look at me like that,' she yawned. 'I'm going to call him as soon as I've charged my phone.'

'Nothing to do with me,' I replied, opening my eyes and my mouth as far as they would go at the baby to try and avoid inappropriate smiling. At least *she* thought I was funny. 'Do whatever you need to do. I'll be here.'

'At the minute it looks like I need to clean up,' Lou replied.

Even though this was as far removed from her mess as it was possible to be, I knew she was itching to get the rubber gloves out and put everything in a bin bag. Possibly some of the partygoers too.

'Hey, cute baby.' One of the girls on the armchair opened her eyes and pointed towards me and Gracie. I looked at my goddaughter who rolled her eyes and shook her head.

'You are very wise,' I told her. She nodded.

'Right, everybody out,' Louisa shouted. I was always impressed at the volume she was able to muster up when she was pissed off. 'Party's over. You all need to go home or at least get out of this one.'

Louisa began walking around the room, shaking people who really didn't want to be shaken and filling up a giant black sack as she went. Of course she already knew where Jenny kept them. The girls on the armchair rose first, seemingly brought back to life by the fear of having to help clear up. They were followed by the girl and her gay who had been crashing on the sofa and a very sorry-looking redhead who looked more and more likely to vom with every step. Christmas parties really were the best. I attempted to help by giving the blond man on the floor another kick, picking up his trainers and tossing them out the door.

'They're my shoes,' he protested, still flat on his back. 'I need them.'

'You'd better go and get them then,' I replied while Grace blew raspberries. 'Merry Christmas.'

'Merry Christmas,' he muttered as he crawled out on all fours. 'Can you ask James to call me?'

'Nope,' I replied, slamming the door shut after him.

'Can you please quit banging doors.' Jenny tiptoed back into the living room as though putting a full foot down on the floor might make too much noise for her poor head. Her curls were tethered to the top of her head and her face had been scrubbed clean. I knew she'd hate to hear me say it but I always thought this was when she looked her most beautiful. Her make-up was always flawless and her hair should probably be considered one of the Seven Wonders of the World but without all the make-up, all the drama, she was just so incredibly pretty. 'Where did everyone go?'

'AWAY!' Grace shouted, leaping onto the sofa and bouncing up and down. I looked at Lou, who looked at Jenny, who shrugged. After what Grace had just walked in on, it did seem a bit pointless to tell her no now.

'Don't touch anything, Gracie,' Louisa warned before scooping up the Jägermeister bottle. 'I don't want you to get hepatitis.'

'No one here has . . .' Jenny began to defend her

friends but her words seemed to fade away. 'Yeah, don't let her touch anything.'

An hour later, with Grace completely unconscious in her pushchair, the four alleged adults in our party were squished into a booth at Scotty's Diner. Jenny and James propped each other up as they mainlined cup after cup of coffee while Louisa and I bartered with each other on the menu.

'Well, if you get fries, we can share,' she suggested, sipping her tea in a far more ladylike fashion than our environment required.

'Or what if I get a side of steamed veggies?' I asked. 'Or a side salad. And you get the fries?'

'I do believe I lost a few brain cells last night so you'll forgive me for asking,' James cut in, pressing his fingers into his temples. 'Are we just pretending yesterday didn't happen then?'

'Oh, can we?' Louisa perked up immeasurably. 'Can we do that?'

'Sure, let's all bottle shit up until we have a stroke,' Jenny said, pouring more sugar into her cup. 'That's super healthy.'

'I came over to apologise.' I snatched the sugar out of her hand and placed it out of her reach, ignoring her death stare. White sugar made Jenny crazy. Crazier. 'And I'm still sorry, I shouldn't have kicked off.'

'No, you shouldn't,' she replied, stirring her coffee. 'I can't believe you sometimes. You're, like, completely incapable of seeing anything from anyone else's position. You don't want a baby, so I shouldn't want a baby. You can't handle a baby, so you think I can't handle a baby.'

'It's not that I don't think you can handle a baby,'

I said, trying to remain calm and measured and not just burst into tears. Yay, confrontation on a Sunday morning! 'It's more that I was worried that you hadn't really thought about how having a baby would completely change your life.'

She dropped her spoon and let it clatter on the table, much to James's dismay. 'Are you serious? Do you think I'm dumb?'

'A baby is for life, not just for Christmas?' I offered.

'I think that's dogs, Ange,' Lou whispered in my ear.

'I know a baby is forever,' Jenny said. 'That's why I want to do it now, before I get any older. How hard has this been for Erin? I don't want to have to wreck my entire body by busting out a million kids when I'm forty. I want to be able to actually enjoy them.'

'I totally get that,' I replied, nodding. 'It just seems like you're going about it in a really difficult way. But yeah, you're right, I'm not ready for kids so the idea of having to have one on my own, doing it as a single parent scares me absolutely shitless.'

'I wouldn't be on my own.' She pointed at the desperately hungover thirty-something man who was currently groaning face first on the table beside her. He wrapped his arms over his head and sobbed.

'Oh dear.' Lou frowned and pretended to busy herself with her handbag.

'You don't think you want to wait a little while and see if you meet the man of your dreams before you get knocked up?' I knew I was risking a slap but I had to ask.

'Ooh, I think that happened in a film!' Louisa's head popped up, looking for confirmation. 'In fact, I think it had Jennifer Lopez in it, you know, the other one.'

'We don't discuss her and we will not discuss that movie,' Jenny declared. 'Not all of us are as lucky as you, Angie. Not all of us will meet our soulmate.'

I opened my mouth but there weren't actually any words waiting to come out.

'Ever,' Jenny added softly.

'Oh, Jenny, don't.' Louisa reached across the table and squeezed Jenny's hand. She was much braver than me. 'That's a silly thing to say.'

'No, it isn't,' she said with a sad smile. 'It's a realistic thing to say. I'm not stupid, I'm cute, I'm successful, I'm freaking awesome in bed—'

'All good to know,' James mumbled from inside his protective arm shield.

'But I'm still single.' She gave James a look before turning back to the smug marrieds across the table. Well, that was me feeling adequately horrible. 'Do you know how many awesome single women there are in New York City? So many. And so many are younger than me, hotter than me and prepared to settle for less than I am. So this seems like a good solution to my problem.'

She turned to look at James again.

'Maybe it doesn't look that great right now but really, when you think about the bigger picture . . .'

'I know I can't go back in time and take back what I said,' I began, briefly wondering whether or not it would be possible to talk to the BBC about me becoming the new Dr Who, although they probably already had someone in mind. 'But I can say new stuff and then we can just ignore all that horrible stuff, yeah?'

'You have such a great command of the English language,' Jenny said, resting her chin on her hand and staring at me. 'It's no wonder you're a writer.'

'I think we all said some things we didn't mean,' Louisa added, playing the peacekeeper as always. 'And as much as I hate it, you were sort of right about me. I did need to call Tim.'

'Did?'

'I called him last night,' she nodded. 'Hence the dead phone battery.'

'And?'

'He says he's not having an affair.' I felt relief coming off her in waves, even if she didn't seem ready to admit that she believed him. 'And he wants me to come home.'

'The asshole didn't even realise you were out of the country for nearly a week! Let him sweat.' Jenny fanned herself with her giant, laminated menu. 'Is it hot in here?'

'No,' I told her, turning back to Lou. 'What did you say?'

'What else could I say?' she asked. 'I've got to go home sooner or later. Gracie needs her dad and, quite frankly, I need him too. I know I've had you two and Erin helped out so much but it's just too hard to be out here on my own with her. I never thought I'd say this a week ago but I miss my life. I just want everything back how it was.'

'So when are you going?' I rocked the pushchair back and forth, trying not to look so upset. Of course she had to go home. Sniff.

'Yeah, that's a bit of a problem.' She let out a tiny laugh and tapped a fingernail against the side of her teacup. 'I looked at flights back home and they are extortionate over the next couple of days.'

'You don't say.'

'Something about a Christmas rush, would you

believe?' she sighed. 'So it looks like I have properly cocked up and might have to stay for Christmas. If you'll have me?'

'Of course I will,' I said immediately. 'Is Tim OK with it?'

'Tim is not OK with it,' she replied. 'But we both messed up here. It's actually really cheap if I fly on Christmas Day but I just can't bring myself to put Grace on a plane to eat turkey off a plastic tray.'

I felt myself shudder and instinctively pulled the pushchair closer towards me.

'That cannot happen.' I was quite insistent. 'We'll sort it out. I'll ask if we can get corporate rates at work or something, I know some people have done that.'

'Doesn't Tim work for a bank or something?' Jenny, never one to understand the value of money, looked confused. 'Aren't you, like, loaded?'

'Working for a bank doesn't mean you're loaded,' Louisa explained awkwardly. Talking about money at the breakfast table was not something she was brought up to do. It was terribly gauche. 'And we've mortgaged ourselves up the arse with the house. And, you know, I might have done some light credit card damage while I've been here. To three different credit cards. My mum's going to go mental.'

'You know you're welcome to stay.' I couldn't imagine how much she was regretting spending five hundred dollars on leather shorts at that exact moment. 'We'll sort the spare room out.'

'And Sadie won't be back, you can still stay with me,' Jenny added. 'No more parties, I promise.'

'Hmm, no impromptu parties once you're on the baby train,' Louisa replied, flicking her eyebrows skywards. 'You'll be too tired for them anyway.'

'I'm too tired to live,' she said, slumping onto James's shoulder. 'It's good, though, right? Get all of this out of my system?'

'I think I'm about to get everything I drank last night out of my system,' James muttered. 'I need more coffee.'

He was staring at his cutlery so hard I was worried he was trying to bend his spoon.

'You all right there, Uri?' I asked.

'The trick is to realise that there is no spoon,' Louisa added.

'You really are going to make the best parents,' I said. 'This is going to be brilliant.'

'I'm not about to take her in the back and knock her up after brunch,' he replied. 'There's a lot to sort out.'

'There's a lot to sort out,' Jenny echoed with a confident nod. But I could already see a glimmer of doubt in her eyes. I just wasn't sure whether it was in the entire plan or her most recent choice of baby daddy. 'I'm too tired to fight, that doesn't mean I'm not still pissed with you.'

'I know,' I said. 'I was a dick. A baby isn't the same as a handbag.'

'A Birkin isn't a handbag,' she gasped, pressing her hands to her heart. 'How many times do I have to tell you?'

'You're not helping your case here, Jen.' Louisa frantically swiped a hand in front of her throat, signalling for Jenny to quit while she was ahead. 'As someone who has already destroyed her own vagina squeezing one of the little monsters into this world, I would have to say, you probably really need to want it more than you want a handbag. Or a Birkin. Or anything.'

'Yeah, whatever.' Jenny winced as the short order

cook bellowed out an order behind us. 'Just don't be an asshole, Clark.'

'I'm just trying to be supportive,' I said, smiling at the waiter as he sloped over. 'I can't wait to hold your hand through all the antenatal classes. I'm totally going to tell people we're a couple.'

'No one would believe you, I'm way too hot for you,' she said, kicking me under the table. And with a bruised ankle and a warm heart, I knew I was forgiven. 'But I'll think about it. You do buy the good coffee.'

'Only the best for my love,' I replied, kicking her back.

'What'll it be, gang?' The ancient Italian waiter parked himself and his dodgy hip in front of our table and pulled an order pad out of his apron.

'Hey, Scotty.' Jenny gave him a tired smile.

'I'm not Scotty,' he replied gruffly. 'How many times?'

'Oh, Scotty,' she said, shaking her head. 'So many, many more.'

CHAPTER FIFTEEN

Monday morning began the way all Monday mornings began, with me rushing around like a maniac, trying to dry my hair without waking Alex and still finding time to eat a very greasy egg and cheese sandwich. The only difference was that this Monday morning Alex had been AWOL when my alarm went off at seven in our new house. I would have called the police to report a kidnapping – he was incapable of getting out of bed before noon unless someone held a gun to his head – but it was my first official day on the job, the first Monday morning *sans* Mary, and I was determined to make a go of it. I found a note on the kitchen counter telling me he was going to be out all day and he'd be home for dinner. I frowned, read it again and set it back on the counter. He was just out. He almost certainly hadn't left me a note in the kitchen and nicked off to another country on Christmas Eve. No one did things like that. Except me. And Louisa. But really, how likely was he to make it a triple? Ignoring the little voice that was doing a dance in the back of my mind and shouting 'TOTALLY

LIKELY', I grabbed my satchel and ran out the door before I had time to overthink things. If I could turn around the Jenny/Louisa fiasco, surely I could manage to send one little weekly magazine to print without too much bother?

At eight a.m. I was the first in the office, which, as far as I was concerned, gave me carte blanche to start playing Mariah Carey very loudly as soon as I walked through the door. It was Christmas Eve and that meant that the season had officially begun and no one could bitch me out for it. The night before, Alex had agreed that my flashing reindeer nose jumper might be 'a bit much' for a busy day and that maybe I could save that for Christmas Day, possibly at home, but I wasn't letting go of my festive spirit that easily. I was decked out in a gorgeous red and green striped cashmere sweater that I'd purchased for an obscene amount of money last time I stopped by J.Crew and a pair of high-waisted black shorts that Jenny had insisted I would never wear, and I was happy to have proved her wrong. Even if this was the first time they'd been out of the wardrobe since I bought them six months ago. Combined with black tights, little black Rag & Bone ankle boots and far too much mascara, I was really quite pleased with myself. Which immediately scared me to death. Because if that wasn't a sure sign that things were about to go spectacularly badly, I didn't know what was.

We always started early on Mondays, and because everyone wanted as much time off as possible over the holidays and possibly because they were a little bit worried about me being in charge (but not nearly as worried as I was), everyone had worked like a demon the week before to make sure press day ran as smoothly as possible. By nine, every desk in the office was occupied. Every desk except for one.

Jesse's.

I'd had my eye on it ever since people started to wander in half an hour or so ago. He was usually one of the earliest around on Mondays – it was his time to shine after all. Without a managing editor, nothing got signed off. This time last week, he was on his third coffee and walking around the office looking over people's shoulders with his red pen.

'Hey, Megan,' I shouted, as his desk neighbour wandered past my office. She spun round to look at me with a biscuit in her hand and fear in her eyes. 'Have you seen Jesse?'

'Oh, thank God,' she breathed out, holding up the gingerbread man. 'I thought these were a test and I was going to get fired.'

'Really?' I tried to forget that I had already eaten three.

'I used to work at *Vogue*,' she explained. 'Jesse isn't in yet. Do you think something happened?'

'It's not like him,' I admitted, not wanting her to worry but worrying myself sick. 'I'll give him a call.'

'Great. I'll get started on the first pages anyway.' She bit off the head of her gingerbread man. 'Beauty should be with you in, like, half an hour.'

'Brillbags,' I said, picking up the phone and then doing absolutely nothing else. What was I going to say to him? *Hi, Jesse, just wondering when you were planning on getting your arse into the office, and, by the way, I still can't believe you tried to lay one on me in the taxi the other night, you massive bell-end.* If only

I had someone who could do awkward things for me that I did not wish to do for myself . . .

With the receiver still in my hand, I pressed the intercom button on my phone and waited.

'Yes, boss?'

'Cici.' Every time I said her name a fairy died. Somewhere out there a fairy died. 'Can you call Jesse Benson and find out where he is?'

'Absolutely, boss,' she replied.

I waited for her to call, watching from inside my office, eyes trained on my new assistant while I nibbled on a fingernail. It wasn't nearly as tasty as a gingerbread man. Since I was shuffled away in a corner, or to be more accurate half a corner, as long as I kept my door open, I could see almost everyone. Of course, I wasn't often allowed to keep my door open because my design sensibilities offended Mary. That and my singing voice.

'Hello, Jesse?' Cici said into the handset. 'It's Cici, Angela's assistant? At *Gloss*? The magazine you're supposed to work at?'

Ouch.

'Oh really?' she pulled a face and looked over at me with a little wave. 'Well, that sounds awful. I can't imagine how awful it must be to be ill at Christmas time.'

She nodded a couple of times and then rolled her eyes. It was something that had crossed my mind before, but sometimes she really did remind me of Jenny. It was quite frightening how someone you loved and someone you were terrified of could be so similar.

'Sounds dreadful,' she said. 'Do you know what else is dreadful? Getting fired at Christmas time. It's press

281

day. You don't call in sick on press day. In fact, you didn't even call in sick, did you?'

'Cici!' I shook my head, making mad 'cut' motions with my hand. 'Don't!'

'Yeah, really?' She was too busy shouting down the phone while the rest of the office looked on in stunned silence. 'Then I'll take that as your resignation. Happy holidays.'

She was carefully replacing the handset and blithely turning back to her monitor as I screeched to a halt by her desk.

'What just happened?' I asked, my heart beating hard and fast. 'What did he say?'

'Something about food poisoning,' she scoffed, eyes still on the screen, as though it wasn't even important enough to bother with eye contact. 'Clearly lying, clearly hungover. And then he was incredibly rude. I don't think he'll be coming back in any time soon.'

'Cici, you can't fire people,' I said, breathless. 'We need Jesse. All I asked you to do was to find out where he was.'

'And I did,' she said, looking up at me with big blue eyes. A complete lack of conscience combined with no concept of the real world made for a distinct lack of dark circles. There wasn't a fine line in sight. 'He was at home when he should have been here. He's clearly not a team player. Dead wood.'

'But you can't sack people, Cici,' I said again. '*I* can't even sack people. There are systems and warnings and HR and lots of annoying paperwork.'

'Technically he quit,' she rationalised. 'So I've saved you all that paperwork. See? I'm super efficient.'

I had no words. The rest of the office was staring

at me but no one had said a word since Cici had picked up the phone.

'A leader needs to make difficult choices,' Cici said, lowering her voice slightly. 'You can't have people taking advantage on your first day in charge, Angela. You don't want to look weak, do you?'

I wasn't sure if it was advice or a threat.

'I will call Jesse back,' I replied as evenly as possible. 'And explain that you had the wrong end of the stick. And you will apologise when he comes into work after the holidays.'

'I don't have a stick.' She looked puzzled. 'Is this a cute British thing?'

'I really wish I had a stick,' I said, trying to look vaguely menacing although I was sure it came off as more constipated.

'Oh, you,' she called as I stalked back into my office. 'I'll get you another coffee, I think you're tired.'

'I'm fine,' I barked. 'Megan, can you come in here, please?'

The little brunette jumped up from her seat and ran into my office, stuck to my side as I shut the door with slightly more force than I had intended. It wasn't quite a slam but it definitely had a distinct air of miffed-ness about it.

'Holy shit, Angie, did she just fire Jesse?' Megan looked horrified.

'She doesn't have the authority to fire Jesse,' I reassured her. 'Honestly, I don't even think I have the authority to fire Jesse. But until I talk to him, I think we've got to assume he's not going to be coming in today. Can you have someone set up the system so I can start approving the pages?'

'Yeah, about that . . .' She wove her fingers together

and twisted them awkwardly. 'We're having a little trouble with it.'

'Trouble?'

Meep.

'IT are coming down, like, any second now,' she said quickly. 'It should be fixed super soon. The pages don't want to load or something. It's stuck on last week's issue.'

'Doesn't the whole company use the same system?' I asked, a trickle of cold desperation running down my spine.

'Everyone's set up independently,' she explained. 'In case this happens. I could maybe call Jesse and see if he knows how to fix it?'

'I'll call him,' I said with a sigh. 'What do we do if the system doesn't start working soon?'

'We'll go with hard copies,' she said. 'Old school. I'll make mock-ups of each page and fix a sign-off sheet for everyone to initial once they've checked them.'

'Right.' I sat back in my chair and cursed the day Mary Stein met Bob Spencer. Bobbity Bob Bastard Bob. 'Let's start doing that now. No one wants to be here all night. And let me know what IT says.'

'Angela,' Megan said, looking at the floor and sniffing, 'is she really going to be sticking around?'

'Who knows?' It didn't take a genius to work out whom she was talking about. Thankfully. 'Honestly, I can't see it. But you don't need to worry, she's not going to fire anyone and if she even looks at you the wrong way, tell me.'

'It's so hard to believe she's related to Delia,' she said in a whisper. No one wanted to be on Cici's shit list. 'I was talking to some of the girls who worked with her on *The Look* and they told me all the shit she used to do up there.'

'She's not going to be doing it down here,' I promised, almost sounding as though I believed it myself.

'I don't want to be an asshole,' Megan smiled awkwardly, 'but if she wants to, who's gonna stop her? She's a Spencer.'

'It'll be fine,' I replied. 'She's a Spencer, she's not Superman. I'm watching her.'

The look on Megan's face did not convince me that the team had faith in my leadership abilities.

'When people told you those stories, did anyone tell you about the time I kicked her arse in London?' I asked.

'Yes,' she said, doubtfully. 'But I wasn't sure. You're so nice.'

'No, I'm English,' I replied. 'Americans often get the two confused.'

Unsurprisingly, Jesse's phone went to voicemail sixteen times in between nine a.m. and midday. By lunchtime, I had given up calling and resorted to sending a short but not terribly sweet email that suggested he give me a call and that I would see him in the office the following day. When he didn't reply to that either, I went for a brief sweep of social media but he had gone to full radio silence so he was either genuinely sick, genuinely pissed off or dead. I didn't know which to hope for as none of them made me feel like I was going to the top of Santa's 'nice' list.

On the upside, the crisis had really pulled the office together. A lot of people, me included, had never sent a magazine to print without our online approval system so Megan's mock-up of the magazine made for a fun novelty. By one o'clock, we were already halfway through the approvals, way further than the average Monday, and whether it was because everyone was shitting themselves or because they just wanted to go home, I didn't care. Even Cici seemed to be pulling her weight after the drama. Or at least she'd been answering the phones, taking messages and hadn't tried to fire anyone in the last three hours. When the intercom buzzed, I answered without looking, assuming she was offering to get me my fourth coffee of the day. I was already shaking from ODing on caffeine but every minute she was in Starbucks was a minute she wasn't in the office.

'Angela, you have some visitors.' Her voice was clipped and cold, making me look up through the glass wall. 'They don't have an appointment and I have explained that you're very busy.'

Held at her desk, I saw a very, very annoyed-looking Jenny, accompanied by Louisa and Grace, both seeming to be struggling to keep their fists under control. And she hadn't even been involved in last summer's brawl, bless her tiny, cotton socks.

'They can come in,' I replied as quickly as I could. 'They can always come in. You don't need to buzz me.'

I watched her quirk an eyebrow before hanging up and waving my friends into my office.

'I'm not sure about this, Angie,' Jenny said, flinging the door open and not even waiting for Louisa to shut it before she let rip. 'Once a psycho, always a psycho. I don't care if they upped her meds, no amount of Xanax can chill a bitch like that.'

'She hasn't upped her meds.' I stood to give them

all a quick hug. 'She went to India. And I know. Everything. All of it. What's up?'

'So, merry Christmas.' Jenny paused and prompted Grace to give me half a chocolate chip cookie and a grin. 'We know you're totally super crazy busy and that it's press day and this makes us complete and utter assholes but could you watch Gracie for an hour?'

'Say if you can't,' Louisa butted in before I even had a chance to explain why it was impossible. I noticed she was in her jeans and sensible shoes again, her ponytail back in place. 'I know today is your mad day. We can just go home and do Christmas things, it's fine really. We could make paper chains.'

I couldn't imagine for a second that Grace knew what paper chains were but the very thought of it was enough to make her bottom lip start to quiver.

'It is a bit mad, yeah,' I said, feeling horrible for taking the cookie. Which I absolutely was not giving back regardless of the lip wobble. 'Where did you want to go that you can't take madam?'

'James got us last-minute tickets to the Christmas thing at Radio City Music Hall,' she explained. 'But Grace won't sit through it, I know she won't. I mean, she's about ready for her nap but if she wakes up and screams blue murder, it'll be a nightmare.'

'They're front row, centre,' Jenny added, waving two tickets in my face. As though that would help her case. I couldn't be more jealous. 'And Erin is out of town at Thomas's parents' place or we totally would have asked her to take Gracie for a couple of hours.'

'We did have a full cookie for you but, well, she ate it.' Lou looked so apologetic and I felt like such a twat. 'Don't worry, we don't have to go. I'm sure James can find someone else to take the tickets.'

I looked at Grace, her face covered in cookie and her eyes drooping in her pushchair. She waved at me lazily and stuck out her tongue. Behind the pushchair Jenny and Lou, wrapped up in scarves, gloves and stylish but not terribly warm-looking coats, huddled together, the light of hope still in Jenny's eyes. Damn them, they knew I couldn't say no to a Christmas-themed activity. After all, if she was going to sleep, what was the difference? I was going to be stuck to my desk all afternoon anyway, and it might be nice to have some sensible English company for a change, even if that company was under two years old and occasionally pooped itself.

'She can hang out here,' I said, immediately regretting my decision. 'What time will you be back?'

'Four, four thirty tops.' Jenny clapped her leather gloves together and did a little dance. 'We'll bring you some shit, I promise. I'll kidnap a Rockette for you.'

'Just go,' I said, rushing them out of the office before I changed my mind. 'Have fun. I'm jealous.'

'She'll go right to sleep,' Lou said, ignoring the fact that Jenny was stood by Cici's desk making hissing noises. Cici was studiously ignoring the two of them and staring at her nails. 'Don't give her any sugar.'

'No sugar, check.' I saluted and waved them into the lifts. 'See you later.'

Ignoring the look on my assistant's face, I turned back towards my office to see the previously sleepy Grace leaping out of her pushchair and grabbing the remaining half-cookie from my desk and shoving it into her face.

'Indian giver,' I said, crossing my arms over my chest.

'That's offensive to native Americans,' Cici said over

288

my shoulder before handing me the updated mock-up magazine. 'Fashion pages. Megan needs them back in fifteen minutes.'

I nodded and tried to pretend Grace wasn't climbing up the bookshelf and throwing herself onto the armchair in the corner of my office as we spoke.

'I might need twenty,' I replied. 'She's nuts.'

'Let me look after her,' Cici offered, crouching down in front of the armchair and clapping at Grace with wide eyes. 'I love children.'

Yeah, right.

'Is that for lunch or dinner?' I asked.

'Really, I have a way with kids.' She made goldfish faces at my goddaughter while she spoke and held out her arms for a hug. Grace immediately leapt onto her new playmate, grabbed a handful of hair extensions and pulled. Hard. I winced, waiting for her to chuck the toddler out of the eighteenth-floor window, but instead all Cici did was laugh. A genuine, sweet tinkle of a laugh, not her raucous LOL in real life guffaw but an actual, honest to God chuckle. I pinched myself and snapped back to reality.

'She's fine,' I said, marching over and grabbing Gracie out of her arms and getting a slap in the face for my trouble. Someone needed to teach that girl some manners. And it wasn't going to be me. 'We'll be fine.'

No matter how tempting it was to palm Grace-sitting duties off on someone else when I was busy, Louisa would end me if I gave her baby to someone who made Cruella De Vil look like an animal rights activist.

'I'll go get her some juice.' Cici stood up and smoothed out the tugs and pulls in her outfit. 'And check back in twenty.'

'That would be great,' I replied, just as Grace sneezed on my shoulder. The amount of crap that came out of someone so small . . . 'But we'll be fine.'

Cici nodded and shrugged, leaving us alone in the office.

'We'll be just fine, Gracie,' I told her as I wiped down my sticky cashmere. 'You would have to get up to some pretty evil shit before I asked Cici for help. And you're not going to do that, are you?'

She sat prettily on the edge of the armchair and shook her head, smiling and swinging her pink T-bar-clad feet back and forth.

'Of course not,' I said, sitting back at my desk with the magazine mock-up. 'You're a bloody angel.'

'Cici . . .' Not even fifteen minutes later, I threw myself around my office door, panting. 'I need your help.'

There weren't many sentences in the English language I'd never imagined myself saying but that was one of them. My shiny new assistant jumped out of her chair and came running as fast as her Louboutins would carry her, which was actually surprisingly fast.

'What's wrong?' she asked, closing the door behind us.

In lieu of more words, I pointed to the corner of my office that Grace was currently terrorising. Everything that had ever been on a shelf was now on the floor, pages had been torn out of magazines, she was covered, head to toe, in slashes of black ink and fluorescent yellow and was traipsing up and down the office with my Jimmy Choo black patent pumps on her feet and my grey suede Gucci Mary-Janes on her hands. This was entirely my fault for keeping such an extensive shoe library under my desk. Of course, she hadn't bothered with the Topshop ballet pumps or the Aldo heels, had she? Oh no, like most terrorists-in-training, this one had great taste. I had got up at six a.m. on the first day of the Saks sale and then fought like a dog to get those Mary-Janes, there was no way they were going out like this.

Things had started off so well. I'd sat Grace in the armchair with an old copy of the magazine, a pad and the closest thing I had to felt-tips – a Sharpie marker and a highlighter – and had gone back to my desk to review the fashion pages. The next time I'd looked up, she'd given herself a David Bowie makeover with the pens and shredded the magazine. Before I could even get to my feet, she was off, tearing around the office and knocking over anything she could get her hands on. At first I thought she was tired and then I put it down to acting out because her mum had stuck her with me for the afternoon. Within three minutes, I decided she was clearly mentally imbalanced and needed electroshock therapy.

'Help me?' I begged. 'Every time I get near her she screams.'

'Oh, I figured that was you,' Cici cooed, waving at Grace who had sat herself in my chair and was happily spinning in circles. Not that I could call her for that, I obviously did it every time the office was empty. 'I thought maybe you were just super excited about that holiday sweater spread.'

'Well, I was,' I admitted. 'But most of the screaming was the baby.'

'Hey, honey.' She tilted her head to the side and smiled at Grace. Grace stopped gnawing on the heel of my Choo and smiled back. 'Want to hang out somewhere fun?'

Of course. It made sense that they would have a kinship – they were both completely mad and dead set on destroying my designer footwear.

Cici held out her hand and Grace clambered out of the chair to take it, gathering up her colouring in as she went.

'Bye, Anala,' she said as they sailed out of my office together. I held my breath and counted to ten, waiting until they had locked themselves in the tiny meeting room, and then ran to the toilet. My bladder couldn't take all this stress. Or the four cups of coffee I'd drunk already.

Post-pee, I immediately felt better. Now, to conquer the fashion pages and get the magazine sign-off back on track.

As soon as I found the fashion pages.

I scoured my desk, searching underneath my keyboard and my mouse pad, even getting on my hands and knees to look underneath, which seemed a bit like overkill when the entire bloody thing was made out of glass, but still, you could never be too sure. I just couldn't work out where they could be. There wasn't enough room in my office to swing a cat, or at least a very nice Alexander Wang handbag, as Jenny had proved the first time she came to visit and did just that. She broke a mug and knocked over a massive jar of Skittles. I couldn't have nice things. But that wasn't the pressing issue at that exact moment. The pressing issue was that ten pages of magazine had completely disappeared from my desk in the three minutes I had taken out to have a wee. This was why we needed Jesse. To stop me from going for a wee whenever I felt like it.

Maybe, I thought in desperation, just maybe Cici had come in and taken them back, thinking I was finished. I looked over to her desk but she wasn't there. She wasn't in the meeting room either.

'Megan,' I said, running over to the door and pasting an unconvincing smile onto my face. 'Did Cici give you the fashion pages?'

'Nuh-uh.' She shook her head and tapped her watch. 'Did you give them to her?'

'No.' I was reluctant to admit I couldn't find them. I really didn't want an arse-kicking. 'Do you know where she is?'

'Should I reprint the fashion pages?' Megan clearly had one priority and one priority only. 'I'd need to get Chloe to go over them again.'

'Let me have one more look.' I ducked my head back into my office. Maybe they had fallen off my desk during Grace's explosive exit. 'And can you see if you can drag Cici up from whatever crack in the floor she's fallen into?'

It wouldn't be difficult to lose Cici – she was so skinny she could easily get stuck behind a filing cabinet or something – but it seemed really unlikely that Grace would be so hard to find. Between the trail of sticky handprints and the banshee-like wailing-slash-maniacal laughter, she was usually a bit of a giveaway. Satisfied, or rather desperately freaked out, that the pages were in fact no longer in my office, I went back to ask for them to be reprinted. Yes, it was going to be embarrassing but it was still going to be better than Megan coming into my office in five minutes to beat me with a massive stick.

'I'm really sorry but I'm going to need those pages again.' I attempted to woo Megan with my shiniest smile, showing almost all of my teeth, and another gingerbread man but for whatever reason she wasn't reacting. In fact, she looked more freaked out than I did. So I pulled the second gingerbread man out from behind my back. Still nothing. This girl had a heart of stone.

'Uh, Angela, did you tell Cici to take that little girl out someplace?' she asked, an incredibly hopeful look on her face.

This didn't sound good.

'I did not,' I replied, magazine panic falling, Grace panic rising.

'Because Chloe said she saw them putting on jackets and taking the elevator.' Megan pointed over at the fashion desk, basically directing me to blame another messenger. 'While you were in the bathroom.'

Seriously, a girl couldn't even go for a whizz around here without the entire world falling apart.

'Right, I'll call her.' I tried to block all images of Cici kidnapping Grace and running off to India to live in a commune from my imagination. Now wasn't the time for it to be active. Now was the time for it to be very quiet and sit in a corner. 'And you print out the pages because all this is fine and they're probably outside getting some fresh air or maybe fetching me a coffee or something and it's fine.'

'Maybe they went out to look at the snow?' Chloe suggested, raising her voice but not daring to stand up.

'It's snowing?' I squealed and ran to the window. Snow! Christmas snow! 'Yes, I'm sure that's it. I'll call her. Me, phone, you, pages, everybody's happy.'

'Sure.' Megan's eyes widened and her mouth narrowed into a tiny cat's arse of terror as she clicked away at her computer. 'Everybody's happy.'

My phone was ringing as I stepped back inside my office and I grabbed the receiver without hesitation, a) because my assistant wasn't there to do it for me and b) because I was hoping it was said assistant calling to see if I wanted two or three sugars in my chai latte and not to explain that she had kidnapped my goddaughter.

'Hello?' I answered, breathless. 'I mean, *Gloss*, Angela speaking.'

'Angela.' It wasn't Cici. Not unless she's gone through a very speedy sex change or possibly been punched in the throat. Oh God, what if Grace had punched her in the throat and run away? 'It's Jesse.'

Ohhh. Luckily for him, he was currently much farther down my shit list than he deserved to be.

'Jesse, I don't really have time to talk right now,' I said, speedily tearing through the online address book for Cici's mobile number. Which of course wasn't there. 'I'll call you tomorrow.'

'Tomorrow is Christmas Day,' he pointed out. 'And I'll be quick . . . I wanted to apologise. For not coming in. And the other thing, I—'

'Then I won't speak to you tomorrow,' I said, fingers flying as they frantically typed out an email to Delia, asking for her sister's number. 'I'll see you on Thursday.'

'I know it was stupid not to come in today,' he carried on, completely ignoring the stress in my voice. 'I panicked about Friday and I'm an asshole and I should have known you'd need me when the system was down but then that bitch-faced assistant of yours—'

'Jesse, I'm not dicking about,' I snapped. 'I really don't have time for this. We're having to do all the approvals by hand, half the magazine is missing and so is said bitch-faced assistant. So I'll see you on Thursday, yeah?'

'Oh, that sounds rough,' he replied, only not nearly as upset as I might like. 'But yeah, Thursday.'

'Hang on.' I stood up sharply. 'How did you know the system was down?'

'Uh, Cici told me?' he said, the line crackling as he spoke. 'I'm on the bridge, I'm losing you.'

'Why are you on the bridge? I thought you were sick?' I was losing my tiny mind.

'Obviously I'm not sick. I said I was sick because I felt weird about the whole scene in the cab,' he explained, beginning to sound a little annoyed himself. Wanker. 'I feel really bad. Should I come? Maybe I can fix Censhare?'

'Can you?' I asked, half hopeful and three-quarters incredibly suspicious. Which made more than a whole but maths was never my strong point.

'I figure maybe?'

'Jesse.' I leaned over my desk, attempting to look intimidating, hoping that it would make me sound the same. 'Did you fuck up the system on purpose?'

'How could I do that?' he laughed, sounding nervous. 'I'm not even there. Sounds more like something Cici would do, doesn't it?'

'Are you in on this?' I barked. 'Are you in on this with her? Because I won't fire you, I will destroy your fucking life. I will literally end you. Christmas or no Christmas.'

And as I said it, I meant it. And the tiny, effeminate whimper down the end of the line suggested he knew I was telling the truth. I knew reading half of the first chapter of *Executive Toughness* would pay off.

'I didn't, Angela, of course I didn't.' He sounded terrified. Good. 'Do you want me to come in?'

'Yes,' I replied, my fingers rolling up the desk until

my hands looked like little claws. At last I felt powerful but not in a good way. More in a 'kneel before Zod' way. And I'd seen all the Superman films – it never went well for Zod. 'Get your arse in here and fucking fix it.'

As I hung up, Delia responded to my email with one word – 'Problem?' Instead of replying, I dialled Cici and prayed that she would pick up, hopefully while laughing at me as she walked out of the lift, holding Grace's hand which still had all of its original fingers. But she didn't pick up and the lift doors didn't open and it was almost two o'clock which meant she'd been missing for fifteen minutes and Louisa would be back in two hours and the magazine had to be completely signed off in three.

Merry fucking Christmas.

CHAPTER SIXTEEN

In my secret, quiet, keep-them-to-myself dreams, I had imagined that Monday might have gone quite well. I'd imagined the magazine going to press without any drama. I'd even fantasised about a bite of a sandwich or something, a little sit-down and three or four seconds to gaze upon my beautiful Christmas tree as a reward for a job well done. It was silly of me really.

Of course I wasn't going to get any of those things. Of course I was going to be running around Times Square without my coat on because I was too much of a twat to grab it on my way out the office, searching for a psycho blonde who had gone AWOL with my goddaughter and was presumably also holding the fashion pages of my magazine hostage. The magazine pages were replaceable. Megan had already got a fresh set to Chloe, who had only sulked and moaned a little bit, before I'd even run out the door. Replacing Louisa's daughter, however, was likely to be a little bit more difficult. Yes, there were a lot of blonde children running around Times Square but I felt a bit weird about picking one up off the street and legging it. Presumably because I wasn't Cici.

I'd left everyone in the office on red alert to call me if the two of them showed up but I'd been running around Times Square in the snow like a headless turkey for nearly twenty minutes and nothing. I'd been to Starbucks but no one had seen them. They weren't in Toys R Us when I pelted around there at top speed, checking everywhere from the Ferris wheel to Barbie's Dream House and quietly congratulating myself for all the recon work I'd done in there in the past, even if I hadn't known it was recon at the time. After that, I found myself stood outside M&Ms World, ready to slap myself. Of course they wouldn't be in there – that's where I would go, not where Cici would go. As if she would spend a second inside an establishment that did nothing but celebrate tiny chocolate nuggets of joy. She was an utterly joyless human being. I couldn't shake the idea that she and Jesse were somehow in on this together, that they had been plotting this all along – to fuck up the magazine and get me fired and then nick off with Grace just to scare me and Lou. There were no lengths that Cici wouldn't go to once she'd developed a plan – she'd proven that more than once before – and I couldn't imagine involving a pre-verbal toddler in her schemes would give her that much pause for thought.

With no better idea, I began to head east, towards Radio City Music Hall. The streets were packed, limiting me to an angry hop, sprinting every fifty metres or so before coming to halt behind some old dears in furs, rattling on about kids today. What should have taken me five minutes took almost fifteen and by the time I arrived at the box office I was freezing my arse off and very, very close to tears.

'Hello,' I beamed at the attendant on the door, adopting my very best 'please trust me, I'm British' accent. 'My friends are inside and I very much need to speak to them urgently. Would it be possible for me to pop in and grab them?'

I clutched my phone tightly, willing it to ring with good news before I had to do this. The man in the white shirt and red waistcoat regarded me with nothing short of utter contempt before clearing his throat, stepping in front of the door and laughing.

'No,' he announced. 'It would not be possible.'

'It really is an emergency,' I replied, pressing my hand into my side to ward off a stitch. Sweet Jesus, I was unfit.

'No way,' he answered.

'I'm not trying to sneak in to see the show,' I explained, attempting to peer over his shoulder and find another, more sympathetic usher. Possibly someone with a couple of ovaries and a heart. 'I was looking after my friend's little girl and she's gone missing and I really need to talk to her.'

He at least had the decency to look distressed, but clearly more at the thought that I would be allowed to look after anyone's child rather than the current predicament before he gave his next pronouncement.

'Sounds to me like that's a matter for the police,' he said, not budging. 'Why don't you call them?'

'Because I'm hoping not to need to,' I said with as polite a smile as I could muster. It wasn't very polite. 'And I really, really have to tell my friend.'

'Why haven't you called your friend?' the man asked.

'Because she's a decent human being and turns her

phone onto silent in the bloody theatre,' I shouted. 'Will you please just let me in? It's an emergency.'

It seemed that shouting was not the way to this man's heart. Rather than smile, soften and let me by, his face hardened and he stepped a little closer towards me. Aah, so that was what intimidating looked like. He really was wasted on Radio City. I was sure that there was some poncey club downtown that was desperate for a bouncer like him.

'You're not going in,' he bristled. 'Maybe I should call the police for you.'

'Oh, that would be brilliant actually,' I replied, waiting for him to step a little closer and then seizing my moment.

As the usher came towards me, he left a tiny gap between himself and the door. A gap that I was now desperate enough to throw myself through and leg it up the stairs, into the main lobby. The usher was just startled enough to give me a head start and, once inside, it seemed like no one gave two shits as to whether or not I had a ticket. I barrelled straight into the main auditorium, just in time to see dozens of dancers dressed like soldiers lined up on the stage. Ooh, the Rockettes! This was one of my favourite bits! But I didn't have time to be distracted by perfect formation dancing, as impressive as it was, as the usher from the front door appeared to have recovered himself and was right behind me. I bolted down the aisle, apologising to everyone under my breath as I went, half hunched over, trying to be as quick and as quiet as possible. Sadly, I was not a church mouse and I was not doing well. Really, I should not have spent all morning eating biscuits. The three-block dash over here should not have left me in such a state.

I saw Jenny and Louisa right away. Jenny, the heathen, was fast asleep, her eyes closed and her head lolling on her left-hand neighbour. Her right-hand neighbour, Louisa, was transfixed. I really, really wished I wasn't about to ruin her afternoon.

'Louisa,' I hissed from the aisle, bobbing down to stay out of sight of the usher. 'Lou.'

A few disgruntled parents turned to look at me while the rest of the front row hardened their faces and stared straight ahead, pretending I wasn't there. I assumed they were English.

'I'm sorry,' I stage-whispered. 'I really need to talk to my friend. LOU.'

But my best friend was completely transfixed by the dancers and couldn't possibly hear me. There was no way I could get to her without actually crawling along the front row to avoid getting in the way of the stage. I sighed, blew a piece of hair out from in front of my face and got down on my hands and knees. Thank God I'd worn shorts and not a skirt. This still wasn't going to be a pretty situation but at least no one was going to have to see my knickers.

I got as far as the fifth person in, just three more pairs of snowy shoes from Louisa, before I felt the very-upset-by-now usher grab hold of my ankle and pull. The floor was slippery and, quite frankly, gross, so I wasn't too happy when he gave me a good yank and my hands slipped out from underneath me.

'Bollocks,' I grunted as my face hit the cold, wet floor and my body began to slide backwards.

As I tried to scramble back upright, one foot held high in the air, face still level with a lovely pair of Manolos on the second person in from the right, I couldn't see an awful lot of point in being coy. I'd already effectively ruined, or made, everyone's afternoon, depending on how you looked at it.

'LOUISA!' I yelled as I felt a second pair of hands wrap around my other ankle. 'LOU!'

Once I had been dragged out to the aisle, the hands let go of my ankles and wrapped themselves around my arms, pulling me roughly to my feet. Really, I'd seen people thrown out of clubs with more delicacy.

'We've called the police,' the usher from outside said in a quiet but firm voice. 'I hope you're looking forward to spending Christmas in a cell.'

'Oh, whatever,' I replied, shaking my hair out of my eyes and trying to see whether or not Lou had noticed the commotion. For fuck's sake . . . she was still staring straight ahead. Stupid British refusal to acknowledge anything even slightly dodgy. 'LOUISA SMITH! TURN AROUND!'

To her credit, she did actually look up but not before the usher bent my arm up behind my back and started to half drag, half carry me out of the theatre.

'Oh shit,' I heard her say as she got to her feet. 'Angela?'

'LOU!' I shouted back, still fighting with the man who had clearly failed the police force entry exam several times over. 'I LOST GRACE.'

She stopped clamouring for her bags and went a very funny colour. Beside her, Jenny snorted, jumped in her seat and opened her eyes, looking around in confusion.

'What do you mean, you've lost my baby?'

The music up at the front really was quite loud. I was surprised the Rockettes weren't deaf, let alone that they could hear well enough for Louisa to distract them. And really, I would have expected more professionalism. Surely someone had stood up in the front of a matinee performance and screamed about a missing baby before today without half of them falling over? Surely?

Every single person in Radio City Music Hall gasped at exactly the same time. The racket on stage as thirty-six dancers all collapsed into each other at the same time was much, much louder than I had imagined it could be. There was no way a single one of them weighed more than a hundred pounds, how could they possibly cause all that noise? The crowd's gasp turned into a ripple of murmurs, finally evolving into assorted tuts, sighs and general displeasure. The people down the front did seem to have the decency to be a bit worried about the baby but the people at the back, who didn't really know what was going on, seemed altogether more excited.

Not stopping to worry about the people in the neighbouring seats, and really, who could blame her, Louisa grabbed her coat and her Jenny Lopez and ran into the aisle while three dozen dancers dragged each other to their feet and attempted to regain formation on the stage.

'Where is she?' Louisa looked terrified and I felt horrible. More horrible than I had ever, ever felt before. 'What? I mean, how?'

'Cici took her out of the office because she was running around,' I tried to explain as quickly as possible but it was difficult when my left arm was about to be broken and I was still being pulled backwards by a man three times taller than I was. 'And then I went out to get her and she wasn't there.'

It was more or less entirely what had happened. I didn't see any point in leaving in the toilet break.

'Cici has my baby?' Louisa bellowed. Jenny rubbed her eyes, slowly waking up and processing what was happening. 'That psycho has my baby girl? Oh my God, Angela, she's probably sold her by now. She's probably on a plane to Guam.'

'Where is Guam?' Jenny asked, blinking. 'I've always wondered.'

'That isn't important,' Lou shouted, punching her delicate fist into my captor's shoulder. 'Will you bloody let her go. My child is missing!'

He glared at Louisa and then looked at the other usher who had assisted in my capture before letting go of my arm. I twisted it back in front of me, rubbing my wrist and nursing it close to my chest. The relief lasted for approximately four seconds before Louisa began raining a torrent of tiny blows onto my arm.

'I cannot believe you lost my baby,' she said, punctuating each syllable with another slap. 'I cannot believe you lost my baby.'

'The police will still want to talk to you,' he grunted. 'We called in a public disturbance.'

'Good.' Lou marched out into the lobby, too angry to even cry. Jenny took my hand and squeezed. I was not too angry to cry. I was sobbing my eyes out. 'I'm about to create a really fucking big one if we don't find my baby immediately.'

Two uniformed officers stood in the doorway as we approached the front door. They looked incredibly bored. I was immediately both thankful for their presence and terrified of how they were going to deal with Louisa.

'We got a report of—' one of them began.

'MY BABY IS MISSING,' she shrieked, throwing herself on the woman officer. 'CICI SPENCER STOLE MY BABY!'

'OK, we were called to a public disturbance?' the male officer said, looking to me and Jenny for answers as he peeled Louisa off his colleague. 'There's a missing baby?'

'Well, there's both,' I said. 'Sort of.'

I tried to work out how I could explain without implicating myself in either potential crime while the police officers stared at me, clearly confused. It didn't take me long to realise it would probably be quite hard, given that I was guilty in both cases. Oh God, I was going to spend Christmas in prison. I'd be someone's bitch by morning. And while I was braiding my prison wife's hair, Cici would be reprogramming Grace to become a complete sociopath on a yacht in the south of France. It probably wouldn't take long, I had a feeling she was already predisposed.

'There's no disturbance.' Jenny woke up just in time to be useful. Both Louisa and I seemed to be suffering complete psychotic breakdowns. 'My friend was babysitting for us in her office and her assistant has absconded with the baby. We need to find the assistant.'

In times of crisis, everyone needed a Jenny Lopez. Who else would think to use the word absconded other than someone who had spent three hours a day for the last six years watching police procedural dramas and dated three different detectives? She was my hero.

The police waited to get confirmation that the theatre staff were happy to drop the disturbance charges but they had clearly already lost interest in me and my Christmas Spectacular crashing antics. Angry usher seemed mostly interested in Jenny and his accomplice looked as though he was only interested in getting the police out before his boss appeared.

'Ma'am, we need to know exactly what happened,' the woman officer said, still supporting a sobbing Louisa with one arm. 'When did you last see the child?'

'It was about one fifteen?' I said as my phone buzzed against my bum in my back pocket. I pulled it out to see Delia's name glowing on the screen. 'Is it OK if I take this? It might be about Grace?'

The cop nodded and turned her attention to Jenny, who was doing a fine job of nodding and looking stern. She would have made a brilliant lawyer if she could have been bothered with going to law school.

'Delia,' I turned away slightly, just in case she told me that Cici had thrown herself off the Empire State Building and taken Grace with her. I wasn't sure I'd be able to control my reaction. 'I've lost Grace. Or I've lost Cici and Cici has Grace. She's kidnapped her, she has totally kidnapped Louisa's baby and—'

'Angela, calm down,' she ordered on the other end of the line. 'I know where she is.'

'You spoke to her?' I shouted, spinning back to Lou, Jenny, the interested usher and the police to give them all a double thumbs up. It was hard to say which one looked less impressed. 'Where is she?'

'I called the office to talk to you and Megan told me what was happening,' Delia explained. 'I'm sorry, she'll be where she is every Christmas Eve.'

'Sacrificing goats?'

'She's at Macy's,' Delia sighed. 'I'll meet you there.'

Of all the places I might have expected to find Cici Spencer on the average Christmas Eve afternoon – Saks Fifth Avenue, Cipriani's, the seventh circle of Hell – the toy department of Macy's was not, and would never have been, on the list. Louisa, Jenny and I leapt out of the police officers' squad car, the siren still blaring, as we pulled up outside the department store. Louisa hadn't said a word on the way over, she'd just kept rocking backwards and forwards, occasionally forgetting to breathe and then having to take a series of short, sharp breaths. Jenny was calmly rubbing her back while I babbled over and over and over. Cici went to see the Macy's Santa Claus every Christmas Eve, had done ever since she and Delia were little girls and became obsessed with *Miracle on 34th Street*. Which was exactly what she'd be needing when I got my hands on her.

Accompanied by our new police entourage, the three of us pushed through the last-minute shoppers, struggling through revolving doors en masse.

'This way.' The male police officer had clearly spent more time in the toy department than any of the ladies in our party and led the way to the escalator. It only took a couple of minutes to find the huge queue of kids patiently waiting to deliver their lists to Santa – altogether too late in my opinion – and right there, at the head of the queue and about to dump Grace into the lap of a questionably motivated old man, was Cici Spencer.

Louisa ran at her with a battle cry, the likes of which I had previously only heard on *Braveheart* or *EastEnders*, and grabbed her daughter right out of the hands of Father Christmas, throwing her at me before launching herself at Cici. But this wasn't her first time. Quick as a malnourished cat, Cici took off around Santa's sleigh, followed by Louisa. Baubles and tinsel and dozens of candy canes flew across the store as Cici pushed over the beautifully decorated trees behind her, trying to slow Louisa down with some sort of festive assault course. But there was no way. Hell hath no fury like a woman scorned but New York had no fury like a mother scared and Lou was currently channelling all the fear that she had lost her daughter into kicking Cici Spencer's arse. It was a form of therapy that I supported.

'Oh, boys and girls!' Santa Claus struggled up from his seat and stepped forward to break up the fight, losing his hat in the process. I was quite impressed to see that his beard seemed to be entirely real. 'Let's not fight at Christmas.'

With Bing Crosby crooning a seasonal backing track, the cries of all the children who had been waiting to see Santa and not two thirty-year-old women chasing each other around a department store growing and the fear that Grace had been sold to Brad and Angelina completely assuaged, I was actually starting to feel quite Christmassy again. I mean, at least I'd seen the Rockettes. On their third go around the sleigh, Louisa finally caught up with her prey, reaching out for a handful of blonde hair and pulling. Hard. Hampered by her pencil skirt and high high heels, Cici went down way too easy. It was disappointing really, she should have known better – this wasn't the first time she'd been beaten up by my mates.

'Really, ladies, not in front of the children,' Santa puffed, falling backwards onto his jolly red bum, wrapping an arm around Louisa as he went.

'Sorry, Santa.' She struggled against Saint Nick's grasp, reaching across to get another slap in. 'She has to die.'

For all the presents he'd been lugging around, Santa wasn't that strong. I glanced over at Jenny to see her calmly popping chocolate-covered raisins into her mouth.

Without taking her eyes off the action, she held out the box. Me and Gracie both helped ourselves.

'Funny Mummy,' Grace whispered into my ear.

'What the fuck is going on?' Cici screeched, shielding her face from Louisa's miniature lady fists. 'Get her off of me!'

The female police officer, or Officer Jackson as I had learned she preferred to be called, pulled Louisa off as gently as possible while the male policeman, or Officer Moretti to his friends, checked that the child I was holding was in fact Grace and that she was in fact perfectly all right. I turned her around in my arms and confirmed her identity as she began pulling my hair.

'She's fine,' I said as she began to laugh. 'Right as rain.'

'Santa!' she shouted, pointing back at a very perplexed-looking Father Christmas. 'Anala, Santa!'

It really was quite the impressive scene. Several huge trees had been upset, their decorations and branches strewn across the store. Santa was still sat on his arse, seemingly unable to get back up again. Three elves were crouched down beside Cici, presumably wondering why the nice lady had just been attacked by three crazies accompanied by the police when she'd been waiting in the queue with the little girl for the last hour. Just as everything seemed to have calmed down, a giant stuffed Rudolph rocked gently for a moment and then toppled over, the light bulb in his nose making a faint popping sound.

'You stole my baby!' Louisa choked, before jumping up from the floor, desperate for another crack at Cici. 'You bloody mental. I'm going to kill you.'

But Officer Jackson and the biggest elf were too quick. They rushed in between her and her target, pinning Lou's arms behind her back as gently as humanly possible. Lou sobbed and sank to her knees, the look of terror in Cici's eyes, seemingly enough punishment for the time being. Lou's own face was covered in scratches from the Christmas trees, her hair full of pine needles. At least she would smell nice.

'Did everyone hear that?' Cici squealed, looking around for witnesses. The lucky cow had a far more receptive crowd than we had at Radio City. No quiet shushing and shocked gasps here, oh no. These people couldn't get their phones out fast enough to take pictures. 'She threatened to kill me. Arrest her.'

'If you can explain to us why you have the lady's child with you,' Officer Moretti said, holding out his hand and helping her to her feet, 'then I'm hoping we can agree that this was a huge misunderstanding and everyone can spend Christmas at home.'

'I'm her assistant,' she said, pointing to me before turning her attention to straightening her hair and batting her lashes. Officer Moretti was very handsome, to be fair. 'And they left . . . left Grace with her so they could go to the theatre.' Cue more accusatory pointing. 'Grace was going crazy cooped up inside so I told Angela I would take her out of her way so she could work in peace. It's Christmas Eve, I thought this would be a nice thing to do. This is all Angela's fault.'

Unhappy with my implication, all the potentially unflattering photos and running out of chocolate-covered raisins, I decided I'd had enough.

'Why weren't you answering your phone?' I shouted. I didn't like pointing, my mother said it was rude. 'Explain that!'

'It was on silent,' she snapped back. 'I always have it on silent in the office, it's company policy.'

Oh. Thinking about it . . .

311

'And why did you steal the fashion pages I was approving?' I demanded.

'What?' Cici looked completely nonplussed for a moment before delving into her alligator-skin Birkin, much to Jenny's displeasure, and producing the pieces of paper Grace had been colouring before they left my office. Along with all ten pages of the fashion section.

'She must have grabbed them off the desk when we walked out,' she explained. 'I swear I didn't know I had them.'

'Next you'll be telling me you didn't sabotage the approvals system this morning to make the magazine late.' More shouting, more pointing. I felt like Poirot without the moustache. 'And that you didn't tell Jesse to kiss me at the Christmas party and that you haven't been having an affair with him all along!'

Louisa gasped and grabbed Grace out of my arms, covering her ears with her hands. The *scandal*.

'Ew, the guy with the glasses?' Cici handed over the crumpled pages from her bag. 'You made out with that nerd? Ha. As if.'

'So you're not having an affair with him?' The pointing seemed a bit like overkill but I persevered.

'Please. I don't date guys from Brooklyn,' she sneered.

And even though it was blatantly an insult, it did seem like a legitimate defence.

'And you didn't sabotage the approvals system?' I deflated slightly, feeling more like Miss Marple, only after she lost at bingo rather than solved a case.

'Angela, I really don't have some epic revenge planned,' Cici sighed, picking pine needles out of her sweater. 'I didn't even spit in your coffee.'

Everyone looked doubtful at that one, including the police officers and they'd only just met her.

312

'I didn't!' she insisted. 'I thought about it, sure, but really it's just not me. I genuinely wanted to make this work. For Delia's sake. And so Grandpa didn't cut off my trust.'

'But that stuff you said at the party,' I reminded her, 'about an editorial position opening up soon?'

'Yeah, because that whore on the fashion desk is pregnant,' Cici explained. 'Don't you know anything about your own magazine?'

Apparently I did not.

I was also pretty certain said 'whore' was married and, in fact, not a whore at all, but then no one had ever accused Cici of being a feminist.

Satisfied that no crime had actually been committed, other than a couple of kids being traumatised by a hot blonde-on-blonde cat fight, Officer Jackson gave us all a stern ticking-off while Officer Moretti took Jenny's phone number. I assumed it was in case he had any follow-up questions-slash-wanted to bone her.

'Excuse me,' Santa suddenly squeaked from his not-so-comfy spot on the floor. 'Could someone help me up?'

'Oh my God.'

Delia arrived just as Cici was hobbling back into her heels, Lou was pulling bits of broken bauble out of her ponytail and everyone was beginning to feel a little bit foolish. The elves were trying to calm the crowds and over Delia's shoulder I saw some besuited Macy's managers staggering towards us, jaws officially dropped. Looking around at the chaos we had created, I could understand why. It must have been like walking in on the nativity scene in bizarro world.

'I passed the police on their way out.' She touched my arm as she ran past me to her sister and slapped her arm, hard. 'What happened?'

313

'Ow, bitch.' Cici slapped her back as the two faced off. It really was disconcerting to see them together. Good twin and evil twin. Nice twin and mean twin. Just like the Olsens . . . 'I didn't do anything. I was just bringing Grace to see Santa Claus like Grandpa always did with us.'

'You don't take someone's baby anywhere without asking them,' Delia said in a low, firm voice. It was just like on all those pet training programmes I definitely hadn't spent hours watching when I didn't have a pet of my own. 'She's not an animal, she's a person.'

'She's fine,' Cici replied, pouting at Grace who waved and immediately stretched her arms out for her new best friend with a whiny squeal. Stockholm Syndrome took hold so quickly when they were young. 'Look, she loves me.'

'Maybe we should get out of here?' Jenny suggested, waving around at the crowd we'd gathered. 'Lou, Gracie must be ready for a nap?'

'I don't know about her but I am,' Louisa said, wiping smudged mascara from under her red eyes and pushing her hair back into something approximating a ponytail. 'Let's just go.'

'I'll take care of everything with the store,' Delia reassured me, her eyes widening at the carnage before her. 'I'm so sorry.'

'It's not your fault,' I said, assuming 'taking care of' meant she was about to get the Spencer chequebook out. 'It was a misunderstanding. No one's actually to blame. Sort of.'

I glared at Cici who beamed at me with renewed enthusiasm.

'Back to the office, boss?' she asked, stepping over a still incapacitated Santa Claus. 'You're probably going to need a big coffee if you're going to get the magazine approved on time.'

'Oh, fuck off,' I said, rolling my eyes at Delia and mouthing my apologies.

'I'll see you in five,' she called as I turned my back. 'Maybe ten if there's a line in Starbucks.'

'You're going back to work?' Jenny asked, looking exhausted. 'And *she's* going back to work?'

'No rest for the wicked,' I replied, resting my head on her shoulder. 'And I have to send a courier to Newcastle to get a mine's worth of coal to put in her stocking.'

'I understood the word courier,' Jenny said, squeezing me into a half-hug. 'But I'll just assume that you meant you're going to kick her ass when you're done with the magazine.'

'More or less,' I nodded as we strolled back outside into a snowy Herald Square.

CHAPTER SEVENTEEN

I wasn't sure who was more surprised to see who when I limped back into the office with Cici at my side. Megan rose as we walked by her desk, but without the necessary brain cells to explain I waved her away and threw myself in the general direction of my desk, hoping I'd land on something solid that would bear my weight.

Unfortunately, I landed on Jesse.

'Oh, fucking hell,' I muttered. 'Fancy seeing you here.'

'I fixed Censhare,' he said as I crumbled into my chair, a broken, empty shell of a human being. 'Everything is uploaded, we just need you to approve the last pages.'

'What was wrong with it?' I asked, wiggling my mouse to bring my computer screen to life. My computer screen and a headache. Bleurgh.

'Megan put my password in wrong and locked it.' Jesse pushed his glasses back up his nose while we both pretended this wasn't massively awkward. 'It just shuts down instead of explaining and she hasn't had to do it on her own before, it wasn't her fault.'

'Shouldn't IT have been able to fix that?'

'Yes,' he replied. 'If they'd known that was what was wrong, they could have reset the passwords but our IT team suck, so . . .'

I nodded, closing my eyes and pressing my fingers into my temples. It was almost four o'clock, I had a lot of work to do, and at the end of all of that I still had to go home, deal with my parents and brine a twenty-pound turkey. I wondered if there was still time to convert to Judaism.

'Angela, am I fired?'

I opened my eyes and tried not to look quite as annoyed as I felt.

'No, Jesse,' I grunted. I was rubbish at staying mad with people but I really, really wanted to get better. I figured this was a very good opportunity. 'No one's getting fired.'

'Oh. OK. Phew,' he smiled and gave me a double thumbs up. 'And yeah, I know I said it before and every-thing but, uh, I feel real bad about the whole . . . thing.'

'You should,' I replied as my head throbbed.

'We just get along, you know?' Some people didn't know when to stop talking. 'And I broke up with my girlfriend a few months ago and I've been real down ever since.'

'Right.'

'She was amazing. So beautiful. Like model beautiful. And you kind of reminded me of her.'

'I did?'

Well, I had been wearing more blusher lately.

'Not because you look anything like her,' he said, kicking my self-esteem in the boob. 'No way. She was, like, six feet tall, long dark hair, so beautiful. So, so beautiful. But you're kind of funny like she was. And you're normal looking. I didn't want to be with someone that into their looks again. I guess I thought maybe it would work out better if I dated a normie. A funny normie.'

A funny normie. I had been called worse. But not in a while.

'Right.' I really wanted this conversation to be over. 'I don't want to talk about any of this again. I just want things back to normal as soon as.'

'Understood.' With a half-smile and a salute, Jesse headed for the door. 'But now you're back we really do need those pages approved ASAP. Everything goes to print at five. I'll be back in an hour.'

Closing my eyes again, I dropped my head onto my desk and whimpered. Maybe things didn't have to be quite so back to normal quite so quickly?

One hour and five minutes later, despite barely being able to read, let alone spell, I ticked the approval box on the last page of the magazine. I never, ever wanted to have to do that again. And looking on the bright side, there was a good chance I would get fired before the end of the day and would never have to.

I was waiting for Jesse to bound into the office and tell me I was free to leave when there was a soft, ladylike knock on the door. Looking up, instead of a sexually frustrated hipster, I saw Delia smiling at me, perfectly turned out as ever.

'Hey,' she said, holding up two huge Starbucks cups. I held out my hands and rejoiced. Just what I needed, more caffeine. Really, my stroke could only be days away.

'Hi,' I mumbled. I was embarrassed. Delia had seen many of my meltdowns but today really hadn't been my finest hour. Well, specifically the last three of them.

Before that I had been operating at an average level of shoddiness.

'Know anyone who needs five eight-foot Christmas trees and five hundred broken tree ornaments?' She took a seat opposite, dropped her bag on the floor and passed me a coffee cup the size of my head.

'I could probably take one?' I replied. 'Sorry.'

'I want to say these things happen but they really don't.' She was trying very hard not to laugh. I couldn't help but feel that I wouldn't have been quite so jovial in the same situation. 'How you feeling?'

'Like shit.'

I didn't believe in lying to Delia.

'Well, you look great.'

She, however, had no concerns about lying to me.

'I can go if you're still putting the pages to bed . . .' She started to stand up again but with my face full of Styrofoam cup I waved her back into her seat and tried to shake my head, but trying to do three things at once was two things too many.

'No, no,' I replied, wiping my coffee spill from the desk. 'It's all done. Just sent it through to Jesse for his final sign-off.'

'Wow.' Delia delicately sipped her coffee. 'What I'm hearing is that you managed to send an entire magazine to print, despite technical difficulties, despite having to work without your managing editor for half of the day, despite having to work with my sister and you still found time to step out and terrorise Manhattan's biggest department store?'

I stared at her blankly, still slurping .my bucket of coffee.

'You sound like you think that is some sort of achievement?'

'You don't think it is?' she asked. 'Angela, I've seen teams here at ten, eleven at night trying to get pages approved and I'm pretty sure none of them brought the Radio City Christmas Spectacular to a standstill in their lunch break. I just wish you'd trust yourself a little more.'

'I do trust myself,' I said, one eye on the door, waiting for Jesse to come in and beat me to death for missing a dirty typo. 'I just don't trust anyone else.'

'Hardly ideal,' she said. 'You're going to have a heart attack if you don't relax a little. The team here is great. You're great.'

'I don't want to let you and Mary down,' I said, a familiar feeling of panic washing over me again. 'I know I'm only looking after things for three months but I don't want to mess up. Mary never gets stressed like I do. Mary never freaks out. Mary is amazing.'

'Mary gets plenty stressed,' Delia said, trying to reassure me. Which might have been easier if she hadn't just given me eighteen Red Bulls' worth of caffeine. 'But Mary doesn't show it. You're just as good as she is, you just don't know it yet. Or you don't want to believe it anyway.'

'I'm English,' I explained with a pout. 'We don't believe in self-congratulation. Just resentment, bitterness and crippling self-doubt.'

'Well, I'm here to tell you you're great. I took a look at some of the pages on my way in and the magazine looks wonderful.'

I wanted to believe her but this was the same woman who had just sat in front of me and told me I looked good.

'The only person standing in your way right now is you.' Delia's words of wisdom settled squarely on my shoulders. I sighed and tried very hard to believe them. 'No one expects you to be Mary, they just want you to be you. You're going to do just fine.'

'Even if I could manage the magazine stuff, I'm a shit boss,' I said, clicking a fingernail against the platinum band of my engagement ring. 'I don't know how to manage people properly. I'm too nice.'

'Good job you've got Cici to practise on, isn't it?' she replied with a smile. 'I don't think you'll be too concerned about being overly friendly with her.'

'True,' I admitted. 'And I know I might have over-reacted a little bit but really, can you blame me?'

'She did steal my cat and give it to a girl in our class when we were kids,' Delia admitted. 'But I do think child trafficking is a little beyond her.'

I raised an eyebrow and said nothing.

'I said a little. And you, Angela Clark, need to start having a little faith in yourself.' Delia picked her handbag up from the floor and stood up to leave. 'Go home, give that handsome husband of yours a kiss and have a very happy Christmas.'

'Actually, I haven't heard from that handsome husband all day.' I scrabbled around in the bottom of my bag, looking for my phone. No missed calls, no text messages, no recent tweets from any of the Kardashians. 'And he was gone when I got up this morning.'

I looked up at Delia, immediately alarmed. 'Oh my God, he's left me. He's run away before my mum arrives. What if he's taken his passport?'

'This is the same thought process that had you believing Cici was crossing the border to Mexico with your goddaughter, isn't it?' she asked.

'I have a very active imagination,' I responded. 'It has not served me well in life.'

'You've done a great job today, Angela. Now go home. Relax.' She pulled her bag onto her shoulder and dropped her empty coffee cup into my rubbish bin. 'Then come back Thursday and do it all over again.'

'All of it?'

'Maybe try to stay out of Macy's?' she suggested. 'Merry Christmas.'

Thirty minutes after Delia left the office, Jesse, Megan and I signed off the final pages of the magazine, sending it to print with a group high five and an awful lot of swear words. I was happy, somewhere inside, but any particularly positive feelings were being choked to death by relief and exhaustion. The rest of the team had already gone, sent off with a hug and a bag of chocolate coins. No one seemed quite as excited about them as I was but that was probably because half of the team didn't eat refined sugar.

'That's it,' Jesse announced, switching off his monitor. 'It's done. We're good to go.'

'You must be super excited to see your folks,' Megan said, grabbing her purse from her desk. 'I know you're super psyched about the holidays.'

'Was super psyched,' I corrected her. 'I mostly just want to sleep until Thursday. Fingers crossed there's some Ambien in my stocking tomorrow morning.'

'I do love a sedative but maybe don't knock yourself out just yet.' It seemed that we hadn't quite cleared out the office. Cici appeared from a dark little corner, holding an envelope. She handed it over, yawning. 'This just came for you.'

I had assumed she'd snuck out hours ago and sort of hoped she might not come back. But there she was, still in her sweater and skirt, still in her torture shoes. Her hair had lost some of its bounce and her make-up had faded dramatically – smudges of eyeliner were caught in the creases under her eyes and her nose was, God forbid, shiny.

'You're still here?' I took the envelope, trying to remember how to check for evidence of ricin while keeping an eye on my assistant.

'I don't leave until you leave,' she shrugged. 'When I worked for Mary, I'd be here all night sometimes. It's part of the job.'

'You're actually going to do this?' I asked, tearing open the letter. The address was handwritten but all in block capitals so I couldn't recognise the handwriting. 'The job, I mean?'

'I don't really know how to do anything else just yet,' she said, glancing over at Jesse and Megan, who both backed away and busied themselves at their desks as soon as they realised she'd clocked them. 'Grandpa got me the job as Mary's assistant because of their, you know, connection. And when I stopped working for her, I was so incredibly bored. I don't want to volunteer on committees or museum boards for the rest of my life. And Grandpa seems to think it's not cool for me to spend the next five years on vacation, so I figure I'd be better off doing something I'm interested in.'

'Ruining my life?' I suggested.

'Working in fashion,' she corrected. 'I thought about getting an internship with a designer or going into PR maybe—'

'Ooh, you should totally do that.'

'But I want to work for the family company.' She finished her sentence loudly. 'And sure, we haven't always seen eye to eye but I think maybe there's something I might be able to learn from you.'

'How to eat carbs?' I couldn't quite believe what I was hearing.

'How to be good at this.' She waved her hand around the office. 'You came in here three years ago without experience and now you're the editor.'

'Interim editor,' I corrected. I couldn't work out what I was feeling. Alongside the confusion and disbelief, there was a tiny, warm glowing feeling in the pit of my stomach. Was that . . . was that pride?

'Whatever,' Cici sighed. 'Delia is just great at this stuff. She's a natural, I'm not. I want to learn how to be good at something.'

'Well, you haven't always used your powers for good,' I pointed out. 'But I have always been quite impressed at how well you've managed the logistics of fucking things up for me. It would be great if you could not refer to other girls on the magazine as whores, though.'

'I am good at organising things,' she said with enthusiasm. 'And I never miss the details. It's always about the details.'

'You do seem to think of everything,' I agreed.

'And I really, really don't want Grandpa to cut off my trust.' She lowered her voice, eyes on Megan and Jesse, as though they didn't already know she was worth millions and might decide to use this information against her somehow. 'I would not be good at being poor. It looks hard.'

It was only when she reached out and patted my shoulder, I realised what she meant.

'Yeah,' I said, sucking in my breath. 'It's not easy.'

'I'm sorry I took Grace without telling you.' Cici

paused for a moment, seemingly shocked by her own apology.

But that wasn't nearly as shocking as her next move. She awkwardly raised both of her arms, leaned towards me and wrapped them around my shoulders in a tight, rigid hug. I flinched as they tightened around my back. I flinched and assumed she was just looking for the right spot to stick the knife. But the stabbing never came. It was just a hug. Part of me was a little bit disappointed.

'It's OK,' I said, patting her back and waiting for it to be over. 'I overreacted.'

She broke off the hug, stood upright again and breathed, her tired face lighting up with a smile that was almost as warm as Delia's. It was a strange sight to see.

'What does your letter say?' she asked, our moment seemingly over.

'Um,' I unfolded the thick, creamy paper and read out the message. '340 Bleecker Street, 6.00 p.m.'

'You only have half an hour,' she said, glancing at her Cartier Tank watch. 'And that's way down in the village. Let me call you a car.'

'Thanks, Cici,' I said, the words thick and uncomfortable on my tongue. 'I'll get my bag.'

'It's what I'm here for,' she sang, picking up her phone.

I waved awkwardly at the remaining team as I jabbed the button for the lift. Cici gave a sparkling little smile and waved.

'Yes, I mean now. She's in the elevator. There had better be a car waiting when she gets down there,' she barked at some poor person in the parking garage. 'I don't care if it's the holidays, find a goddamn driver.'

As the lift doors opened, I stepped inside, strangely reassured that she hadn't undergone a complete personality switch. The hug was quite enough for one day. If we could crack 'please' and 'thank you' by Easter, I'd be ecstatic.

I was so busy apologising for Cici's behaviour, all the way from Times Square to the West Village, that I didn't realise where we were when the driver pulled over and announced that we had arrived. Stepping out into the snowy street, I pulled my coat tightly around myself and slung the long strap of my satchel over my head. I was at Manatus, the restaurant where I had first met Alex three and a half years earlier. Asking the driver to wait, I pushed open the wood and glass door, letting a gust of freezing cold air announce my arrival. The people sitting in the booths closest to the windows shivered and involuntarily turned towards the door, shaking their heads and sipping their wine. I made an apologetic face and looked around, waiting to recognise someone. But there was no one. No one I knew at least. I took the letter out of my pocket and read it for the millionth time. This was definitely the spot and this was definitely the time.

It was strange being here again. Erin had suggested it, way back when. I'd walked past a few times since – it was very close to Marc Jacobs – but I'd never been back inside. I looked over at the table where we'd eaten breakfast, gossiped about boys. Where she'd offered to introduce me to Mary and had started my whole adventure. And there in the back was the tiny table for one where Alex had been sat, drinking his coffee and pretending to listen to his iPod when really he'd been eavesdropping on our conversation the whole time. He's never told me what he was doing way over here in the West Village on his own on a random weekday morning. I could only imagine that meant I didn't want to know. He had been such a boy whore pre-me.

'Are you Angela?' A small, red-headed Greek lady tapped me on the arm and looked at me through her wire-rimmed glasses. 'You're the lady?'

'I'm Angela,' I said, taking the small, gold box that she thrust into my hands. 'I'm not sure if I'm the lady. Or a lady to be honest.'

'Man said to give you box and letter,' she shrugged. 'You want table?'

'No, thank you.' I tore into the second envelope, identical to the first. Inside was another piece of paper with another address. 'Is the man still here?'

'He left,' she said, pointing at the door. 'He gives me box, he buys a coffee, he leaves a big tip, he says you will be here around six thirty. He says you might be late.'

I smiled to myself, developing an inkling as to who the man might be.

'Thank you,' I said, folding the second letter back up and putting it back into its envelope. 'Merry Christmas.'

'And happy New Year,' the woman replied automatically.

I tapped on the driver's window with what I hoped was a face he would take pity on. As soon as he rolled it down, I realised he was not a man to take pity on anyone. But he was a man who was scared of Cici and I wasn't above taking advantage of that.

'Where to?' he asked, unlocking the passenger door.

'Broadway, between 13th and 14th,' I said, hopping

in and ripping the gold wrapping paper off the box. 'I need to be there by six fifty.'

'Traffic is heavy,' he replied as he pulled away from the kerb. 'I'll get you there as soon as I can.'

'That's OK,' I said, marvelling at the brand new iPhone in my lap. There was a small Post-it note on the front with the words 'play me' written in marker pen. 'He's expecting me to be late.'

There was only one song loaded onto the phone. It started with a guitar and some sleigh bells and then there was a voice I recognised.

'Dude, this is so gay.'

It was Craig. Presumably on bell duty.

'Shut up.' Alex's voice streamed into my ears and into my heart, washing away all the rest of the day's stresses. I laughed lightly and pressed the earbuds in tighter. I didn't want to miss a second of whatever he had to say. 'So, this is one of your presents, Angela. Merry Christmas.'

As he started to sing a heartfelt acoustic rendition of 'All I Want For Christmas', I felt the first tear slide down my cheek. I wiped my tired, gritty eyes once and then let the tears fall. All that was missing was my recorder solo.

The traffic was bad on the way back up to Union Square but I didn't mind. This time I knew where we were headed and, after all, I had my song to listen to and a new iPhone to stroke. When we finally stopped outside Max Brenner, I couldn't get out of the car fast enough. I'd done some light repair work to my make-up but my eyes were still red and my lips were still chapped. I had a feeling that it didn't matter.

The site of mine and Alex's first date was much busier than Manatus. Maybe not quite as busy as the time we'd come for the best hot chocolate in the city but still bustling with families and excited tourists in the city for the holidays. My stomach rumbled as I approached the hostess stand. I hadn't really eaten anything proper all day and I sent up a silent prayer to the birthday boy that Alex had included a snack with this part of my present.

'Hi, I'm Angela.' I approached the hostess with the same 'please don't think I'm mad' look that I'd given the driver. 'I think you might have a package or something for me?'

'Angela Clark?' she asked, running a finger down a list of names in front of her. I nodded as though my head might fall off. 'I don't have a package but the rest of your party is already seated. This way.'

The rest of my party?

I followed the waitress through the busy tables, dodging children who had consumed more sugar than I had caffeine and trying to inhale the chocolatey goodness all around. It was only when we went up a set of stairs I hadn't noticed before that I spotted the rest of my party.

It was only my bloody parents.

'You're late,' Mum said, refusing to stand up. Or make eye contact. Or smile. 'And you look a right state.'

'Merry Christmas, love.' Dad put down his cup of tea and opened his arms for a hug. Still in shock, it took me a moment to realise they were really there. I threw myself at my dad, almost knocking him into the wall, squeezing him as hard as I could. Not fancy holograms, not muggers in elaborate fancy dress, they actually were my mum and dad.

'You're here,' I whispered in his ear. 'I'm so happy.'

And I was. The second I had laid eyes on my miserable-looking mother, it really began to feel like Christmas.

'We're here,' she replied, her lips still a thin tight line as I wrapped my arms around her neck and gave her a hug of her own, whether she liked it or not.

'Alex called,' Dad explained while I breathed in my mum's perfume. Eventually she relaxed and patted me on the back. It was as good as I was going to get for the time being. 'He explained you've been under a bit of pressure.'

'But you cancelled your flights?' I finally let go of my mum and dropped into a chair opposite, taking a sip of Dad's tea. Good and sugary, just how we liked it. 'I can't believe you're here.'

'I didn't cancel them,' Dad admitted. 'And I'm glad I didn't. It's bloody good to see you.'

'It's good to see you too,' I said, trying to tidy up my hair. 'Are you all right, Mum?'

'Hmm,' she nodded, utterly stoic. 'I'm fine.'

'I'm sorry about the message,' I said as earnestly as possible. 'It wasn't OK. And I am glad that you're here. We haven't had Christmas together for ages, it'll be nice to do it properly.'

'As long as we're not in the way,' she sniffed. 'I'd hate to put your majesty out.'

'Annette.' My dad gave her a look and a nudge. Incredibly brave on his part. 'What did we agree?'

'I'm just tired,' she replied in her stiff, awkward voice. 'But I'm glad I'm here.'

'I'm glad you're here too,' I said, leaping back up for a second round of hugs. It was too early to ask if she would make her special roast potatoes for lunch tomorrow but I was hopeful. 'I love you.'

'Oh, get off,' she half laughed, pushing me away. 'Don't make a scene.'

'Why don't you come home and go to bed?' I suggested, straightening her scarf. 'You should be resting.'

'We're going,' Dad said, handing me another box, wrapped in gold paper just the same. 'Alex asked us to meet you here and give you this. And, well, we wanted to give Louisa and Tim a bit of privacy.'

'Tim is here?'

'He came on our flight,' Mum replied. 'Alex sorted it all out apparently. Moved our flights so we could all come out together and then told us to meet you here. You didn't know he was coming?'

'I did not know he was coming,' I confirmed. 'Is he here? Alex?'

'Oh no.' Dad grinned and tapped his nose. 'We cannot say a word.'

'Honestly, I don't know who's worse, you or him,' my mum said, picking up the cup of tea in front of her. 'Can you believe this only came with lemon. Honestly, Angela, lemon. I had to ask for milk. *Ask* for it.'

I resisted the urge to shout *That's how they serve it here!* and forced myself to remember that my parents were old, set in their ways and had only just got off a plane. Besides, I was too happy to see them to get annoyed. I felt another layer of stress melt right off me and I smiled.

'You, madam, need to open that and be off on your travels,' Dad said, patting the gold box and attached envelope. 'I think you've got somewhere else to be.'

'I hope it's my bed,' I replied, tearing into the envelope.

'You'd think she'd been down the mine all day,' Mum tutted. 'It's only seven o'clock. Midnight at home. And here we are, sat in a bloody café instead of putting our feet up on Christmas Eve.'

'I'll see you at home,' I said, leaning over the table to kiss her on the cheek. Kissing was better than punching, I was sure. 'Have you got keys?'

Dad nodded and gave me another hug. 'Now get off before you're late.'

'Again,' Mum added.

'It is nice that it doesn't matter how long goes by between our visits, you're always yourself,' I said. 'Love you too, Mother.'

'Oh, sod off,' she muttered. 'Let me drink my horrible tea in peace.'

Mustering up a smile, I headed back down the stairs and out into the snow.

CHAPTER EIGHTEEN

I could not have been any happier to find three Max Brenner cookies inside the second box and had already inhaled half of one before I even opened the accompanying envelope.

'Oh,' I smiled, face covered in chocolate, lap covered in crumbs. 'Rockefeller Plaza, please.'

The driver nodded in the rear-view mirror and pulled out into traffic, turning right onto 13th Street and then heading up Sixth Avenue. I sat back in the plush leather seat, enjoying the warm air blowing around my feet, and imagined for a moment how it must feel to be as rich as Cici. No wonder she considered me poor. I lived in Brooklyn, I bought clothes on sale, I worked because I had to, not just because I wanted to. I took the subway, ate two-dollar slices of pizza at three in the morning on my way home from a dive bar where the drinks were two for one all night . . . and I wouldn't have swapped it for anything. I had no idea what her romantic status was but I had to assume it wasn't terribly happy. Anyone getting laid regularly wouldn't have the energy to put into making other people so incredibly unhappy. I wasn't rich but I wasn't poor and, most importantly, I was happy. And I had a cookie and an iPhone five as well, but all of those things were definitely related.

Rockefeller Plaza was almost forty blocks north of Union Square but most of the bad traffic was leaving the city and so I hopped out of the car on Sixth and 50th less than fifteen minutes later. I hastily chomped a piece of dried-out old chewing gum I'd found at the bottom of my poor, abused Marc Jacobs bag in an attempt to de-cookie myself, hoping that I was about to find Alex at the Rockefeller Christmas tree. It was, after all, where he had proposed two years ago. The plaza was busy. It seemed like every tourist in New York who wasn't at the Christmas market on Union Square was lining up to ice skate but it wasn't hard to spot the person waiting for me underneath the tree. It was never hard to spot Jenny Lopez.

She'd got changed since our excursion to Macy's and was wrapped up in a bright pink wool coat, knee-high black leather boots on her feet and her hair tied up and away from her face to stop it frizzing out in the snow. And to show off her white fur earmuffs.

'Jenny!' I waved madly as I approached, a little worried by the scowl on her face. Maybe she was still mad with me? 'Jen?'

'Angie,' she sighed and gave me a standard kiss on the cheek, pulling the earmuffs down and wrapping them around her neck. 'I'm so glad you're here. You get hit on by crazies hanging out here on Christmas Eve.'

Relieved that the filthy look wasn't for me, I kissed her back and held out my arms.

'So what's the deal here?' I asked.

'OK, so you need to get some skates, do three laps around the rink and then you'll see your box is dangling from the tenth branch of the Christmas tree,' she explained, laughing at the look of horror on my face. 'Nah, I'm fucking with you. Here.'

She handed me another gold box. This was even smaller than the previous two. There was definitely no cookie inside this time.

'Your husband is crazy,' she said, punching me in the arm. 'You lucky bitch.'

'You're the one who's having a baby with a Hollywood actor,' I replied, smiling. 'That's pretty lucky.'

'Yeah, we'll see,' she shrugged. I started to raise my eyebrow but this wasn't the time or the place. 'Maybe.'

'You're both still coming for dinner tomorrow, yeah?' I asked, slipping the box into my pocket. I could open it back in the car – there was some one-on-one Jenny time needed, no matter how brief.

'I am,' she said, poking my nose gently and smiling a smile that I knew was a complete cover-up. 'Who knows where Mr Jacobs might be. He's kind of unreliable.'

'Kind of,' I agreed. 'Thank goodness you're completely sane and entirely dependable at all times.'

'Thank goodness,' she agreed, setting her hands on my shoulders and pushing me away. 'Now go, you have a date to keep.'

'I'll see you in the morning,' I called over my shoulder as I left. 'I want you there to open presents.'

'I'll be there,' she promised, slipping the earmuffs back over her ears. 'Merry Christmas, Angie baby.'

The last box was so small that I couldn't imagine what was inside. The directions on the letter told us to head towards 350 Fifth Avenue and even though I promised the driver this would be the last stop, he still sighed and turned the radio up a little louder as soon as I got in the car. I gave him half of my last cookie out of guilt and immediately regretted it when I saw him toss it onto the passenger seat. Bastard.

Inside box number three was what seemed to be a credit card. I turned it over again and again but there was nothing written on it, it was just a white plastic card with a black magnetic strip. It wasn't anything special.

'350 Fifth Avenue,' the driver announced as the car stopped in the middle of a boring-looking block. 'This is it.'

'Really?' I said, looking around. 'Do you know which building it is?'

'It's the big one,' he replied. 'Goodnight, miss.'

I hopped out of the car, narrowly avoiding an extremely slushy puddle, and looked up. It was the big one. The biggest one in fact. It was the Empire State Building. I fingered the credit card, turning it over in my hand and shaking my head. I didn't even want to know how he'd managed this or what was waiting for me. I just wanted to remember this moment for the rest of my life. The before, the almost. The way my heart was beating even faster than the first time he'd brought me here and the way I always wanted to feel.

The attendant grinned when I walked through the door and showed me straight into a lift, passing all the crowds waiting in the queue.

'Ms Clark.' He held open the doors and pointed towards my key card. 'That's gonna take you right up to the eighty-sixth floor. No need to switch.'

'Thank you.' I knew I was blushing but I couldn't help it. For the first time in an age, I was nervous about seeing Alex. Not because I'd ruined his favourite shirt at the laundrette, not because I'd eaten the last doughnut after promising I would leave it for him and not because I'd been an absolute moron and risked our relationship with my appalling interpersonal skills. Well, not just because of that. It felt like our first date all over again. It felt like the day he'd taken me out and shown me his city, only the last time it was so sunny I'd burned the back of my neck and this time it was so cold I could hear my own teeth chattering. I looked down at the hand holding the key card and saw my wedding and engagement rings. I supposed they made things different as well. It just didn't feel like it sometimes.

The butterflies in my stomach were sorely tested by the speed of the express lift, and when I stepped out onto the eighty-sixth floor observatory, they had vertigo, travel sickness and were buzzing around as though I'd done nothing but drink coffee and eat sugary cookies all day. Oh, wait . . . but there was no time to be nervous. The crowds were sparse on the open-air terrace – it was snowing and temperatures were dipping below freezing after all, but everyone up there was so happy. All I could see were smiling faces and shining eyes. Christmas in New York did that to people. It was one of the reasons I loved the season and loved the city so much. But not nearly as much as I loved the man I saw leaning against the wall opposite me. Alex raised a bare hand and curved his lips into a smile, his hair highlighted with snow that sparkled red and green from the lights above.

'Hey,' he said as I approached, pulling me in close, his chest still warm even though he was only wearing a leather jacket. It was bitter this high up but Alex was never cold. He was always warm enough for both of us. 'You found me.'

'You sang Mariah for me,' I whispered into his neck as I nestled my face under his chin. 'This is amazing. You are amazing.'

'It's Christmas,' he replied. 'Miracles can happen.'

'You are a miracle,' I said, running my arms around his waist and rubbing my cold hands against the soft wool of his sweater. 'I can't believe you did this.'

'I know things have been tough lately,' he said, pressing his forehead against mine and kissing me lightly. 'I wanted to remind you of some of the good times. How we got here in the first place. How I fell in love with you.'

'I've never forgotten that,' I promised, kissing him back harder, hoping that I could explain without words. 'And I never will. I know I get caught up in other stuff and I know I clam up and don't talk when I'm stressing out but I am always, always in love with you.'

'I was pissed that you didn't tell me about the doctor stuff,' he admitted, pressing a hand against my cheek. 'I was pissed that you were keeping it from me. And then I was pissed at myself for making you feel like you couldn't tell me.'

'Oh God, don't.' My blue eyes met his green ones and not a single sight in all of Manhattan could have torn them away. 'It wasn't that. I had to process it all first, that's all. I know I can tell you anything. I was just being stupid.'

'And you've made an appointment to see the doctor?' he asked, brushing my hair away from my face, his fingers catching carefully in its snowy tangles. 'And we'll go together?'

'Not yet,' I admitted. 'But today was something of a write-off. I will, on Thursday, I swear it.'

'And you know it doesn't matter what she says, right?' Alex looked super serious for a moment. It didn't happen that often so when those sleepy eyes were open and alert, I paid attention. 'Because I already have everything I want. I had it from the day we met in that coffee shop. I knew it the day we came up here together and I knew it for sure the day I gave you that ring.'

I looked down at my engagement ring and bit my lip. The snow was already making my mascara work so hard, there was no need to push it to the limit with tears.

'And what about Max Brenner's?' I asked.

'Oh man, I just needed to send your folks some place,' he laughed. 'Get them out of the house.'

'They're here for a week,' I reminded him. 'I think they'll be hanging out there a lot.'

He leaned over me, shielding me from the snow as it began to come down in big, heavy flakes, and pressed his lips against mine. His mouth was warm and familiar and the feeling in my stomach began to spread all over my body as I pulled him towards me, standing on my tiptoes to get as close as humanly possible to the man I loved.

'If you carry on like that we're gonna get arrested,' he said in a low, broken voice as he pulled away. 'Save it till we get home.'

'How about the cab on the way home?' I replied,

grabbing his collar and pulling him back into me. 'Home seems very far away.'

'You're all talk, Angela Clark,' Alex said, the same longing in his words that I felt in myself. It seemed as though it had been a long time since we'd been together. 'Let's get out of here so I can give you your real present.'

'You do mean we're going home to do it, don't you?' I asked as he took my hand and led me back towards the lifts. 'Because a girl's got needs.'

'Yes, that's what I meant,' he said, shaking his head as we went. 'We're going home to "do it". You and your romantic soul.'

'One of a kind,' I said, poking myself in the chest. 'They don't make them like this anymore.'

'They really don't,' he replied. 'Thank God.'

Christmas Day was exactly what Christmas Day was supposed to be.

Grace woke us all up far too early and when she jumped on top of me at six a.m., I was thankful that Alex had remembered to put his underwear back on after our late-night stealth sex session. Louisa and Tim emerged from the makeshift guestroom in the basement holding hands and looking incredibly awkward but clearly we weren't going to be having any epic conversations while my mother was marching around insulting my selection of vegetables and preheating the oven to nuke the turkey.

While me and Lou helped Grace open her pile of presents, my dad poured the boys an Irish coffee while my mum wasn't looking, and pretty soon everyone had a bacon sandwich in one hand (except for me who was a third of the way into a Terry's Chocolate Orange, as was tradition) and a drink in the other. Once the mountain of presents Grace had managed to amass were open and strewn across the apartment, Alex allowed us all to open one gift each, having been brought up by abusive parents who only let him open his presents after lunch. I sat impatiently, watching everyone else 'ooh' and 'aah' over their gifts while trying to select the most likely-looking box under the tree. I picked the gift bag that contained a six-pack of knickers from M&S and three pairs of black opaque tights. I was not amused. After making the usual complaints when I turned on the TV, insisting that Christmas was family time and we didn't need the 'goggle box' on, Mum eventually piped down when I gave her the latest James Bond on DVD and told her she could put it on while we all got showered and dressed in our nice clothes.

While some quiet time might have been what I wanted, it wasn't what I needed. The idea of lounging around on the sofa with nothing better to do than annoy Alex all day long still sounded pretty great, but nothing could have made me happier than seeing my dad bouncing Grace on his knee while my mum and Alex, both resplendent in aprons Mum had brought from home, argued over whether or not to cut tiny crosses into the bottom of the sprouts before boiling them.

It was a proper Clark family Christmas.

Or at least it was until Jenny, Craig, Graham and James arrived with a bottle of tequila and a half-eaten pizza. According to Jenny, it was a Lopez family tradition but if it was, it was the first I'd ever heard of it. Not that a little thing like bullshit stopped me from taking a shot, obviously. Almost eight hours after the turkey had been brined, basted, cooked, carved and then microwaved out of my mother's sight to get rid of any red bits, and our new dining table was covered in nothing but remains of the carnage that had been Christmas dinner, we left Mum with her two favourite Jameses – Bond and Jacobs – and let Dad pass out on the sofa while the rest of us headed out for a post-lunch stroll-slash-drink.

'Everything's all right then?' I asked Louisa as we climbed the stone staircase. 'With you and Tim?'

'I wouldn't say all right,' she said, sniffling a little from the cold. 'But he isn't cheating. He is mates with that girl who's been texting him and I'm not convinced she's not having a go at him but he says she's got a boyfriend and she's just one of the lads and there's nothing to worry about. But he did admit he's been a bit shit lately.'

'A bit shit doesn't send you running off over the Atlantic,' I replied, too much turkey straining against my jeans. I wondered if I could pop open the top button without anyone noticing.

'Very shit then,' she bargained. 'From what I can gather, he's been sat in front of the PlayStation in his boxers and feeling sorry for himself. He says he thought I wasn't coming back.'

'Then why didn't he try to get you back?' I asked, a very clear picture of Tim's bachelor week in my mind. 'Hasn't he completed *Grand Theft Auto* yet?'

'He says he was scared,' she whispered. 'He actually said he was too scared.'

'Ohhh.'

We both stared in wonder. An English man. Having feelings. And admitting to them. Scandalous.

'And I have to admit, I haven't been on my best

wife-ing behaviour either,' Louisa said. 'I've been too preoccupied with Grace and we fell off the radar. We both need to try harder if we want it to work. I feel so silly for overreacting now.'

'It's so easy to fuck it all up, isn't it?' I blinked as we reached the top of the stairs and walked out onto Brooklyn Bridge. 'It happens before you know it.'

'I think a lot of the time, it's not one big thing,' Louisa said. 'I think it's loads of little things. By the time the big thing comes along, it's already dead. I hope we've caught it in time. I really do love him.'

'I know,' I said, squeezing her hand. 'And he knows. Like you said, you just have to try sometimes. I've thought about getting it tattooed onto the insides of my eyelids.'

'What are you guys whining about?' Jenny crashed hard into the pair of us, throwing her arms around our shoulders and jumping up and down. 'It's CHRISTMAS!'

'We were just deciding whether to throw you off the bridge now or on our way back,' I replied, pushing her away. She was far too strong for such a small woman. 'What do you think?'

'You're supposed to wait an hour after eating before you swim,' she replied, sticking out her tongue. 'So let's do it on the way back. And then I'll swim back to your place and kick your ass.'

'She's going to make a great mother,' Lou said, smiling against the sunlight.

'Yeah, maybe just not yet.' Jenny pushed into the middle and linked arms with us both. 'I think maybe I'm gonna hang in there and save up for that Birkin this time.'

'You're getting a handbag instead of a baby?' Lou was rightly confused.

'I'm gonna wait a little while longer and see if I can't find a Birkin of a boy to knock me up,' she explained. 'Not that I don't love the shit out of James but I need someone who will be around. And he can't promise that he will be. Or rather he will promise and then he'll flake and if that's the way it's gonna be, I'd rather hit up the sperm bank.'

'I told you, I'll make a baby with you.' Craig appeared at my elbow and pulled Jenny out of the chain, tossing her over his shoulder. 'It'll be my Christmas gift to you.'

'Because you didn't get me anything, you cheap bastard.' Jenny pounded on his back with small fists but she was laughing as he charged forwards, running off across the bridge.

'I really, really hope that he's joking,' Alex said, taking my free hand in his. 'That is not a christening I want to go to.'

Lou squeezed my arm lightly and let go of the other side, jogging to catch up with Graham and Tim. I raised my hand over my eyes to see the outline of Grace, happily swaying from side to side on her daddy's shoulders.

'And you know we'd be putting it through college,' I replied, smiling at the happy-ish family. 'And taking it to college. And picking it up from college. And feeding it and clothing it and everything else-ing it.'

'I'll get him sterilised first thing in the morning,' Alex said gravely. 'And you can get the Pill injected, right? Can you make your doctor friend give her that?'

'I'll give it to her myself,' I promised. 'I'll tell her it's Botox to stop her arse from sagging.'

'She does have a great ass,' Alex admitted, tilting

his head to the side to get a better look. 'I've got to give her that.'

I shoved him a little but he was right. She did have a great arse. That was one of the reasons I wasn't worried about her finding a man.

'But it's not as great as yours, my love,' he said, kissing the top of my head.

'Obviously,' I replied, lifting my face up towards him for a proper kiss.

We stalled for a bit, hanging back while the rest of the gang walked on and leaned against the barrier, looking out at the Statue of Liberty. It was hard to see anything when the sun was so bright but the sky was blue and the water glittered beneath us, keeping Brooklyn and Manhattan at a safe distance. Close enough to wave but not near enough to start any trouble. The spiky skyline of the city was completely greyed out as the sun leaned over into the west but Brooklyn sparkled. The windows of the warehouses and fancy apartment buildings on the waterfront glowed orange with the reflected late afternoon light and there were patches of snow that had settled on Christmas Eve and gone undisturbed overnight. I imagined me and Alex taking our child there and building snowmen or throwing snowballs. I imagined taking him or her over to the carousel in the summer and taking pictures to send to my mum and dad. Playing in the park, taking them to school for the first time, sitting on our stoop and watching Alex teach them to ride a bike on our new street. For the first time, I really imagined what it would be like to not just be us anymore, but to be a family.

'You're quiet,' Alex whispered into my ear.

'It's a Christmas miracle,' I replied in a voice just as low.

'You're having a good day?' he asked, turning his back on Lady Liberty and leaning in towards me. 'Or at least a better day than yesterday?'

'I'm having the best day,' I said, meaning every word. 'And Mum remembered to bring my pork pies so it's only going to get better.'

'I'm going to make every day better,' Alex promised, rubbing his thumb over the back of my hand. 'That's my job. That was part of the whole marriage deal.'

'I missed that part of the vows,' I smiled. 'But it sounds nice.'

I looked over to see Graham throwing Grace high in the air while she screamed with laughter. Tim and Louisa were holding hands, her head resting on his shoulder, and Jenny and Craig were stumbling alongside them, stopping every few steps to kiss like teenagers. Probably because they were drunk like teenagers. It felt good to see everyone smiling and I couldn't imagine how I could possibly be happier than I was at that exact moment. I felt as though someone had emptied out all the stress and the worry and the panic and filled me up with light and sunshine and assorted Disney characters. That or I was very, very drunk.

'Merry Christmas.' Alex kissed the top of my head and pulled me by the hand, hurrying to catch up with the others. 'Come on. You can open the rest of your presents when we get back. I've heard a rumour that there might be shoes.'

'I'm coming,' I said, letting him drag me along. 'You don't have to bribe me with footwear.'

'Since when?' he asked, eyebrow arched. 'Shoes, Angela Clark, there are shoes waiting for you.'

I laughed and I picked up my pace but I wasn't in a rush. I wasn't in a rush for anything. I had everything I needed right there with me on that bridge, and it was more than enough.

Angela's Guide to
Christmas

I can't tell you why I love Christmas as much as I do but
sweet Jesus, I'm giddy just thinking about it. The tree,
the lights, sequins on every item of clothing and the
Boots Christmas Catalogue...

Mostly, I love Christmas because it's the time of year when
people are a little bit happier and there's one more smile on
every street. And now that I'm in New York, and winter here
can be an absolute demon, you sometimes need an extra
reason to smile: whether it's a cup of coffee in a red cup,
an eight-foot fir tree or a Christmas cocktail with your
best friend, I'm sold.

Angela

x

New York Christmas in a Day

You could easily spend all of December wandering around New York and getting your Christmas on but if your time is limited, this would be my dream festive day in my favourite city on earth.

You're going to need a big feed so make a reservation and head downtown to **Balthazar** in **Soho**. It's a super swanky spot but way more laidback at breakfast and since you're (probably) not drinking, it won't hurt your wallet as much as dinner might. Once you're done, head up Broadway to the F train all the way to the 57th street stop and walk a couple of blocks to **Central Park** for a lovely wander or, even better, a quick turn around the rink. Nothing burns off calories like **ice skating** – word to the wise, wear jeans. Only idiots (like me) go ice skating in a dress. More than once. After your best Torvill & Dean impression, hang up your skates and cab over to **Bloomingdales** for some essential Christmas shopping. Don't miss the Christmas shop, the limited edition tree decorations make great gifts. And if you're hungry again (I would be, but I'm a pig) the burger bar in the basement, **Flip**, is all new, all improved and completely delicious.

After lunch, walk down **Madison** to **Barneys** and then over to **Fifth Avenue** to check out the gorgeous store windows. From **Bergdorfs** to **Saks**, there are some real beauties: **Cartier** all wrapped up in a big red bow, **Henri Bendel's** brown and white stripes... ohhh. Cough, sorry, got distracted. Anyway, after all your wandering and window shopping, it's time for a sit down. Book tickets to **Radio City Music Hall's Christmas Spectacular** and get ready to feel as seasonal as humanly possible without putting on a santa suit. It's the best. After the show, it's dinner time and you deserve something nice so I'd go with **Benoit** for classic French food on 55th street or the dining room at **The Modern**, the restaurant at MoMA for modern American. With dinner and cocktails taken care off, it's time to top off your day with a trip to visit the **Rockefeller Center Christmas Tree**. The crowds won't be so manic later in the evening and you'll be so full of dinner and happiness that it will make the world's best tree (other than mine) even more fantastic.

Gingerbread Christmas Trees Recipe

I have a desperately unhealthy love of gingerbread in whatever shape it may come in but, I have found, if you make gingerbread Christmas trees, you can feasibly eat them all through December without ever feeling guilty. But you will get fat. You have been warned.

350g plain flour

1 tsp bicarbonate of soda

2 or 3 tsp ground ginger (I like super gingery gingerbread)

115g butter

175g light brown sugar

4 tbsp golden syrup

1 medium egg, beaten

icing sugar to decorate

1. Preheat the oven to 190C

2. Sift together the flour, bicarbonate of soda and ginger. Add the butter and rub it until it looks like breadcrumbs. This bit is boring, then stir in the sugar, slightly less boring, just because it's sugar.

3. In a different bowl, beat together the golden syrup and the egg then stir into the dry ingredients and mix to a dough. Turn out onto a floured surface and knead until smooth. I like to pretend the dough is the face of someone I don't like but that's just me.

3. Roll the mixture out on a lightly floured surface until it's about 5mm thick. Using a tree shaped cookie cutter, cut out 12 gingerbread trees and transfer to baking trays lined with parchment paper.

4. Bake for 12-15 minutes until golden. YAY! GINGERBREAD! Allow to cool slightly before transferring to a wire rack to harden.

5. Decorating is entirely up to you. I like to ice strings of lights or dust the sugar like snow or smother the things and chuck a load of silver balls on there. More sugar = better cookies, fact.

Santa's Favourite Fudge Recipe

As everyone knows, you cannot gain weight from calories consumed in December. Cough. So that makes this the perfect time to make this super awesome, super easy fudge.

500g vanilla baking chips

1 can (400ml) sweetened condensed milk

½ tsp peppermint essence

1 ½ cups crushed candy canes

dash red food colouring

butter for greasing the tin

---

1. Line an 8 inch square baking pan with tin foil and grease the foil. Mmm. Butter.

2. Combine the vanilla chips and condensed milk in a saucepan over medium heat. Make sure you stir until almost melted, then remove the pan from the heat and continue to stir until smooth. When chips are completely melted, stir in the peppermint extract, food colouring, and candy canes. Don't touch it, it's hot. Even though it looks amazing.

3. Spread the fudge evenly in the bottom of the prepared pan. Chill for 2 hours, then cut into squares and eat until you feel sick.

Top Five
Christmas Movies

You truly know that Christmas has arrived when you turn on
the TV and one of these movies is on. And you truly know you're
off work when you watch three of them in one weekend.
This selection has been carefully curated to please the whole family,
from Christmas-a-holics like myself, right through to grinchy
boyfriends who 'hate Christmas'. Idiots.

✓ ***The Nightmare Before Christmas***
Granted, this isn't the most fluffy Christmas movie but it's
a great one to break yourself in with. Plus, awesome songs.
Just awesome.

✓ ***Ghostbusters***
This movie has everything. Bill Murray, Slimer, Christmas
joy, Sigourney Weaver with amazing hair and a giant Stay
Puft marshmallow man. What's not to love?

✓ ***Scrooged***
More Bill Murray! More Christmas! A super cute, super
violent ghost of Christmas present! That super awesome
song at the end! Scrooged has been my favourite Christmas
movie forever and ever and ever.

✓ ***Die Hard***
I've got some weird crushes but really, who doesn't love
Alan Rickman and Bruce Willis? Nothing says merry
Christmas like a dirty vest and a visit to Nakatomi Plaza.

✓ ***A Muppet Christmas Carol***
I. Love. The Muppets. As if their interpretation of this
Dickens classic wasn't enough, Kermit and co even throw
in Michael Caine. Perfect fun for all the family.

Angela's Super Awesome Christmas Mix

You never know when an unexpected Christmas dance party is likely to take off and when it does, you need to be prepared. I like to keep this little mix handy on all devices (I'm not kidding) in case I need to bust out a move at any given moment. Pros will want to download *A Christmas Gift for You* by Phil Spector and then you're covered in case of any eventuality. Just try not to think about that whole thing where he shot someone in the face.

- ◎ *Last Christmas* – Wham!
- ◎ *Christmas Wrapping* –The Waitresses
- ◎ *I Wish It Could Be Christmas Every Day* – Wizzard
- ◎ *Merry Christmas Everybody* – Slade
- ◎ *Driving Home For Christmas* – Chris Rea
- ◎ *Sleigh Ride* – Bing Crosby
- ◎ *Santa Baby* – Eartha Kitt
- ◎ *Lonely This Christmas* – Mud
- ◎ *What Are You Doing New Year's Eve?* – Ella Fitzgerald
- ◎ *All I Want For Christmas Is You* – Mariah Carey

Thanksgiving vs Christmas

One of the reasons Christmas doesn't seem to be quite as big a deal in the US is that Thanksgiving sneaks in at the end of November and tries to steal a lot of the fun. I mean, to someone who didn't grow up with it, Thanksgiving doesn't really seem to make so much sense – it's another turkey dinner with your relatives, only a month before Christmas, and you don't even get presents. Yes, there is a kick ass parade down 5th Avenue in New York with giant balloons but aside from that and obviously all the food, it seems to be the bad, obligatory, family resentment parts of Christmas without the joy of the gift giving, tree or baby Jesus shenanigans.

Obviously, my Jenny sat me down and explained the whole 'celebrating the meal that the pilgrims shared with the Native Americans' thing but she also told me to shut up when I asked to explain the bit where the pilgrims slaughtered all the Native Americans.

My favourite part of Thanksgiving (aside from all the food) is when everyone goes around the table and says what they're thankful for. Traditionally, Jenny and I do this twice. Once at the beginning of dinner and once at the end. Last year, Jenny began by being thankful for friendship and President Obama and New York City. On her second pass, she went for gel manicures, Ryan Gosling and her iPhone 5. All these choices are valid.

British Traditions vs American Traditions

Tree Trimming

Every year, my friend Erin has a tree trimming party. When I got my first invite to this bad boy, I was confused. I am not green fingered. BUT it transpired that trimming means decorating (idiot, Angela) and while I love my Christmas tree, I have to admit, decorating it is much more fun in theory than in practice. In America, tree trimming parties are a great excuse to have your friends over, get them good and liquored up and then dress the tree. Of course, I'd have to rearrange everything after people left so it's tricky. But still, a habit worth adopting.

Candy Canes

Candy canes have become pretty universal now but they're much more available here in the States than the UK. You can literally pick up a box of twelve for a dollar in any drugstore after Thanksgiving. I want to say all mine go on the tree and stay on the tree but in reality, I eat them all. Plus, they look awesome if you chop them in half and stick them in candy cane martinis or peppermint schnapps spiked hot chocolate… or regular hot chocolate. If you must.

Christmas Movies

America really, really loves a themed cinematic experience. Christmas isn't Christmas until you've seen *It's a Wonderful Life*, *A Christmas Story* and *A Charlie Brown Christmas*. Fact.

Brining the Turkey

Now this one really weirded me out. The first time I bought a turkey in the States, it came with a brining kit. This basically means you chuck your turkey into a bucket of seasoned water OVERNIGHT, wash it the next morning and then whack it in the oven. I was epically doubtful but it turns out this shiz is amazing. A-Maze-Ing.

Crackers

America doesn't have Christmas crackers. It breaks my heart that this is a people who cannot understand the joys of a tissue thin paper hat, a small metal finger puzzle and a terrible knock knock joke. That is all.

Advent calendars

America also does not really have proper chocolate advent calendars. And if they did, they would suck because they don't have good chocolate. Sniff. I get them sent over, it's all OK.

Boxing Day

Boxing Day is a mystery to Americans. While they get the day after Thanksgiving off work JUST TO GO SHOPPING (legit, it's called Black Friday and everything's on sale) they don't get Boxing Day. Most people think it has something to do with boxing, which of course it doesn't. But since it does have everything to do with eating yourself blind on leftover turkey, ham, pork pie, pickled onions and assorted cakes and pies, I have made it my business to really force this down my American family's throats. What's Christmas without a day to lie on the floor watching James Bond films while massaging your food baby and choking down one more sausage roll?

CATCH UP WITH

I heart

THE REST OF THE SERIES!

'Fans of the I Heart series will instantly fall
for this gorgeously funny and romantic read'
Closer

Tess Brookes has always been a Girl with a Plan.

But when the Plan goes belly up, she's forced to reconsider.

After accidently answering her flatmate Vanessa's phone, she decides
that since being Tess isn't going so well, she might try being Vanessa.
With nothing left to lose, she accepts Vanessa's photography assignment to Hawaii
— she used to be an amateur snapper, how hard can it be? *Right?*

But Tess is soon in big trouble. And the gorgeous journalist on the shoot with her,
who is making it very clear he'd like to get into her pants, is an egotistical monster.
Far from home and in someone else's shoes, Tess must decide whether
to fight on through, or 'fess up and run…